Summer
SHEIKHS

Three exotic, exciting and intense novels
by three super writers: Alexandra Sellers,
Abby Green and Marguerite Kaye

Summer
SHEIKHS

Alexandra Sellers
Abby Green
Marguerite Kaye

M&B™ and M&B™ with the Rose Device
are trademarks of the publisher.
Harlequin Mills & Boon Limited, Eton House,
18-24 Paradise Road, Richmond, Surrey TW9 1SR

SUMMER SHEIKHS © Harlequin Enterprises II B.V./S.á.r.l. 2010

Sheikh's Betrayal © Alexandra Sellers 2009
Breaking the Sheikh's Rules © Abby Green 2010
Innocent in the Sheikh's Harem © Marguerite Kaye 2010

ISBN: 978 0 263 87465 5

009-0810

Harlequin Mills & Boon policy is to use papers that are natural, renewable and recyclable products and made from wood grown in sustainable forests. The logging and manufacturing processes conform to the legal environmental regulations of the country of origin.

Printed and bound in Spain
by Litografia Rosés S.A., Barcelona

SHEIKH'S BETRAYAL

Alexandra Sellers

Alexandra Sellers is the author of over twenty-five novels and a feline language text published in 1997 and still selling.

Born and raised in Canada, Alexandra first came to London as a drama student. Now she lives near Hampstead Heath with her husband, Nick. They share housekeeping with Monsieur, who jumped through the window one day and announced, as cats do, that he was moving in.

What she would miss most on a desert island is shared laughter.

Readers can write to Alexandra at PO Box 9449, London NW3 2WH.

Dear Reader,

I wonder how many men and women hold in their hearts the image of their first love while they carry on lives that bear no relation to that dream? For every story that we hear of true love reunited – after years, even decades, of separation – there must be many, many more who remember, but never take that risky first step towards rediscovery. If the chance was offered, though, would we be able to resist?

My heroine, Desi, hasn't kept the dream alive, at least not consciously. A painful betrayal changed her passionate young love, first to its opposite and then to indifference – or so she imagines. It would take wild horses for her to seek out her old love, Salah… wild horses or a best friend's desperate need.

Salah, now a powerful Cup Companion who has the confidence of a prince, also thinks himself immune to the siren call of rediscovered love. But still he is driven to meet Desi, the first love whose memory has haunted him all these years. And once met, he's driven to taste the bittersweetness again…

There's another kind of reunion for me in this book – it's my first SONS OF THE DESERT story in nearly five years. I am very glad to be back writing for you again and I hope you'll find the rediscovery as thrilling as I do!

Love,

Alexandra Sellers

For you

Again

PROLOGUE

THERE were two immigration officers at passport control, and a short line of travellers in front of each. A man stood behind one of the desks, scanning the faces of the disembarking passengers. His watchful stillness was a hub for the busy flow, as if the scene somehow revolved around him.

He looked straight at Desi, and a buzz of warning sounded in her bones. She was wearing sunglasses, but even so, she turned her head to avoid meeting his eyes. Passport and landing card in her hand, clutching her elegantly travel-worn leather bag, she joined the other line, and resolutely did not look his way again.

But it had taken only one glance for his image to get stuck in her memory, as irritating as a fishbone: desert dark and harsh-faced, wearing an immaculate white cotton kaftan under a flowing burnous and the traditional headscarf she knew was called a *keffiyeh*. A chiselled mouth. Cheeks carved out of the rock she'd flown over in the desert, a scar across one cheekbone.

'Passport, please,' a voice said, and Desi came to. It was her turn. She stepped forward and handed up her passport. She was tight with nerves.

Desirée Drummond. He read the name without a flicker of recognition, and she breathed a little easier.

'Take off sunglasses, please.'

She had to comply. She held her breath while the agent's eyes roved over her face with sudden eagerness. She let it out slowly when it was clear he didn't recognize her face, either. He didn't ask her to take off her hat. He picked up his official stamp and flipped through the heavily stamped passport for an empty page.

'What is porpoise of visit?'

'Pleasure.' *And that's the first lie done and dusted,* she told herself. *Pleasure is the last thing I expect from this little outing.* Then, an inexpert liar, she rushed to add detail. 'I'm a student of archaeology. I'm going to visit a dig.'

'Deeg?' he was clearly pleased to have an excuse to prolong the encounter. He might not have recognized her, but he clearly liked what he saw. 'What is *deeg*?'

'Oh…it's a—a place where they find an ancient city or something and…archaeologists, you know, they dig to find out about history.'

His eyes widened with sudden alertness, and Desi cursed herself. Why hadn't she just left well enough alone?

'Where is the dig?' he asked, in the voice of a man determined not to let beauty distract him from duty.

'Oh!' Desi laughed awkwardly. 'I don't actually know. Someone is meeting me….'

'Stamp the passport,' a deep voice commanded in Arabic, and both heads snapped up in surprise.

Him. The man who had been watching her. Standing by the immigration officer now and looking at Desi with a black gaze that sent nervous ripples down her spine.

Then she gasped, her head snapping back in sudden shock. The face of the stranger in front of her dissolved and reassembled. Her heart kicked like a million volts.

'I don't believe it!' she croaked.

'Hello, Desi,' he said, in the same second.

'Salah?'

He was nothing like the boy she remembered, nor the man she might have imagined that boy becoming. He looked closer to forty than thirty. There were deep lines on his forehead, a scar high on one cheek, and the once-generous mouth was tight and disciplined. The thin boy's chest and shoulders had filled out with mature muscle.

And those were only the superficial changes. He had an aura of unquestioned authority, a man used to commanding and being obeyed. Power came off him like heat, distorting the air around him.

But it was the harshness, the cold disillusion behind the eyes that shocked her most.

Salah, but not Salah. She could not imagine how he'd got here from who he had been. She was looking at a stranger.

A stranger whose name, she knew, was His Excellency Salahuddin Nadim ibn Khaled ibn Shukri al Khouri, Cup Companion to Prince Omar of the Barakat Emirates, one of the dozen most influential men in his government.

The childhood sweetheart she had come here to seduce, and betray.

CHAPTER ONE

'BABA'S a gineer.'

That mystical communication, imparted to Desirée by Samiha on their first day at school, had entranced Desi with its exotic otherness and bound her instantly to her pretty, dark-eyed new friend. Soon she learned that *Baba* meant *Daddy*, and that *gineer* meant he had come to the west coast to build something big. But the magic never quite faded.

It was the first day of what grew into a lifelong friendship. Desi and Sami were inseparable all through school. They spent their summers together, too, on a small island off the B.C. coast, where the Drummond family's lakefront 'cottage' was a century-old black clapboard farmhouse with outbuildings.

Her ex-hippie parents were hoping to turn the place into a year-round home, growing their own food, and hosting retreats, healing courses and dream workshops in the summer to see them through the winter. But the project never generated enough income for her father to give up his university post and permanently move the family from Vancouver.

Every summer Desi and her brother and sister were

each allowed to invite a friend to stay. Every year from first grade on, Desi took Sami.

The summer Desi turned nine, Samiha's cousin Salah came from Central Barakat to stay with Sami's family and improve his English. Salah was twelve, the same age as her brother Harry, and for some reason no one could afterwards remember, he was invited to the cottage.

Salah and Harry became friends, and after that every year it was somehow taken for granted that Salah would be a part of their summer adventure.

Salah was deeply attractive, a fascinating boy. Those first few summers, Desi hovered between hero worship and competitiveness in her feelings for him, half determined to prove she was braver and brighter than any boy, half wishing Salah were *her* friend instead of her brother's.

Such feelings were a perfect primer for something deeper, and it wasn't long in coming. At the end of the summer she turned fourteen, Desi was just entering on puberty, and a new awareness between herself and Salah beckoned. The next summer, Salah didn't make his annual visit to Canada.

During those two years, Desi grew up. Her breasts formed, her waist appeared, and her height shot up six inches that was almost all leg. Her face shifted from sweet roundness to a haunting elegance.

The just-sixteen-year-old who greeted her old sparring partner the following summer was tall, very slender and quirkily beautiful—so 'unusual' that she had been spotted in the street by a scout and signed with a modelling agency.

As for Salah, at nineteen he showed more clearly the man he would be: slim but powerful, with broad, thin shoulders, a dark, intense gaze and a voice that came from his toes. He was also broody, inscrutable and very sure of his opinions.

Of course she fell in love with him. Of course she did. The friend of childhood whom she already adored, transformed into a romantic hero? Salah was now intensely good-looking, darkly masculine—and so much more adult than the boys at school. And his innocent integrity was a complete contrast to the predatory male sleaze her father and minders kept at a distance in the modelling world.

He was clearly sunk by the new Desi, whose flowing hair moved even when she didn't, whose creamy skin glowed with sensual promise, whose bikinis showed off the curve of full small breasts, fabulous legs, smooth abdomen and firm rump, and who could scarcely eat for fear of gaining an ounce.

That was the year, by an unlucky coincidence—though they thought it perfect enough then—that both her brother Harry and her friend Sami missed the usual holiday on the island. Samiha had gone back to the Barakat Emirates for a visit, and at the last minute Harry had got a summer job to earn money for university. He came to the island only on odd weekends.

It was only natural that Desi and Salah should spend their time with each other.

That summer, too, there was a heat wave, and maybe it was the exhaustion factor that meant her parents didn't notice the building chemical reaction between them, or maybe it was just their hippy laissez-faire attitude; Desi never knew.

On the mainland there were forest fires, but the islands, although oven-hot during the day, mercifully got rain at night. Mornings began cool and fresh, with mist lifting off the lake, but by ten the temperature was soaring, and by eleven most of the paying guests were prostrated by the heat.

Everybody hated the intense heat—everybody except Desi and Salah. Salah was used to such temperatures, and as for Desi—she felt she was waking from a lifelong sleep. The heat energized her, made her blood sing, her muscles flex, as if she were a runner waiting to begin a race she knew she'd win.

Not just the heat, of course, contributed to the feeling.

They became inseparable. Looking back on that summer, Desi remembered bright hot days lasting forever, and an all-encompassing joy in sheer being. They ran together, swam together, talked, explored.

They didn't stop competing with each other, of course. But that only added to the intensity, spiced their meetings, kept them on their toes.

'Salah?'

They gazed at each other for a frozen moment, and suddenly, treacherously, against all the odds, the warm, sweet, sensual memories of a decade ago stirred to melting in her. The sun-burnt warmth of his naked chest against her trembling hand. Black eyes filled with love and need. The intoxication of desire that he had tried so nobly to resist....

Kiss him hello. You need to knock him off balance right at the start, before he gets his lines of control in place.

Desi couldn't have moved to save her life. She couldn't have kissed Salah to save the world. All she could do was stand there, her gaze locked with his, and wonder how she would ever manage to do what she had come here to do, while yesterday's vision of a full, young, passionate mouth and eyes intense with longing arose to confuse the impression of tight control and harsh judgement she saw in his face now.

Then his mouth moved.

'Who were you expecting?'

'Not you.'

If he had expected anything, it was not that his heart would leap so painfully at his first glimpse of her. This fact annoyed him almost as much as her daring to come here. It argued a weakness in him, and he would not be weak where she was concerned. He was no longer a boy, to be at the mercy of his own needs, and hers. He would not be manipulated by her sexuality, practised as it was. He was a man, as she would discover.

Her right eyebrow flared up in the nervous way he remembered. Her eyes seemed slate grey now, as if her anxiety had drained them of colour. She had chameleon eyes, a fact he remembered well. He had never met a woman whose eyes changed colour in such a way. In his memory they were mostly turquoise, deep and rich, like the jewel. Green sometimes when they made love in daylight…and sometimes this green-tinged, slate grey….

'I was not expecting you, either,' he said grimly.

'Then I wonder who you're here to meet.'

'I hoped that you would change your mind. You should have.'

'Excellency,' the passport officer murmured, and His Excellency Salahuddin Nadim al Khouri surfaced to take her passport from the outstretched hand. A muscle in his jaw moved.

'Come, Desi,' he said, turning to lead the way. He pronounced it, as he always had, *Deezee.* The memories it summoned up skated on her nerves. *Desi, I love you. I will love you longer than the stars burn.*

Now that the gaze was broken, she could move. She fell into step beside but a little behind him. *Like a good Muslim wife,* she told herself, and with an irritated little skip that was totally unlike her, she caught up with him.

Her heart was in turmoil, not least because of the way he had changed. Was this what the desert did? Was this the kind of man it grew? Fierce, hard...dangerous to cross?

But she had to cross him. She had come here to cross him.

I'm sure he never got over you. He'd probably give his right arm for the chance to kiss you.

She had even believed that she would enjoy settling scores with him. What a fool she was. If anyone was going to suffer from their encounter, it would not be this closed, proud man.

He led her through a door marked with an elegant sweep of Arabic letters above *Private* in English. They passed along an empty corridor in charged silence. She tried to think of something ordinary to say. If only he would ask her about the flight! Couldn't he feel how the silence built tension? Or didn't he care?

'We flew in over the Barakati desert,' she offered, stupidly, because how else would a plane get to the capital of Central Barakat? 'It's the first time I've seen desert like that! It's so...well, *beautiful* is the wrong word. It has a haunting...'

He turned his head and her little speech died as the black gaze collided with her own.

'People have strong reactions to the desert,' he said. 'But whatever your feelings for it, the desert does not change. It is dangerous whether you love it or hate it.'

The clear attempt at intimidation irritated her. He might as well have said, *I am dangerous whether you love me or hate me.*

And I've done both, Desi told him silently. *But no more. I got through having any feeling for you a long time ago.*

'Funny, so is the Arctic,' she said aloud, because two could play at the innuendo game. 'Would it be better to freeze to death, or fry, do you think?'

His mouth tightened. 'It is better to survive.'

For a moment the scar showed white against the skin drawn tight over his cheekbone. It traced a path to above his ear and was lost in the thick black hair under his *keffiyeh.*

'And I guess you'd know,' she said.

Salah's been wounded. For one unguarded moment she relived the overwhelming anguish that had hit her with those words. She was astonished to discover how shaken she was by the evidence of how close he had come to death. Her hand ached suddenly, as if with the need to touch. But she wasn't here to soothe any hurt of Salah's.

'Yes,' he agreed.

As they reached the end of the corridor a uniformed guard, clasping a fist to his chest in salute, opened the door for them. Salah paused to issue instructions to him as Desi passed through into blinding sunlight.

She stopped. 'My bags!'

Salah continued without pausing. 'Come,' was all he said, and his burnous streamed out behind him like a king's cloak as he stepped out into the hot desert wind.

The heat smacked her, a living thing. Desi stopped to take her first breath of the dry, orange-scented air with its tang of plane diesel.

And suddenly here she was. The place he had promised to bring her, ten long years ago. The place she had dreamt of, yearned for—believed would be her home. The desert, he had assured her, where men were men, where life was lived and love was loved with the deepest intensity. Where passion was a part of nature and human nature.

Where his passion for her would never die.

How many times, under his urgent, loving guidance, had she visualized herself in the desert, and how often, long after it was hopeless, had she wished and pleaded for life to have worked out differently! Begged fate to allow her to retrace the steps that had taken her away from that life with him. Ten long years on, she was here.

And she would give a year of her life to be anywhere else.

'So *hot*!' she cried, trying to shake the feeling. 'It's only ten o'clock!'

'This is not a good time for foreigners in Central Barakat,' Salah said.

'By *foreigners* do you mean any foreigner? Or just me?'

'Are you so different from ordinary people, Desi? Has fame made you weak?' he asked, but didn't wait for an answer. 'Not many foreigners come at this time of year, unless to work in the oil fields. Next month will be cooler.'

Next month would be too late. *It'll be hell on earth, Desi, but if you don't go now, I'm lost.* She would never forget the mixture of rage, grief and exhaustion in

Sami's voice, the voice of a woman driven to the edge, fighting not to go over.

She glanced at Salah, wondering again how a boy of such passion as she remembered in him could have turned into a man ready to contemplate what he was now contemplating. But his face was closed, impossible to read.

Ten years ago she had understood every expression as it crossed his face. Now he was unreadable. As well read stone. What had done this to him? His injury? War itself?

A white limousine hummed in quiet readiness at the bottom of the steps. A chauffeur in black trousers, white polo shirt and a headscarf like Salah's leapt out to open the passenger door. As she slipped inside with Salah, an airport official arrived, carrying the two battered leather satchels that had accompanied her around the world over the past ten years. They were stowed in the trunk, doors banged, and the limo moved off.

And suddenly she was the last place in the world she would ever have chosen to be again: alone in a small space with Salah.

CHAPTER TWO

AT THE height of the heat wave, Desi's father had accompanied her to Vancouver on a two-day modelling gig. Hating to miss one moment of time shared with Salah, she would have cancelled the engagement if she'd dared, and in the stifling heat of the city, she had wondered, not for the first time, why her friends envied her. She missed Salah with a desperate intensity, and could not wait to get back to the island. When they returned, it was Salah who met them at the ferry dock.

'Your mother is a little sick with the heat,' Salah explained, but when he looked at her, Desi knew. The knowledge was like chain lightning in her blood, striking out from her heart again and again, every time she thought of it: he had to come. He couldn't wait even the extra half hour to see her.

'It has not rained since you left,' he told her, and Desi's heart kicked with what he meant.

'You'll want to tell Salah all about your trip,' her father said, with masterly tact, or, more likely, masterly insensitivity. So she got in the front with Salah while her father sat in the back reading the local paper. But they did not talk much. There was a killing awareness between them, so powerful she felt she might explode with it.

The tarmac was practically steaming in the heat, as if it would melt the tires, and when they turned onto the unpaved road that led to the cottage dust billowed up around them in an impenetrable cloud.

'Like my country,' Salah said. 'Like the desert.' And Desi half closed her eyes and dreamed that they were there, that he was driving her across the desert to his home.

'I wish I could see it,' she whispered. 'It must be so beautiful, the desert.'

'Yes, beautiful. Like you.'

He might as well have punched her in the stomach. She had never dreamed love would be like this, gasping for air, every cell of her body ready to burst.

'Am I?'

'I will take you to see it one day,' he promised. 'Then you will know how beautiful you are.'

'Yes,' she said softly, and they looked into each other's eyes and it was as if the promise were sealed with a kiss.

The kiss came later, as they sat on the dock, wet from swimming, watching as the sunset behind the trees painted the lake a rich gold.

'In my country I will show you an ocean of sand,' he said. 'The shadows at sunset are purple and blue. And every day it is different, because the wind—what do you say?—makes it into shapes.'

'Sculpts,' she offered.

'Sculpts, yes. In the desert the wind is a sculptor. I wish I were a sculptor, Desi,' he breathed, and his hand moved up to explore the line of her temple, cheek, chin, and then slipped behind her neck under the wet hair.

It was her first kiss, and it was unbelievably, piercingly sweet. It assailed her body as though a thousand tender mouths touched her everywhere at once. With Salah bending over her, their mouths fused, she melted down onto the dock, and the sun-warmed weathered wood against her back added its mite to the overwhelming sensation that poured through her.

Her hand lifted of its own volition to the warm skin of his chest, his shoulder, and a moment later Salah lifted his mouth to look at her. His face was gold and shadow, the most beautiful thing she had ever seen. They gazed into each other's eyes.

'Desi, I love you,' he said; she breathed, 'I love you, Salah,' and all around them was perfection.

She had never seen real desert so close before. Mountains and sea were her natural background; from her childhood she had never questioned the rightness of that.

Until now. Now, as she watched an eternity of dusky sand pass, smoky tendrils of longing and belonging reached out from the stark landscape into the vehicle, into her being, her self, and clasped her heart.

'So,' Salah said, in a harsh voice that immediately brought her back to the now. 'So, Desi, you come to my country at last.'

She could feel her emotions rising to the bait, and fought down the impulse to rake over their ten-year-old history.

'Well, I guess you could…'

'After ten years, what have you to say to me?'

'I didn't ask you to meet me, and I've nothing to say to you,' she said, forgetting Sami, forgetting everything except basic life-saving procedures.

'You lie. What do you come for, if not this?'
This?

'What are you talking about?' she demanded.

He looked at her for an electric moment, his eyes blazing as if he were struggling against some powerful impulse, and she held her breath and awaited the outcome.

'You know what I mean.'

She licked her lips. 'Didn't your father tell you why I'm here?'

Salah snorted. 'My father's work! Even the immigration official knew better than to believe it. Why do you come to me now? What do you want? What do you hope I can give you? You are too late.'

She couldn't believe this. What was time, then? Ten years since they had spoken, but here they were, picking up the argument as if scarcely an hour had passed.

'I don't want anything from you! Who told you I wanted—?'

He pulled her sunglasses off, flinging them down on the seat between them.

'Do not hide behind darkness and tell me lies.'

'What do you think you're doing?' She grabbed the glasses up again, fumbling to unfold them.

'When women veil their hair it is to protect their modesty. When they veil their eyes it is to conceal deceit.'

It was impossible to put the glasses back on, after that, impossible to leave them off. She glared at him, anger rising in her.

'And when men accuse women it's to avoid facing their own guilt. What do *you* want?'

'We will discover. But I did not go to you, Desi. You came to me.'

'That's a Napoleonic ego you're nursing there, Salah. I came to your *country*.'

The flesh on his face tightened. 'To visit my father,' he said, measuring every word.

'Exactly!' she said. 'I think we're back where you started, aren't we?'

He was not fazed.

'Why do you deny it? There is no shame in returning to your first love when other men are unsatisfactory. If your first love has waited for you, all is well.'

'Do you have any idea how pompous you sound?'

'Do you regret our unmatched passion, Desi?' His black eyes burned into hers. 'That day in the cabin—do you remember it? What could ever reach it, if we lived a thousand years? Is that why you are here?'

The memory of that summer welled up in her at his words. Heat burned her blood. That incredible, bone-deep, never-to-be-repeated yearning for the touch of another human being—it was as if she had sat by a fire she thought was ashes and dust, and with one measured kick he had set it roaring into an inferno again.

'I regretted it for a while,' she said. 'And then not. What about you?'

'Your hair,' he said. 'I want to see your hair.'

Her head twitched back. 'Don't touch me!'

'Ten years.'

She could not prevent him. He reached out to grasp the brim of her hat and slowly pulled it off. At his bidding, the ash-blond hair came tumbling down around her shoulders. It was like being undressed by any other man.

'Still the colour of the desert at the edge of the mountains.'

One strong finger reached for a lock, curled around it. He had said it ten years ago. *Not the golden sand you see on postcards, Desi,* he had whispered as they lay in each other's arms, and he kissed a lock of her hair, *more beautiful than that. The colour before sunset, just where it flows into purple foothills. I will show you.*

Her skin shivered with unbearable sensation. He was watching her with half-lidded hawk eyes, the better to see her with. She lifted her chin to draw back, and could not.

Time, the great trickster, stopped altogether then, and they stared at each other, unmoving, his hand locked in her hair, her eyes wide, hypnotized. Outside the car, blinding sun and a harsh, unforgiving landscape. Inside, the unforgiving landscape of the heart.

The car went over a bump, kicking time into motion again. Desi lifted her hand and pulled her hair from his grasp.

'Don't touch me,' she began, but even as she spoke the command his control snapped. One strong dark hand clamped her wrist and his other arm went around her waist to pull her into his embrace, thigh to thigh, breast to chest, her hands helpless, her body arcing against him as if in erotic submission.

For a moment they were frozen there, eyes fixed on each other's face, but if it was the past she was yearning for, there was nothing of the tender boy she remembered in the angry blackness of a gaze that seemed to swallow her every attempt at conscious thought, fatally weakening her resistance.

At last she found the use of her hands and lifted to push them against his shoulders. Still he held her, resisting the pressure with frightening ease. His *keffiyeh* fell forward over one shoulder, cocooning them in their own little world.

Their own world. It had always been their own world.

'Salah!' she protested, but the name was lost in a gasp as his lips took possession of hers.

His mouth was strong and hungry, and her body heat went instantly to melting point as the kiss devoured her. Need like a starving child rose up in her then, an ancient, unfamiliar yearning—hunger, and thirst, and the bone-deep ache of a decade bursting a heart that had been locked tight against feeling for too long.

Terrified by the force of her anguished need, gasping at her overwhelming response, she resisted the powerful urge to wrap her arms around his neck and drink deep of what she had been deprived of so long, and instead struggled and pushed against him, dragging her parched mouth away from water in the desert, fighting against instinct and compulsion like one who knows the source of all they need is poisoned.

He lifted his mouth at last. Again they were still, staring into each other's eyes at point-blank range, her hair flowing over his arm, his black gaze over her face.

'I always liked to taste my name on your lips,' he said, remembering.

Something like panic gripped her. 'Let me go.'

Salah breathed as if for ammunition in the battle for self-control, and opened his arms. She flung herself back indignantly, flicking her hair, tweaking her clothes straight, avoiding looking at him for fear of what he could read in her eyes.

With all her heart she wanted to avoid confrontation, pretend this had never happened. But it would be fatal to let it pass. At last she could raise her eyes and stare at him.

'If you kiss me again I will hit you,' she said between her teeth.

'Beware of chain reactions, then.'

His voice was like iced gravel. A thrill of something that was not quite fear went through her.

'Can we leave it out?' she cried. 'I've been flying for most of a day and I'm tired!'

He nodded, lifted up and opened a briefcase, pulled out some papers, and began to study them. Suddenly he was the stranger again, in the unfamiliar *keffiyeh* and desert robes. He looked like an oil sheikh.

Just like that, it seemed, he could dismiss her from his consciousness. Desi resisted the sudden, mad urge to go for him and tear off the intimidating headgear, as if that would restore him to the boy she had known.

But there was more than a *keffiyeh* between this chiselled, haughty face and the Salah she'd once over-whelmingly loved.

CHAPTER THREE

PERHAPS if her parents had been more awake to what was going on, Desi's personal disaster might have been averted. But the house was at peak capacity, with every bed full, and in the heat there seemed to be twice as much work, with guests demanding fresh towels, cold drinks and extra service.

They had a retreat, a place that the children had used as a hideaway for years: under the old wooden pier that lay on one side of the lake a few hundred yards from the house. Every summer Desi and her brother dragged an air mattress underwater and up onto the rocks beneath, and then inflated it so that it lay half floating, half moored.

They called it their clubhouse. Sometimes, when avoiding household chores or ignoring mealtimes, the children had hidden there, giggling and listening to their mother call.

In sunlit hours, the spot was pleasantly shady. In rain, they could pretend it was dry. And in the evening it was perfection to sit there with a small smudge coil keeping the mosquitoes at bay, talking about life, death and destiny, and what they would do when they grew up.

Salah and Desi spent many hours there that summer, away from the paying guests who wandered up and down at the lake's edge. In the searing heat, it was pleasant to lie there, while shafts of burning light pierced the gloom, the air mattress bumping lightly against the sides of the pier or the rocks as the water lapped. In the evenings they lay in each other's embrace, watching as stars and moon appeared.

With her head resting on his shoulder, his fingers threading her hair, they dreamed together about the future. They would get married as soon as she finished high school. She would move to the Barakat Emirates to be with him, and make her life there. They would have four children, two boys and two girls.

Neither Salah nor Desi meant for it to happen, though it was always Salah who drew back, when Desi was too much in love, and too drowned in sensation, to know where the point of no return was.

'We have time, Desi,' Salah would say gently. 'All our lives. We can wait.' And of course she agreed.

But everything seemed to conspire against this determined nobility: the heat, their innocence and the fact that they were always together, so often alone.

It was there under the dock, when he told her about the war in Parvan, that their control finally broke.

Brave little Parvan, which had been invaded by the Kaljuks, and had long been fighting an unequal war with little help from its friends. Prince Omar of Central Barakat had formed a company of Cup Companions and joined the war on the side of Prince Kavian of Parvan.

'The Kaljuks are monsters,' Salah told her. 'Prince Omar is right—we can't let them do what they are doing to Parvan. He is right to join the fight.'

Desi's heart choked with a sudden presentiment of doom.

'You—*you* wouldn't go, would you?'

'My father has forbidden me, he says I must finish one year of university first. He thinks the war will be over this winter. The Kaljuks are tired and Parvan will never give up. But if it is not—what else can I do, Desi? I must join the Prince. I must help them.'

Tears starting in her eyes, she begged him not to go to war. She pleaded her love and their future. The life together they would never have if he were killed. Those four children who would never be born.

'Marry me now, Desi,' he said roughly, drawing her in against his chest and holding her tight. 'Then, if I die, I will leave you with a son to take care of you when he grows up. Come home with me! Marry me now!'

He kissed her then, when all their barriers were down. And amid the perfect silence of nature, that silence that is wind and birdsong and still water, they could no longer say no to the wild desire in their blood.

She always marvelled, afterwards, at the coincidence. After two weeks of utter joy, of living in their own secret, magic world, on the night before Salah's departure, her brother Harry arrived for the weekend bringing a magazine.

'Baby, it's you!' he said proudly, opening it to show them all something that the family was still a long way from being used to: a full-page ad with Desi's photo.

It had been her first high-fashion assignment, shot in Toronto months before, and it had been a very different world from any she had experienced up till then. Desi had been awed by the arrogance of the makeup artist, never mind the photographer, who everyone said was the absolute best...

The results, too, were different: the peak of professional skill evident in the ad, which was all in shades of bronze. Desi sat on a director's chair with her feet sprawled wide, her knees angled in, in a trench coat, buttoned and belted, but exposing a V of sensual dark lace at both breast and hip. With her elbow resting on the arm of the chair, propping up her chin, Desi gazed at the viewer with limpid beauty. Between her feet was a fabulous leather handbag. Glossy shoes matched the bag.

The family and guests crowded round. 'You look absolutely stunning!'

'Oooh, very sexy!'

'I'll buy one! Just show me the money!'

Everybody was delighted, thrilled for her. Only one voice was silent. Desi looked shyly up at Salah, expecting his proud approval.

His face was dark with shock.

'They exploit you,' he said quietly, and it was a terrible slap, all the worse because it was public. The babble in the room damped down as Desi gasped and blushed bright red.

'*Exploit* me? Do you know how much I was paid for that shoot?' she cried indignantly. 'And the hotel where they put us up...'

'They put you up in a fine hotel and pay you to expose yourself,' Salah said.

'Expose? My *legs*!' she cried. 'Everybody does it! I'm not nude, you know!'

'Yes,' he said. And it was true that the positioning of the bag between her feet, with the innocent vulnerability in her eyes, was disturbingly erotic.

For once her mother rose to the occasion.

'Isn't it wonderful the differences you still find in cultural perceptions, when we're all so worried about American monoculture sweeping the world?' she said, picking up the magazine and flipping it shut. 'Congratulations, darling, we'll look at it again later. It's a cold supper tonight, everyone, shall we eat now?'

Tears blinding her, Desi got up and banged out through the screen door into the star-filled night. The door banged a second time behind her, but she did not stop running.

He caught up with her down by the water's edge.

'Desi!'

'Why did you do that? Why did you humiliate me in front of everyone?' she demanded.

'If you are humiliated, it is not me. That picture, Desi—'

'Oh, shut up! Shut up! There is nothing wrong with that picture! It's a fashion shoot! I was *so* lucky to get that job, girls wait years for something like that! It'll open so many doors for me!'

That was her agent talking. The truth was that modelling, the teenage girl's fantasy, had never really been Desi's dream. Perhaps it was the impact of her parents' ideals on her, her island upbringing, for what she had seen of the life so far she did not like. But, perversely human, when pressed, she defended what she did not believe in.

'Desi, we are going to be married. You will be my wife. You can't pose like this for other men.'

'Men?' she cried. 'That's not a men's magazine! It's fashion! It's for *women*! I'm advertising a *handbag*!'

'No,' he said levelly. 'You advertise sex.'

He had the outsider's clarity, but it was too much to expect that she could see what he saw, or that he would understand the intimate connection between sex and sales.

'You don't know what you're talking about!'

'Desi, one picture is not important. But this work you do—will it all be like that? Is this what a modelling career means?'

'All like *what*, for heaven's sake? I was fully dressed! Wait for it, Salah, next month I'll be in an *underwear* catalogue! What is your problem?'

'Desi, a Muslim woman cannot do such things. It is impossible.'

She was silent, listening to the crickets. Then, 'I'm not a Muslim woman,' she said slowly.

'Desi!' he pleaded.

She burst into tears. 'And if that's what it means—that my photograph is seen as disgusting, then…and if that's what *you* think—if that's what *you* see when you look at that picture of me…oh, God, you make me feel like a…like a…'

They were too young to see that what had motivated his outburst was not religion, but jealousy. Sexual possessiveness.

'And if you're so high and holy, Salah, what about what we've been doing? How does that stack up with your principles?'

'We love each other. We are going to be married!' he said, but she thought she could see doubt in his eyes.

She said accusingly, 'You think what we're doing is wrong, don't you?'

'No, Desi!'

She cringed down to the bottom of her soul.

'Oh, *God*! That is so *sick*!'

ALEXANDRA SELLERS 35

If he felt guilty about their lovemaking, what did that mean about how he saw her? Shame swept through her. And the stupid fragile dream she'd been dreaming cracked and split open, and the real world was there, beyond the jagged edges, telling her she'd been a fool.

Suddenly she was saying terrible things to him, accusing him of tricking her into sex, and then judging her for giving in. Horrible things that she did not believe, but was somehow driven to say.

His face grew white as he listened, and then Salah erupted with things about the corrupt West which he did not believe and always argued against with friends at home.

Corrupt. The word hung in the air between them as they stared at each other, bewildered, their hearts raw with hurt, and far too young to make sense of what was happening.

'You mean me!' she cried then. 'Well, if I'm corrupt, you're the corrupter! I hate you!' She whirled and ran back into the house and up to her room.

She locked her bedroom door, and buried her head under the duvet, trying to drown out the sound of pebbles hitting her window during the night, the whispered pleadings at her door.

She did not come down again until after breakfast the next morning, just in time to say a cool goodbye to Salah, with all the others, before her father took him to the ferry. As he got into the car he looked at her with the reproach of a dying stag who cannot understand what has motivated his killer.

Salah never came to the island again.

CHAPTER FOUR

THE palace clung to a rocky slope above the winding river and the city between, brooding over the scene like a dream of white, terra cotta and blue. From the plane, in all the glory of its dome and its arched terraces, the palace had looked like something out of a fairy tale, but approached from below it had the air of a fortress.

It was some time before she understood that they *were* approaching it. They drove through the centre of the city, past the bustle of a market, through a small herd of reluctant goats driven by a grinning urchin, then along wide streets bordered on two sides with high white walls topped with greenery. So entranced was she with the unfamiliar sights that it was only after they left these walls behind that she realized there was only the palace ahead.

'Where are we going?' she asked, when the answer was already obvious.

The car stopped at a gate and the chauffeur exchanged words through the window with an armed guard.

Salah put the papers away, snapped the briefcase shut and set it aside. After a moment, as if at a thought, he reached out and spun the locks. She felt it like a slap.

'You can never be too sure,' she said sarcastically. 'But really, the state secrets of little Barakat are safe from me.'

He looked at her with a black gaze that revealed nothing.

'What is this place, Salah?'

'It is Prince Omar's palace.'

'Am I staying *here*?'

'What else? Should I put you up in a hotel? Do you think I forget what I owe your family?'

'Won't I be meeting your family?'

They moved up the incline, past an unmanned sentry post, then under a broad archway and into a courtyard where there were several parked vehicles.

'Except for my father, who is at the dig, my family go to the mountains in summer. The heat is bad for my mother's health. Only the poor remain in the city in summer, and they move down by the river.'

His eyes were hard. She remembered the very different look in his eyes the last time they had met, on the morning that he left the island for the last time.

Never got over her? On the contrary, the boy who had loved her had disappeared. He was changed out of all recognition. *You had a lucky escape!* she told herself.

Her heart, contrarily, mourned a loss.

'So why are *you* still in the city?'

He lifted one corner of his mouth and looked at her as if she were being naive.

'You stayed in the city to meet me? Why? What do you want?'

'Not what I want, Desi. What you want.'

He opened his door as two servants appeared through a doorway. The men seized her bags from the trunk and disappeared. The chauffeur opened her door. The heat slapped her again as she got out.

'What has it got to do with me?'

'I will be your guide to my father's dig. Did you not expect it?'

Of course Salah will be your guide. The entire plan depended on this, and yet, somehow…not until this moment had Desi really believed that it was going to happen. That she'd be travelling across the desert for hours with only Salah for company.…

Her eyes hurt as she gazed at him, as if they were letting in too much sun.

'Well, I'm sorry. Your father said a guide. I didn't expect…'

'No?' His manifest disbelief infuriated her, even though he was right.

'I'm sorry, but this is the only time I've got. It's when I normally go to the island.'

The word was electric between them.

'And the case is so urgent,' he said.

There was no answer she could make to that, without looking even more of a selfish idiot. She turned her head to escape his cynic's gaze, and a panel of exquisite, ancient tilework met her eyes.

She had stayed in some pretty fabulous places in her time: a hot modelling career opened a lot of doors. But not so far an active royal palace. Never a place with such an aura of power, past and present.

'Will I get to meet them?' she asked. She knew that Prince Omar and Princess Jana had children of their own, as well as two daughters from Omar's first marriage.

Salah led her under a worn, intricately arabesqued stone archway onto a tiled path.

'They go to Lake Parvaneh in summer. Princess Jana asked me to assure you of your welcome here, and apologizes for her absence.'

He opened a door and ushered her along a path bordering a formal garden and thence into an internal courtyard so entrancing Desi stopped short and gasped.

Columns, floor, stairs and walls were covered with beautiful, intricately patterned mosaic tiling. A perfectly still reflecting pool in the centre reflected greenery and sunlight and the balcony above, with a mirror's clarity and water's depth. Cloisters ran around the walls on all sides; an ancient tree rose up in one corner, its gnarled branches and thick leaves shading the space from the morning sun. More tumbled greenery cascaded down from the balcony, or entwined the tall columns and latticework.

It was compellingly beautiful, deeply restful. The temperature seemed to have dropped by at least ten degrees. Desi heaved a sigh of sheer wonder.

'Isn't it spectacular!'

'It is more beautiful in spring, with the flowers,' said Salah and, pausing under the archway, he threw a switch.

She heard a rumble, a groan, as if some great underground creature had been disturbed in its rest, and then the perfect reflection in the water shimmered and was lost as fountains leapt up into the air from the centre of the pool.

The fine spray damped her face as she stood smiling up at the vision.

'Now, that's what I call air conditioning!' Her spirits lifted and she laughed for sheer pleasure.

Watching as the fine mist damped her lips, as if a kiss had moistened them, his face closed. He turned away to lead her through the spray up a flight of stairs and along the balcony.

A sudden gust caught his cloak and it billowed around him, the image of the hero in an ancient tale. Desi was struck by the same promise of timelessness and belonging that the sands had whispered to her, as if they had met here a thousand years ago....

He opened a door.

She stopped to catch her breath again at the doorway. It was a magnificent room, huge, but divided into comfortable niches by the artistic use of rugs, furniture clusters, and intricately carved antique room dividers in cedar, ebony and sandalwood.

Above the doorway and windows, panels of stained glass threw patterns of coloured sunlight onto the white-painted walls. Fat brocade cushions forming sofas and armchairs were interspersed with low tables; on the walls above hung fabulous paintings and patterned mirrors, with niches holding burnished bronze plates and pitchers that glowed like gold. Covering the dark polished wood floor was the biggest silk carpet she had seen outside a museum. A Chinese cabinet looked as if it had been painted for an emperor.

The plates and jars that glowed like gold, she realized with a jolt, were gold.

A sweeping arch gave onto a farther room, and against the opposite wall a soft breeze coming through the jalousies of an open window disturbed the silk canopy of a low bed whose pillows and spread were patterned in turquoises and purples.

The luxury was suddenly and profoundly erotic. So different from the bed under the old dock ten years ago, but pulsating with sensual and sexual promise. As if that other bed, those places they had made their bed, had been a foreshadowing, a dream of which this, now, was the living, breathing, full-colour reality.

They stood gazing at each other, locked in the moment, as the tentacles of memory reached out from the thing called *bed* and began to entwine them.

She had thought herself immune. She had imagined that hatred had blanked out the love that had once consumed her, and that in the intervening years indifference had wiped out hatred.

Desire, it seemed, was independent of such considerations. It operated outside them, it must, because right now his eyes were as hot on her skin as the desert sun.

Desi thought wildly, with a kind of panic, *If he kissed me now...*

A woman appeared silently, suddenly, as if from nowhere, and murmured a greeting. Salah drew in a controlled breath, spoke a few words to her, and when he turned back to Desi all sign that he had been affected by the moment was blanked out behind obsidian shutters.

'I have a meeting now. Fatima speaks a little English. She will look after you and bring you lunch later. It will be best if you remain in the palace today. We will have dinner about sunset. Do you wish something to eat or drink now? Fatima will bring it.'

'Nothing, thanks. Do you live in the palace?' she asked, not sure which answer she was hoping for.

'I have rooms here, yes,' he said. 'We all do.'

'"We"?'

'Prince Omar's Cup Companions have offices and apartments in the palace.'

Desi remembered all about the Cup Companions. In ancient times holders of the title had had duties no more onerous than to carouse with the monarch and take his mind off affairs of state.

'Now they work very hard,' Salah had told her, that day he confided his dreams of one day serving with Prince Omar. 'They are the Prince's working cabinet. One day, *inshallah*, I will achieve this—to work with Prince Omar.'

I don't know what Salah's exact mandate is, but my brothers have heard he's in Prince Omar's confidence, Sami had explained more recently. *They're convinced he's very, very VIP.*

'We heard about your appointment, of course. Congratulations, Salah, I know it was always your dream,' she said now. 'Your parents must be proud.'

'*Mash'allah,*' he said dismissively. *It was God's will.*

In another life, he would have come to her first with the news.

Looking up at the shuttered face, the arrogant tilt of his chin, the hanging judge's eyes, Desi could well believe that Salah had a Prince's ear. But she herself wouldn't marry him now for all the power and influence in six continents. She was suddenly violently, intensely glad she'd agreed to help Samiha. Marriage to Salah would be a hell of a life.

CHAPTER FIVE

'THEY want me to marry Salah,' Samiha had said.

The harassment had begun during the last year of her undergraduate degree, after Sami's father had been killed in a work accident. With his death, her eldest brother, Walid, became 'head of the family'. The trouble started almost immediately, and because her mother caved in under the pressure, Sami had had to give in. First she had been forced to wear the head covering called *hejab* whenever she was out of the house. Other restrictions followed, in a steady erosion of her freedom.

But when Walid, supported by their brother Arif, started to suggest that the headscarf was not sufficient to protect her from men's lusts or show her devotion to their religion, and that Sami really ought to wear *niqab*, the full face veil, Sami had finally found the courage to introduce him to Farid, her fiancé. The couple hoped that Walid would be happy to pass his troublesome ownership of his sister to a husband.

This had been a tactical error. The secrecy of it, her brazen determination to make her own choice, outraged Walid. It violated his right as her protector and guide to choose a good husband for her. Farid al Muntazer, though a Muslim, did not meet with his approval.

Samiha should marry someone from back home. Someone connected to them. Family.

'But Salah's your *cousin*!' Desi had protested, scandalized.

In her distress, Sami had turned to Desi as naturally as breathing. They no longer lived on the same street, but there were ways of keeping in touch that were almost as good as walking home from school together. Wherever Desi was in the world, the two friends always spent a couple of hours a week on the phone.

'All the better!' Sami informed her bitterly. 'The old ways are best, you see!'

'They're crazy! Sami, you can't give in to this!' The idea filled her with primitive horror. Sami and Salah, married? It couldn't be allowed! 'You're twenty-seven! It's none of their business who you marry. You've got to refuse!'

'I am refusing. But my mother is being very weak. My brothers keep telling me how lucky I am, can you believe it? Salah's got everything—he's rich, handsome, Prince Omar's right-hand man.'

'I don't care if he's Prince Omar himself. He's your cousin!'

'If he were Prince Omar himself, Des, he wouldn't be my cousin.'

'That's what they call gallows humour, is it?'

'I knew there was a word for it.'

'What can you do to make your refusal stick?'

'I know what I can't do. I can't marry anyone but Farid. I'll drink bleach first. But Walid is pretty crazy right now, and Arif is right behind him. Full-frontal confrontation is probably not a good idea.'

'Can you just tell Salah himself? He must think you want this. Surely if he knew—'

'Maybe, but, Des, I'm actually scared to risk it. I don't know what *his* reasons are. Maybe he needs a Canadian passport or something.'

'*What?* He's a Cup Companion! Why would he need—'

'Des, I can't risk telling Salah!' Sami protested in a tight voice. 'I don't know what's in it for him! If he told Walid…'

'Do you really think Salah would—'

'I don't know who to trust!' Sam cried, and Desi suddenly realized how close her friend was to outright panic. When your own brothers could turn rabid, what was safe?

'Oh, I feel so useless! I wish I could help!'

'Des, you're the only one who can.'

Her heart had started to pound right there. '*Me?* What—'

'It's no good challenging the noble protectors of Islamic purity head-on. I figure I have to start from the other end.'

'I'd be very happy to kneecap them both for you, Sam, but I think it's actually illegal.'

'Not that end.'

Desi's heart seemed to feel she was trying for the thousand-metre world record.

'You want me to kneecap…Salah?'

'That's the one! Do you think Salah ever got over you, Desi?'

'Yes,' she said crisply. 'Without a doubt. In ten years he hasn't lifted a finger in my direction.'

'He hasn't married, either.'

'Clearly the women of Central Barakat are not stupid.'

'I don't think he ever really got over you. And that was then. Look at you now. Did you see what *Everywoman* called you this week? Hang on a sec, I've actually got it here.' There was the sound of rustling paper, then Sami started reading.

'"Perhaps the most iconically beautiful of all the supermodels on the world scene today, Desirée Drummond—Desi to everyone caught in the intimacy of that smile—projects the haunting vulnerability of a woman who has never learned to hide her heart."'

'How wrong can one sentence be?' said Desi.

'Whatever reasons Salah's got for wanting the marriage, I bet if he thought he stood any chance with you…'

'Along the lines of an icicle's chance in hell…'

'…he'd walk away from this deal so fast we'd see smoke at his heels.'

The bottom fell out of Desi's stomach. She tried to laugh.

'Sami, I haven't seen Salah in ten years!'

'Yeah, but he's seen you! Your face is everywhere, isn't it? You can bet *he* hasn't forgotten.'

Her face on a magazine cover would only serve to remind him of why he'd rejected her, but Desi couldn't embark on that now.

'You aren't dating anyone, are you? I wouldn't ask if you were involved with someone. At least—I hope I wouldn't,' Sami admitted with disarming honesty.

'Are you joking me, Sam?'

'Des, all you'd have to do is—let him think there's a chance. Talk about those carefree summers on the island. Remind him how you used to hero-worship him. You know you can do it.'

Desi took a deep breath, and reminded herself that Sami hadn't been there. And afterwards she'd told no one, not even Sami, all of it.

'Oh, Sam…' she began pleadingly.

'Des, I know it's a terrible thing to ask. But this is the rest of my life, and you're my only hope. Just think if your father wanted to force you to marry—Allan, say.'

Her cousin Allan was a blameless stockbroker in Toronto, but Desi shuddered.

'I understand. You know I understand. But honestly, Sam—'

'All we need is some excuse for you to visit Central Barakat. Could you be looking for locations or something?'

'Models don't scout locations. Anyway, even if I did visit, why should I run into Salah? The country's not that small.'

'After all your family did for him all those years! Of course you'd get in touch and ask for his help! Wouldn't you?'

'When pigs fly,' Desirée said grimly.

'But why? Of course you'd call him! Harry did, when he was over there. Salah treated him like royalty, he told me.'

'Sam, if I did go, if I did see him, it wouldn't do any good. Ashes are ashes. They don't stay warm for ten years.'

'They do. Salah used to act as if…'

She would not ask. She didn't care how he used to act.

'As if what?' Desi blurted.

'As if his heart was broken, I guess. For years when I mentioned your name he'd stiffen, the way people do when they're protecting a sore spot.'

'I'd be happy to think Salah suffered, but I think it was probably gas.'

'Hey—that's it!' Sami said. 'Two birds with one stone! Think of how sweet revenge would taste.'

'It's tempting to consider myself a worthy successor to Sharon Stone, but come on, Sam!'

The wind went out of Sami's sails abruptly.

'You're right. It's crazy of me to ask. Sorry, sorry. But, Desi, what can I do? Tell me what to do!' And again, the flame of desperation was there, licking around the edges of her voice. Desi's heart contracted.

'God, Sam—can't you and Farid just elope?'

'Walid is not above making threats. Maybe—probably he'd do nothing, but you know I can't count on that.'

'Making threats? That's disgusting!' Desi exclaimed. 'Is Walid completely insane?'

'Don't get me started.'

'What about talking to your Uncle Khaled?' Uncle Khaled was her father's younger brother, and since her father's death, Sami had explained, was the head of the extended family. Uncle Khaled was also Salah's father.

'I've thought of that. But Uncle Khaled and Aunt Arwa are really keen on me and Salah. They've told my mother they're thrilled. So I can't just ask Uncle Khaled straight out, either, because if that went wrong… But, Des, if you were there you could sound him out for me—'

Sami broke off with a gasp. 'Oh, *Allah*, I've got it! I've got it!' she cried. 'Uncle Khaled's dig!'

CHAPTER SIX

THE servant led her through the palace to the foot of an external staircase running up to a large terrace backed by the dome, and left her. Desi went slowly up, gazing entranced as the vista was slowly revealed.

The sun was just disappearing behind the horizon of deep-purple desert on the right, pulling a cloak of fiery, furnace-red sky after it; to the left the last of its rays caught the mountain tops with liquid gold. Below and beyond the palace the city was lighting up, a swathe of glittering jewels cut in two by the darkness of the great river that carved its way from the mountains to the sea. As the sun's last light faded, the tree-lined river began to reflect the myriad lights from its banks.

Desi drew a long breath as she arrived at the top and sighed it out. Magic.

Salah was standing halfway along the terrace, looking out over the city. He turned, and at once she was locked by his gaze. Desi put one foot in front of the other and, as helpless as if a magnet were drawing her, slowly moved towards where he waited.

Her hair was loose, he saw, caressing shoulders and neck; her skin was without a flaw. She was wearing sea-blue silk that turned her chameleon eyes to turquoise: a clingy slip top bared the smooth skin of her throat and the shadow between her breasts; flowing trousers caressed the tantalizing shape of hip, thigh and leg when she moved; a matching jacket, the collar standing up under her chin, showed purple and gold embroidery. Gold and amethyst glinted against her neck and ears. Her sandals were delicate straps of gold across her insteps.

But it was her eyes where the true beauty resided—that wide level gaze that once had shown him all the truth of her soul, the gentle sweep of mobile eyebrows under a broad, pale forehead. The curve of her cheeks like wind-sculpted sand, and the mouth—wide, full, sensuous. Her face had always held this contradiction, as if her eyes held no awareness of the sensuality promised by her mouth and body.

Long ago, he had awakened something else in that gaze. Joy, sensual gratitude and love had mixed in a gaze for him and him alone. He had believed he was the only one to see it.

Falsely, as it happened, for it was exploited by every advertiser she posed for. But men had been fools before him, and would be fools when he was dust.

And still in ten long years he had not seen beauty to match it. But he would not fall victim to that beauty again. He had been weak earlier, but he would be that much more on his guard now.

Her gaze was guarded, her beauty remote. But something more: in her eyes was more than a simple veiling of the inner. She was lying to him.

What lie? Well, he would find out.

'Good evening, Desi,' he said.

He had dispensed with the *keffiyeh* and the oil sheikh's robes. Now he was wearing flowing cream cotton trousers and a knee-length shirt, the outfit called *shalwar kamees*. The shirt was open at the neck and rolled up at the wrists, leaving his dark throat and his forearms bare. His head, too, was bare, black curls kissed into gold by the setting sun.

Without the *keffiyeh*, he was less a stranger. She looked up into the harsh face, searching for traces of the fresh-faced boy she had loved, and wondered if he, too, was looking for the awkward, naive girl of ten years ago.

The boy was gone forever. The eyes she remembered could never have looked at her as these eyes did: hard and suspicious, even as they raked her face with a hunger so blatant she shivered.

'It's a fabulous view,' she said, to defuse the sudden tension. But his jaw only tightened. She felt a sudden jolt of heat against her back—his hand, guiding her.

They moved silently along the terrace and into a roof garden. In the centre of the space was a small fountain, its splashing sounds a caress to the ears in the twilight.

He led her to an alcove surrounded by trellis, enclosed in greenery, where a low platform was luxuriantly spread with carpets and pillows. He kicked off his sandals, stepped up onto the platform and sank down on the lush carpet amongst silken pillows.

Lying back against the cushions, dark and arrogant, he suddenly looked like a sultan in a storybook.

She hesitated, without knowing why. With a regal gesture he indicated the cushions opposite him in the little enclosure. Desi slipped off her own sandals, stepped up along the soft carpet and melted down into the luxuriously comfortable cushions opposite him.

'You are beautiful tonight.' The words seemed choked, as if they came out in spite of his intentions.

He had said it before. *Tonight—and always,* he had said then.

'*Mash'allah,*' she said, with a wry half smile. He had taught her the traditional Barakati response to a compliment. *Like crossing your fingers,* he'd said, *you have to avert the evil eye.*

His eyes darkened, suddenly, like a cat's, but his lips tightened, as if the fact that she used the expression gave him pleasure but he would not allow himself to feel it.

Beyond the trellis and greenery, sky and sunset created a backdrop of magnificence. Intimacy closed around them like a velvet paw, trapping them for the gods' amusement.

The desert was deep purple now in the darkness. A soft breeze lifted her hair as she gazed at the scene, tossed it lightly across her face. Shaking it back, Desi sighed in pure delight. A feeling of peace invaded her bones, and she searched for something innocuous to say. She did not want to fight with him.

'This must be the most unusual dining room in the world.'

'Princess Jana designed it for private use. It is Omar's favourite retreat. No state business is ever conducted here.'

'I hope food is coming soon! I haven't eaten since London, and I'm ravenous.'

'I apologize. Fatima should have offered you lunch.'

'She did. I wasn't hungry. Then.'

'And you didn't eat on the plane?'

She shook her head. 'I don't usually.'

There was a curious amplified clicking noise, and then down in the city the haunting voice of the *muezzin* began to recite the call to prayer. The reciter's deep tones, half singing, half chanting, poured out over the city, echoing in the distance. They sat in silence, listening, trying not to remember how, long ago, he had lovingly described this sound to her....

A waiter came, spread a tablecloth on the platform between them and set down a couple of jugs and four goblets. He half filled the goblets and disappeared again.

Allahu akhbar. Allahu akhbar. Hayya alas salaat.

'What is he saying?'

'God is great. Come to prayer,' Salah translated softly.

'Curious to hear so many echoes! Does the desert do that?'

'Echoes?' A smile twitched one corner of his mouth and he shook his head. 'Each mosque has its own *muezzin*, so that no one lives beyond reach of the call. Up here we hear them all.'

The last note sounded as darkness covered the sky. Desi leaned back and looked up through the tracery of trellis and leaves at the stars just beginning to appear.

'This is magic,' she breathed again, and then, with a little frown, 'It reminds me of somewhere! What is it? That sky is pure velvet. I can't think when I last saw such a— *Oh!*'

Heat burned up her chest and into her face like a flash fire, and she instinctively jerked upright.

'What is it?' Salah said.

'Nothing.' She coughed unconvincingly. 'Something in my throat.'

'You are reminded of something? A place? A time?'

'No, not really.' She coughed again and reached for a glass.

'Yes,' he said harshly, as all his intentions for the

evening went up in smoke. 'The island. I, too, Desi. The first time I sat here under the trellis at night I remembered those nights under the dock. We looked up at stars glowing with endless beauty, telling us it was the right time, the right place, the right one.'

Desi gazed at him, frozen, the glass halfway to her mouth.

'You remember, Desi?'

'Do I?' she asked bitterly. Tears were ripping at the back of her throat, but she was damned if she would give him that victory.

'Yes!' he said fiercely. His face was shadowed in the candlelight, his eyes hidden, his mouth hard. 'Yes, you know how our love was! Tell me! I want to know that you remember.'

'Why, since *you* forgot?'

'I thought the stars would die before my love for you. I told you that, didn't I? *When each of those stars is a blackened lump, my love will still be burning for you.* Isn't that what I told you?'

Her throat closed tight. She set the glass down again without drinking. 'I don't remember,' she said, her eyes shadowed and grey.

'Ah, that is well. Because I was wrong. My love did not last.'

'No kidding. And are you proud of that fact? I've always wondered.'

'Proud?' His eyes flashed. 'Why should I be proud? I was shamed, for you and for me. My love did not die honourably, like a star, consuming itself in its own burning. You know how it died.'

'Your love died because it was fantasy from day one. The stars going out? It wouldn't have withstood a hiccup.'

The waiter appeared out of the night, shocking them both into silence, and set down a basket of bread and another filled with sprigs of greenery before disappearing again.

'Tonight,' he said, 'they will bring us the foods I told you of, in those starry nights when we lived a dream.'

She closed her eyes and breathed for calm as memory smote her. 'Why?'

'Because it was a promise. A man keeps his promises,' he said. 'Even ten years too late.'

A kiss with every mouthful.

She had not expected this. Of all the reactions she might have imagined in Salah, the last would have been that he would actually want to bed her. Flames burst into life in her stomach. No. No.

'Just so long as you don't expect me to keep mine,' she said grimly.

He smiled. 'But I know well that you do not keep your promises, Desi. Who knows better than I? That other one you promised to marry and then did not?'

The bitter memory was bile in her throat. 'I changed my mind there.'

'Yes,' he said with emphasis. 'You changed your mind.'

Why was he doing this? What did he want? She was miles from understanding him. For years she had waited for his call, hoping against hope. Until her love died and nothing was left but dust and ashes. He must know that. The choice had been his.

'And you didn't, I suppose?'

He stared at her for a long, electric moment during which his eyes seemed to pierce her soul. A hard, angry gaze that was nothing like the boy she had loved. Then he tore off a bit of bread, plucked up a sprig of the greenery, wrapped it expertly in the bread, and held it out to her.

'This I told you of. *Sabzi-o-naan.* This is traditional in the mountains.'

Desi took it and put it into her mouth. The pungent taste of a herb she didn't recognize exploded in her mouth and nostrils, sweet and fresh, and she made an involuntary noise of surprise.

His eyelids dropped to hide his eyes for a moment, then his dark gaze burned her. 'I taught you to make that sound,' he said hoarsely. 'I thought it would be the music of all the rest of my life.'

Heat rushed through her at his words, tearing at defences she now saw were pitifully weak. 'Stop this,' she said.

He reached for the herbs again, pulling off a sprig that he put into his own mouth.

'Stop?' He handed her another little bouquet of *naan*-wrapped herb. 'How, stop? You are here in my country, where you promised to come. Now I keep my side of the bargain. I promised you would delight in these herbs. Do you?'

She took it from him again, and put it in her mouth, because there was nothing else to do. Not even in her nightmares had she imagined such ferocity as this.

'Very nice,' she said woodenly.

'The freshness in your mouth. I told you then that I would kiss you after every bite.' Her lips parted in a little gasp. 'A kiss with every mouthful. You remember, Desi? Shall I keep that part of the promise, even though ten years have passed?'

'No, I don't,' she said woodenly, and 'No,' again.

'No?' he said. She couldn't see his eyes. 'That is not what you came for, my kiss? But then, what did you come here for, Desi? Why do you come to my country, to the heart of my family, if not for this?'

He offered her another little twist of bread and herb, but she shook her head and reached into the basket herself.

'Why did you get involved?' she countered. 'There was no need!'

'But yes!' He lifted a palm. 'My father was determined to allow you to visit. The rest followed.'

'He said he would arrange a guide. Why should it be you?'

'Who else? You know what I owe your family—so many years of hospitality! You know that such hospitality must be reciprocated.' A fleeting instinct told her there was something else here, but she was too bombarded to be able to pin it down. 'So, Desi, I say to you that you knew your guide would be me. Our meeting was inevitable. And I ask again, why are you here? What do you want from me?'

'I want nothing from you, Salah.' She opened her mouth to tell him that she would hire someone else to be her guide, thought of Sami, and closed it again. He was right, after all. This was all according to plan. He was only mistaken in whose plan it was.

'Why do you lie? What you come for is no shame. A woman has a right to experience pleasure. If her Western lover can't give it to her, she must look for one who does.'

'I'm sure you're right,' she countered. 'But believe me when I say I really don't need to search so far afield.'

He lifted his hands. 'How can I believe it, when you are here?'

A puff of irritated laughter escaped her.

'And even if I did, you are the very last person I'd come to.'

'No,' he said, with such certainty she almost believed he could read her mind.

'Trust me, Salah,' she said. 'You are imagining this. Every part of what you imagine is the product of your own fantasy. I am not remotely interested in reviving old times with you.'

He laughed and before she could stop him, clasped her wrist. She felt her pulse hammering against his thumb. She thought he was going to pull her against him again, it would be so easy, but abruptly he let go.

'It is in your blood. In every part of you. As in me,' he said, with a kind of angry self-contempt. Her heart kicked.

He waved a sultan's wave and a waiter came from nowhere and cleared the little baskets away.

Now there was nothing but space between them. He lay resting on one elbow, looking at her. He didn't move, but he seemed to come closer. Drawing back was agonizing to her, an iron filing trying to move out of the magnet's powerful field.

'Shall we make love here, Desi, as we did under the dock?'

'Don't be—'

'I can tell them to go. We will blow out the candles. There will be only you and me and the stars.'

'And your conscience.' She felt desperate, grasping at anything that would keep him away. 'Wouldn't that get in the way?'

'My conscience?'

'Aren't you engaged to Sami?' she said.

CHAPTER SEVEN

SHE hadn't meant to blurt that out. She had planned to act as if she didn't know. Some things she could do. Pretend to be someone who would go after her best friend's fiancé wasn't one of them.

But Desi was grasping at any defence. It had become sharply clear in the past few minutes that she could not trust herself if Salah made a serious assault. The armour that had served her for years was not up to this challenge. Her heart was melting with grief and regret, her skin was electric with feeling.

She wouldn't let it happen. It would be a betrayal of everything. It would kill her to make love with him.

'But isn't that why you've come just at this moment, Desi?'

'What do you mean?'

'Your timing is too good to be coincidence. You know I can never again make love to you once I am married. Our chance would be lost forever.'

'You don't think being engaged to my best friend puts you out of bounds already?'

'We are not engaged. No discussions have yet taken place. And a man must come to terms with his past before he marries, isn't that so?' Salah said. 'So that he can go to his wife without…regret. You have haunted me, Desi, how can you imagine otherwise? If I am going to marry, first I should have—what do you call it?—closure.'

Her heart was beating in hard, painful thumps. In her worst imaginings she had not foreseen losing control over the proceedings so quickly.

'And how, exactly, would sex with me give you closure?' she asked bitterly. 'Is it an ego thing? Are you hoping to hear me say that sex with you set the bench-mark and nothing since has lived up to it?'

'Is it true?'

'No, it is not!'

'You always lied badly,' he said.

'And you always had an ego as thick as butter.'

'I judge by my own experience, Desi,' he said.

The admission rushed through her like wildfire. She felt faint.

'I don't believe you! A few weeks, ten years ago!'

'And what about you? Don't you, too, wish for this closure?'

'I got closure long ago,' she lied. No closure was possible for a blow like the one he'd delivered. 'The day you told me I was soiled merchandise.'

'And this old man, was he a good lover?' Salah asked, an expression in his eyes she couldn't read.

'What old man would that be?'

'The one you nearly married, Desi. Do you forget lovers so easily? Did he please you as I did?'

'Leo was forty-five!'

'Was it—'

'And it's none of your bloody business!'

She picked up one of the glasses and took a gulp of water. It blasted into her mouth, burned her throat, stung her nerves. She gasped and coughed.

'My God! What *is* this?' she cried, staring down at the glass in horror.

Salah laughed aloud. 'Wine, Desi,' he said, just as her brain belatedly interpreted the taste and gave her the answer.

'Oh, that's wild!' The tension of the past minutes exploded into laughter as she sank back against the cushions. 'For a minute there I thought you...' She broke off when she saw where she was heading. 'Have you ever done that?'

'Tried to poison you?'

'Drunk one thing when you were expecting something else!'

'In England, once,' he confided, 'I drank what I thought was coffee. It was not coffee. For two seconds, I thought, *They have given me pigs' urine to insult me!* Then I realized it was tea.'

She let out a whoop. The incident shook them both out of the mood of angry recrimination. They lay laughing together over nothing, like the old days, the old nights, under the moonlit dock.

They had always laughed together. It was one of the things she'd loved most, missed most...

Laughter shared with a lover. It didn't get better than that.

And now, when he was no longer threatening, when her guard was down, the layers of protection she had laid down over the past tore away. In one moment she was naked again. Her heart coiled with yearning. Oh, what had they done? What had they lost?

The waiter arrived with the next course, a tray with a dozen little dishes that all looked impossibly succulent. Just as Salah had promised, ten years ago.

She had to stop this. Salah was already dangerous enough without help from her own feelings. If there was one thing she was not going to do on this trip, it was get seduced into sex for the sake of closure.

For him it would be closure. For her, she saw suddenly, it might be just the opposite.

Desi sat up and tucked her feet under her.

'So, when do we go?' she asked in a bright voice, as the dishes, one by one, were laid on the cloth between them. 'Do we leave first thing in the morning?'

He jerked his chin in the way she remembered. 'Not tomorrow. You need at least a day to acclimatize before going into the desert. Maybe two.'

'But—'

'And I have business tomorrow. The day after, if you insist. At sunrise.'

She nodded agreement. 'How long does it take to get to the site?'

'How long?' Salah was examining the various offerings with close attention. 'That depends.'

'It *depends*? On what?'

The last dish was set down, the waiter bowed and left, and Salah began spooning various bits of food onto a small plate.

'On what?' he repeated absently. 'Oh—it may depend on the weather, the wind…'

'The *wind*? What, we'll be sailing?' she asked ironically.

'You are not so ignorant about the desert that you do not know that wind can be a dangerous enemy.'

'I suppose weathermen predict the weather in Barakat as well as elsewhere.'

'Climate change impacts the desert as well as elsewhere, also.'

'So a big wind might blow up from nowhere and we'll get stuck in the sand?'

'It is not unknown. Not even unusual. Try this, Desi,' Salah said, reaching out a long arm to set an array of taster-size morsels in front of her.

The odour of the food reached her nostrils then, utterly intoxicating.

'Oh, that smells amazing!' she cried, scooping up a morsel of something mysterious, then heaved a sigh as the flavour hit her taste buds. 'That's delicious. That's the food of the gods!'

You make it sound like the food of the gods, she had said.

He looked at her, and she knew he was there again, too. She sought for something to say to dislodge the time shift.

'So do we—'

'Why does my father's work interest you, Desi?'

Her heart sank. She tossed her hair back to look at him. 'It was all in my letter. Didn't your father tell you?'

'You tell me.'

Damn. This wasn't fair. The letter, mostly composed by Sami, was supposed to have paved the way, established all the lies. Desi was all right about *living* the lie, since so much depended on it, but she hated having to *tell* it, face to face. Especially to Salah. Especially now.

Especially as it was, she knew, so ludicrously unlikely a lie.

'Did he tell you that I'm going back to university to do a degree?'

'Now?'

She nodded uncomfortably. 'I'll start part-time this year…if I can. Middle Eastern history and archaeology.'

'Why? Don't you have a very successful career?'

'Modelling won't last forever,' she said, and it was perfectly true. 'I want a smooth transition when the time comes.'

'A smooth transition into archaeology? What awoke this sudden interest?'

'Not that sudden. I've been curious about archaeology ever since that summer the university came to dig on the island,' she said. 'Remember that First Nations site they were digging? We used to go and watch every day. I never forgot the thrill of seeing someone uncover an arrowhead!'

That part at least was true—eleven-year-old Desi had been fascinated as the past was unveiled: the discovery of the floor of the longhouse, the settlement's refuse mound, the arrowheads of chipped stone. One of the students had encouraged her interest, telling her what each find said about the people who had lived on the site, showing her how the history of two hundred years ago could be discovered even without written records.

'Two hundred years?' Salah had said in youthful disdain. 'In my country we have cities five thousand years old!'

Desi had reacted to the challenge with predictable outrage. 'So what?' she had cried. 'I bet there are lots of countries where they have them *ten* thousand years old!'

His mouth smiled when she reminded him; his eyes were too shadowed to read.

'You made me so mad! But I think I made up my mind then that one day I'd come to Barakat and see what you were talking about, a city five thousand years old!'

'And now you are here.'

She hated the way he said it.

'Won't you find archaeology tame after a career as a supermodel?'

'It beats marketing a perfume called *Desirée*,' she said dryly. Her distaste for that at least was no lie. '*"Feminine, delicate, but with a smouldering hint of sensuality."* Or a chain of restaurants: *Desi's Diner.* How would *you* like it?'

He had the grace to laugh.

'But isn't a chain of restaurants with a smouldering hint of sensuality just what the world needs?'

She rolled her eyes. 'Not from me.'

'And only an urgent visit to my father's site will save you from this fate?'

How she hated the lies! But Sami's anguished voice was there in her head... *I've only got one chance to derail this thing...*

'I told you—it's the only time I have free,' she said. 'This is the time I go to the island every year. I thought how great if I could get in on the ground floor with your father and he let me volunteer on the site for a couple of seasons. That's a requirement of the course.'

The explanation had sounded halfway reasonable during the planning stage. She wasn't sure now.

To her relief, Salah hardly seemed to hear. He was tearing at a chicken wing.

'Try this,' he said, leaning right over to hold up to her mouth a piece thick with a purply-black sauce. Desi automatically opened her mouth and bit into the tender flesh, then grunted at the rich, melting flavour.

'Mmm! What *is* that black stuff? I've never tasted anything so yummy in my life!' she said when she could speak.

'Pomegranate sauce. Another speciality of the mountain tribes.'

A drop of sauce was on her cheek too far for her tongue to reach. Salah caught it with a fingertip and presented it to her mouth. She licked instinctively, then her eyes flew to his.

He slid his wet finger deliberately across her lower lip.

The hoarse intake of her breath told him everything. A jolt of electricity zapped the night air. In his black eyes two tiny golden flames were reflected, as if to warn her his touch would burn. His white teeth tore off a bite from the same piece he had offered her, and the sensual intimacy of that hit her another blow.

Desi dropped her eyes and made a business of wiping her cheek with a napkin. She tried to think of something to say, but her mind had been tipped onto its back and lay there, kicking helplessly. She felt gauche, inexperienced. As if the ten years were smoke and mirrors.

Silence fell, a silence thick with feeling, expectation, a question asked and answered.

She began to eat.

The little lamps on the cloth lighted his hand as he ate, emphasizing the strength of his fingers, the fluid grace of his wrist that transformed into power whenever he grasped a bit of *naan* or a goblet. Involuntarily the memory came to her of that same hand, painted in moonlight and shadow, rough and tender with inexperienced passion as they lay under the dock.

Sometimes, too, his mouth and jaw were touched with gold: a stern mouth, a full lower lip that the chiaroscuro painted in more sensual lines than was revealed in ordinary light. His eyes were mostly shadowed, except for a black glinting in the darkness.

'You go to the island still?' he asked. She wished he had started any topic but that one, but she had to answer.

'My parents live there full-time now. I spend a month there every summer, and Christmas if I can.'

He asked after her parents, her young sister, after Harry, her brother. Softly, softly, he drew her into remembering. She knew it was deliberate, to prove some point, to set some mood—but she could neither prevent it, nor resist.

The shadows, the stars, his voice, the talk of those island summers—everything conspired to take her back to the sweet hours they had lain undetected and undisturbed in their refuge under the ancient dock, their world of two. She began to feel like that child-woman again, on the brink of discovery of self and other, of love and desire, of her own sexual power, and another's.

He had been her lover. She knew what it meant for those hands, with light and shadow playing on them like this, to caress and stroke her. Sometimes when his hand disappeared again into shadow, her body shivered in the unconscious expectation of a caress.

Desi sank into the embracing cushions as they talked, her legs folded with unconscious grace, naked toes curling as she rested on one elbow and ate with her fingers. All her guard had come down. She was eating more food than she'd had at one go for a decade. This was a total sensual delight.

He watched her soften, and the predator in him gloried in his success even as he told himself it meant nothing.

The last course was put in front of them then, a pastry oozing with the promise of sweetness, and she summoned resistance at last. 'That looks lovely, but I never eat sugar,' she said.

'This is made with honey.'

'Or honey.' But for once she could not resist. 'Just a taste,' Desi said.

Fatal mistake. 'Oh, that is just too delicious!' she exclaimed, hastily dropping the little gold fork.

Salah bent his head, and she saw his eyes clearly. They glinted amusement at her, and something else, and her blood leapt so painfully in response she almost whimpered.

'Do you push temptation away so easily, *Deezee*?' he asked, his voice caressing her nerve endings like soft sandpaper.

She looked at him, a hard man if there ever was one. 'Don't you?'

'Not such temptation as this,' he said. She knew he did not mean the little honey-crusted sweet. Flame flickering in the black eyes, he picked up the sweetmeat from her plate with his fingers, tilted his head back and caught it on his tongue.

It nearly flattened her. Sensation roared over her skin, bringing every cell to attention.

His gaze caught hers before she could turn away, and

it was all there in her eyes. She saw him read it. The heat rose up in her cheeks, but she could not tear her gaze from his.

Her eyes were emerald with desire. He smiled like a wolf, dark and determined, and said what he did not want to say….

'Shall I come to your bed tonight, Desi?'

Warmth flooded her body. Oh, how could she be so weak? She'd had ten years to get over this!

'No.'

He shrugged. 'Then you must come to mine.'

'Mmm. I'll be riding a flying pig.'

She was falling apart, and it was only the first day. Desi took a deep, trembling breath. She was headed out of her depth here. The sooner she got out of the palace and onto the dig with other people, the better.

She sat up, drew her legs under her, pressed a cushion behind her back.

'So, you never actually told me—how many hours will we be on the road?'

'Hours? What do you mean?'

'What do *you* mean?'

'Desi, the trip across the desert will take four days at least, probably five.'

CHAPTER EIGHT

How was flight? Have you seen HIM yet?
  Where R U?? Please call!

There were five texts from Sami on her BlackBerry, each one more frantic than the last, and a half a dozen missed calls. Desi should have texted Sami from the Arrivals hall or, failing that, the car, and was stunned to realize she had forgotten. She'd completely forgotten her phone, if not her life, from the moment she'd met Salah.

Has he murdered U? What is going onnnnnnnnnn?

Desi sat with the thing in her hand. She should call Sami to update her, but…she just did not want to talk about Salah and their meeting and the dinner she'd just shared with him.

Or the fact that she had turned down the chance to share his bed.

Meanwhile, she had to respond.

Sry, sry!! Horrible jetlag. S picked me up, going to sleep now. Ttyl, she sent.

She ruthlessly shut the phone off before Sami could call. Then she lay in the fairy-tale bed, surrounded by soft lamplight and ancient luxury, trying to think.

Trying to get distance on the evening she had just experienced.

Five days in the desert alone with Salah! How was it possible? How had Sami not known?

What would she do, alone with him day after day, night after night, a forbidding stranger who somehow shared a past with her? A man who thought making love with her would give him closure?

He wanted her. His love might be dead—he said it was, and she believed him—but Salah wanted her. She was alone now because she had chosen it. He would have come to her bed if she'd wavered for one second. If she'd flicked an eyelash.

Might he still come? She couldn't be sure. She had said no, but—he might think that if he came to her room she wouldn't be able to keep on saying it.

And he'd be right. Desi was afraid. All the defences she thought she'd built up over ten years had disappeared in the space of one short breath. She was vulnerable in a way she hadn't been with any other man. And she didn't know what he really wanted.

Closure. That was such an extraordinary thing for a man like Salah to say! What closure would sex give him? *You have haunted me, Desi.* Was it true? Or did he have some ulterior motive for saying it?

Desi flung the sheet back, swung her legs over the edge of the bed, and sat with her head in her hands. After a moment she got up and began to pace.

The intimacy of the roof garden. The constant harking on the past. The fact he had ordered food he had lovingly described to her ten years ago. The irresistible way he'd chosen tidbits for her, fed her. Painful reminders of their love, scorching tokens of intimacy, the actions of a man determined to win back an old love.

All false. All stage dressing. Salah did not want to win her back. He had made that very plain, a long time ago.

Why, then?

He wants revenge. The thought dropped into her head with an almost audible click. Four days. Five. He could find a dozen ways to get revenge, she was sure, alone with her in the desert for five days. But what could he want revenge *for*?

Everything that happened had been his own doing.

A few days after he left, Salah had phoned her. He begged her, he pleaded his love. He knew now that it was jealousy that had motivated him. He had believed that look in her eyes was only for him, and there it was in the photo, for anyone who looked at her. He had taken refuge in blaming her, too easy to do.

'But I will never do anything like that again, Desi. I will understand myself better.' If only she would forgive him.

The call came too late. Their argument had shaken Desi to the core, and suddenly all the changes that before had seemed so easy frightened her. Move away from her family and friends, to a country on the other side of the world whose language she didn't speak, whose people and culture and religion she knew nothing of, where she knew no one save Salah? Have children who would be citizens of another country?

History was against them, too. That week there had been a graphic television documentary showing a woman stoned to death in the capital of Kaljukistan. Television news was full of the atrocities towards women there. Women dying because no male doctor was allowed to attend them. Girls' schools closed, women teachers and doctors thrown out of work. Women beaten in the street by armed policemen for showing a lock of hair.

Desi was deeply frightened. How well did she really know Salah? How could she love him when she didn't know who he was?

She was too young by far to handle the terrible, contradictory feelings that raged through her at the sound of his voice.

'I don't love you,' she cried.

'You do,' he insisted, but he was young, too. 'You love me, Desi. We love each other. I love you! I love you more than the world. Please, please, Desi, we are going to get married!'

But her wild fears had proved stronger than his young courage.

'You're just like the Kaljuks!' she accused him at last. 'You want to stop me doing anything except stay at home and have babies!'

Two weeks later she learned from Sami that Salah was in Parvan, fighting alongside Prince Omar and the Cup Companions. The agonizing pain in her heart told Desi the truth of her own feelings, but there was no way to tell Salah now.

Desi had felt utterly helpless. She had destroyed something precious, and now that she saw her mistake, there was no way back.

Before she could think what to do, Leonard J. Patrick came to town.

Leonard J. Patrick was *the* hot North American modelling agent. He had a nose for what he called raw star quality. When he came gunning for Desi, her future was practically guaranteed: supermodel status, celebrity, stardom. And just then, it seemed like the answer.

He swept Desi off to the best consultants on the continent, gave her a movement coach and a personal trainer. He created a signature look for her.

Desirée. Leo launched her with fanfare, and his nose wasn't mistaken.

Sometimes she had the feeling, almost too deep to reach, that just because others envied her didn't mean the life was right for her. She ached for Salah with a need so deep it burned her.

Salah's been wounded.

Standing by an ocean, plugging one ear against the music and laughter floating from the balcony above the exclusive stretch of beach, Desi had stumbled and almost fallen, as if the ricochet from the bullet had hit her.

'Wounded? How?'

'He was leading the charge on a Kaljuk position,' Sami sobbed out. 'Baba's trying to find out more. We think he's in a field hospital…'

'A friend of mine has been wounded in the Parvan-Kaljuk War,' Desi told Leo. 'I have to go there. Please don't take any more bookings for me right now.'

But hard as he tried, Leo never managed to make space in her booking calendar….

'He's back in Central Barakat,' Sami told her, sobbing with a mixture of relief and grief. 'He's in the best hospital, Uncle Khaled says. Oh, God, Desi, it's his *head*!'

Desi sent a card, a cute one with a patched-up teddy bear. Too shy to say all that was in her heart, she wrote only a few lines. If he answered, *when* he answered, she would be braver. She knew he would answer.

If he could...

At night she dreamed of him. She dreamed he was lost somewhere in the darkness, needing her, calling her name. But she couldn't find him, and when she opened her mouth to call, she had no voice.

'He's out of danger,' Sami reported, after three nightmare weeks. 'They've taken him home, my aunt is nursing him there now.'

At last a letter came with a Barakati stamp. She knew, she knew it could only be from Salah, and she knew, too, that now she would have the courage to face Leo and tell him what she must: her life here was over. This was not the life for her. She belonged with Salah.

She tore it open in all innocence, her heart wide open.

It was short. Her eyes ran over the few lines, grief clawing at her even before she took in the meaning. *Why do you write me? What can we be to each other now? You betrayed your honour. A man must marry a woman of honour, or regret his foolishness all the rest of his life.*

CHAPTER NINE

THE moonlight coming through the fan of coloured glass over the door threw shadows of red, blue and green onto her face as Desi pulled open the door and stepped out onto the balcony. All was still. Moonlight bathed the courtyard, was reflected from the smooth surface of the pool below, bright against the black water, shimmering a little as wind dusted across its surface. The tree rustled, touched by the same soft wind.

A sleepy bird asked the time. A night insect clicked and buzzed in the tumbled greenery.

The wind pressed the silk of her nightshirt against her body, the moon outlining in white gold everything the wind revealed. Wind and Moon conspiring in the revelation of beauty.

No wonder the pagans worshipped them, he thought, *when they grant such favours as this.*

She shivered, as if sensing his presence, but did not turn to the shadows where he stood waiting.

He had known she would come. True desire would always draw the desired. *Desirée.* The nightingale sang for the rose...the rose gave up her perfume to the night.

The moon rode fat and heavy in the sky, a few days to the full. Desi leaned on the parapet and looked up to where the dome glowed purple. The palace looked so different in moonlight. Mysterious, its beauty shadowed.

She had loved him so much. She had forgotten just how much. Made herself forget. But he had not killed her love. No, her love had survived that brutality. She had had to kill it by her own hand. Deliberately, so as to be able to live. It was the only way she knew to survive.

Or believed she had killed it. Tonight she understood that her love was a river driven underground, but no less a raging torrent for being secret. Now it flooded up from the fertile earth of her being, smashing its way into the light, gaining strength from the years of being suppressed.

Hot tears stung her eyes. 'Salah,' she whispered. 'Oh, Salah.'

And in that breath he was there, hard and real, his strong arms wrapping her in a sudden, fierce embrace against his naked chest.

'I knew you would come,' he growled, and even as she protested, his lips came down hard and possessive on hers. He kissed her until her protest was a moan of deliverance, until the hand that pressed against him melted into submission against his chest, moved up around his neck. Then he swept her up in his arms and carried her back through the doorway to the tumbled bed.

He laid her down among the tossed sheets, but did not take his mouth from hers for a moment. With one hand he tore off the sarong that was the only garment he wore, releasing his hot, hard flesh to press against her thigh as he flung himself against the length of her.

He was consumed with need. He was a fool, but this had been inevitable from the moment he saw her. Her power over him had only increased with time and absence, though he had believed it would be otherwise. Now memory was conspiring with her beautiful sensuality to bring him down.

But at least he would take her with him: she, too, was lost....

Never had she met such ferocity in a kiss. His lips devoured her, setting fire to her blood. He had laid her on the bed and stretched his long body beside her, and still his mouth did not let her go.

One hand caressed and held her throat, pushed at the silk collar, the heat of flesh on flesh. Then there was the high shriek of a tear, and cool air breathed over her breast, for a moment before the fire of his hand clasped her and stroked her.

Her flesh was scorched by the burning need in his touch. Her body arced under his kiss and lifted hungrily against the hungry palm enclosing her breast.

His hand slipped from her breast then, moved against her back, her stomach, her hip, discovering and defining at the same time. Then his hand moved to her thigh, and he cupped her sex with ferocious possession. She melted as if that statement of ownership alone would be enough to bring her to the peak.

He began to stroke her, his fingers hot and strong and knowing, and her body lifted wildly to the pleasure of his touch. She whimpered with pleasure and yearning, the sounds he remembered, and still he did not lift his hungry mouth, but drank in those little mews like wine.

She opened her mouth wider then, as pleasure climbed in her, and he thrust his tongue into the warm hollow, till the double assault left her sobbing with pleasure.

His mouth tore away from hers, and he lifted his head, and looked down into her face for one long, tortured moment before his mouth found hers again, plunging, hungry, devouring.

She was aflame, melted, an inferno of need. A fire of desire she hadn't known existed roared up in her, consuming thought, reason, everything except the fact that he was there and she needed him.

His body was hard and urgent against her, as if with the need of years, and her hand found and encircled the hard, seeking flesh, and his groan shivered along her nerves to send her joy a notch higher.

Still the silk of her shirt thwarted his intent. He lifted away from her, grasped the fabric in two hands and ripped it again and again until it parted for him from top to bottom.

She lay with her body exposed now in the soft lamplight, exposed to the fire of his gaze, her throat arched and inviting as she looked up at him. His eyes ran greedily over the perfection of her, painted with the golden glow—hair, eyes, mouth, breasts, waist, hips, sex, thighs, ankles…sex.

He drew her against him then, the whole length of her bare skin aligned with his, and his arms wrapped her. Her face pressed into the hollow of his shoulder as his hand curved behind and between her thighs. Gently his fingers slipped into the moist depths that waited for him.

He stroked the delicate lips while her moist breath panted against his throat in little pleasured moans. His touch was sure, as if he had known her body intimately for ten years, or as if it had been waiting for this moment all that time. In what seemed like seconds she lifted against his expert touch, crying and sighing, a sound he remembered as if from yesterday.

She mewed and slid down from the peak, and then he drew away from her. Then his hand clasped her thigh, lifted her leg up, and his body shifted against her and, with a thrust that made her cry out, he pushed his way home at last.

He filled her to bursting. She cried out, arching into a pleasure that she had not experienced in ten long years. 'Salah!' she cried, in a voice he remembered, and a groan was torn from his own throat.

His body thrust again and again into the hot nest of her, and with each thrust they cried out together. His hand cupped her neck, so that they looked into each other's eyes. She stroked his strong chest, his arms, greedily, hungry for the feel of his skin, and every caress drove him higher.

'How I have waited for this!' he cried then, gazing into her eyes, then down at the place where their bodies met, and his look held such passionate hunger that her pleasure began to peak in an overwhelming burst and she sobbed with too much pleasure.

It was too much for them both. The pitch of their joy, and their need, was overwhelming. He grunted, pushed in again and again, and as she melted into powerful, sobbing release, his head lifted, his neck arched up, his body swelled harder, made a convulsive thrust, and then he cried out with her, a long, involuntary sound that was half weeping, half joy, and fell down against her.

* * *

Desi awoke to shaded sunlight and lay for a moment in a mood of lazy well-being, wondering why it should be so. Behind her head the breeze blew in through the wooden slats shading the window, cool and fresh. As she yawned and stretched a muscle protested, and she remembered what had happened in the night. A smile played over her lips and she turned her head.

The bed beside her was empty. It was late, and he had said he had work today. She was not sorry. She needed time to think.

Ten years. She stretched like a cat, feeling that her arteries carried warm honey instead of blood from her heart to her body. Ten long years since she had felt this magic in her limbs.

He wants to marry Sami.

Her heart contracted at the thought, withdrawing the honey from her muscles, and Desi flung herself to her feet. What had she done? What kind of fool was she?

Sami was right. Salah had never got over her. The thought touched her in some deep part of herself that she was afraid to look at more closely.

She hadn't got over Salah, either, that much was obvious. It might have been better if she had had some suspicion that that was the case, Desi reflected. She had been totally unprepared for the onslaught of his feelings, and her own. And she had fallen at the first fence.

Closure. If Salah now felt he had closure, she had done Sami no good at all. Instead of putting up a roadblock, she had only paved his way to marriage with her friend.

And as for her—what grief had she stored up for herself?

* * *

Breakfast was served to her in her suite, where she sat on cushions at a low table, beside a window open onto the fountain. Salah, Fatima told her, had arranged for one of the chauffeurs to take her on a tour of the city if she wished.

Desi spent a restless day, wandering through mosques and gardens, around the magnificent tomb and gardens of a thirteenth-century Barakati poet. It was all beautiful and impressive: soaring domes, exquisite mosaic and delicate stone arabesques, but Desi could take it in with only half her awareness. She kept thinking about what had happened last night, and what might be going to happen tonight.

Was once enough to give Salah the closure he was looking for? How could she bear to be with him for so many days and nights, with this bottomless need assailing her, if he no longer wanted her?

Another bout of the heartbreak she'd suffered ten years ago would kill her.

In the late afternoon, as she got into the car after a visit to a small, breathtakingly ancient mosque, her phone beeped with a text. Sami, just waking up in Vancouver.

How RU? What's happening? Talk to me!

OK. Nothing to report, lied Desi, who just could not talk about what had happened. *Sightseeing in city today, with guide. Leaving 2morrow 4 site.*

Who is guide? Sami wanted to know.

Today, Faraj. Tomorrow, Salah. TRIP TAKES 5 DAYS ACROSS DESERT!!! WHY DIDN'T YOU WARN ME?

OMG! I had no idea. Vry sry but at least will give u lots of time to work your magic! Car will be air conditioned, LOL.

It's not the heat, it's the COMPANY!

ROFLMAO. Good luck. U know I wish u every success...

That was, oddly enough, the first time it occurred to her that if, for reasons of his own, Salah really was set on marrying Sami, he would not be very happy if she, Desi, managed to sabotage his plans. If she succeeded in getting permission for Sami to marry Farid from Khaled al Khouri against Salah's wishes, five days in his company on the way to the site would be nothing compared to five days in his company on the return....

She could only cross that bridge when she came to it.

She arrived back at the palace at the end of the day sunburnt, tired and hungry, and desperate to see Salah again. Desperate to know that something had been awakened in him by their lovemaking.

'His Excellency not come. All meeting very hard all,' Fatima said. 'He say tomorrow come up at *fajr*, breakfast very quick. You live after *fajr*. In summer go early!'

'Get up at *fajr*?'

Fatima shook her head with her inability to translate the word. Thinking it must be a number, Desi held up fingers. 'Seven o'clock? Six? Eight?'

Fatima, too, began to use sign language. She looked up and moved her hands in a broad arc. 'Sky night, not sun. Sun—' She stretched one arm out to indicate the horizon and wiggled her fingers.

'Sunrise? Get up with the sun?'

Fatima shook her head vigorously. 'Before sun! *Fajr. Muezzin!*'

Muezzin, she remembered, meant the call to prayer. The first call to prayer came when the world was still dark. So they would set out before daybreak.

That entailed no particular hardship for Desi, who

might not wake up for less than ten thousand dollars, but who, when she did so, was often required in Makeup while the sky was still black.

But it was difficult to wait so long to see Salah. The more so as she suspected he was deliberately avoiding her. She would like to know why. Because he feared his own reactions, feared to be tempted again? Because he was feeling guilty about what had happened?

Or, worst—because once was enough, and now he would find it a burden to be with her?

Desi felt confused, at odds with herself. What did it mean, that she still wanted Salah, in spite of everything? That the sexual bond was as powerful now—more powerful, perhaps, with maturity—after ten years of thinking she hated him?

Why had she come here, and stirred up this hornet's nest?

She ate alone, listening as the evening *muezzin* made his call, turned down Fatima's invitation to watch television, and went to bed early. She was still jetlagged, and dawn would come early.

She phoned Sami, and was relieved when she got her friend's voicemail.

'It's me. We're leaving tomorrow at first light, and apparently there's no coverage in the desert without a satellite phone,' Desi said. 'So I'll be incommunicado for a few days. I know you wish me luck.'

She was restless. She read for a little, then knelt up on the bed, turned out the lamp, opened the wooden jalousie, and rested her elbows on the window sill, gazing out on the silent courtyard and the stars.

If only she could get a sense of where she was headed! But the future was as black and impenetrable as the sky. She felt nothing—no sense of impending doom anymore, no promise of release. Only an intense, unbearable yearning for his presence. His arms, his mouth, his body. *Please, please, let him come to me...*

After a while she slipped down into bed. She didn't notice when sleep came.

She woke suddenly. Through the open window above her bed she saw stars in a clear black sky. A cooling breeze blew in over her, shaking the wooden jalousie, but that sound was not what had awakened her.

She leaned up and put her hand out to the lamp. Before she could turn it on, he was there, kneeling beside the bed.

'Desi.' His voice was hoarse with the struggle against longing. *'Deezee.'*

She reached for him, and in the next moment his body was hot against hers and she was drowning.

CHAPTER TEN

THE sun flamed up in the sky on the right, a perfect circle of burning fury that promised the greater ferocity to come, and the grey line of the mountains' shadow rushed towards them, chased by golden sand.

'That's quite a vista,' Desi murmured. It was a dizzying view all the way to white-topped Mount Shir, brooding high above the foothills like the lion it was named for.

Salah glanced at her, and away again. She looked like what she was—a beautiful woman who had known passion in the night. And he realized, from the change he saw in her, that it had been a long time since she had experienced the kind of lovemaking he had given her. Her skin had a glow that had not been there before; her eyes were soft with remembered pleasure, her mouth was swollen with the memory of kisses.

His kisses.

He felt a burst of masculine satisfaction. That was the measure of a man, or one of them: to give his woman true pleasure—so that afterwards she was sweet, like honey. His own body ached and sang with the thought of her sweetness, and for him, too, it had been lovemaking like nothing he had known for ten years.

'I told you once that you would like it,' he said, but he was not talking about Mount Shir.

Then he heard his own thoughts—*his woman.* But she was not his woman, not now, not ever again. And he was a fool if he let sex cloud his thinking about her. She had betrayed him once, when he needed her most. She was almost certainly betraying him now, betraying his country, perhaps—for although he had no proof of what she really wanted here, he could be very sure at least that she was lying to him.

Sex made fools of men. He knew that, he had seen it happen to others. He would not be of their number. He would keep a clear head. He had four or five days to get the truth from her. Desire must not blind him to the need to do it. Sex must not be allowed to interfere with his plans. He reached out and pressed the radio into life, to puncture the mood in the truck's cabin.

He had been ten times a fool to think he could undertake this task without risk.

Desi smiled and stretched in her seat, letting the incomprehensible chatter from the radio blend into the background like music. Every muscle in her body simultaneously protested and relayed a honeyed memory of the lovemaking just past.

Salah had been wild with need in the night, seeking the solace of her body over and over, as if to make up for ten lost years in a single night. When they arose at daybreak Desi had no idea whether she'd slept. The mix of languor and energy in her body was like nothing she'd ever experienced before.

The memory of their lovemaking was in the vehicle

with them now, heavy in the air, liquid in her cells. She was sensitive even to the pressure of the air against her skin; any movement was slow dancing in honey.

A few more minutes of driving in shade, and then, with a little explosion of light, they were in full sunshine.

There was a smile in her being, and it played with her eyes and the corners of her mouth. Desi leaned lazily back and watched the landscape. Silence fell for minutes, during which she savoured shimmering crystal sharp air, blinding light, purple-grey shadows under distant foothills.

Watching the shadows retreat across the desert as the sun climbed higher could almost be a life's occupation, she reflected. And again she had that strange feeling of belonging, as if the desert had been waiting for her and would now claim her.

He had not mentioned the letter, but she thought he would soon. He had to. Could he explain, would he apologize? Surely now they could discuss what had happened so long ago with some detachment?

She shifted nervously. Everything was too over-whelming, happening too fast. If he did bring it up, where would that lead them? Was she ready for that?

Would she end up telling him about Sami? she wondered suddenly. No real explanation was possible between them without that, but…how would he react? She had promised Sami she would not tell Salah. If she risked betraying that…she had no idea where the discussion would go.

'So much traffic!' she said. 'Does everybody start early, or have they been driving all night?'

'This is the main road to the oil fields. In summer everyone avoids driving in the middle of the day.'

In his voice she thought she heard a reflection of her own nervous reluctance to start on something where they could not be sure of the end. Well, there was time. Five days they would be alone. Five days to try to sort her thoughts. No hurry.

They drove in silence. Now and then Salah pointed out an ancient ruin in the desert, or a distant nomad encampment. Desi laughed aloud when they came up behind a pickup truck carrying a young camel which was hunkered down with its legs folded beneath it, complacently regarding them over the tailgate, chewing its cud.

'And my camera's packed in my case!'

'You have a camera?'

'Of course! I want to—'

'You will not be able to take photographs at the dig,' Salah said.

'Oh! Is—' But she was afraid to ask why for fear of exposing her ignorance. 'Have you been to the dig before?' she asked instead.

'A few times,' Salah said. 'When it was first discovered.'

'What can you tell me about it? I couldn't find any information. Sami said it might be contemporary with Sumer. It sounds really exciting.'

It was barely three weeks since Desi had first heard of Sumer, the ancient civilisation that thrived between the Tigris and Euphrates Rivers five thousand years ago, but she wasn't faking her interest. There was something about five thousand years of history that sparked her imagination now as much as when she was eleven.

She had crammed a lot of study into the short time she had to prepare. But although she could bone up on the Sumer period and archaeology in general, she had found absolutely nothing about the site Salah's father was working, so far from where ancient Sumer had prospered. Some mysterious outpost, some far city?

'My father is maintaining very close secrecy until he can publish,' he said. 'You he could not refuse, but no other outsider has been allowed to visit. No media. A hand-picked team. You understand.'

'I see,' Desi said lamely, who didn't know what it meant to 'publish' a site, couldn't imagine why an ancient site would be kept secret, and was dismayed to learn she was on the receiving end of such a massive favour. 'I didn't realize what I was asking for. I mean...'

'Are you sure?'

'Sure?'

'Sure you didn't realize what you were asking for.'

His voice was hard suddenly. In anyone else she would have called it suspicious, but what could he be suspicious of as far as the dig went?

'I'm new at this,' she pointed out mildly.

'And just by chance you happen upon the most tightly kept secret of archaeology of the last thirty years and discover an interest.'

It *was* suspicion. She couldn't imagine what he suspected her of, but after last night, how could he speak to her in such a voice?

'I didn't go looking for this, you know,' she pointed out calmly. 'Sami is my best friend. Why shouldn't she tell me about her uncle's work when I told her what I was planning? I'm sure she has no idea how secret it is. She'd have said something.'

'Sami should not know about it herself.'

'She knows because it's the reason marriage negotiations aren't taking place yet. Till your father gets back from the dig. But by all means let's not discuss the dig if you'd rather not!' Desi said. 'Let's talk about something else. We've made love two nights running. Have you got the closure you wanted?'

Immediately she wished the words unsaid.

Salah turned his head and looked at her with a look so smouldering she felt physical heat. Memory roared up, making her weak.

'Have you?' he countered.

'I wasn't the one looking for closure. Why won't you give me a straight answer?'

'You were looking for something. Have you got it yet?'

'I was looking to go to your father's dig,' she snapped. How much hurt he could still inflict! 'Are we there yet? No? Well, then, not.'

He flicked a glance into her eyes.

'So you didn't come here to see me?'

'Salah, how many times do you need that question answered?'

'Truthfully, only once.'

'By which you mean, you won't accept any answer till you hear what you want to hear. I'm happy to oblige. What answer would you like? Let's get it out of the way.'

'Desi.' His voice was almost pleading, and her eyes jerked involuntarily to his face. 'I know that you are not here for the reason you say. I know you. You can't tell me a lie and I don't know it.'

'You don't know anything about me,' she said, as bitterness welled up in her throat. 'You don't know me now, you didn't know me then. You couldn't have written that letter if you'd known the first thing about me.'

He shook his head at the attempt to derail him. 'Tell me why you have come.'

'Not from any motive you are contemplating.'

'Is that an admission? What motive, then?'

'Oh, leave it alone!'

The honeyed languour was gone from her body. Sunlight was beating into the car with such ferocity she was getting a headache. Heat and sun rarely bothered her, she blossomed in the heat, but this was different. A strip of chrome on the wing mirror was reflecting the sun straight into her eyes. She realized she hadn't put on her sunglasses, opened her bag and pulled them out.

'Hiding your eyes won't help.'

'On the contrary, it may prevent a headache,' she said sharply. A herd of camels grazed on nothing in front of a settlement of half a dozen mudbrick houses. Tourists pressed cameras against the windows of a bus, snapping pictures as they passed. The highway curved around to the west; Mount Shir was behind them now. Ahead was an endless stretch of sand, shimmering in the heat, the highway a silver-grey ribbon laid across the vastness.

The road to nowhere, she thought.

After lunch in a small village restaurant, where they waited out the midday heat for another hour, Salah turned the four-wheel drive vehicle off-road and struck out across the dunes.

Now they were completely alone. Within a few minutes they had left all signs of civilisation behind, and were surrounded by the rich emptiness of the desert. Heat shimmered over the dunes; the sun was a white blast furnace against a blue of startling intensity; the pale sand, broken by rocky outcrops now and then, stretched to infinity. Only when she turned to look back at Mount Shir was there any relief for her eyes.

After several hours, the sun began to set ahead of them, the sky turning fiery red and orange and the sun getting fatter and heavier as it approached the horizon. As she watched, the sky shaded to purple, and now the sun was a massive orange ball, larger than she recalled ever seeing it before. When it began to sink behind the horizon, the sky above turned midnight blue.

The sun disappeared in a blaze; the sky went black very quickly. And still they drove.

Salah did not put on the headlights. The world was shadows. There was no human light visible anywhere, just stars and a moon almost at the full, bathing the dunes in ghostly purple. Desi was seized with a sudden, atavistic dread.

She shifted nervously. 'When do we stop for the night?'

'Soon,' he said. 'An hour or so. Are you tired?'

She shrugged and took a sip of water from the bottle ever present between them.

'A little. Aren't you going to put the headlights on?'

'What for?'

'Can you drive in the dark?'

'Why not?'

'But how do you know where you're going?'

Salah laughed. 'There is only one way to navigate in the desert, Desi—by the sky. In daylight, by the sun. At night, by the stars. My forebears have done it for many thousands of years. Don't worry—if my ancestors had not been good navigators, I would not be here.'

She laughed, and the strange dread lifted. They

spoke little, but a feeling of peace and companionship settled over her as they drove on into the night. She almost forgot the harsh accusations of the morning in her pleasure at being with Salah in a world of two.

She had no idea how long they drove when at last a flickering light appeared in the distance. 'What's that? Is that a town?'

'You will see,' he said, and flicked on the headlights.

A cluster of strangely patterned tents met her eyes: a Bedouin encampment. By the time they reached it, a party of tall robed men was there to welcome them. Under instruction, Salah parked the Toyota against the wire fence of an enclosure, and they got out to be greeted by the men.

They were a tall race, clearly. The men towered over her in their flowing robes and turbans, with the dignified bearing of those who have never lost their connection to the land. They chatted with Salah in soft welcoming voices and led them past the wire enclosure, which proved to be a camel corral. In the flickering torchlight as they passed she saw a dozen beasts crouching on the ground, chewing and whuffling, their outrageous long curling eyelashes made even more seductive by moonshadow. Her heart leapt with the alien magic.

They were led to the centre of the encampment of tents, where there was torchlight and a charcoal brazier. Other men were moving about, laying a carpet with plates and food. Another took their bags and disappeared.

'Is this a hotel?' Desi asked in amazement.

'It is a nomad camp. But the people are by tradition very hospitable. They are used to strangers appearing out of the desert. There are guided tours of the desert for foreigners. Such tourists nowadays often stay with the desert nomads like this.'

Desi was enchanted. A tall moustachioed man of impressive bearing and impregnable dignity bent to offer her a silver basin and a bar of soap, poured water over her hands as she washed, then gave her a weather-beaten square of cloth to dry them.

'Is this a work camp?' she asked. 'Why are there no women?'

'Women do not serve strangers,' Salah said. 'In the morning probably some will come and show you their craft work.'

'Lovely! What sort of things do they make?'

'Dolls, pottery, maybe. You will have to wait and see.'

Very soon food was laid before them.

'Is it the desert air, or is this food totally delicious?' Desi demanded, falling on it with a reckless abandon that she would have to pay for by eating starvation rations soon.

'We haven't eaten since lunch,' Salah pointed out mildly.

'Yes, but I'm so used to going without food, it shouldn't get to me like this,' Desi said. 'I've been eating far too much since I got here; at this rate I'll have to fast completely for a week!'

'Not on this trip, please. The desert is dangerous enough without that.'

Desi nodded, taking his point, and consciously slowed her eating.

'They use so much oil!' she protested. 'In the palace, too. Is that what makes it so flavourful? How on earth does everybody in this country not turn into an elephant?'

Salah laughed aloud. 'Olive oil,' he corrected her, as

if he were talking about gold. 'Olive oil is very healthy, as well as giving its delicious flavour to food. We grow our own species of olive. Barakati olive oil is rare but very prized in the world, and very little is exported. Its flavour is excellent.'

When the last of the food had been presented, they were politely left with only each other and the stars. Above them a shooting star rushed along a golden pathway to oblivion.

Suddenly the night air was heavy around them, weighted with awareness. And now that there was nothing to cloak it, their hungry need rose up like heat from the sand to cloud the space between them.

'They are preparing our tent,' Salah said, his voice low and hoarse. 'Will you sleep with me, tonight, Desi? I want you.'

CHAPTER ELEVEN

HER heart leapt with yearning, her body melted into instant need. But she looked at him for a moment, resisting, remembering his harsh words earlier in the day.

'Tell me what it means to you, that you want me,' she said quietly.

'It means you are a beautiful, sensual woman.'

'Not good enough. Next answer.'

'What do you want to hear?'

'You've thought yourself too good to talk to me for something like ten years. Now you're sleeping with me. Have you looked at that fact?'

'Is this why you came? To prove something to me?' he asked.

'My interest in proving anything to you runs in the minus figures, Salah. I find that when a person makes an accusation, he's usually talking to a mirror. Are you trying to prove something to me?'

'You forget that I did not go to your country. You came to mine.'

'You forget that I did not go to your bed. You came to mine.'

'Why did you come out to me? You came to me. You knew I was waiting.'

'I think we've agreed the old sexual fire still has live coals amongst the ashes,' Desi said. 'Still, I don't call stepping out of my room to get some air "coming to you", exactly.'

'You called my name. You knew I was there.'

'I didn't, actually. Why were you there?'

'You know it,' he said.

'Closure, you say. What do you need closure on, exactly, Salah? Because you look as though you've had closure on everything in life. You look as if you've shut down everything except the food intake. What's left?'

He put out one hand to catch her chin and turned her head. For one tremulous moment his eyes met hers.

'You know what is left.'

Honeyed sweetness flooded up her body, making her neck weak.

'You stirred up what was frozen, Desi. Until you came, I had forgotten how much I once loved you.'

'Salah!' she whispered.

'And how little you loved me.'

'You think?' she said bitterly.

'You did not love me at all. You said so, and you were right.'

'I was sixteen!'

'Yes. You were young. I also was young, too young for such powerful feelings. I could not control what I felt. You said I was like the Kaljuks, and my only thought, Desi, was to prove to you that I could never be like them.'

'Is that why you joined Prince Omar?' she breathed, horrified.

He shrugged. 'I was running across a rocky ledge, looking for a way down to a Kaljuk gun emplacement that had been shelling a mountain town for a week.' Unconsciously he stroked the scar that ran across his cheekbone to above his ear. 'There was an explosion of light in my head, that's all I remember. I woke up in the hospital.

'You were there with me day and night, Desi. You were my solace and my torment, in one. I dreamed of you, sleeping and waking. I wanted you more than anything in the world. I begged you to come to me. You did not come.'

'I tried, but Leo…' Immediately she wished she hadn't pronounced the name.

'Yes, Leo,' he said in a different tone. 'Sami sent me a letter with pictures of you in your new life with this old man. Then I understood. You did not love me, you could never be mine. I wrote you the letter to tell you I knew it.

'But I could not defend myself against the knowing. It went straight into my heart. The pain was like the end of the world, Desi. I did not recover, not even after I told myself I did. When you love someone the way I loved you…. Every day and every night I yearned for you. In the bed of other women, I dreamed of you.'

Suddenly she had to choke back tears.

'Why did you never tell me? Never try to get in touch?' she demanded. 'It was up to you, wasn't it? After that letter did you expect me to try to contact you again?'

'No,' he said. 'I expected nothing. You were with Leo. My love died, a terrible, painful death that I thought had killed my heart.

'One day, I awoke from the pain. But still I was not

free of you. Then it was the memory of love itself that haunted me. Fool that I was, I wanted to find this feeling again, with another woman. I thought you could be wiped from my memory forever and I would feel alive again.

'But that is impossible, I learned that. I can never feel such an impact again. I don't know why it is so, but it is. I was ten times a fool to wish it. Such love is weakness. An addiction.'

He paused, but she had no words.

'I thought it was dead, Desi. Before you came I thought there was nothing left, not even ashes. When my father told me he would let you come, I was angry, that was all. I thought, it is over. What business does she have, to come to me now?

'Then you came, and it was not what I expected. Anger was only the first of many feelings. I understood things I did not understand before.

'Our love and its death has affected every decision of my life from that moment, every breath I took, every woman I rejected as a wife. I understand it now.'

'God,' she whispered. Her heart was choking her.

'I want to free myself, Desi. My parents urge me to get married—for ten years they have wanted this. Now even I see it is time. But I can't go to my future wife with such a burden of the past. Not now that I feel its weight.'

Her mouth opened in a soundless gasp as she took in his meaning.

'It is time to leave this behind. We have a few days together. I want to finish with these broken hopes. I want to bury the past once and forever. I want to go to my new wife with a heart free and ready to accept her.'

She was silent, struggling with feeling. A sound like

gunshot startled her as one of the flaming torches fell to be extinguished in the sand, and its dying spark shot skyward like a soul going home.

'And how will sleeping with me for a few days free your heart?' she asked at last.

'I have been haunted by you, Desi, by the memory of lovemaking that moved the earth. Nothing has matched it, but it is because nothing can match it. You can't match a dream. It is a fantasy, I know it, born from the fact that you were my first experience of love.'

She wanted to tell him how it had been for her. The tearing grief, the bottomless yearning for that soul-deep connection, the determination to forget. Then Leo's terrible betrayal, and afterwards, the emptiness, the feeling that that part of her had died. And the terrible shock, seeing Salah again, to discover that it might still be there.

'I want that haunting to stop. Can you understand this? And I think—to put out my hand and know that it *is* you, and that the sex is what it is and no more—then I can close the book. I want to close it, Desi.'

'You're going to marry my best friend, feeling like this?' she protested.

'Don't you see, it is not feeling? It is a memory, that is all.'

'What if it worked the other way? What if this revived your love? Then what?'

Salah shook his head. 'Do not fear for me, Desi.'

'And what about my feelings? They don't matter?'

He was silent, his eyes meeting hers. He didn't believe she had any feelings to be hurt, that was obvious. And she just could not open her mouth to tell him. What would he do with such knowledge?

'You're sure this is not a disguised desire to punish me?' she pressed.

'How would this punish you?'

'You might think I'm vulnerable. You suspect me of coming here to see you. What did you imagine I wanted?'

An odd expression crossed his face in torchlight. 'What power do I have to hurt you?'

Before she could answer, one of the Bedouin came and spoke to him.

'Our tent is ready,' Salah said. 'Come to bed.'

And in spite of everything, her heart kicked with cell-deep anticipation.

The interior of the tent was softly lighted in the glow of two hurricane lamps. The earth was covered with reed mats and carpets, the space was divided into two sections by curtains of mosquito netting. On one side there was a large basin and two jugs of water behind a curtain. The other side held cushions and a thin mattress spread with a clean striped cloth.

A small spade was placed discreetly by the entrance, and Desi picked it up and went out to walk into the dunes. When she returned Salah had washed and was behind the netting, zipping their sleeping bags into a double. He turned and looked at her, and suddenly she was remembering the night they had spent in a little cabin on the island. Then, too, they had lit hurricane lanterns.

Then, too, the air between them had been thick with anticipation, and her limbs had been heavy with it.

They did not speak. He got up and went out.

Desi got out her sponge bag and went into the little space to bathe. She had packed unperfumed soap, to avoid enticing insects, but now she wished she could risk using some scent. Nor could the cotton pyjamas she had packed be called anything but plain.

She knew she was being a fool. She was storing up heartbreak for herself.

But if for Salah lovemaking was a necessary way of coming to terms with the past, for her it was thirst in the desert.

All those years of telling herself it had been nothing to him. That if he had truly loved her, he could never have written what he did. What he told her this evening was like a firestorm in her. He *had* loved her.

If she had known that, would she have had the courage to write back, to shout at him for his despicable attitude? To fight?

But how could she have been happy with a man who harboured such alien, archaic views? Would he ever have treated her as an equal? A man makes love to a virgin and then calls her a slut? When she looked at it squarely, she knew she had had a lucky escape.

If only it felt like that.

When Salah returned to the tent, she was lying in the sleeping bag reading by the light of one of the lanterns. She looked up.

He stood gazing at her from the other side of the heavy netting, a shadowy silhouette, tall and powerful in a flowing robe, perfectly still. For a moment, as they stared at each other, the world stopped. There was no past between them, no future, the silence whispered, there was only the moment. Then he lifted the netting and stepped inside her little cocoon.

The little slow intake of her breath as she watched him was perfectly audible in the silence. Rivulets of anticipation coursed through her. She put down her book.

Lamplight caressed his curling black hair like melted gold. His desert cloak was open. She took in the vision of a flat, hard stomach, snug boxers, legs that were powerfully muscled. So different, and yet still there was the shadow of the eager young body that she had first seen so long ago.

A thin pale mark ran from his abdomen, over one hip and down his thigh almost to the knee. That was the line that marked the frontier between then and now: his battle scars.

He had a light dusting of hair on his forearms as well as a neat mat of chest hair. A delicate line of black curls tracing the middle of his abdomen gathered momentum as it reached his shorts. His flesh stirred as he looked at her.

It was unmistakably, primitively male.

And primally, powerfully erotic. She could not remember a time when the mere sight of a man's body had affected her so deeply, drawing her irresistibly.

Salah shrugged off the robe and dropped it on the carpet. His shoulders looked even more powerful now. He sank down onto his haunches, and then he was beside her, his mouth searching for hers, his heat enveloping her.

Her hand went of its own accord to the flesh at his groin, and she stroked him hungrily as it turned to marble, drunk on the knowledge that her touch had such power over him. She had seen statues of gods with erect sex, and tonight she understood the primitive urge to worship such flesh.

His head fell back at the assault of pleasure, and she slipped her fingers inside the elastic of his waistband, to draw the black fabric down and off his body. Then he lay naked in glowing lamplight, his eyes watching her with a black fury of need that stirred her to the depths. Her hand enclosed him again, and she bent down over him and almost without conscious volition, because in some deep part of her she was compelled to it, took him into her mouth.

His breath caught, and the sound shivered over her skin. She closed her eyes and gave herself up to the pleasure of giving pleasure. She felt his hands in her hair, cupping her head, felt the intensity of his need.

'Too much,' he said hoarsely after a few moments. His hands moved to catch her shoulders, and he drew her up into a fierce embrace. 'Too much.' He leaned away from her for a moment, she heard the puff of his breath, and then the tent was in darkness.

In another moment, she was wrapped in his embrace.

CHAPTER TWELVE

THE haunting sound of a distant *muezzin* woke her. Desi slipped out of bed, leaving Salah still sleeping, wrapped herself in her bathrobe, and went out.

The sky was showing the first signs of morning, the moon palely giving way to her ferocious brother as the sky paled. The air was deliciously fresh and crisp. Beneath her feet the sand was cool. When she dug at it with her toes, the layer underneath proved to be still warm, as if the earth were a living creature and she had burrowed under its fur. She stood, shivering a little, her feet warm in the sand, savouring the lonely sound of the *muezzin*'s voice against the utter peace of the desert, until it fell silent.

Then she took the spade and went into the dunes. When she returned, the camp was beginning to stir.

It was her first desert dawn, and Desi was moved by its perfection. She went back into the tent to discover Salah up and gone, and the pitchers filled with fresh water. She hurried with her washing and dressing, not to miss a minute of the morning.

When she got outside again, dressed in khaki shorts and a T-shirt but still barefoot, the sky was the colour of smoke, with a straggle of cloud and a swathe of rich, deep pink at the horizon. She set off running. Overhead slowly the sky revealed itself as blue, while above the horizon the pink expanded into red, gold and yellow, setting the cloud alight, and a tiny burning arc of fire appeared behind the dunes.

She jogged out towards the camel corral, where the beasts regarded her with placid condescension as she passed, and up the steep side of a nearby dune, her feet sinking deep into the sand, which brought her to the top breathless.

She stood looking out over the vista as the newborn sun painted the tops of the dunes in bright gold. The camp was revealed as a few broad, low tents pitched around a small central area where a pit had been dug to form a brazier. A man was stirring the coals into life.

Not far away from the camp, women were drawing water from the concrete housing of a well. In the light wind of morning their brightly patterned robes and scarves fanned out against a backdrop of endless pale sand. A herd of white and black goats clustered around, eagerly pushing towards the broad troughs that the women were filling. Their bleating was the only sound on the morning air, a dozen different pitches and rhythms like strange music.

The women were covertly watching her. From her vantage point on the dune she waved, and two of the older women smiled, one of them shyly waggling her hand at chest height. The younger ones drew their scarves up to cover their mouths and dropped their eyes.

Back in the tent, she found Salah, looking handsome and intimidating in desert robes, seated lotus-position on the ground, consulting a map. When she came in, fresh-faced with her exercise and the morning chill, he looked up and smiled. Her breath caught with surprise. It was the first time she had seen him so relaxed. The frown was gone from his eyes.

'Ready for breakfast?' he asked.

'Ravenous! Is it going to be local fare again, or do they provide the usual tourist stuff?' she asked as he led her outside to where someone had placed a carpet for them with cushions side by side in the sun. A man in flowing robes and turban was setting down plates.

'They aren't so changed yet. The few travellers they see are still the sort who want to experience what the world has to offer, not impose their own lifestyle on it. We will be offered the best of their own food.'

'Can't wait!'

As last night, the only utensils were spoons, and again she washed her hands under the stream of water poured for her from a ewer.

Little bowls of yoghurt and a curious mud-coloured paste were set before them and Desi was negotiating with the yoghurt when the pièce de résistance arrived: a huge, deliciously sizzling, buttery, puffy pancake that had been grilled over charcoal. Something that looked suspiciously like honey was drizzled all over it.

On the pure desert air the scent of it was tantalizing.

'Oh, *totally* too fattening! I must remember to ask before I go around demanding the local food,' Desi exclaimed helplessly.

'You can eat all the yoghurt.' Salah grinned and tore off a large chunk of the pancake, expertly rolling it up in one hand before taking a bite. Honey dripped onto his lower lip and he licked it off, his eyes closing with enjoyment.

He turned his head and looked at her from under lowered eyelids. 'Hot. Sweet.' *Like you.*

The thought of what those long, strong fingers, his tongue and mouth had done to her last night stormed through her. Her neck was suddenly too weak to hold up her head.

She took a hasty mouthful of the yoghurt and shivered as a blast of sourness reached her nerves. 'I give in!' she cried, reaching to tear off a bit of the pancake and dipping the end in a little pool of honey that had collected in the lower levels of its bubbly terrain.

'Delicious! That's so yummy it should be classed as a dangerous weapon! Is every meal over the next few days going to be diet sabotage?'

'Boiled camel feet sometimes lack that certain something,' he advised. 'Eat while you can.'

'Between the suntan and the fat, my agent will kill me.'

'Start a fashion for voluptuous,' he suggested.

'You don't understand. I *am* voluptuous. I abandoned the waif figure years ago. Do you think this body is size zero? Think again.'

'What is size zero?'

'That's the size models try to be. I'd have to lose ten or twelve pounds to get there. As a model I'm considered borderline fat, as my agent keeps warning me.'

Salah stared at her for a moment, then began to laugh. It started as a chuckle, but quickly descended to his belly, where it took on a deeply contagious quality that drew her irresistibly into laughter, too. With great gusts and hoops, they were caught so helplessly that finally Salah fell backwards into the sand.

She turned to look down at him, at the black curls dusted with sand, sun-crinkled eyes, white teeth and laughing mouth. A new expression came into his eyes, and the laughter died on her lips.

He lifted his hand up her back and clenched it in her hair.

'You are perfectly beautiful,' he said, and for an uncharted time they were still, gazing at each other through ten long, wasted years.

Then Salah's eyes widened in something like alarm. His face became shuttered and he sat up.

'It is time to leave,' he said flatly. And only then did Desi breathe again.

As he had predicted, several of the older women were sitting near the camel corral as they left, with their crafts and other wares spread out for examination.

Desi crouched down in front of the spread. Dolls made of bits of cloth and coloured thread, stones with fossils embedded in them, some pottery bowls with a curious design, and, best of all, some beautifully etched and painted bits of camel bone.

Desi oohed and aahed over everything, miming her admiration, and, unable to disappoint such dignified, open people, who clearly were very poor, carefully chose several items.

The camel bone work was exquisite: carved and engraved rings and pendants, and little etched scenes on flat strips of bone that looked for all the world like ivory.

Desi picked up an oval medallion bearing a delicately etched camel. Brown paint had been rubbed into the etched lines, so the outlines were dark against a smudged paler background blending into the creamy white of the bone.

'This stuff is gorgeous!' she said over her shoulder to Salah. 'Where did she learn to carve like this?'

Salah briefly spoke with the artist, a middle-aged and weather-beaten woman with a thin face and calloused, graceful hands.

'She learned it from her father. He learned it from his own father, and as none of her brothers survived childhood, he taught her. Her father used to colour such etchings in many colours, but she can no longer find the substances to make the paints, so she paints mostly in monochrome. She misses having the colours and apologizes because the work is not very pretty.'

'It's lovely. Can you find out her name for me, please?'

As Desi drew out her wallet, one of the women signalled to her, then opened a bit of cloth to show her something.

A small clay statue of a woman with a large tiara and hair exquisitely moulded in tumbling curls down her back and over her shoulder. She had prominent breasts, and her pubic hair was clearly marked, but her body had been given a dress of paler clay that flaked easily when she picked it up.

Desi examined it curiously.

'How old is this?' she asked.

'"Very, very old",' Salah translated for the women.

'Do you think that's true? I mean, if so, wouldn't it be in a museum?'

'It is unlikely that anyone in this tribe would make a forgery of that kind. They would consider it blasphemous. That is why they have given her a modest cover-up before selling her.'

Forgery or not, Desi was taken by the little figure.

'How much is it?'

Again a short colloquy. 'Twenty dirhams.'

Desi blinked. 'But it must—it has to be a forgery. If it were genuine they'd be asking a lot more, wouldn't they?'

'They find such things in the sand as they travel. They used to destroy them, thinking them some sort of witchcraft. Then they learned that foreigners liked them. For them, twenty dirhams is a lot of money, especially for a found item. They don't understand why tourists like things that are old and broken like this.'

'Well, I certainly like her.'

When she had paid and everything had been wrapped in rags or bits of old newspaper and put in a very distressed plastic bag, she thanked the women and got to her feet. With many goodbyes they were on their way.

'Where do they spend the money?' she asked later, as they headed out over the desert.

'Taxis sometimes come and take them to town.'

'What, such a distance?'

He flicked her a look. 'They are not always camped so far from civilisation. But mostly they buy from the travelling shops—trucks loaded with every kind of merchandise, which service the nomad communities.'

'But no chance for that artist to buy manufactured paints?'

'Probably not.'

'If I found her some paints, would there be a way to send them to her?'

After a short silence, Salah asked, 'Why do you bother with this?'

'Because she's an artist, and art this good has a

right to the proper materials. Are you going to answer my question?'

'If you sent her something, eventually it would find its way to her. Tell me, when did you develop an interest in the indigenous art and antiquities of Barakat?'

'I do a lot of travelling in my job, Salah. Half the time I don't get to see anything more than the inside of my five-star hotel and the shoot site. It's not the art so much as the people. I rarely get to meet real people in a real environment. Those women are lovely people, so friendly, and they look as though they can use the money.'

'But the goddess is a collectors' item. Are you a collector?'

'The goddess? Is that who she is? How do you know?' Her interest sparked, Desi dug into the bag of goodies and unwrapped the little clay statuette. She held it cupped in her hand.

'What's her name?'

'It depends on where she was found. It's almost impossible to say with certainty. My father would say, a love or fertility goddess.'

Desi frowned, accessing recent memories. 'Inanna! Wasn't she the goddess of love?'

Salah flicked her a look and said gravely, 'In Sumer. Yes.'

'Could it be her?'

'You would have to ask my father.'

'Oh, but it's impossible. It would mean this was five thousand years old!'

'It probably is.'

Desi gasped. A feeling of wonder flooded her, and a strange energy, as if the little goddess's locked-up power had suddenly been released into her palm.

'That's amazing,' she whispered. 'But—why...I mean, how is it I can buy something so valuable just like that?'

'She might be taken away from you at the airport.'

'Really?'

'It is illegal to take antiquities out of the Barakat Emirates. It is part of our cultural heritage. We have museums where such pieces belong.'

'Seems a pretty poor way to manage resources. Wouldn't it be better to stop the sale in the first place?'

'We can't police the entire desert. Instead tourists are searched before they leave, and such valuable items as your little goddess are confiscated. This discourages tourists from making such purchases in future.'

She laughed. 'So I'll have to give up my little talisman?'

'Not everything is found, of course. Perhaps less than forty percent. If you pack it carefully, you might get away with it.'

She looked at him quizzically. 'What makes you think I would want to "get away with" taking something that belongs in the country's museums?'

'You seem to like it.'

'You think I steal everything I like? Have you noticed me wearing any of the Crown Jewels?'

'You paid for it. Most people would not consider it theft.'

'Oh, give me a break! We make love at night, and in the morning you salve your conscience by suggesting I'm dishonourable, is that it? We've been there before, Salah, and I got enough of it last time. Can't you just enjoy the sex for what it is and leave your condemnation in your pocket?'

His jaw tightened. 'No, that is not it. I apologize. In my work I see many people who consider themselves honest but who are without any conscience at all in this area.'

'In your work?'

'One of my areas as Cup Companion is antiquities security.'

'Say what?'

'My task is to prevent the smuggling of antiquities to foreign markets. Both West and East have many wealthy men who are interested in the ancient cultures of the Barakat Emirates. Organizers pay what to poor nomads and farmers seems a good price for any artefact they can steal or dig up, then sell them on to unscrupulous dealers for many times more. They in turn sell it on. By the time it reaches the collector, he is paying thousands of times the sum the finder got. Our heritage is in danger of being destroyed by this practice.'

'Are you saying your personal mission is to stop it? How do you go about it?'

'In various ways, none of them satisfactory. People mostly rob the sites of ancient cities and settlements which have not yet been studied, near the villages where they live. It is a big problem for archaeologists like my father. As you know, once something is dug up and removed, its provenance can never be discovered. So even if we recover that piece, its historic value is lost.'

'Of course.' Archaeologists must know exactly where something is found before it can shed light on history: Desi had learned that in her researches. A jug was just a jug unless you knew what else it was found with, its period, of what civilisation it had formed a part.

'But theft is not my father's biggest worry.'

There was something in his tone that caught her attention.

'Really? What is, then?'

'The answer is in your hand.'

She thought it was a covert challenge, that he wanted to know if she had any real archaeological interest or understanding. She held up the little statue.

Goddess of love. What did she know about the goddess of love? Worshipped as the one who made animals and land, as well as humans, fertile. Her sexual characteristics painted over by whoever had found it, because now her blatant sexuality was seen not as powerful, but immodest.

'Oh my God!' Desi whispered.

Found in a land where to worship the divine in any form but as Allah was blasphemy.

'Tell me I'm wrong!' she begged. 'Is your father afraid that religious fanatics might... Oh, no!'

'There is a significant risk. My father thinks the site is a city devoted to a love goddess. It could rewrite history. But if the Kaljuks and their supporters here in the Barakat Emirates hear of this find, and learn where it is located, the risk is worse than ordinary theft—they may try to sabotage the site itself. They would want to destroy it completely.'

Desi's strongest emotion after dismay was exasperation. 'For God's sake! Four thousand years before Islam even happened!'

'They do not care about that.' Salah slowed the vehicle and turned his head, and his black eyes found hers. 'That is why, Desi, I ask you if you have any other reason for wanting to visit this dig.'

'What?' she asked blankly.

'If someone has asked you to try to find out what you can about the site my father is digging, you must understand that it is unlikely to be for genuine academic purposes.'

'What are you trying to say?' She blinked at him.

His voice was rough now, his eyes probing.

'I know you are not here for the reason you have given. Do not be the innocent tool of villains, Desi. If someone wants to know about this project, it is because they want to steal our history from us, one way or the other. Tell me who asked you to use your connection with our family in this way.'

She felt as if he had slapped her. She had to open her mouth twice before she could speak.

'What do you imagine you're talking about?' she cried. 'No one asked me to visit the dig! No one asked me to come here!'

'This is not the truth, Desi! Tell me their names! Such information can be invaluable to us.'

'I am not anyone's tool, innocent or otherwise!' she cried indignantly. 'Do you imagine I could be so stupid? Or maybe you think I'm the cheat myself? Is that what you think?'

'Why are you here?'

'I told you why!'

He was silent, watching the guarded look come into her eyes. The lie was in her tone; even she could hear it. But she had to glare back at him with the best outrage she could muster.

'I am not anybody's tool,' she insisted, hating the expression on his face, hating the lie she was living. How she wished she could throw the truth at his head.

He said, 'I will take you to my father, if you insist,

Desi. But I tell you now that you will not learn where the site is, even though you see it with your own eyes— the desert does not tell the uninitiated where they are. You will learn no village name. Do you still wish to make the journey?'

'Of course I do!' she cried. 'And I couldn't care less about knowing the compass coordinates! You can blind-fold me if you want to. That's not why I want to visit the site. I told you—I had no idea how important it was till you told me the other day. I thought it was just another site. I had no idea I was asking for such a big favour.'

'My father could not say no.'

'Well, I'm sorry. I wish I'd known.'

'And now that you do?'

With every fibre of her being she wanted to say, *Forget it! I don't want anything from you or your father.*

But she couldn't. She said lamely, 'Well, aren't we nearly halfway there now?'

He nodded without speaking.

'Salah, I swear to you I am not here to steal any secrets for anybody.'

He looked at her as if there was nothing in the world he wanted more than to believe her. But when he said, 'Good,' she knew he was still doubting.

'You always did judge me,' she reminded him bitterly.

'Not without cause.'

'Then, as now, the cause was all in your own head.'

He laughed, seemed about to say something, then changed his mind.

For one powerful, compelling moment Desi had the conviction that she should confide everything to Salah—should just tell him, *Samiha doesn't want to marry you, she's in love with someone else.*

She half opened her mouth and closed it again. If she were wrong, she would not be the one to suffer.

Or at least, not more than was already on the cards.

CHAPTER THIRTEEN

THAT day was spent crossing the bleakest imaginable desert, emptier than she could ever have dreamed. For miles they saw nothing but sand and rock. No animals, no trees, not even any scrub.

The sun was scorching. The Land Cruiser was air-conditioned, but that did not stop the sun coming through the windows, and setting her skin on fire. Desi had always loved heat, but this was something else. There was no shade anywhere, it was hour after hour of burning sand, till her eyes grew hypnotized and her brain tranced.

She would not protest or complain, because she suspected he was waiting for just that. Nor did she want to give him any excuse for turning back. *It'll be hell on wheels, Desi,* Sami had said, but even she could not have foreseen this.

Desi lifted the bottle of water to her lips for the fiftieth time that day, and took a long swig. She'd never drunk so much water in her life.

'I suppose if we ran out of gas or water out here, we'd be dead in an hour,' she observed mildly.

'It would take longer than that. But we will not run out,' Salah said.

At noon they stopped only briefly to eat and drink. Salah, wearing his desert robe and the headscarf she had learned to call *keffiyeh*, got out to stretch, but Desi remained in the vehicle. To step outside in this heat would be tantamount to suicide, or at the very least, instant second-degree burn. She had put on shorts and a T-shirt in the nomad camp this morning, and now she was sorry. But it was too much effort to think of changing into something with sleeves.

After only fifteen minutes they were on their way again.

In late afternoon Salah pointed through the wind-screen. 'We'll camp there,' he said.

Desi frowned and shaded her eyes till she saw it: a large outcrop of sand-coloured stone ahead. She would not have seen it if he hadn't pointed it out. The best way to see anything out here was by the shadow it cast, and there was no shadow.

'Will there be some shade? Why can't I see a shadow?' She was desperate to be out of the sun.

'On the other side. The sun is behind us now.'

'Are we heading east?' Desi frowned and looked at the sun. They were. She hadn't noticed him change direction. 'Why?'

Salah glanced at her ruefully. 'I'm sorry. I overshot. We should have reached it an hour ago.'

'Thus the great desert navigator whose ancestors survived to produce him!'

'As long as the mistakes are not fatal, of course, one survives.'

'You can't imagine how comforting.'

At least they could laugh.

Ten minutes later—how deceiving distances were

when you had no real landmarks!—they reached it.
The mound was much bigger than she had imagined, a
small hill, the size of a substantial building. As Salah
slowed the Land Cruiser and pulled around to the other
side, Desi gasped in relief.

'An oasis!' she cried. 'A real, true blue oasis!'

'At this season the water will be brackish.'

Two dozen palm trees surrounded a large pool of
water in the rock's welcome shadow.

'Heaven is a relative construct, I see,' Desi said.

Salah pulled the vehicle up underneath a rock
overhang and Desi tumbled out.

Even in the shade it was boiling hot. She gasped.
'Wow! How right you were about travelling in this
heat! Is it all going to be like this?'

'No,' he said, opening the back and beginning to
unload supplies. When Desi moved to help him he
waved her away. 'Leave it to me for now. You are too
hot. Go and sit in the shade.'

He was right there, and she could assume he was
more used to this heat than she. She sank down on a
rock and watched him heave out the tent.

'I think I've drunk four litres of water today! Do we
have enough?'

'We have plenty. When did you last take a salt tablet?'

She told him, and he nodded approval.

She knew she must be sweating, but she'd never
have known it by her skin. In such dry air, sweat seemed
to evaporate before you saw it.

'I suppose this is as good as a detox cure,' Desi mused.

When Salah had unloaded the equipment and supplies, he slammed the tailgate and turned to look into
the sun.

With his eyes narrowed, his chiselled face outlined by sun and shadow, he looked fiercely handsome, a face from another century. Desi felt lightheaded, almost drunk, with his beauty.

'You're the image of the desert,' she said dreamily.

Salah flicked her a glance. 'You need food,' he said.

He bent to pick up the roll that was the tent, and carried it to a flat spot among the trees. Desi set down her bottle, dusted her hands on her butt, and moved to help him.

An hour later the tent was up, the sleeping bags unrolled, and Desi was watching the sun go down to glory over the desert as she scooped up the last morsel of lamb and aubergine stew.

'Does this place have a name?' she asked dreamily.

'It is called Halimah's Rest.'

'Halimah? Didn't you tell me she was a great queen or something?'

'Yes. After her husband's death, she held the throne for her son against all comers for years.'

'What was she doing out here in the middle of nowhere?'

'Queen Halimah and her army got lost during a battle. A local Bedouin boy led her to this oasis. The army camped here and refreshed themselves and went on to win the battle the next day. Later Halimah commanded that the pool be banked with brick and a well dug, to the great benefit of the Bedouin. You can still see the remnants of the brick walls.'

'Who was she fighting with?'

'Adil ibn Bilah, her dead husband's nephew, who wanted to take the throne from her.'

'He didn't succeed?'

'No. He was killed, and Halimah made an example

of his generals. No one challenged her rule for some time afterwards.'

The sun was all but gone now. Salah got up and moved among the trees, collecting palm leaves and bark. Desi sat and watched the desert change from gold to red and then to purple.

The desert went on forever. A sense of unreality settled over her. What stories the sand whispered to the secret ear!

'This is so weird,' she murmured, after a long silence.

'What?' Salah began laying a fire with what he had collected.

'I feel as though I've plugged into a mindset that's been sitting here forever. As if time is nothing, only the desert exists.'

'The desert has many effects on the mind. You've never been in the desert before?'

'I've done a couple of photo shoots in the more obvious places. Golden beaches and palm trees. Once we went out to an old battlefield and I posed by burnt-out tanks. That was horrible. But never right out in the middle of nowhere, never where the desert could really get to you. Never anywhere I felt like this.'

'There is more than one sort of mirage,' Salah said, setting a match to the fire.

'Meaning?'

'People see what they want to see in the desert.'

'And what do I want to see?'

'That in the desert time is transcended, perhaps. That time does not matter.'

She went still with the truth of it. There was silence between them, and then, as if driven, he went on.

'If there is only the desert and eternity, how can ten

years matter? Do you yearn for that time of innocence, Desi? I, too. We drive across the desert together, and I know that, if only we had been more *thabet*—what word is it?—stead…steady…'

'Stea—' Her throat closed. She cleared it. 'Steadfast.'

Darkness was settling around them as the first stars appeared. Thick, roiling smoke curled up from under the stacked leaves, and then a puff of yellow flame.

'Steadfast, yes. We might still be here together, but how different it would be. You would be my wife. Our children would be sleeping in the tent. Do you feel their ghosts, Desi, as I do?'

Baba, Baba, I want a drink!

Her heart convulsed at the nearness of the dream. Desi opened her mouth to breathe.

'What is there in that moment that still traps us, after so many years?' he pressed. 'A few weeks out of a lifetime. Why is it so close?'

The question hung on the air like smoke, symbol of the fire that lurked beneath.

Desi moved her head. Something burned her eyes and the back of her throat. 'I don't know.' The desert at night was like nothing she had ever experienced, and yet there was something about the campfire, the stars and his nearness that brought those island feelings close. Love—the *memory* of love! she corrected herself—tore at her heart.

A moment later he was beside her on the blanket, his voice hoarse and low.

'Here there is no time, Desi. You feel it. I feel it. Time has disappeared. Here we can be what we were. Let us make love once more as the innocent children we were. Let us remember the love we felt, just once; let us make love as if ten years had not passed, as if you had come to me then.'

Her heart was caught between melting and breaking. A sob burned her throat. 'What do you want, Salah?'

She felt the approach of heat, and then his hand was on her breast, cupping it tenderly.

'Do you remember the first time I touched you, Desi? How my hand trembled. Let me touch you like that again.'

Slowly he drew the loose shirt down her arms and tossed it to one side. Under her T-shirt she was naked, the heat was too much for a bra, and he knew it. Gently he pushed her down onto the blanket, his hand slipping up under the thin cotton to find the silky curve of her breast and encircle it as if coming home.

'The first time I touched you like this, Desi, how my blood leapt! The magic of your soft breast, the way your flesh answered me—' He stroked his palm over the shivered, hungry tip that responded to his urgency with aching need, then pushed the cloth up and bent his head.

The firelight shadowed his chiselled face, showed her the tortured passion in his eyes, so that she could almost believe he was again the boy he had been, passionate, loving, accepting, burning with need of her. She melted at the thought, body and soul, and as his lips gently encircled her flesh, she whispered his name, as she had so long ago.

Salah.

Her voice held the surprise of awakening passion, as if he heard it down the years and she were still a virgin, and he closed his eyes as the power of it struck him a blow straight to the heart.

As they had then, his hands became urgent, his tenderness struggling with the need that moved in them both. He pushed the T-shirt over her head and off, and his eyes devoured the beauty of her perfect breasts, her skin's creamy smoothness caressed by the flickering blaze that stroked her even as his hands did. Then he was jealous, primitively jealous of the fire's adoration of her, and moved over her, so that she lay in his shadow, as he urged off the shorts that had no right to touch her legs...

But starlight, too, adored her, glowing on her white forehead, her dampened lips. He bent to take possession there, too, his mouth hungry and urgent.

The hunger of years rose to her lips, and she opened her mouth tenderly, willingly, hungrily, and as innocent now as then, for in the desert time disappeared. Her hands wrapped him, fingers clenching on his shoulder, his head, clasping the rich black curls in the newness of that passion she had learned only with him. Each move of his mouth and tongue and lips was answered by hers, and his blood pounded through him and he struggled against the urgent need to take her, consume her, be one with her, now.

He shrugged out of his clothes, and then stretched out beside her, naked and gleaming in firelight. Her hands stroked the length of his chest and flank, and in the darkness and flickering shadow the honing of maturity and even his battle scar somehow were lost, so that his body was as fresh and perfect as at seventeen.

His fingers caressed her cheek, her temple, stroked the silky hair back from her brow as he gazed into eyes that reflected the night sky and all eternity. Stars glinted in her gaze as she smiled fearlessly, trustingly into his face, in a way no woman had done again. It touched him to the depths of his soul, and he gathered her wildly up in his arms, clumsy, inexperienced, like the boy he had been, and crushed her to him, drowned her mouth with his own, drank in the sweetness of her like wine.

His hands were strong, holding her as if he could never let her go, as they pressed her back, her shoulder, her head, desperate to bring her closer and closer, till she was part of him. She melted with yearning, with ful-filment, with need, crying her joy to the night air, to the desert that saw all, knew all.

His mouth drank and drank of the nectar of their kiss. Her body was pressed so tightly against him they were one flesh, and the hands that wrapped and caressed her sent sensation like honey through her, and in her response he felt the honey return and pour into his own flesh.

Still it was not enough for either; the last, the final union was still to come, and she began to plead with him as she had so long ago, soft murmurings in his ear that resonated in his heart, *please, Salah, please, please,* as she pressed closer and closer, as her body moulded to his and his to her.

He drew away a little then, unable to wait longer, for what they needed was to sink into each other, and remember who they had been.

He drew away, and his flesh fitted to hers with the hungry knowing of the key for the lock, and pushed inside, and they cried out together in surprise and completion, one voice that drenched their nerve ends with sweetness. And then they were locked together, gazing into each other's star-filled eyes, unmoving with the surprise of passion.

He stroked her face, her hair, she touched his full lips

with a questing fingertip, and that moment of wonder and surprise was the same as it had been ten long years ago, that moment of feeling the pulse of an ancient rhythm burn up inside them, the summons of that urgent, age-old necessity that is the heartbeat of life. It began to move in them, through them, and they were helpless on the current of its urgency, the pulsing, pushing beat that took them closer and closer to the place where time is destroyed in eternity.

The fire watched greedily, coating their limbs with light and shadow, as they moved and embedded deeper and deeper into each other's being, towards the one.

They cried out as they approached it, cried their helpless pleasure, their consuming need, to all who would hear: earth and water and fire and air, and sky and time and nothingness and all, and then they were there, and all need, all urgency, exploded in a blaze of honeyed light that swept out from the tiny space where souls and bodies met, to enrich all creation. And, bathed in its glow, blinded by its brightness, for that place cannot be seen by mortal eyes, for one moment of perfection they cried out their gratitude, and then, slowly, because they must, sank back together into the abode of separation.

The firelight died, and still they lay entangled, unwilling to let the world enter between them again. But soon the desert chill invaded both body and soul.

'Now we know,' said Salah, and there was something in his tone that chilled her even further, because it told her nothing had changed.

'Do we?'

'It was real,' he said. 'It was there. We destroyed it, but it was real.'

'Is it better to know?' she asked bitterly, feeling somehow that it was tonight, not ten years ago, that she had created the real heartbreak for herself.

She stiffened to ward off pain, but Salah didn't answer. He sat up as night insects, drawn by the scent of honey, approached, and threw a few more dried fronds onto the dying blaze before disappearing down towards the pool, now shrouded in darkness.

Desi dug in her pack, got out her night gear and pulled it on, then sat there as smoke and flame curled up on the air, trying to see her way into the future.

He came out of the darkness like a pagan god, naked and strong, his body glistening with wet. As he pulled a towel out of his own pack and rubbed himself dry, she watched with detached admiration, as if at a work of art, until he had put on his night clothes and sat down again.

'Are you going to marry Sami?'

Salah shrugged and lifted a stick to stir the fire. 'It is not agreed yet. But why not? I must marry someone.'

'How can you talk about it so calmly? You know what love is. You remember how it feels. How can you contemplate marrying someone you don't love?'

In the firelight her eyes were dark, watching him. He turned his attention to the fire.

'The best love comes after marriage,' he said. 'You create a life together, and love each other within that life. It is easy to love the mother of your children.'

'You don't sound convinced.'

'I told you once, Desi!' he growled. 'I will never love again in the way that I loved you. It is impossible. I do not wish it. It is better to marry in the old way—find your wife first, and then learn to love her. The other way is heartbreak.'

Who had he first heard it from? His uncle? His grandfather? He couldn't remember now, but that it was wisdom his own life had proven. It was best to marry calmly. Strong feelings could always turn into their opposite.

They sat in silence for a few moments. 'Is it because of your parents? Are they pressing you to marry?'

'I told you, my parents have been pressing me to marry for ten years. They have given up asking me. But they are right, it is time. I am nearly thirty. I am the eldest of my family.'

'Why now? Why Sami?'

'There are reasons why a wife born and educated in the West is a good idea.'

'What reasons?'

The moon was rising. Salah, his arms resting on his knees, gazed at her for a long moment. In firelight her face was hauntingly beautiful; no wonder that fingers of flame and shadow warred to caress it. He could not love her again, all that was past. But through the curls of smoke still she was a dream, a ten-year-old dream. And he could almost believe he was that boy again.

He must resist that temptation. The truth was elsewhere.

'Why do you ask these questions, Desi? What is it you want to know?'

'Because I don't believe it! Something doesn't add up.'

'Why not?' He raised an eyebrow.

'I—I just think it's an extremely odd match, you and Sami. You're cousins!'

'By our tradition, that is the best match.'

'But do you and Sami think so?'

'Some women raised abroad seek to retain connection with Barakat in this way. It means their children will have the right to citizenship in two countries. With the world so uncertain, that is not a bad thing.'

'Is that what Sami wants?'

'Perhaps.'

'And what about your own reasons?' she asked again.

He tossed something into the fire that crackled and sent sparks up to the treetops. 'This comes at a time when I may have to move abroad and it will be best not to go on a diplomatic passport.'

He felt her shock and wondered why it struck her so forcibly.

'You're going to be living in the West?' she gasped.

'Why not?'

'But you're a Cup Companion! Your life is here! At least—isn't it?'

'My duty is elsewhere, however. I did not become a Cup Companion for the privileges, but to do what is necessary for my prince and my country.'

'And what duty requires you to move abroad?'

'This I cannot discuss with you, Desi.'

'How long?'

'Why are you asking? Why do you want to know?' he asked, and watched as her face closed. With distant anger, he wondered who had asked her to ask these questions, which he should not have answered. His guard was down.

Salah tossed the stick he was holding onto the fire.

'Let's get some sleep,' he said.

Desi lay sleepless beside him long after his breathing told her Salah was out.

I still love him. I could tell him so. Ask him to love me again. The thought tortured her. She was half convinced that he was lying to himself when he said his love for her was dead. She, too, had believed herself immune, and how wrong she had been!

He wanted to move to the West. He wanted a Western wife. If she confessed the state of her heart might he pretend to love her for such a reason? At least he could be sure the sex was good. What if he thought, why not marry Desi, as easily as Sami?

Why not? whispered the voice of temptation.

Desi had never really understood what had motivated his letter. When the first flush of guilt and grief had passed, she had been almost sure that it was something to do with his illness. He had been shot in the head, she knew that. He'd been very ill for weeks. So for a long time she'd lived in hope that another letter would come, telling her he'd been delirious…but it never came.

But that was ten years ago. Why hasn't he got some distance on it? How can he still judge me the way he did? Is it just habit? Did he really never take it out and look at it? I'll talk to him tomorrow.

She must be careful. Because if what he really wanted, unconsciously or not, was to punish her for his inability to love another woman, she might offer him the perfect means. She was so vulnerable, yearning for his touch, melting at his nearness. How much more vulnerable she would be as his wife!

But…her heart whispered…he's determined to love his wife, whoever she is. If he could love me again…he's planning to live in the West, who knows for how long? Maybe we could live in two worlds. It's doable.

She argued with herself while the moon tracked her serene path across the heavens, and came to no conclusion.

CHAPTER FOURTEEN

THEY were up before the sun. Desi bathed in the oasis pool, but the water left her skin feeling sticky, and afterwards she rinsed as best she could in a tiny ration of bottled water. Still feeling slightly grubby, she got into clean white cargo pants and a loose long-sleeved white shirt, hoping by this means to keep the heat off better than yesterday. She stuffed her hair up under her straw hat and felt a welcome morning breeze caress the back of her neck.

What she'd give for a shower!

Just before noon the desert monotony was broken by distant rocky hills and a long line of green on the horizon. Mount Shir towered above the scene, remote and majestic. They must have been travelling north for some time, but she had been too involved with her thoughts to notice.

'What's that green I see?' she asked.

'That is Wadi Daud.'

'Wadi—does that mean *oasis*?'

'Wadi means a valley, or a riverbed, where there is water only in the rainy season. But Wadi Daud has underground water and there is an irrigation project there, so it is green all year round. Not so green now as it will be in a few months, but still pleasant.'

Desi was surprised when a paved road appeared in front of them; she'd thought they were miles from such niceties. Salah turned onto it in a cloud of dust, and not long afterwards it slanted down into a broad, flat, rough-hewn valley with steep walls of purple-grey rock and a floor of green that stretched for miles in both directions. In the centre of the valley a stream trickled over a stony bed.

'In winter that is a torrent,' Salah said. 'In summer it often dries up completely.'

Soon they were driving through palm and olive groves. Along the other side of the valley she saw a small village amongst the greenery.

'Is that where we're headed?'

'I have friends who will give us lunch.'

The house was like those she'd seen in the city: low, white and domed, set in the middle of a broad court-yard surrounded by a high white wall. A servant opened the outer door to them with a murmured *'Marhaban,'* and the blistering heat of the midday sun was instantly mitigated by the shade of numerous trees and the sound of a fountain.

A strikingly attractive woman with flashing black eyes and black curls cascading down her back came out of the house, smiling and calling what was obviously a warm greeting in Arabic. In a cotton summer dress, she had bare legs and feet; her arms were bare save for a few bracelets.

'Marhaban, marhaban jiddan, Salah! Nahnou...'

'Desi, Nadia,' Salah said, just as Desi took off her

hat to wipe her forehead and her fair hair came tumbling down. 'Desi doesn't speak Arabic, Nadia.'

'Oh, I'm sorry!' Nadia's level gaze met hers with a frowning smile as the two women shook hands. 'Hello, how are you? Welcome! You are very welcome! Salah, it's so good to see you!' she said. 'Ramiz will be here in a minute. Come in, come in!'

She led them across the shady but still hot courtyard and into the cool of a large, airy room whose decor seemed to blend West and East, modern and ancient, with perfect ease. It was a massive, spreading space obviously covering most of one floor of the house, protected from the midday sun by green-covered canopies and thick walls.

The furniture was a mix of Western and Eastern, with conventional sofas and chairs and coffee tables in a cluster at one end, and cushions on a massive knotted silk carpet at the other.

The right-hand wall had sliding glass doors looking out on to an obviously antique, mosaic-tiled pool with a fountain that reminded Desi of what she had seen at the palace. The left wall was a stunning row of pillars and delicately fluted arches through which could be seen an endless maze of pillars, arches and mosaic floors, and the corner of a distant, sunny courtyard.

It took Desi a moment to realize that the entire scene was a *trompe l'oeil* painting. She was looking at a solid wall.

'This is spectacular!' she exclaimed involuntarily, stopping to gawp as Nadia, happily chatting to Salah, led them along the length of the room down to a sofa at the far end.

Nadia and Salah turned in surprise, then, seeing what had caught her, laughed.

'I love it, too,' Nadia confessed with a smile. 'You haven't seen it since it was finished, Salah, yes? That shows how long since you visited us! Anna finished it almost three months ago. She's a perfectionist, she kept coming back with her paints to put on "the final touches"! But now it's done.'

'It's magnificent,' Salah agreed.

'Like living in a palace,' said Nadia, grinning up at him. 'Or is it?'

'It's like a page from a fairy tale!' Desi said, still gazing, and feeling a little as if she'd been put under an enchantment. 'Who is the artist?'

'You may have heard of her. She is English, but she lives here in Western Barakat. Her name…'

'Oh, my God, is this an Anna Lamb? Of *course*!' Desi exclaimed. 'She did one in London for Princess Esterhazy, and then everyone was after one! Fabulous, too, but not nearly as extensive as this.'

Nadia stared at her for a moment, then smiled broadly.

'Oh my goodness! I *knew* I'd seen you before! You're *Desirée*! How amazing!'

'I didn't expect to be recognized so far from… home.' Desi laughed. She was glad she had stopped before saying *civilisation*.

'We read *Vogue* in West Barakat, too! But what are you *doing* here? How do you come to know Salah?'

At that moment a dark, thin-faced man came into the room, closely followed by two servants carrying trays.

'Salah! Great to see you!' he cried, as the two men embraced. 'What are you doing in Qabila?'

Salah turned. 'Desi, this is my very good friend Ramiz.'

Soon the four were seated on sofas around a low table, on which had been placed jugs of juice and water, and tall glasses.

'So why are you here? Just touring? Or is it a modelling assignment?' Nadia asked eagerly. 'That would be exciting for us, to have Barakat used as a background.'

'No, something much more interesting, as far as I'm concerned. I wouldn't spend days camping out in the desert for a shoot, let me tell you!' She paused and looked at Salah, wondering if his friends knew about his father's site.

'Camping out in the desert?' Nadia repeated in amazed tones. 'In this heat?'

'Desi wants to see an archaeological dig in progress,' Salah filled in. 'I'm taking her to Baba.'

Ramiz's eyebrows went up. He exchanged a look with Salah, and then his eyelids drooped, masking his expression. The sound of a child's voice came from the next room, and for the first time Desi realized that one of the doorways under the painted arches was real.

'But I don't understand,' Nadia said. 'Why are you...?'

'You haven't seen Safiyah for a long time,' Ramiz said to Salah, over her. 'She misses you. You'll be surprised by how much she's grown. Tahir, too.'

'Ayna Safiyah?' Salah called. *'Ayna walida jamilati?'*

The child's high shriek answered him, and then a little girl came tearing into the room and ran straight into his arms, followed by a woman carrying a baby.

'Aga Salah! Aga Salah!' the child cried.

Desi watched as Salah swung the shrieking child up

into the air. His face was suddenly soft, his expression relaxed and warm. The face of the Salah she remembered.

He was not lost, the man she had loved. He was still there, underneath. If only she could reach him.

'Have you really been camping out in the desert at this time of year?' Nadia asked Desi against the background of the child's chatter. 'What's Salah thinking of?'

'He did warn me, but I insisted. This is the only time I had to visit. The first night we stayed with nomads. Last night at Halimah's Rest.'

Nadia frowned and shook her head. 'Was the water clean enough to bathe in?'

'Call it a large puddle.'

Nadia looked at her. 'And then you drove all morning in the desert to get here? Salah must be crazy!'

'I haven't felt so grubby and sticky since I was five and my father took me for a day at the fair.' Desi laughed.

'Desi,' Nadia said hesitantly, 'would you like to take a shower now? I am sure…'

'Oh, *could* I?'

So Nadia showed her to a bathroom, gave her towels and soap, and left her to indulge herself. Never had water been such bliss! She could have stayed under the cool flow for half an hour, but even here in Wadi Daud water must be a precious resource at this time of year. She restricted herself to five minutes.

She came out feeling human again, her newly washed hair twisted up on top of her head, her face cleansed, her skin breathing for the first time in two days. Heaven.

In the sitting room, meanwhile, Nadia took a protesting Safiyah away to get her lunch. Ramiz and Salah were left alone.

'Two days through the desert, via West Barakat, to get to your father's dig?' Ramiz asked softly.

'And we're only halfway there,' Salah replied blandly. 'It's a four-day trip. Nadia's not likely to mention where the dig is, is she?'

'Does she know? I don't, not with any accuracy. Subtle form of abduction, brother? She's very beautiful.'

'Subtle form of interrogation. I want to know why she wants to see it.'

'Ah.' Ramiz pursed his lips. 'Nadia recognized her. Supermodel? She would have a lot of connections among the wealthy.'

'Got it in one,' Salah said.

'Could she be an innocent pawn?'

'No. I tried that one. She's hiding something.'

Even as he spoke he wondered why he had brought Desi to this house, where the least slip would expose the truth of this expedition. Was he tired of the deception, had he somehow accepted that she was innocent, that last night had taught him her real reason for coming? Or had he merely fallen victim to her wiles in spite of his best intentions?

'The big mystery is, why has your father allowed it? Isn't the site completely shut down to outsiders?'

Salah nodded. 'I advised him to refuse. His sense of justice wouldn't allow it. Desi's family in Canada hosted me very generously every summer for years when I was a kid learning English. He couldn't say no, even though we have to assume that whoever is behind it chose her for that very reason.'

'So the desert is going to sweat the truth out of her?' Salah nodded.

'And what else?' Ramiz asked.

Salah raised his eyebrows in surprise. 'What do you mean?'

'There's more going on between you than just a spy story, Salah. The air catches fire every time you look at her. What else are you trying to sweat out of her?'

'I have an idea!' Nadia said.

After a delicious cold lunch of various kinds of salad, Salah and Desi were making moves to go.

'We have a very interesting site close to Qabila. Rock carvings, two thousand years old, Desi! If you stop the night with us, Salah, you can take Desi to see them this afternoon.'

Desi glanced at Salah. It was tempting, the thought of a comfortable bed and cool sheets and a shower in the morning. But she was unsure what such an offer of hospitality meant. Was this one of those moments when you were supposed to protest three times before accepting?

'Thank you, that's very kind,' Desi said with a smile. 'But it's such a long trip, and I am really eager to get there as soon as possible.'

'But if you leave now, you will not get to the site till nearly sunset, maybe even after dark,' Nadia said. 'You may as well stay here and go tomorrow morning. Anyway, the road is safer in daylight.'

A funny little silence fell over the table. Ramiz and Salah exchanged glances. Ramiz started to say something in Arabic, but Desi was already asking, 'The road?'

'Yes, in the dark, you know, you can hit blown sand before you see it. Salah is a very good driver, but when sand grabs your wheels, it can be very uncomfortable.'

'What road would that be?' Desi asked carefully.

Nadia smiled and waved vaguely with her hand. 'The main road to Central Barakat, of course! I really don't understand why—'

'The dig is on the main road?'

'No, didn't you tell us once it's an hour or two off piste, Salah? But the secret is knowing where to turn off!'

'Really. A whole hour off the main road.'

'*Shokran*, Nadia,' Salah said. 'But we'll go on. I prefer to do the last leg under cover of darkness. Harder to track us, if anyone is trying.'

CHAPTER FIFTEEN

A FEW minutes later they were in the Land Cruiser again, heading down the valley.

'So, are we going to continue the circular tour for another two days?' Desi asked as soon as she was sure she could control herself. She had never been so angry in her life, mostly with herself. What a fool she had been! Dreaming dreams about a man who had already proven himself a selfish, faithless monster. A man, clearly, who was obsessed with honour because he had none.

'Desi…'

'Since your ancestors were faultless navigators, I assume the detour was planned. Did you mean me to get to the dig at all? Or was the great navigator planning to get lost and spend two weeks driving around in circles?'

'I told you I would not let you discover the way, Desi.'

'Five days? Was that much bluff really necessary?'

'I have told you from the beginning that I am concerned about your motives. I thought after a few days in the desert you might tell me the truth.'

'Your own particular brand of endurance test. Is that why you made love to me, too?' Her heart convulsed so that she felt sick. 'To try and break me down? Hoping for a pillow confession?'

'I warned you there was no future for us.'

She began to laugh unhappily. 'Oh, you're as noble as they come! A true mountain warrior—what's the code you once told me? Generosity, hospitality, bravery in battle, and a good lover? Oh, yes, everything's there, except the generosity, the hospitality and the bravery! What a cowardly way to fight a battle against a woman! God, you make me sick!'

A cloud of sand billowed up around the car as Salah slammed on the brakes and pulled off the road under a cluster of date palms. He turned to her, his black eyes blazing.

'What did you expect, Desi? You come to me with lies, but you want truth from me! I *have* to know why you came here, why you want to visit this place! My father could not say no to you, because I owe your family such a debt! Was it noble in you to take advantage of him in this way?'

'I am not taking advantage of him! Why do you suspect me? Why won't you believe me?' she shouted.

'Because you are lying to me. I know it. Do not deny it again, Desi, it makes you more of a liar!'

'How can you make love to me at night and then in the day believe I could be a cheat?'

'Because you are a cheat. You cannot be trusted. You are weak. This I learned ten years ago.'

Her jaw fell open. Her eyes blazed outrage at him.

'*Me!* How dare you? I'm *sick* of this accusation, Salah! You're ten years older now, isn't it time you got a handle on what happened? All I did was love you, and if that's a sin, well, I've paid for it in spades! You're the one who was weak! You're the one whose love didn't last past the first hurdle. Not me!'

'Do you pretend to rewrite history with me?' he demanded. 'Do you pretend to forget what you did?'

'What *I* did? What did I do, exactly?'

'Why do you want to open this? You did not love me.'

'That's what I said, all right. I was sixteen years old. You're the one who wrote the letter. You're the one who decided that we were not after all married in our hearts and therefore I wasn't pure enough for you!'

He narrowed his eyes at her. 'Do you pretend still? You could not have gone to the bed of this old man if your love had been real. You know it.'

'*Old man? Bed?* What are you talking about?'

'You know. The one they called your agent. Why do you pretend with me?'

'*Leo?*' she screeched incredulously. '*Three years later*, Salah! How long did you expect me to wait for you to see the light?'

'*What?*' he whispered.

But she was in full flood.

'Three years during which you never once tried to get in touch! What was I supposed to do? You rejected me in the most humiliating, shaming way possible! Was I supposed to beg? To promise to give up my too demeaning career? Grovel because I was weak and slept with you before we were bound in holy bloody matrimony?

'I waited and waited in the hopes that when you wrote it you were delirious or something, but no! Your self-righteousness was fully conscious! I don't know what the *hell* you think you had a right to expect…'

'What do you mean, three years later?' Salah finally found his voice, and it rasped like gravel against a screen.

'I was nearly nineteen before Leo's master plan came to fruition! Are you really presuming to blame me for that? You didn't want me, but I should remain virgin forever? What was it, some kind of sanctity test? No one else got near me for three years, Salah. Did *you* wait that long? I'd like to know.'

His eyes were hollow with shock.

'He was your lover from the beginning! You went from me to him.'

Her face convulsed with distaste. 'No, he was *not*! I was sixteen, for God's sake! He was forty-two!'

'It wasn't true?' He was hoarse with horror.

'What?' Desi stared at him blankly. Then her eyes narrowed as suspicion took hold. 'What do you mean? *What* wasn't true?'

'Sami sent me a magazine clipping. A picture of you with this old man. It said…'

Her head went back as if he had hit her. She stared at him, and for a moment they were frozen there, locked in mutual horror.

'You *believed* it?' She was open-mouthed with shock as the fact sank in. She stared, shook her head to try to clear it. 'Is *that* why—?' she whispered. 'How could you believe it?'

'Desi—'

'You, of all people! Did you really imagine that within a few weeks I could—? With you on a battle-field, for Christ's sake! You thought I had—' Suddenly feeling came rushing in to fill the blankness and her voice found its feet.

'You read something about me in a damned cheap-thrills sell-your-soul-for-a-dollar celebrity magazine, and you *believed it*?' She drew in a shuddering breath. 'My God, it was bad enough when I thought...'

She didn't know where to look. She turned away from him, lifted her chin, breathing with her mouth open like a wounded animal, trying to get air. Chills rushed over her skin.

'Oh, God!' she moaned. 'This can't be true! This is a nightmare...'

She closed her eyes. Opened them again. Fury flooded her.

'*That* was why you wrote that letter. Wasn't it? You—you faithless...*my* love not strong enough? How dare you talk to me as if— *You!* What was *your* love worth, if you could believe *that*? Without asking, without even accusing—you just read some innuendo in a photo caption, and believed it? Leaving me to the mercy of those vultures who were surrounding me! *Nothing!* I had *nothing* to defend myself with, if you didn't love me! Did you think of that?'

Salah looked like the survivor of an explosion. He stared at her, his eyes black with shock.

'No,' he said.

'A caption under a picture! Not even a story! I wanted to deny it, but Leo told me if we made a fuss it would only confirm it in people's minds. It was better to let it pass. Anyway, he said, this would make it easier for him to protect me from predatory men, the way he'd promised my father!

'And it did give me protection—of sorts! I was sixteen and pretty and not engaged to you. If Leo hadn't been in the background I'd never have had a moment's peace!'

With an upsurge of the sick bitterness that Leo's betrayal of trust had created, she added, 'It didn't protect me from Leo himself, of course. He was the most predatory of all, but he could play the long game.'

'Ya Allah,' Salah whispered. She had never seen his face the way it looked now.

'I hated it all. I'd never wanted the life, never! I always felt I was living some other girl's dream. But because it was so fantastic I somehow had to live it. I missed you so much! I wished and wished I'd never done that stupid ad. Then you'd never have said what you said, and we'd have been married and I wouldn't ever have met Leo. But I was so nervous. Over and over I started a letter to you, but each time I thought...

'And then you were wounded, and I knew none of that mattered, because I loved you and I would never love anyone else, and if you died, I died, too. I waited for you to answer my card, wondering if you would live, praying—God, how I begged for you to recover! And when I saw your letter lying there—!' Her eyes squeezed shut. 'I nearly died from joy. I thought my heart was going to burst out of me and fly.

'Then I read it—and you know what? He may have waited three years before he physically climbed into my bed, but Leo got me in spirit the day I read your letter. I gave up that day. I gave up thinking what we had was special, that anything was special! I gave up what I'd believed about myself. I wasn't good enough for you, Salah. I'd loved you and wanted you too much, and because of that you thought I—'

She began to sob helplessly, feeling as if all the tears of a lifetime were waiting to be shed.

'I felt so cheap! I thought, well, if Salah can say such horrible, disgusting things…then it was all nothing. What I thought we had was nothing. It was never real. *You betrayed your honour.* It burned me like an iron. I'll remember that feeling till the day I die. I'd have given up that life in a minute, if you'd asked, but that letter told me it was more than being a model. I'd demeaned myself in your eyes by making love with you, too, that's what I believed. What we had wasn't beautiful at all, it was cheap and dirty. That was the end of everything.'

He was silent, his eyes black, watching her, knowing without doubt that what she spoke was the truth.

'And now you tell me you wrote that filth because you believed—*how* could you believe it? And not even to ask me if it was true!' she cried, as the barriers gave way and all the hurt rushed into her throat, demanding release. 'How could you think for a moment that I could go from you to him? I couldn't stand any other man touching me! Even three years after—the first time Leo… I was sick afterwards! I ran into the bathroom and threw up!'

She stopped and groped in her bag for tissues, then lifted her head and looked at him.

'It was bad enough when I thought you despised me for loving you or for being a model, but *this*! It's too much, Salah. This is unforgivable. You destroyed the most beautiful… What a cold, judgmental, untrusting bastard you were. Are. Well, I'm glad I know at last. And to think I've spent these few days with you regretting what we missed!' she added, in a self-disgust so total she could hardly breathe. 'Imagining that we still had something that could…but we never had anything, did we? It was all a lie from the get-go. I'll never regret it again. I was lucky. I had a bloody lucky escape.'

Then there was silence, broken only by the sound of her weeping.

CHAPTER SIXTEEN

SALAH felt blank, the way one feels after a bullet has hit: the emptiness of waiting for the pain.

He sat staring into the past, as all the carefully constructed armour of ten years collapsed into rubble around him. He had destroyed the dream by his own hand. Feeling began to blast in, a storm of grief and self blame.

She was completely blameless. The fault had been entirely his from the beginning.

She was right. He had acted towards her without generosity, without honour, all the while pretending that the lack of honour was hers. Even the least degree of decency had required that he ask her for the truth before judging her. And even believing it true, shouldn't he have tried to understand the pressures of that new world? A man of forty-two, a girl of sixteen. What chance would she have stood? Why hadn't he seen it before? Why hadn't he judged differently when he got a little older?

He opened his mouth three times before he could speak.

'Desi. There isn't a word strong enough. What have I done? Desi, forgive me.'

He put his hand out to her but, still weeping, she twisted away.

'*Forgive?* How can I forgive it?' she howled.

'Desi.' His voice sounded completely unlike him. 'My God. What a fool I am. Worse than a fool. A devil.'

She was sobbing inconsolably. 'You said you loved me, you say now it was the biggest thing in your life— how could you think such a thing? How could you begin to believe it? Why didn't you at least give me a chance?'

He swallowed. Ten years. What could make amends for such a waste of life and love?

'Desi, I am sorry.'

'Oh, great. Yes, that makes all the difference!'

The car was insufferably hot. Sweat was pouring off her, and she wound down the window and tried to catch her breath.

Salah started the engine. 'We can't stay here.'

He put the vehicle in gear and backed out onto the road again.

The sun was in the west, streaming into the car now from the front, now on the right, as the road curved and turned. It was burning hot, in spite of the air conditioning, and Desi felt sick with the brightness and the heat on her skin. For a few miles she twisted the sun visor this way and that, trying to block the rays, and then Salah pulled over again.

He got out, rummaged in the back for a moment, then came around to her side. Without a word he opened the door, lowered the window, tucked a cardboard window protector over the glass and rolled it back up. It covered the passenger window and a few inches of the windscreen, putting her in welcome shade.

When they were moving again, she said, 'Thank you.'

He nodded, swallowing, as if he could not trust himself to speak.

'You could have done that any time over the past three days, I suppose. But then, you had to sweat the truth out of me.'

They drove in silence, passing other cars on the road, glimpsing herds of camels and goats at distant nomad camps in the bleak, bleak desert. After a while Salah turned off the road and headed out over the sand again.

She wondered how she could ever have imagined such a landscape magnificent. It was nothing but emptiness.

RU still in desert? RU seducing Salah??? What is happening? Plz call as soon as U get coverage.

Desi read this message from another life dimly, hardly taking it in. Reception was poor, and she shut off the phone without answering.

Another hour passed, and then they were winding through a curious forest of rocky outcrops and into a valley between high walls of rock. Green scrub clung to the rock face here and there, and in places the wheels sank into mud or splashed through a stagnant puddle. In other places a thin trickle gave promise that this was a river bed.

'In winter there are flash floods here,' Salah said. 'It is very dangerous.' It was the first word that had passed between them for over an hour. 'Two years ago all this area flooded for the first time in living memory. Even in the tribal traditions there was no history of such flooding.'

'Ever the travel guide,' she said.

Just before sunset the rock walls fell away and the vista opened up. The sky in the west was a brilliant fire of gold, with Mount Shir shining in white majesty over the growing shadows in the desert. In the distance she saw a collection of tents nestled beneath a stand of rock.

'My father's camp,' said Salah.

It was as if a nomad encampment had entered a technology warp, and half its tents had been converted into air-conditioned caravans and trailers. All the modern equipment was nestled into the protective shadow between two large outcrops of black rock that jutted up from the desert floor. In front of them was ranged a nest of tents, half modern and half the low-slung nomadic type. And in front of that was the massive ancient site, where workers in straw hats toiled in rows, as if the nomads had taken to terrace farming. As they approached, an armed guard sitting on a rock peered at Salah's face for a moment and waved the vehicle on.

'I have to find out what arrangements have been made for us,' Salah said, pulling up to park in the shade of a white trailer. 'They are not expecting us yet. You can wait in the mess tent, Desi, or I can take you to my father.'

It was far too hot to sit in the car, though that was what she would have preferred. Desi squeezed her eyes shut for a moment, struggling to find focus in her shell-shocked, blank state.

'There will be people in the mess tent?'

Salah nodded.

'Is there anywhere I can go and sit by myself?'

'Not till I find out which trailer they have arranged for you.'

'Your father, then.'

He led her to the long white caravan that served as the site office. Inside it was air-conditioned to a comparatively refreshing twenty-five degrees, nearly eighty Fahrenheit. Desi was desperately grateful to get out of the sun.

The archaeologist Dr. Khaled al Khouri was sitting at a desk inside. He was a solid, square-set man with grizzled grey hair, a face with deep lines furrowing his forehead and carved from his strongly cut nose to the corners of his mouth. When they entered he was engrossed in examining a dirt-impacted object with the sunburnt, intent young woman standing beside his chair.

Neither noticed them enter. They watched for a minute as the professor's strong, competent fingers prised off the dirt of millennia to fall unheeded on his papers, and revealed a goblet.

With caressing strokes that reminded Desi of Salah's hands on her body, he dusted down the little cup, turned it over, then held it still, gazing at the face of the bowl.

'You're right, Dina,' he said at last. 'Congratulations. Well done.'

'Thank you, Dr. al Khouri.'

'Leave it with me. I'll take it to Hormuz later.'

As the young worker slipped through the door beside them, her eyes fell on Desi and she turned around to gasp in disbelief before continuing on her way. At the sound, the doctor lifted his head.

'Yes?' he said, and then, 'Salah!'

'Desi, meet my father,' said Salah. 'Father, this is Desirée Drummond—Desi.'

'Desi! Hello!' Dr. al Khouri exclaimed, getting to his feet. He put out his hand, giving her the same focussed attention he had bestowed on the found object. The clasp of his hand was firm, reminding her of Salah's. The black eyes were friendly, but uncomfortably piercing.

'I am very happy to meet you at last. We have heard so much about you! It is kind of you to come to visit us.'

He did not sound in the least like a man who suspected her of conspiring to steal priceless objects, and Desi flicked a glance at Salah.

'It's very kind of you to let me come,' she said, and under the warm intensity of his gaze, she managed to find a smile.

Her hand had collected a certain amount of dirt during the handshake, and she absently dusted it down on her khaki shorts. Dr. al Khouri frowned, looking at his own hand.

'Too much dirt in this job!' he said, dusting his hands. 'I must go out now and make my round before they down tools for the night. Perhaps you will like to come with me, Desi. You have come a long way, and I know you will be eager to see the site as soon as possible.'

She nodded agreement. It was long past time to get away from Salah. Salah seemed to agree.

'I will check on the sleeping arrangements,' he said. Their eyes caught for a moment, and she sent him a cold warning with her eyes. Then she saw that he did not need it: he had no more interest in their continuing to share a bed than she did. Well, he'd had his closure, of course, she reminded herself bitterly.

If only *she* could feel closure. But for Desi it was all still boiling up inside her, rage and heartbreak and a deep, abiding sense of betrayal.

A moment later she was out in the late sunshine, listening as Dr. al Khouri began to explain the site. He spoke as if she were the student she was pretending to be, and in spite of everything Desi began to be intrigued.

'Look at this,' Khaled al Khouri told her, as they paused by a worker who was carefully excavating a massive slab embedded in the hardened soil, on which she could make out, faintly, an etched image. 'This piece is our pride and joy.'

Desi peered at it. 'Is that a woman?'

'Not a woman,' he said, with the air of a man used to correcting students. 'All we can say with certainty at the moment is that this is a female figure. In fact, she is probably our goddess. We believe this lady might have been the tutelary deity of the whole civilisation.'

She bent down to see more clearly. The figure showed the hint of a tiara in the intricately curled hair that fell down over her shoulders above wide-spaced breasts, a curving waist encircled by some kind of string or thong, broad hips and a prominent nest of pubic hair. One hand was at her side, the other held up in what might be a gesture of greeting, palm towards the viewer. She was standing on an animal that Desi could not distinguish.

Excitement bubbled up as she recognized her little goddess.

'Who is she?' she demanded.

'We think, the deity of this temple.' The archaeologist waved his hand at the long shape marked out in the earth with stakes and string. 'We don't know her name yet.'

'Is she a fertility goddess? A love goddess?'

'We think so.'

'Inanna?'

He lifted an eyebrow at her, in a gesture so like Salah her heart kicked a protest. 'Possibly, but if so it's an unusual depiction of her that would be specific to this people, and she might have had another name. What made you think of her?'

Desi laughed. 'She's the only ancient love goddess I know!' she confessed. 'I bought a little statue from some nomads a couple of days ago. I think it's the same woman...female figure!'

Dr. al Khouri shook his head, sighing. 'You bought her from nomads?'

'Yes, for twenty dirhams. She's in the truck.'

'Then tomorrow you will show her to me. This, we suspect—' he waved his arm to take in the entire site '—was her particular city. Perhaps the people came here on pilgrimages.'

'The goddess of love was the chief god?' Desi asked, amazed.

'Yes, and such worship left its mark on later genera-tions. In antiquity, Barakat has had many ruling women, and even after Islam, we often allowed queens to rule us. You have heard of the great Queen Halimah?'

'Yes.'

'Her path was of course paved by the goddesses and queens of antiquity, who still exist in the psyche of Barakat.'

'Oh!' Desi said in surprise.

'Your own little goddess probably came from this area, but not this particular site. The flooding brought many things to the surface all along the valley. We have seen evidence for at least two more large settle-ments not far away.

'That is why it is so critical to keep this secret for as long as possible. We can never hope to police every potential site in the valley, and if we lose too many of them...but we start with the largest, hoping that it is also the most important.'

'Salah says looters aren't the worst threat, though,'

she said, remembering. He had said it only a day or two ago, Desi realized in distant surprise. She seemed to have lived a lifetime since then. Then she had felt alive, that was why it seemed so long ago.

'That is true.'

The archaeologist guided her over a narrow bridge of land between two square holes, smiling and nodding at the diggers below, who were starting to call to each other about the happy prospect of downing tools and cold beer.

'Looters take what they find for their own enrichment. But the others, the fools who cannot bear to know that once the feminine was worshipped as fervently as the masculine is today, the idiots who must force the past to match their ideals as well as the present—they are a different kind of danger. They want to destroy the evidence.

'Whatever we find here, Desi, it is the heritage of the whole world. It is our collective history. These madmen—they want to forget that all of Mohammad's line comes through a woman. Fatima. Without his daughter, there would be no sharifs at all, no descendants of the prophet. But still they want to wipe the feminine out of the world.'

'And you thought I might be helping these people?' she asked in quiet bitterness.

He stared at her. 'Help them? What intelligent person would help such lunatics?'

'Salah said you suspected I wanted to come here because—'

'Oh!' he said, in a different tone. His eyes moved to her face. 'My wife said that if we wanted Salah to be happy, I had to let you visit, in spite of Salah's objections. And I had to pretend to suspect your motives, too. I am only an archaeologist, I don't really understand these things. But you will know—is my son happy now?'

Her heart was suddenly beating in hard, heavy thuds. 'How would I know?' Desi protested. 'Isn't he going to marry Sami?'

He shrugged. 'My wife says not.'

Desi took a deep breath and sighed it out. *Promise me you'll tell Uncle Khaled only if you're absolutely certain he'll be all right with it,* Sami had said. And here was Sami's chance. This at least she could accomplish. This at least she could pull from the wreckage. No happiness for herself, that wasn't possible now, but…

She said, 'Dr. al Khouri—'

'But you must call me Khaled!'

'Khaled, I have something to tell you, and something to ask you, from Sami.'

'Ah, yes, my niece is your friend! My wife said. Let us sit here, then.' He guided her to a bench beside a table under a canopy, where they had a view over the whole dig. 'Now. What has to be said that my niece could not say to me herself?'

Desi stared out over the scene, watching long shadows move and dance as the workers moved out of the field and headed towards the tents.

'It's about…the marriage.' Her voice grated on the word. 'Sami asked me to tell you that she—doesn't want to marry Salah. She's already engaged to a man she loves, but her brothers wanted to choose her husband. It was they who chose Salah. She's told them she doesn't agree, but they…'

'Do you speak of Walid and Arif?' the scientist interrupted in amazement.

Desi nodded. 'She asked me to beg you to overrule Walid and send your permission for her to marry the man she loves. Otherwise she's afraid Walid will do something…really stupid.'

Khaled al Khouri's eyebrows went up as he inhaled all this, and when she stopped speaking he sighed explosively.

'Well, they are fools, these young nephews of mine! If they do not control themselves, they will soon be among the madmen who come to destroy history for the sake of their convictions. What is his name, Samiha's fiancé?'

'Farid Durrani al Muntazer. His family is originally from Bagestan, but he's Canadian.'

'*Madthe?*' Khaled threw back his head and laughed a loud, boisterous laugh. 'Well, they are worse than fools. They are ridiculous! This boy is a member of the royal family of Bagestan!'

Desi stared. 'What?'

'This is one of the names the al Jawadi took decades ago when they went into exile. Why does he not tell them so? It is no secret anymore. They are on the throne now, as the world knows.'

The Silk Revolution. Desi, like everyone else she knew, had been thrilled when handsome Sultan Ashraf had been restored to the throne of Bagestan. And Farid was related to him?

She smiled, and her heart lightened a little with happiness for her friend.

'I don't think Walid rejected him on his merits. It was the principle of the thing.'

'Well, I will give her my formal permission, it is the only way with such young men as this. But I will also have something to say to them.'

He stood and lifted a rope barrier for her.

'And now you have done your duty, Desi. Come and look at the lady's temple before the sun goes.'

Salah stood in the doorway of the mess tent, a cup of coffee in his hand, watching from a distance. The grace with which she moved up the long buried slope of that ancient temple where his distant ancestors had once worshipped love. In the shimmer of heat he seemed to see her through millennia. As if she belonged there, the high priestess of the religion of love.

Once he had worshipped at that shrine, had drunk from the honeyed chalice. Then with his own hand he had smashed it to fragments.

All the pieces of his life had come apart a few hours ago, and no new image had yet formed. He seemed to himself to be still staggering under the blow. All his landmarks were gone, blown down by the whirlwind of the horror of what he had done.

But the answer was here. He gazed at the lithe beauty of her as she talked earnestly to his father. She lifted her arm to point into the distance, and a last ray of the setting sun caught her suddenly, haloing her figure with flames of red gold, imprinting the shape on his heart, where it matched some shape already there....

The answer would be found here.

'Everyone eats in the food tent,' Salah told her a little later, leading her across the moonshadowed desert towards the trailer where she would sleep. 'Supper will be ready in half an hour. Or someone can bring you a tray here.'

Desi heaved a breath. Everything was suddenly catching up with her, and she knew she couldn't sit through a meal with the bunch of cheerful, enthusiastic volunteers she had seen in her tour of the site, especially as it seemed all the starstruck girls were going to want her autograph. She would feel stronger in the morning. Right now she felt she would burst if the least demand were made on her. She desperately needed to be by herself.

'I'm not hungry. If I can have a glass of water I'll go to bed now.'

'There's water in the trailer. Desi, I—'

'No,' she said, flinging up a hand, her voice cracking with emotion. 'Please. There's nothing to say.'

'There is everything to say,' Salah said. 'Do you think we can leave it where it is?'

She couldn't take any more. Not tonight. Not ever. 'I'll say good night, Salah.'

But his hand closed on her arm, heat burning through her skin to war with the coldness in her heart.

'Walk with me,' he said. *'Deezee!'*

Even now, even after what she had learned, his voice roughing up her name had power over her, like a cat's tongue on a sensitive spot. The knowledge filled her with distant fury. That nickname in his mouth was like blasphemy now. Bitter hurt welled up in her, choking her so that she could not speak to resist.

'Come with me.'

And she turned and went with him out beyond the cluster of caravans and trailers, into the empty desert.

A full moon was climbing up the sky. The giant rocks threw heavy black shadows onto the sand, making a landscape unlike anything she had ever seen before, strange and otherworldly.

'Desi, I was blind. Blind and a fool.'

She closed her eyes as a sense of waste and devastation flooded her. She shook her head.

'Too late,' she choked. 'Too little, too late.'

'Don't say it!' he commanded. 'It can't be too late, Desi. I won't let it be too late! We are still young, we have so much life in front of us.'

'Are you young? I'm old. I feel a hundred years old. I'm tired and life has passed me by. And I don't want to talk about this. Is that all you wanted to say?'

He stopped and turned to face her. Moonlight carved his face like rock.

'What are you saying? Do you think we can just walk away from this? You loved me once. Love is still possible. That I know. When we make love, you tell me so in everything but words. Desi, I—'

She felt exhausted, bruised. 'I think our watches must be out of sync, Salah.' She glanced down at her wrist in the milky gloom. 'Yeah, by, let's see—about ten years.'

'A mistake destroyed those ten years,' he insisted. 'A stupid, ignorant mistake. And if we don't mend it now, it will destroy the rest of our lives. We have to find our way through this.'

'The only mistake that would destroy the rest of my life would be to listen to you.'

'You know it is not true. You would not be so hurt now if you did not… Please. Let us not go on in this terrible error. Look into your heart, Desi, and hear me.'

Like a wounded animal goaded beyond its endurance, she rounded on him.

'Look! You wanted closure, am I right? That's what you wanted! Now you've had closure. You're going to get married, I think you said. Well, off you go, and good luck to you!'

'Do you think I can marry Sami now?' he almost shouted.

'But it doesn't matter who you marry, does it?' she reminded him harshly. 'What happened to "the best love comes after marriage"?'

'How can I marry another woman *now* in the hopes of learning to love her?'

'I have no idea. But then I never understood the principle in the first place.'

'Desi, I made a mistake. That mistake has ruined our lives for ten years.'

'You're a powerful Cup Companion who lives in a palace. I don't wake up for less than ten thousand dollars. I don't think we can call this ruination.'

'You speak of the world. I speak of the heart.'

'Do you?' Desi gave vent to a snort of bitter laughter. 'That's a good one!'

'Desi, you have to forgive me! Forgive me and let's leave this in the past, where it belongs. Stay with me tonight, Desi. Let me love you again. Love me. Let us find our hearts' truth together.'

Panic choked her. Her heart was kicking like a drum, and there were too many words in her throat.

'Love you? Love the man who only yesterday believed I was conspiring to destroy his country's history and culture? The man who for ten years judged me by a piece of trash magazine gossip and never bothered to find out the truth? Gosh, I wonder what I should say to this? Will a simple *no* do, or should I point out that I wouldn't touch you again if you were the last man standing after Armageddon?'

'Desi—'

'And that if you so much as touch me, I will blast

you down so hard Armageddon will look like a tea party. Please, I can't take any more of this! If you've said what you had to say, I want to go back.'

He gazed down into her anguished face in the moonlight, lifted his head for a moment, breathed deeply, then turned their steps. Their moonshadow moved ahead of them now, disguising the path, making it harder to find their footing. Desi felt seasick, as if she'd had too much sun.

'Can you understand that I was suspicious of your motives because I didn't trust my own?' Salah asked quietly.

'What the hell's that supposed to mean?'

'You know what I mean. You said it yourself. When I said I only wanted closure I was lying to myself. When I accused you of lying I was looking in a mirror.'

'I'm thrilled for you if you see it, however belatedly.'

'Desi,' he commanded.

She turned her head to look at him, her jaw tight. His shadowed eyes glinted moonlight at her.

'I told you once that we were already married, in our hearts. That we would be married forever. Do you remember?'

'*I* never forgot.'

'Once I forgot it, Desi. I am sorry. Please don't—'

'You forgot it a lot more than once.'

'A man may not live up to the truth, but the truth is no less true.'

'Whatever that means.'

'We are married in our hearts. We always were.'

'Didn't we get a divorce?' she asked brightly. 'I think I remember that.'

'We can fix that mistake now. Think how many more

years there are ahead of us. What if we live to eighty? Ten years of misunderstanding will be nothing.'

They had reached her trailer now. Desi went up the step, then turned and faced him, her hand on the latch.

'The last ten years will never be nothing to me,' she said stonily. 'But you will, Salah. You are. Nothing to me. Good night.'

She went in and closed the door.

Sleep would not come. She lay like one fatally wounded, reexamining her life and her ten lost years. The shame she'd carried for so long after reading Salah's letter. That miserable year-long affair with a man almost as old as her father. And afterwards, feeling so permanently degraded it was as if all sexual life in her died. Until Salah himself had brought her to life again.

Leo could never have succeeded, of course, had she not felt so despised. She remembered her stunned shock at the gross betrayal of trust after three years of acting like a father to her. There was no one she'd trusted more.

'Oh, come off it!' he'd said impatiently. 'Don't try and tell me you haven't been expecting this! Why do you think I've invested so much time and money in you, Desi? Building a career you would never have had without me. You're not quite as fabulous as we've got them saying, you know! Without me you'd still be posing in cheap anoraks for catalogues in the backwoods.'

She'd accepted it, too stunned to resist either the judgement or his advances. She accepted his marriage proposal, too. That ten months of being Leo Patrick's fiancée had been three hundred days of humiliation, until she had found the courage to break with him completely, find her feet and a new agent.

Salah's judgement of her had become a self-fulfilling prophecy.

If Salah had trusted her, that awful year could not have taken place. Her life would now be something else entirely. The possibility of happiness would not seem so distant.

Was it only yesterday she had realized she had never stopped loving him? Where was that feeling now? He had betrayed the past, and it ran like a seam all through her life.

And now he wanted her again, he said. Not just physically, this time: no, now he wanted her love.

But he'd killed that. A love that had survived, buried but intact, for ten long desperate years, had finally been put out of its misery. *You killed it with your own hand,* Desi told Salah silently. *And all things considered, I should be grateful. One day I will be. When I've recovered, I'll be glad.*

Then she turned to bury her tears in her pillow.

CHAPTER SEVENTEEN

'WE KNEW there was a VIP coming,' the girl gushed happily. 'We thought it would be the French Culture Minister or somebody like that. I mean, who would have thought it would be *Desi*?'

The noon sun painted the world a painful, bright white outside the open-fronted mess tent, where she was sitting with Salah and his father and a couple of the dig supervisors over lunch. She had awoken with a headache and stayed in the trailer to miss breakfast. Then she had done the rounds with Salah's father again, keeping all possibility of conversation with Salah at bay.

But she had to face Salah sometime, so when Khaled had mentioned lunch, Desi hadn't protested. She and Salah still had not spoken, but in the bustle no one seemed to notice.

She glanced at him once, and that once was enough to tell her she'd had no need for evasive tactics: the window of opportunity was closed. Salah was back in control. The anguish of last night was gone, his face today was shuttered stone. He was the Salah she had met at the airport once more—harsh, forbidding, a man who was nobody's fool.

That was good, of course. She was glad. Now all she wanted to do was get away from him as soon as possible.

Desi smiled and signed her autograph in the thick, grubby notebook labelled FIELD NOTES for the young volunteer, who had finally summoned the courage to approach the table and speak to her. Others were watching from a distance and it was clear they would join their friend in another minute.

'So are you going to be having pictures taken here? Is it, like, a modelling shoot?' the girl asked.

Suddenly there was the sound of a vehicle engine approaching, and everyone sat up with ears pricked as it came to a stop outside the tent.

'Are we expecting someone?' Dr. al Khouri asked. Everyone at the table shook their head. 'I hope the guards were awake,' the archaeologist said grimly.

A car door slammed, and a moment later a woman's figure appeared in the tent opening, features indistinguishable against the light. She paused briefly in the entrance, swept a look around the tables, then headed firmly towards the table where they were sitting. Desi saw an elegant woman with an aristocratic face and alert black eyes.

'Mother?' exploded Salah in disapproving amazement. 'What are you doing here in such heat?'

'I came to meet Desi, of course,' said Arwa al Khouri.

'This is my husband's home on site,' Salah's mother said a little later, as they entered a cool, if rather cramped and untidy trailer. 'I am not often here, because the heat is bad for my health.

'So. You will call me Arwa, yes?' she said, shifting a pile of papers from the sofa to the floor so that they could sit down. 'I feel that I have known you a very long time already! It is only bad luck, after all, that we have not met long ago.'

'You speak such good English!' Desi said brightly, nervously steering the conversational boat towards the shallows.

Arwa was an elegant, aristocratic woman whose black hair had been cut probably, Desi guessed, in Paris, where she doubtless also bought her clothes. Her skin was firm and clear without any sign of surgical or chemical assistance, and Desi thought she must be about fifteen years younger than her husband. Wearing a smart pink linen tunic and trousers, she made Desi feel grubby and underdressed in her khaki shorts, T-shirt and the loose khaki shirt.

'Not so good. But I am glad that you and I can talk without an interpreter. I am so glad to meet you at last, Desi! Because I go every year to Paris for the shows, I have seen you several times on the catwalk. And I so wanted to meet you! Each time I thought, if I just send a note…but always I lacked courage.'

Desi had heard this kind of thing many times, but from a woman like Arwa al Khouri it surprised her.

'Why did you want to meet me?'

'Because you were the woman who had my son's heart, and there was trouble between you,' Arwa said simply. 'I am so glad to meet you at last, Desi.' She reached out to pat Desi's arm. 'So glad you have finally come.'

Desi stared, discovered that her mouth was hanging open, closed it, felt it open again of its own volition.

'What—what are you talking about?' she asked stupidly.

'Now, you won't worry that I am his mother,' said Arwa. 'You will tell me everything, yes? Because I look into your eyes, Desi, and I think I see that you do love my son. As of course he loves you.'

Desi shook her head, because suddenly she couldn't trust herself to speak. She thought of the stony face that had greeted her at lunch today. Whatever he had briefly imagined yesterday, she knew Salah was impervious to love. For one treacherous moment Desi regretted last night's outburst. If she had let him speak when he wanted to...

No. She'd been right before. She'd had a lucky escape ten years ago.

'Tell me,' Arwa invited.

A moment ago she had imagined she was in control of herself. Now, suddenly, Desi was horrified to find herself close to tears. She gulped and shook her head, but it was all too recent, she couldn't contain her grief. She had never told anyone the whole story, not even Sami knew. But now the words began to spill out, as if with a will of their own, until she had unloaded everything. The letter that had destroyed her ten years ago, the discovery of why he had written it. His baseless accusations about her motive for the visit.

'Never once did he take me on trust! Never once in ten years! I don't call that love!' Desi finished at last.

Salah's mother did not speak till Desi had stopped talking. Then she sat shaking her head.

'And in this way he has nearly destroyed himself, and you, too,' she said. 'Men can be such fools when they love too much. But I think I understand my son. I see how it happened.'

'So do I,' Desi said, hiccuping. 'It's no mystery, is it?'

'He was very young and our two cultures are so different. Ten years ago such advertising pictures of women were rare here in Barakat, Desi. Even now they do not appear often. So to see you in such a way was a shock for Salah. Of course he did not react well, but he regretted it almost immediately, you say. He did beg forgiveness. And then you, from your own cultural distance, mistrusted Salah in return.'

'*I* mistrusted *him*?'

Arwa smiled. 'But what else was it, when you feared—on the evidence of one jealous outburst!—that he was like those Kaljuk fools who punish women for their own inadequacies? He believed you were being sexually exploited, but you feared he could be a madman.'

Desi went still as it sank in. She had blamed Salah for not trusting her, but she had never recognized her own fears as mistrust of him. On what evidence had she judged him? One argument, and he was sharing a mindset with the lowest of the low.

'When he returned from his visit with your family that year, I knew he was very unhappy,' his mother recalled softly. 'But he would not talk to us. And the next thing we knew, instead of going to university as he should, he enlisted in Prince Omar's troop of Cup Companions and went off to fight the Kaljuk War.

'And a few months later, he was wounded. The bullet missed killing him by a centimetre and he fell down the side of the mountain and suffered more injuries. The first time I saw him…'

She put her hand up and massaged between her eyes as if the memory still haunted her. After a moment she went on.

'And you tell me it was at this time—just when he was at his weakest, when he was in terrible pain and fear and had only his own determination to tell him he would recover—that he read something that told him you had gone to another man. And he believed it.'

Arwa paused, but Desi's throat was too dry for speech.

'He should have questioned it, of course. But in the Barakat Emirates, again, we do not have such magazines as these. How could he know that they publish rumour as fact?'

Desi felt as though all her certainties were so many logs in the rapids and she could no longer keep her balance on them.

'Did he tell you about this? Is that how you know?' she asked.

'No,' Arwa said firmly. 'How I wish he had! We did not know at all what had happened, except that he loved you and you had broken his heart.'

'If he didn't tell you, how could you know I broke his heart?'

Arwa smiled sadly.

'Desi, ten years ago, I sat beside my son's bed when we did not know if he would live or die. Every day and every night he called your name. He begged your forgiveness. He told you he loved you.

'We knew who Desi was—the young sister of his friend Harry. We knew you were only fifteen or sixteen. We discussed it many times during those terrible days, my husband and I, whether to get in touch and ask you to come to him.' She shrugged. 'We were afraid, and we did nothing.'

'I wanted to come to him,' Desi whispered. 'But my agent said…'

But she had known. If only she had listened to her heart, and walked away from Leo and his 'important bookings'! Then there would have been no room for misunderstanding. Why had she been so weak?

Salah was right—it was Leo who had come between them. He had not come to her bed then, but he had taken possession of her as surely as a lover.

Arwa sighed. 'After these few weeks there was a big improvement. We brought him home. He was happier then, he was recovering. And then one day I went into his room, and my son was gone. Someone lay in the bed who looked like him, but it was not Salah. It was as if his inner self had died. I never learned what had happened, Desi—but I think perhaps today I know.

'And for ten years I never saw my son himself again—until the day his father told him that Desirée Drummond was coming to visit the dig. In that moment, I tell you, a mask was ripped away, and I saw that inside the stranger we had known for ten years was still my son Salah, and that you had the power to bring him back.

'Today I see that my son is alive again. His heart is breaking again, but at least it speaks to him. Salah recovered physically a long time ago, Desi, but today, for the first time since that terrible war, his spirit is alive.

'You ask how I know he loves you. That is how I know. Your presence has touched him as no one else can do. He doubted your love at a time when he was ill and vulnerable, it is true. And that weakness has led to misery for both of you. But if you love him—and why else have you come here?—you must find a way to forgive him, don't you think?'

Desirée gazed at her, torn between hope and grief.

Was it true? Did his mother see something she herself had not seen behind the cold mask of Salah's face today? Could it be unhappiness, not coldness, that had turned his face to stone?

Her heart was being torn to ribbons, but one thing at last was clear. She could admit it now. She loved him. She did love him. And if he loved her…

What shook her most was the knowledge that the change she had seen in Salah, the thing that had turned him into the harsh, closed man she had hardly recognized at the airport was—herself. His conviction that she did not love him.

That was so much to absorb that she wasn't sure it would ever sink in completely.

CHAPTER EIGHTEEN

'WILL you walk with me, Desi?' Salah said.

It was sunset, and the air was cooling quickly. She looked up into his face and nodded once, then looked away again.

The setting sun coloured the great outcrops of rock all across the desert deep pink and gold as they walked out into the deserted ancient city. It was easy to feel the pull of another age, feel that she had almost slipped in among the people who had worshipped the feminine principle.

Easy to feel the female power that was deep in the fabric of the temple under her feet burn up through her.

They climbed the brick steps of the exposed remains of the great temple, and as her feet pressed into the ancient brick, built by hands dead five thousand years, Desi was flooded by a sense of otherness, a different way of being. A feeling of uninhibited joy embedded in the brick seemed to lift a burden from her.

She yearned to know these people. Who were they? How did they worship the divine they revered as Goddess?

Desi said, 'I asked your father this afternoon—he's agreed to take me on as a volunteer next season. There's something about this place. I want to be in on the discoveries. I want to know about her.'

He thought of how it would be, to know she was here, day after day, if she were not his, and his heart clenched, but he could not protest.

Salah said softly, 'You are the representative of the Goddess on earth, Desi, do you know that? She has to come to the world in disguise now, to hide her true face in a masculine world. So she manifests as a supermodel or a cinema star. This is the secret way the world now worships the feminine.

'I was wrong, ten years ago. It is not demeaning. They try to demean it, but in a woman like you, this female power comes forth unsullied.

'When they admire you and yearn for you, Desi, it is my father's lost Goddess that they seek. You keep her alive in the world. If she were not always alive in the world, the world would have been destroyed by human stupidity long ago. I see that now.'

There was no answer she could find to that. But he did not seem to expect one. They stood and watched in silence until the sun had disappeared and stars spangled the blackness.

'Listen, Desi,' he began urgently, as night settled around them, shrouding the sound of voices from the tents. 'Please listen. I want to tell you how it was with me. Maybe if I tell you, your hurt will be less. I want to tell you.'

'I'm listening, Salah,' she said quietly.

'In the hospital you were there with me day and night. You were so much with me that finally it was as if I was thinking your thoughts. Then I learned with certainty that you did love me. It was fear that had made you deny it. And for the first time, Desi, I understood those fears. I thought of the savages in Kaljukistan and understood why my outburst had made you think I was like them. You knew so little of me, of my people.

'But I was not like them. I never could be. I never admired such men, openly or secretly.'

'I know you couldn't,' she whispered.

'And I knew, I *knew*, that our love could overcome everything. My jealous stupidity, your fear. We loved each other so much, we had touched a deep well that most people never reach. I knew it would be forever. I knew I had to get better, go and find you, and make it happen.

'From that moment, I began to recover. They brought me home.

'I was writing you a letter. I could write only a little at a time, but I was filled with confidence. In the letter I told you what I had learned, what I knew. I asked you to come.

'Then, before it was finished—so close, it was almost done! What demon interfered at that moment, Desi?—they brought me some mail, letters that had been following me for weeks, from home to Parvan, to the hospital and back home again.

'There was a letter from Sami, weeks old. From before I was wounded.'

Sami, excited by her friend's success, had enclosed pictures cut from a magazine of Desi in her new life. He looked at the pictures and into another world. Desi was a different woman—polished, glossy, her hair perfection, diamonds at her ears and around her neck, her dress tight and short, her heels impossibly high. But worst of all was the smile, a smile he didn't recognize. It was wide, but it didn't reach her eyes.

'I went cold, Desi. I started to shiver. My heart stopped with the fear that my feeling was wrong, that it was too late for us. The longer I looked at the pictures the more I was afraid. My certainty crumbled. I thought, she belongs to this other world now, she will laugh at my letter.'

But still, he would have sent the letter. It was better to be laughed at than not to try.

The last photo showed her with a man with a fake tan and a stitched-on smile, hovering over her with predatory possessiveness. Underneath, there was a caption. He still remembered it word for word.

"'Leo J. Patrick with his latest discovery, the stunning Desirée. He's calling her the find of his life. Reliable sources suggest he's not talking strictly business. Apparently it's a May-December romance.'"

'I didn't understand *May-December* until I asked. But I understood *romance*.' He closed his eyes at the memory, opened them again. 'It was worse than death, Desi. The pain carried all my confidence, all my security away.'

Two days later her own card had come. It was stilted and awkward, and made nothing clear. *With love, your friend, Desi,* it said.

'I had lost all my insight into your thoughts. I thought this was your way of saying we should be friends. But I could not be friends with you, Desi. I wanted to be your lover, your husband, not your friend while another man was your lover.'

He stood gazing out over the purple-shadowed desert.

'I don't know what happened to me. I don't know why I never questioned the truth of it. Fool that I was. Did my illness make me crazy? I don't know. I only know the pain was much worse than my physical wounds, and that I wished the bullet had killed me.

'I wrote that letter. When it was sent I regretted it. And then I didn't again.'

Desi's heart was kicking in her breast, pumping hope and fear in equal measure through her system. She couldn't speak, couldn't look at him. She bent her head, listening with every cell of her being.

When he recovered, he was to go to university abroad. His parents suggested Canada, but Salah rejected the idea. He chose London instead. But London was not the place to escape from thoughts of Desi. Her picture was in every magazine and newspaper, her name in too many gossip columns. One day he read that she was engaged to Leo J. Patrick, a year later he heard of the breakup on television.

Even then a part of him had wanted to go to her, fight for another chance. But he had struggled against the desire as foolish weakness, and won.

'I was a fool. So much worse than a fool. I killed it with my own hand. And now you hate me, and how can I complain? It was not you, Desi. I see it now. It is myself I have been angry with all these years. I was the one who killed our love.'

It was not true, of course. He had been living a lie. Nothing had killed his love. He had loved her from that day to this, without ceasing for the space of a breath.

'Salah, I...' But she could not put anything into words.

'If you come to my country, Desi,' he said, 'to work with my father, you must understand that I will be here, too.'

'Yes?'

'And when I see you, Desi, I will try to make you

love me again. No more now than ten years ago am I capable of being your friend.'

'No?' she whispered.

'Desi, I love you,' said Salah. 'Tell me I'm not too late. Tell me there is a way to make you love me again.'

The moon was rising, fat and full-bellied, lighting the sand with her own particular glow. Her heart climbed with it, up among the stars. Her eyes burned with unshed tears.

Below them in the compound, lamps were lit. The table in the dining tent was being laid with food. Men and women came out of their tents, refreshed by the cool night air and the shower each was entitled to at the end of the working day. Their voices rang back and forth in the darkness, cheerful and ordinary, belying her feeling of mysterious communion with the distant ancestresses who had built this place.

He waited, gazing at the shadows below, listening to her soft breath, closer than his own heart, waiting for her answer.

'It wasn't all your fault, Salah,' she began softly, struggling for calm against the wild fluttering of her heart. 'For a long time I thought so. But I'm as much to blame as you are. So let's not talk about fault anymore. I'm tired of guilt and blame.'

He turned her to him, and gazed into her face. Moonlight both revealed and cloaked it in mystery, and she was as haunting and elusive as the great feminine power that had once been worshipped here. He would spend the rest of his life in pursuit of her mystery.

'Desi?' he said.

She said, learning it even as she spoke, 'I've been realizing something. It was never my own dream, to be a model. All the girls at school were so thrilled when I was "discovered", when I started getting jobs, they all fantasized about supermodel stardom, and it was great, but...it just had never been my particular dream.

'When we fell in love, you and I, that was the dream I recognized. And I see now that I could have changed everything that night, if I'd only admitted it to myself, if I'd said to you—it doesn't matter about that ad because we're going to get married and it won't happen again...none of it would have happened. But I was caught in someone else's dream.'

He said, 'I attacked you. How could you answer but by resisting the attack? It is human nature.'

'You didn't kill my love, Salah,' Desi breathed. 'Sometimes I wished you had. It hurt so much. But I know now I never stopped loving you. I was as wrong and weak as you were. But we were so young, and it was so powerful. I suppose we ought to be grateful it didn't kill us both outright.'

'Desi,' he said, in a voice suffocated with hope, 'I love you. I will love you forever.'

'I love you, too, Salah. Forever. I know it now.'

Then his arms wrapped her in a fierce embrace, pulling her tight against him as he gazed hungrily down into her face. 'Say you will marry me!' he demanded. 'Tell me!'

Moonlight spangled the tears on her lashes, but she smiled at him.

'How can I say no? After all, we're already married in our hearts, aren't we?'

'Yes, beloved,' he said, as his lips touched and tasted hers. 'We are already married in our hearts.'

EPILOGUE

'MISSION accomplished,' Desi said into the phone.

They had driven back to the palace in the morning, and Desi had called Sami to tell her the news.

'Oh, you *magician*!' Sami cried. 'Thank you, thank you! How did you manage it, Des? Did you—what did you do?'

'It was easy. I just had to agree to marry Salah in your place. No sacrifice too great.'

Sami screeched.

'I knew it! I knew he still loved you! I knew if he just saw you he'd... I've always thought it wasn't over for you two! That's wonderful, Des! Do you love him? Have you loved each other all this time?'

'Yes, and yes.'

'I am over the moon for you! And what about Farid?' Sami demanded anxiously. 'Did you...did you get a chance to ask Uncle Khaled?'

'He said something kind of interesting. Did you know your fiancé is related to the Sultan of Bagestan?'

'My *fiancé*?' Sami caught it instantly. 'Has Uncle Khaled actually given his consent?'

'He's going to tear a strip off Arif and Walid, too, as I understand it.'

'Oh, that's wonderful, Des! Oh, thank you, thank you!' Her voice caught, and for a moment she couldn't speak. 'I am so—but I knew it would all come right, if you would just—I knew you and Salah would…'

'Sam! Are you telling me you were *counting on—*'

'*Allah*, I'm delirious with relief!' Sam sniffed loudly and laughed on a sob. 'Are you as happy as I am, Des? You sound…wait a minute! *Des! What did you just say* about Farid? He's related to *whom*?'

He held the wife of his heart in his arms, and looked into her eyes, and nothing came between them. No shadow of the past, no fear for the future clouded the perfect communion of that gaze.

Her hair lay spread over his arm and the pillow, where the lamplight kissed it tenderly. She smiled up into his face, and he marvelled at the trusting openness, the vulnerable offering of the deepest parts of the soul he saw in her eyes, not realizing that the look was reflected in his own gaze.

'Beloved,' he murmured, and bent to brush her perfect lips with a kiss. Gently, sweetly, as tenderly as moonlight, his lips caressed her mouth, her cheek, her temple, her throat.

Melting followed every lightest touch, and she smiled and heaved a long, slow breath. She wrapped an arm around him, drawing him close, and pressed her own mouth to his cheek, his strong throat, his mouth.

'I love you so much, Salah,' she whispered. 'Please love me.'

His body stirred and pushed against her, and she melted deep inside, in anticipation of his homecoming. His hunger tightened his arms around her, his mouth grew more demanding, drinking deep of the delights of those soft lips, that eager tongue.

He began to stroke her, but she did not want delay. She wanted union. She pressed up against him, slipped impatiently under his body.

'Love me,' she said again. 'I want to feel you inside.'

He could not resist such a command. Was this how the Goddess had treated her worshippers? Demanding her pleasure of them?

He would always be a worshipper at this shrine.

He slipped into the cradle of her hips, lifted himself while she fitted up against him, and hungrily pushed home. They gasped together as the blow pushed pleasure into every cell, and lay for a moment of surprise, looking into each other's wide eyes.

In the moonlight she was both mysterious and known, both his and the other, the unknowable. He realized he must make her his, all his, and his body instinctively rose and pressed home again, to repeat that burst of joy, for this, he knew, was the way to own the lady. Her weakness for pleasure would always make her his.

He drew away and then home again, over and over, listening to the rhythm of her cries, guided by her hands, her mouth, her eyes, the hiss of breath between her teeth.

His own pleasure was his at any time, such power she had over him. But it was his delight to withhold it while he pushed her closer and closer to the source of the lady's mysterious power.

Melting pleasure flooded through her with each thrust of his body, and stored itself up in her cells, waiting for release. She lifted her body in response to the rhythm that had been created before the world. This was the rhythm of the birth of worlds, she thought dimly, this was how it happened—this endlessly repeated, endlessly building heat and joy, the sending of light into her heart, her muscles, her cells, her atoms. The pushing and pushing against the barrier that divided body from spirit, soul from soul, the barrier that only joy could defeat.

The pleasure built up in her till there was no room for any more, and still it built, overflowing from her cells into the world, till they were surrounded by an aura of sweetness and light and warmth that was all and everything, a warmed honey that glowed with its own light, an all-embracing delight-in-waiting.

And still he pushed, and pushed more, till she was sobbing with her inability to contain the pleasure, and then, suddenly, there was an explosion of heat and light, of love and joy, of delight and honey, and the wild need to be both self and other.

Pleasure blasted its way through them, and then what they hungered for was within their grasp, and they reached for it together, clasped it and brought it down to their bed, and held it for that brief, endless moment that was all that was allowed to mortals.

Afterwards they lay in each other's embrace, talking and silent, loving and still.

'Prince Omar has asked you to go and live abroad?' she asked. 'Why?'

'He wants me to set up as an unscrupulous collector, and let it be known I'm interested in Barakati antiquities, whatever their provenance.'

'With the goal of?'

'We hope it will allow us to trace the lines of supply right back to source. With luck we might bring down the whole chain.'

'And what happens when you've finished the job? Salah, you won't expect me to live in Barakat full-time?' she asked.

His arm tightened around her.

'I know your career means you have to be in Paris and London. We'll find a way, Desi.'

'Only a few more years,' she admitted. 'I'm very tired of the life. But I've been thinking for a while that I'd like to get a place on one of the islands and spend a few months of the year there. Not too far from my parents. Would you go for that?'

'I always liked the island,' he said. 'Summers there were always more pleasant than here in the desert.'

She grinned. 'I don't think I ever understood quite how much until these past few days.'

'And what about your work with my father?'

'Yes, I'm looking forward to that! I'm definitely going to see if I can fit in some part-time study this year. Sami says everything gets taped now and you can download lectures. So it should be doable.'

'I'm glad you have found a new career with my father, Desi. And I have another apology to make. How many times did I accuse you of lying? I was so sure I knew you!'

'Yes,' she said curiously, tilting her head to look up at him. 'What made you so sure?'

He smiled and lifted a strand of her hair to tickle his mouth.

'Even when we were children and you came in to tell the rest of us stories, or when you said something to challenge me—I always knew when you'd made it up, remember?'

'Oh!' Desi cried, remembering. '*Yes*, how infuriating that was! Harry would have swallowed anything, but for you! How did you always *know*?'

'Well, I will tell you, though perhaps it sounds impossible in the cold light of reason. The colour of your eyes changed. When you had something to hide, your eyes were grey.

'I was already suspicious of your motives before you came. I told my father so, and he agreed it was suspicious. But when you were telling me your reasons for coming here, and your eyes went grey…then I was sure you were lying.'

'Ahhh,' Desi said. 'No one's ever told me that before.'

'I could think of only two reasons for you to be here. I told my father you were the tool of thieves—I told myself that that was why I had to be your guide. But I couldn't suppress the hope—not that I saw the feeling as hope then!—that you had really come here for…'

'For you? You secretly wanted me to say, *You can't marry Sami because I still love you*?'

'Things might have proceeded more quickly if you had.'

'Sami made me swear a terrible oath that I wouldn't tell you the truth. Otherwise I'd have cracked a dozen different times.'

It took a moment for that to filter in. He propped himself up on one elbow and stared down at her. In the lamplight clear turquoise eyes smiled up at him.

'What? What truth?'

'You were right, Salah. I *was* lying to you. Not for my own ends, though—well, not consciously. I came here because of Sami.'

She felt his surprise. 'Sami?'

'I guess your father never had the chance to tell you.

Sami has a fiancé already. She doesn't want to marry you. Please don't break your heart. She asked me to—well, to try and…sidetrack you. And to try to get your father's permission for her to marry Farid instead of you.'

'But this is crazy! It was they who made—'

'It wasn't Sam's doing, though. Her brothers have forced her into a lot of observant practice over the past few years.'

He wouldn't rest till he had the whole story out of her. Then he lay back laughing.

'You were supposed to compromise my bid by seducing me?'

'I know it sounds crazy…'

'*Sounds?* What if I obliged you, and then denied it afterwards? Were you going to the media to expose me? Think of the headlines!'

'I was never very happy about it,' she said meekly. 'But Sami was so desperate.'

'But why not speak to me directly? She could have phoned me!'

'Because she was convinced you had reasons of your own for wanting the marriage. She wasn't sure how you'd take it, or if you'd tell Walid. As soon as I saw you, I understood her fears. Let's face it, you're a bit intimidating these days, Salah.'

She kissed his shoulder to soften the words.

He lay in silence for a moment. 'And she was right. I did have reasons, not that I understood that then. I think now that I felt it was a way to bring you back into my life. And it did.'

'But only because Sami begged me. I wouldn't have come otherwise. What would have happened if I hadn't?'

'I would have found a way, Desi. I know it now. Something had begun to speak in me, and it would not have been silenced until I saw you again.

'But still, I think, we will be grateful to Sami all the rest of our lives. And I am very glad to know that I was not mistaken. I do know you, my heart.'

She said thoughtfully, brushing his cheek with a curl of her hair, 'It could be a problem, though, never being able to lie to you.'

'You foresee that you will want to tell me lies, *Deezee*? When? Why?'

'Well, for instance…when I'm trying to throw a surprise party for your eightieth birthday,' she said. 'It's going to be a bit of an anti-climax, isn't it, if you know all about it right from the get-go?'

* * * * *

BREAKING THE SHEIKH'S RULES

Abby Green

Abby Green got hooked on Mills & Boon® romances while still in her teens, when she stumbled across one belonging to her grandmother in the west of Ireland. After many years of reading them voraciously, she sat down one day and gave it a go herself. Happily, after a few failed attempts, Mills & Boon bought her first manuscript.

Abby works freelance in the film and TV industry, but thankfully the four a.m. starts and the stresses of dealing with recalcitrant actors are becoming more and more infrequent, leaving her more time to write!

She loves to hear from readers and you can contact her through her website at www.abby-green.com. She lives and works in Dublin.

Look for Abby Green's latest novel,
In Christofides' Keeping,
in November from Modern™ romance.

Dear Reader,

When my editor first asked me to consider writing a sheikh story, I was reluctant. Why? Because the prospect was daunting to say the least. These books, to me, have always delivered the ultimate fantasy – the heroes are impossibly autocratic, hardened by their harsh environments; the heroines have to be strong enough to withstand their particularly delicious brand of arrogance. And there is a well-loved list of names who do them so well: Penny Jordan, Jane Porter and Sandra Marton, just to name a few. Not to mention the sheer task of creating that evocative world! Deserts and oases and stupendously gorgeous palaces.

But...the lure became too great. I'd had an idea in my head for some time about a sheikh who comes to Ireland to buy a thoroughbred horse and so that became the start of my story...not in the arid desert, but in the lush green fields of Ireland.

And whilst in the process of writing the story, I found myself encountering two more arrogant heroes: one a sheikh, the brother of Nadim in this story, and the other a sultan from a neighbouring sultanate. So, far from my initial trepidation, it looks like I'm going to be inhabiting the land of sheikhs and sultans for a while longer.

I hope you enjoy Nadim and Iseult's story as much as I enjoyed writing it...

x *Abby*

This is for Peter Commane – thank you for answering all of my questions and for showing me around Goffs, and for demonstrating how to bid on a yearling in the process; here's to Sheila's Wish!

Thanks also to Nemone for taking the time to answer my queries.

CHAPTER ONE

SHEIKH NADIM BIN KALID AL SAQR'S dark eyes followed the horse and rider as they exercised on the gallops. He was blinded not only by the sheer magnificence of the colt, which had quickened his pulse and sent a thrill of triumph through him as soon as he'd seen its exquisite lines, but also by the intense green of everything as far as the eye could see. Softly falling rain covered everything in a fine mist, even though it was an unseasonably warm September day.

For a man who considered himself hewn from the uncompromising aridity of mountains and desert, he hadn't expected to feel a kinship with this inclement part of the world, but strangely, standing here now, he felt its lushness pull on his soul in a way he hadn't anticipated.

Up until now he'd been content to confine his interest in thoroughbred racing and breeding to his home on the Arabian peninsula, trusting his aides to buy in Europe and transport the horses to him. But now it was time to set up a European base, and he'd chosen Kildare, the Irish capital of thoroughbred breeding and training.

Ireland's reputation as home to the world's best horses, breeders and trainers was not in doubt. The man beside him, despite his florid appearance, which more than hinted at a drinking problem, had reputedly been one of the best trainers in the world, but until very recently had all but disappeared from the racing world.

The silence grew taut but he didn't speak for a few moments longer, unperturbed, studying the two-year-old.

His eyes drifted up from the horse to the rider. He could see that not only was the horse perhaps one of the most magnificent he'd seen in a long time, the rider too was one of the most accomplished he'd seen—and that included his own carefully handpicked staff back home. He looked to be about eighteen, slim build, definitely young. Yet he exuded an effortless way of handling the horse which Nadim knew only came from true talent, sheer courage and experience. And the animal was spirited.

The man moved restlessly beside him and Nadim took pity, saying finally, 'He's a stunning colt.'

'Yes,' Paddy O'Sullivan said with more than a hint of relief in his voice. 'I was sure you'd see it straight away.'

The horse they observed and spoke of was one of the main reasons for Nadim's visit to Ireland, and the reason why he was about to buy Paddy O'Sullivan out of his failing modest-sized training grounds and stud farm.

'It'd be hard not to see it,' Nadim murmured, his eyes once again mesmerised by the sleek move of powerful muscles under the thoroughbred's glossy coat. Already he was imagining the lineage that such a stallion and his brood mares could produce one day.

He'd sent his most senior equestrian aide to research this part of the world for him, and had instantly seen the potential; the stud was about two miles down the road from the house and training grounds. Perfect for his European base.

His mouth firmed when he recalled how his aide had been all but run off the beleaguered property by some angry woman with a rabid dog—hence his advice to steer well clear. But Nadim had made sure that his people had approached Paddy O'Sullivan directly and made an offer that no drowning man hoping for a life-raft could refuse...

The O'Sullivan stud had once been very successful, breeding numerous winners. It was that pure bloodline which had produced this colt, who was already making a name for itself, having won two of Ireland's highest-profile flat races in recent months. Excitement kicked low in Nadim's belly—a sensation he hadn't felt in a long time—making him aware of how rarely spontaneous emotion impacted on his day-to-day life. Just the way he liked it.

O'Sullivan spoke again, 'Iseult has been working with him tirelessly. He wouldn't be the horse he is today without her.'

Nadim frowned and took his eyes off the horse for a moment to look down at the much shorter man beside him. He hadn't heard that name before, and assumed it had to be of Irish origin. 'Ee—sult?'

The man gestured with his white head to the field, blue eyes fond. 'Iseult is my daughter—my eldest. She's got the gift. Been able to communicate with and control every animal she's encountered since she was barely walking.'

Nadim's eyes went back to the rider on the horse. He

felt slightly stunned. That was a *girl*? And this *girl* had trained this colt? Impossible; he'd worked with plenty of female trainers, but never one so young. Too young—no matter how innate her talent might be.

He shook his head, mentally trying to take it in, and only then started to see the subtle differences. Her waist dipped in and out more than a boy's should. The silhouette of her shoulders was slight, the hint of her neck delicate. Apart from that he couldn't tell much else, because she was covered up in jeans and a fleece, hair tucked up and under a flat cap. His belly clenched as he tasted the old fear when he realised belatedly that she wasn't wearing a hard hat. He drove it down. This wasn't Merkazad. The ground was soft here—not fatally hard.

But still she should be wearing adequate protection. A surge of irritation prickled across Nadim's skin. If she was at *his* stables right now she'd be seriously reprimanded for not wearing appropriate head protection.

O'Sullivan said now, *sotto voce*, even though no one could overhear, 'I'm sorry about what happened…with your assistant. Iseult's not happy about the sale…of either our stud farm or Devil's Kiss.' He continued nervously, 'She's very attached to her home and her…' The man blustered for a moment and corrected himself, 'That is, *your* horse.'

Nadim's blood started to boil ominously. *This* girl was the person who'd practically set a dog on his assistant Adil? This was intolerable. Where Nadim came from daughters were dutiful. Independent, yes, but not openly wilful and opinionated. And they weren't trainers who looked to be barely out of their teens. He thanked his lucky stars that he'd come now. This girl, if left to her own devices, could have ruined all his chances for acquiring this property.

She was clearly bent on obstructing a sale, and right now he wouldn't put it past her to sabotage the horse he wanted so badly. He was well aware that the racing world was littered with great two-year-olds who peaked too early and never went on to achieve anything else.

Those thoughts made his voice more autocratic. 'He is about to become mine, as is your property—unless of course you've changed your mind?'

O'Sullivan blustered and stuttered, '*No*, Sheikh Nadim. I never meant that at all. It's just that Iseult has been training Devil's Kiss...so she's attached.'

Nadim flicked the man beside him a dark look, hiding the fact that he was taken aback anew to hear it confirmed that she'd trained him. And he had to admit, despite his misgivings, that the horse looked good.

'I would hope that the advantage of keeping the training grounds and stud in your name, along with being kept on as manager, is benefit enough compared to the alternative—which is that your bank is ready to throw you out on the street.'

The older man was all but wringing his hands, clearly terrified he'd offended the new landlord. 'Of course, Sheikh Nadim...I never meant to imply anything... It's just that Iseult—well, she's a bit head-strong. I hope that she doesn't offend...'

His voice trailed away as the rider slowed and came to a halt, turning the horse slowly to face where Nadim and Paddy O'Sullivan stood. Nadim watched as they approached, and the rider became more obviously a young girl. Just how old was she, anyway? he wondered as they drew closer and closer. It was impossible to tell.

He noted with increasing displeasure that she wasn't jumping off the horse to make his acquaintance.

For some reason, when his attention should have been taken by the horse, he found his eye resting curiously on its rider, his thoughts staying on her. A face was partially revealed beneath the lip of the cap. And something in his chest kicked once. Like an electric shock to his heart.

He could see that her face was exquisitely sculped—high cheekbones and a delicately firm jaw, straight nose. Her eyes were hidden by the cap, and her mouth was set in a mutinous line, but Nadim imagined that in repose it would be sensuously full. His gaze dropped and he saw the unmistakable line of slight but feminine curves beneath her T-shirt. He felt another kick then, in a more base part of his anatomy, and was astounded.

He expected such responses when he moved in sophisticated circles where mature, experienced, sensually confident women abounded. Not here in a strange country, on the edge of a green field, looking at a girl he'd moments ago dismissed as a boy. And who was irritating him more with each passing minute. Anger at his own unbidden response made the muscles in his face tighten.

Iseult O'Sullivan had hated every minute of having to exercise Devil's Kiss for the man who had come to inspect the spoils of his takeover—especially when he didn't even care enough to see what he was buying himself before he came today to sign the deal.

He'd sent an assistant to trespass on their land and take photographs, after which he'd quietly bought the adjoining land some months previously. And since then he'd been biding his time, waiting to strike—like a vulture circling over a decaying carcass—until they'd had no choice but to announce the sale. But as she looked down now, her boiling anger seemed to drain away.

She was suddenly absurdly glad to be sitting astride Devil's back, because she knew if she was standing she might not be able to remember why she was angry. Her hands gripped the reins and Devil's Kiss moved restlessly underneath her, sensing her inner agitation, his highly strung nature never too far from the surface.

The man was like something from another planet, and nothing like the stereotypical Arabic Sheikh she might have imagined if she hadn't already Googled him for information and seen pictures. And, despite having seen pictures of him, it was still hard for her to deal with the reality. He looked to be in his mid-thirties, and was as insanely good-looking as his pictures had promised. Tall, handsome, and dangerously dark.

He was wearing faded jeans which clung indecently to powerful thigh muscles, and a dark long-sleeved polo shirt, its sleeves rolled up to reveal muscled forearms. His biceps bulged against the material of his shirt, and the fine Irish mist settled over him like a glittering diamond coat. His darkly olive skin stood out against the lush backdrop like an exotic hothouse flower.

One booted foot was lifted to rest negligently on the bottom rung of the fence. His hair was short and dark, but thick, as if it would lean towards unruly curls if allowed to grow any longer.

She took in all this in a second, with an accelerating heartbeat. Virile sexuality drenched the air around him like a tangible forcefield and Iseult shivered involuntarily, recognising a base sexuality that seemed to resonate with something equally base within her.

He carried an air of authority and power suited to the monarch he was, ruling over a wealthy sheikhdom where he owned one of the most exclusive thoroughbred stables on the Arabian peninsula. The kind of stables where legendary winners were bred and trained.

With her heart stuttering in her chest, Iseult watched as the Sheikh calmly and gracefully vaulted over the fence, not a hint of strain on his face even though the fence was over five feet. Immediately Devil's head reared back, nostrils flaring, and he stepped sideways with a skittish move. Iseult patted the horse and murmured encouragement for him to not make this easy on his new owner.

Her father, standing just a few feet away, was sending fervent silent signals to Iseult: *Please behave.* But she was too heartsore to behave, no matter how she'd been momentarily thrown. This man was coolly and calmly taking everything she'd ever known and loved, and there wasn't a thing she could do about it except not make it easy for him.

The Sheikh was looking up at her, and she could see the expressions crossing his face, and his anger mounting that she wasn't jumping off, jumping to attention. While she'd have liked to think that she was consciously making her displeasure known, she knew her inability to move had more to do with his sheer male charisma than any rebellion. Finally her father's voice intruded, and she could hear the fear. 'Iseult, please allow Sheikh Nadim to ride Devil's Kiss. He's come a long way.'

With much less grace than she was used to Iseult slipped off the horse and came around his head to hand the reins to the Sheikh. Her legs turned to water when she recognised just how tall and well built he was. Like one long, lean and hardened muscle, with shoulders so broad they blocked out the background.

She felt innately feminine next to his superior build. It was very disturbing when she'd long ago given up any attempt to explore that side of herself, assuming she just didn't have it in her. Reaction to her thoughts made her all but thrust the reins at him. 'Here you are.'

His black eyes glittered dangerously, and Iseult was glad of the protection of her cap. She desperately wanted him to take the reins before he could see how her hand was starting to shake, and to her intense relief he did. But not before his fingers touched off hers, and she jerked back so quickly that Devil's Kiss moved skittishly again.

Before she could lose it completely she turned and walked away through the soft damp grass, and climbed over the fence jerkily to stand by her father, who was radiating waves of disapproval. She'd never felt so out of control of her own body and emotions, and she didn't like it one bit.

She watched with a thumping heart as Sheikh Nadim coolly and calmly walked around the horse, lengthening the stirrups and running a large brown hand over his flanks. Iseult's belly tightened and she felt a flare of something hot in her abdomen.

Then he vaulted onto the horse with a fluid grace she'd never seen before, and nudged Devil's Kiss straight into a canter. Iseult's throat dried up completely. Devil's Kiss was an absolute traitor; he'd shown not even a flicker of rebellion at seating this man, clearly recognising his skill and authority.

Sheikh Nadim al Saqr was considered something of a rebel in horse breeding circles, as he'd been slow to set up a base in Europe, preferring to keep his horses in his home country, out of sight and highly secret. The world of flat racing had been sent into a tailspin when he'd entered one of his three-year-olds into the most prestigious race in Europe at Longchamp the previous year and it had won. A rank outsider, who had only raced previously in Dubai, it had stunned everyone and made the racing world sit up and recognise Sheikh Nadim al Saqr as a serious contender.

Beside her, her father chuckled softly and said, 'Weren't expecting Devil's Kiss to take to him like that, were you?'

The backs of Iseult's eyes stung with hot tears, which was so unlike her—after everything she'd been through she rarely if ever resorted to tears, and suddenly she was a bag of weeping hormones. This was the ultimate betrayal, coming on top of everything else. With an incoherent grunt she turned and stormed off, back up the drive to the house they no longer owned, away from the field they also no longer owned.

Her father hissed after her desperately, 'Iseult O'Sullivan, come back here right now. You cannot just walk away—what will he think?'

Iseult turned, but kept walking backwards and flung her arms up. 'We've lost everything, Dad—I'm not going to bow and scrape after that man. Let him take Devil's Kiss back to the stables and scrub him down if he wants him so badly.'

Years of looking after her father and her two younger brothers and sister had put her in a position of unspoken authority in their home. Even her father knew when not to push her; he owed her too much.

It was only then that she noticed the sleek silver

Jeep with dark windows and an officious-looking body-
guard standing to attention nearby, intermittently scanning the surroundings from behind black glasses. It
made her even angrier, reminding her of the sheer arrogance of his pushy assistant, who'd had the gall to
come and look the place over, as if it was a slave girl
being sold at an auction, before they'd even publicly announced the sale.

Iseult turned and kept walking, tears blurring her
vision. A part of her balked at her extremely uncharacteristic lack of grace and manners, but something about
the Sheikh had all her defences raised high and on red
alert. She simply couldn't stand there and watch him
steal her horse from right under her, and then deal with
the undoubtedly arrogant and smug way he'd hand her
back the reins as if she was nothing more than a stablehand.

Iseult's tears cleared as she fumed and stomped up
the drive; that might be what he was used to in his own
country but he wouldn't get away with it here. She
imagined him coming from a barbarically foreign
place, where he had harems of scantily clad women at-
tending to his every need, and where he lounged on
plush velvet and silk cushions in lavish tents in oases
in the desert, gorging himself on decadent foods and
wines. The man clearly believed himself important
enough to merit bringing bodyguards to a quiet and
rural part of Ireland.

Her overblown imagination mocked her as she
recalled the sliver of hard, olive-skinned, muscle-ridged
belly she'd seen as he'd vaulted onto Devil's Kiss, when
his shirt had ridden up for a moment. He didn't have
the body of a louche decadent, and he didn't strike her

as the kind of man who required protecting. Her belly tightened again, and a disturbing pulse throbbed between her legs.

She entered the stableyard and tore off her cap, releasing her hair, breathing hard. Damp sweat pooled uncomfortably between her breasts and trickled down her back. She knew they'd been fighting a losing battle for some time, and that the culmination of it was today. And she knew rationally that she had no real reason to feel such antipathy towards this Sheikh other than the fact he happened to be the new owner...and that he disturbed her on a level she didn't like to think about.

As she looked around the unbearably shabby yard the fight suddenly left her, and she felt overwhelmed with fatigue and grief at seeing all the empty stalls. The stud down the road was equally desolate-looking. The homestead stood to the right of the yard. Once it had gleamed from top to bottom, a grand country house, but now it was a mere shadow of its former self. Everything was peeling and crumbling. She'd worked so hard to try and keep them afloat, but everything had gone against them—not least the global economic crisis.

They might have won two prestigious races recently, but that money had barely made a dent in the huge debts that had built up from years of mismanagement. The one ace up their sleeve had been Devil's Kiss, and now he was gone. Quite literally. The Sheikh had come to transport him to his own country on the Arabian peninsula, where he had plans to train him, race him, and eventually use him to breed even more winners to add to his arsenal. He was going to overhaul their small stud farm and gallops and turn them into something homogenous: a conveyor belt outfit that would 'perform' and meet 'targets', and make a profit and breed winners.

While Iseult had no problem with expansion, and turning their property around so that it functioned properly again on all levels, she'd always loved the fact that they'd remained true to their own identity long after many other farms had sold out to rich Arabs and huge syndicates. Now they were no different from the rest.

Desultorily, Iseult made her way to Devil's Kiss's stable, to get it prepared for his return. She grimaced as she turned on a hose and started to sluice down the yard, thinking of her beloved grandfather, who would have railed against this day too… She'd followed him everywhere until his death; she'd been ten when he'd been struck down with an awful illness and everything had started to unravel…

Iseult diverted her mind away from painful memories. As soon as Devil's Kiss had raced and shown his pedigree as a stunning two-year-old the spotlight had been turned onto their stud—especially as it had been so long since they'd produced a winner. Everyone knew that their backs were against the wall, and that they'd sold all but their oldest mares to concentrate on Devil's Kiss. That buzz was undoubtedly what had brought them to the attention of the Sheikh. And Iseult had to admit bitterly that he'd snapped them up like the bargain they were.

Ridiculously, tears threatened again—too much buried grief swimming up to the surface. And that was when Iseult heard the familiar clatter of hooves in the yard behind her. She hurriedly blinked away her tears and turned around warily to look up. The sun chose that moment to peek out from dark, oppressive clouds and Iseult shivered—because she was momentarily blinded and all she could see was the intimidatingly broad-shouldered silhouette of the Sheikh on Devil's back. Like a portent of doom.

For a second Nadim was utterly transfixed. The girl was revealed fully without that unflattering cap, and she was most definitely a girl—beautiful enough to make his breath catch. Not a scrap of make-up marred her pale alabaster skin and that amazing bone structure. And he'd never seen such unusual colouring: long dark red hair was pulled back into an untidy ponytail which must have been stuffed under the cap, and tendrils drifted and clung to her cheeks and neck. Tight jeans and the fleece did little to disguise the fact that she was tall and slim, lean as a whip, her body sleek and toned.

But it was her eyes that caught him as if spellbound. Huge and almond shaped, with long black lashes, they were the colour of dark liquid amber. And as he watched, fascinated, those stunning eyes flashed a warning and her chest rose and fell, making him want to drop his gaze and inspect those delicately feminine swells again. He sensed instinctively that she was more voluptuous than she looked, and wondered why she hid her curves. But he cut off his wandering mind there, when it had a direct effect on his anatomy. The kick of desire in his blood made him feel disorientated. It was unwarranted and completely inappropriate.

Her full mouth had tightened back into the mutinous line. 'If you've quite finished your inspection, I'll take Devil's Kiss now. I'm not part of the inventory of your newly acquired assets.'

Her voice was surprisingly husky, but Nadim didn't dwell on that further enticement now. Her haughty look forced a surge of anger upward and drove Nadim off the horse to the ground. Once again he'd been mesmerised by someone who was little more than a stablehand. *Unthinkable.* He deliberately ignored her hand, outstretched for the reins, fixing her with a harsh glare.

It was a struggle for Iseult to stay standing as the Sheikh came off the horse and stood far too close for her liking. His slow appraisal just now had turned her insides to jelly. And now, facing her like this, he was far more devastating than she'd acknowledged before. He had to be at least six foot three and, while she was relatively tall, she felt minute in comparison.

'Correct me if I'm wrong, Miss O'Sullivan, but I believe that you and your father are very much part of the *inventory*. Part of the agreement for the sale of this property outlines the fact that all working staff will be retained to ensure a smooth transition. Are you not part of the staff?'

His deep voice and softly drawled words, with more than a hint of a seductively foreign accent, made Iseult's knees feel curiously weak. Anger at her response made her lash out. 'I'm more than just staff. Perhaps where you come from you're used to buying and selling people, but in this country we've outgrown such antiquated practices.'

His face tightened perceptibly. 'Be very careful, Miss O'Sullivan. You're in danger of going too far. As it is, your insolence is intolerable. I don't appreciate *employees* who talk back or use guard dogs to intimidate.'

Iseult flushed at being reminded of the recent incident with his emissary. 'Murphy isn't a guard dog.

He's just protective. Your assistant was trespassing; I was here on my own.'

The Sheikh's mouth was a grim line of displeasure. 'You ignored a perfectly polite request from him to come and see the property even though it was common knowledge you were close to advertising a sale.'

Iseult couldn't meet that blistering dark gaze. She felt about two feet tall. How could she explain to this autocratic man the violently visceral feeling she'd had not to give up and admit defeat? And how his arrogant assistant had effortlessly raised her hackles by being so pushy, making her dread a soulless takeover by a faceless buyer?

He continued, 'Do I need to remind you that very soon I will own everything you see around you, and could have you thrown off this property for good?'

Iseult could feel the colour drain from her face, and saw something flash in his eyes. He even said something that sounded like a curse under his breath and moved towards her. Did he think she was going to faint? Iseult had never fainted in her life. She moved back jerkily, and the Sheikh stopped, his eyes gleaming obsidian.

Nadim had to curb a reflex to apologise—although he couldn't remember the last time he'd had to apologise for anything. He hadn't meant to speak so harshly, but when she'd gone white and looked as if he'd put a knife through her heart his immediate reaction had been one of remorse and to protect. He couldn't believe that this girl had taken him in even for a moment. He allowed no woman to get under his skin so easily.

He shouldn't be demeaning himself by engaging in dialogue with someone like her. She was about to become just one more of hundreds of employees scattered across the globe.

He finally handed her the reins and said curtly, 'Devil's Kiss travels tomorrow. See to it that he's ready.'

CHAPTER TWO

A SHORT while later, her belly still roiling with tangled emotions, Iseult went through the back door into the house, toeing off her boots and muttering under her breath as she walked into the warm and welcoming kitchen, where their housekeeper, Mrs O'Brien, was looking flushed and harried. Their infamous family dog, Murphy, was not doing much to help by getting in her way.

Iseult shooed him out through the door and turned back. 'What's wrong?'

The older woman blew some hair out of her red face. 'Your father informed me barely an hour ago that the Sheikh will have lunch here, along with himself and their solicitors. That's lunch for five people—more than I've had to cook for since the kids went back to college.'

Everyone in the family affectionately referred to Iseult's younger siblings—Paddy Junior, and the twins Nessa and Eoin—as the kids. But now anger bubbled up again to think that the Sheikh, with a mere click of his fingers, was putting them under added pressure. They barely had the money to stock the fridge and cupboards for themselves. Iseult longed to tell Mrs O'Brien to ignore the decree, but she knew her father would die of embarrassment. The fact was, they had no choice but to accept their predicament.

It was the Sheikh or the bank—neither one a palatable option, but at least, Iseult had to concede grudgingly, the Sheikh was keeping her father on as a manager and had offered a decent wage. She didn't like how that concession made her feel guilty now. She knew she'd behaved badly. But right now she didn't want to look at the cause of the irrationality of her response.

Defeatedly she reached for the spare apron and started to help Mrs O'Brien, who sent her a grateful smile as they worked together to bring lunch up to some kind of acceptable standard for a Sheikh.

Carrying a tray of soup starters a short while later, Iseult hesitated at the dining room door for a moment, and had to ignore the shiver of sensation that shot through her body when she heard the low rumble of the Sheikh's sexy voice. *Sexy?* Since when had she been aware of *sexy?* Gritting her teeth and jaw so hard that it hurt, she pasted a bland smile on her face and went in.

Silence greeted her, and she deliberately avoided any eye contact. Her heart ached to see that her father had allowed the Sheikh to sit at the head of the table. Once, in her grandfather's heyday, they had run a hugely successful and thriving business. Renowned horse-breeders from all over the world had come and paid exorbitant sums of money just to have their mares stand at O'Sullivan's stud to be covered by their pure-blooded stallions.

This moment, right now, couldn't make it any clearer how far their fortunes had fallen.

With a shaking hand Iseult served the solicitors their bowls of soup, then her father, and lastly the Sheikh, though she knew she ought to have served him first. Barely holding it together, she somehow managed to grab the tray and go to leave again. But then she heard her father clear his throat.

'Iseult, love, aren't you going to join us?'

She heard the plea in his voice. He depended on her for so much—she was the one who knew the farm inside and out—but in all honesty she hadn't expected to be included in this. Her father remained the public figurehead of the stud despite everything, and Iseult had every hope that one day he'd assume his role fully again. The look in his eyes spoke volumes, though. He was terrified these men would see how little control he had over the place. And he was terrified that they'd renege on the agreement to keep him on as manager.

Iseult hesitated for a second, but then that deep drawling voice came. 'Since when does a stablehand who doubles as a server sit at the table with the new owner? I think not, Mr O'Sullivan. Your daughter can hardly be expected to be party to our private discussions.'

Iseult turned to the Sheikh, the tray still held by her side, and had to restrain the urge not to smash it on his arrogant head. She smiled sweetly, while mentally apologising to her father. She deliberately made her Irish brogue even stronger. 'I couldn't agree more, Sheikh. I know my place. And I've a horse to get ready for the travelling tomorrow—straight after I've finished serving the lunch, of course.'

With that she bobbed a curtsey, and as she left she could have sworn she heard a muffled snigger coming from where their own solicitor had been sitting.

Iseult thought it best to let Mrs O'Brien retrieve the soup bowls and serve the main course. But when she got busy making Irish coffees and asked Iseult to get the plates she couldn't avoid going back.

The silence was thick with tension when she walked into the room, and Iseult's skin prickled under the weight of one particularly heavy gaze. Somehow she managed to take the plates while avoiding all eye contact. She could see that her father's face was slightly flushed, and her belly clenched in an automatic reaction of anxiety. But to her relief she saw that he was still drinking water. He'd been dry for years now, but she knew something like this had the potential to send him back to a dark place. Her conscience struck her hard. She wasn't exactly helping matters.

With all the plates balanced precariously in her arms, Iseult got to the door—only to find that it had closed on her. She had a split second of wondering what to do, and then she felt a large dark presence loom behind her. A tantalising scent of something sensuously foreign tickled her nostrils, making her belly clench again—but this time for a very different reason. In utter surprise, she watched as a tautly muscled brown arm reached around her to open the door.

She had to step back closer to the Sheikh in order for him to open it, and for a very disturbing moment the entire length of her back was pressed against his hard chest and belly. It was like a wall of steel. She nearly dropped every plate, but in a smooth move he ushered her out and pulled the door after them, coming round to stand in front of her. Iseult wanted to avoid his eyes, but drummed up all her courage to meet them.

His voice was low, and tore strips off her. 'I didn't

appreciate the ham acting, Miss O'Sullivan. Try a cute move like that again and neither you nor your father will have anything further to do with this place. Your name will be history overnight. I'm beginning to feel that I've been entirely too generous where your father is concerned, and I have serious doubts about his capability to run this place.'

He continued with a blistering tone. 'I have no idea where your misplaced animosity has sprung from; your farm's demise was not by my hand and we've never met before. I suggest you have a think about that before we meet to talk after lunch.'

The plates trembled ominously in Iseult's hands. She found it hard to think straight. 'What do you mean, *talk*?'

'After just ten minutes of conversation with your father it's become clear that he's no more in control of things around here than that homely housekeeper. It would appear that I have underestimated you, Miss O'Sullivan. You will meet with me in your father's study in one hour and you will explain everything to me.'

With that he brushed past her and went back into the room, shutting the door again with a firm click. She stood motionless for a long moment, her heart hammering, until she heard Mrs O'Brien huffing up the stairs with a tray full of desserts and Irish coffees. In a state of shock, Iseult put down the plates on a nearby table and opened the door for Mrs O'Brien before escaping back to the kitchen. She couldn't have helped give out the desserts even if she'd wanted to. She knew that something hot or cold would have ended up in someone's lap because she was shaking so hard with reaction.

She dumped the plates in a dishwasher that had seen

better days, and fled outside after stuffing her feet back into her mucky boots.

Once in the yard, sucking in deep breaths of fresh air, Iseult put her hands to her hot cheeks. What was wrong with her? The Sheikh was absolutely right. It wasn't his fault they were in this position; this had been coming for a long, long time. He'd just taken advantage of their weakness in a challenging market. And, as she'd conceded earlier, being bought out by him was infinitely preferable to being bought out and sold off in pieces by the bank.

So, apart from the heartache of losing their family business, what was wrong with her? She knew more than most people how things changed, and plenty of their neighbours had undergone similar buyouts to survive. In a way, they'd been lucky; thanks to Devil's Kiss they'd survived far longer than anyone had thought they would—long enough to see the kids settled at college in Dublin.

Iseult walked instinctively towards the stables, where Devil's Kiss heard her coming and put his head out over his door with a welcoming whinny. Iseult smiled sadly and went over, rubbing him affectionately on the nose. 'This is our last day together, Devil. You'll be gone tomorrow…'

A huge lump constricted Iseult's throat then, and she fought not to give in to the grief when she thought of how she'd hoped and prayed for a different outcome. But one good horse could never have turned their fortunes around. They'd have needed ten winners for that. Everyone had depended on her for as long as she could remember, so it was second nature now to bottle it up, swallow the lump down.

Her thoughts gravitated back to the Sheikh, and how

threatened she'd felt just now with his tall, hard body
against her back. She shivered. She couldn't explain it,
but from the moment she'd heard he was coming to get
Devil's Kiss himself her hackles had risen for no good
reason. She'd put it down to the fact that she'd have felt
that way about whoever the new owner was, but it was
almost as if some sixth sense had warned her that he
would threaten her on many more levels than that of just
being the new owner of their stud, which was ridiculous.

Her conscience struck her again; she'd felt that way as
soon as she'd seen the pictures of him on the internet. It
had been a physical reaction to his image that had no
basis in logic or rationality. She'd never been one to sigh
over and lust after pin-ups; those normal rites of passage
were something she'd never had time to indulge in as a
teenager.

But then today her fears had been confirmed. From
the moment she'd seen him out of the corner of her eye
as she'd exercised Devil's Kiss on the gallops every
sense had gone onto high alert. Which had only got
worse when she'd actually seen him up close. He was
hard and implacable. Unreadable. And yet…some
deeply secret and feminine part of her had *thrilled*
inside when she'd seen him in the flesh.

Her mouth compressed as she continued to rub
Devil's Kiss distractedly. After losing her mother at the
tender age of twelve, she'd never had anyone to encourage her out of her naturally tomboyish state. Her one
failed attempt to be feminine had ended in abject humiliation, after which she'd vowed never to let anyone
make her feel so vulnerable again…

Iseult cursed herself now. *Why* was she thinking of

that memory? An image of the Sheikh's hard, beautiful face came into her mind and her belly quivered. She resolutely refused to acknowledge the fact that this complete stranger seemed to have unlocked something deeply feminine within her, bringing back painful memories. It was preposterous, because there was no way on this earth that a man like him would ever notice someone like her. She'd seen pictures of his women on the internet: all stunning, polished, *gorgeous*. Everything Iseult wasn't and never would be.

She turned and walked back to the house reluctantly, driving down the mounting feeling of dread at the thought of facing the Sheikh again. She would have to apologise to him for her behaviour.

After taking off her boots again, and replacing them with trainers in the room beside the kitchen, Iseult walked through the house and paused outside the study door. Taking a deep breath, she knocked lightly and went in.

The Sheikh stood looking out of the big window which took in a view of rolling green fields as far as the eye could see and the gallops in the distance. Iseult's breath hitched and her heart took up an unsteady rhythm. And then he slowly turned around, and heat climbed up her chest and into her face.

She stayed near the door and saw one ebony brow arch imperiously. She was reminded in that instance who she was dealing with, and who she had trifled with. She swallowed. 'I owe you an apology.'

The brow stayed arched. He wasn't going to make this easy.

'I'm sorry if I gave you the impression that I was—'

He cut in then, and she could hear the anger vibrating in his voice. 'Rude? Obnoxious? Behaving like a petulant teenager?'

Iseult fought to clamp down on a renewed surge of anger and clenched her fists. The Sheikh walked over to sit against the huge desk, crossing his arms over that formidable chest. In her peripheral vision Iseult could see the material of his jeans straining over his powerful thighs, and for a dizzy second she forgot what he'd just said.

But then she remembered. Her vision cleared, the red mist lifted. She lifted her chin. 'I'm apologising now for my behaviour. I had no right to treat you with such disrespect.'

'No, you didn't.' He sounded a little surprised, and looked at her assessingly. 'But I can appreciate that this must be a difficult situation, so I'm prepared to give you the benefit of the doubt. For now.'

His eyes dropped for a moment, in a long sweep down her body. Iseult could feel that clammy sweat break out again. Why did she feel as if he'd undressed her every time he did that?

'After all,' he drawled, his eyes on hers again, 'you can't be more than…what? Eighteen?'

That red mist hovered close again. Iseult had to will it down and bit out, 'I'm no child. I'm twenty-three.'

Nadim had to quell the surge of reaction when he heard how old she was. She was the same age as Sara had been when she'd— He ruthlessly cut off his thoughts there, uncomfortably aware of how different the woman in front of him was from his late wife. He didn't appreciate being reminded of her now, and it made his voice harsh.

'Clearly a very immature twenty-three-year-old,

who can't abide the thought of no longer being the mistress of the house.'

Iseult felt hysteria rising. '*Clearly* you've not taken a close look at your new property, Sheikh. It's been a long time since there was a mistress of this house the way you're implying. Everyone here works day and night to keep the place running. Even Mrs O'Brien hasn't been paid in months; she's here out of loyalty and because we provide a roof over her head.' Her voice took on a bitter edge. 'But evidently sheer hard work wasn't enough to bring us through tough times.'

'Or a good horse…' Nadim said.

'Or a good horse,' Iseult repeated, unable to hide the weariness in her voice.

Nadim was taken aback by the sudden jump from passion to defeat. He'd clearly hit a nerve. Taking a closer look for the first time, he could see that Iseult was actually bordering on being painfully thin. And when her face wasn't flushed with anger, as he'd seen it often enough today, it was pale…too pale. He could see faint purple shadows under her eyes. Something shifted in his chest, and a protective instinct nearly overwhelmed him with its force.

'Is your father still drinking?' he asked then, so abruptly that Iseult's face flushed again. Curiously, it made Nadim feel somehow comforted.

She shook her head fiercely, her eyes flashing a warning. 'He hasn't touched a drop in seven years. And he won't—ever again.'

Nadim's mouth quirked, but not with humour. 'Not even you can guarantee that—and I saw your worried glance earlier, before you saw he was drinking water. How do you know this transition won't send him off the rails again? After all, isn't that what precipitated your decline?'

Iseult wondered dimly how he'd so effortlessly articulated her own innermost worries, how he knew so much, but then had to concede that her father's drinking problem had been common knowledge within their circles—despite her attempts to hide it and take his workload onto her shoulders.

Reluctantly she explained, 'We started to do badly when my grandfather became gravely ill—nearly thirteen years ago. We'd had a run of bad luck…disappointing foals and yearlings. The owners of the horses we were training got nervous after my grandfather died and sent them to other trainers.'

Her mouth twisted. 'We were suddenly *unfashionable*. And we were up against much more successful studs with infinitely more resources than we had. Not long after my grandfather died my mother passed away, and that was when my father…'

She didn't have to finish. She couldn't finish. In truth, she was a little stunned that she'd just shared what she had. But some instinct had warned her that the Sheikh would dig until he got to the very bottom of their *modus operandi* and how they'd got to this dismal state of affairs. And if he went through the paperwork it wouldn't take him long to trace events back to her grandfather's death, and then her mother's.

He was frowning at her now. 'What happened then? Who did your father bring in to keep this place running?'

Iseult shook her head, feeling shame mount for the first time in her life at hearing their history articulated so baldly. At knowing that she had failed. 'No one. We all pulled together. I...' She faltered, and then hitched her chin again. 'I helped until my father could get back on his feet again...and since I left school I've been working here full-time.'

There was no expression on the Sheikh's face, but Iseult could see a muscle pulse in his jaw. 'Your brothers and sisters?'

'I've two brothers and one sister. They're away in college in Dublin. They helped out when they could.'

Nadim reeled inwardly. At the mere age of twelve she had taken on that burden, along with school? If what Iseult was saying was true, then she'd more or less single-handedly helped keep the stables afloat. He could tell that she was embarrassed, and he could also tell that she was used to protecting her father. He felt a surge of anger towards that man now, and couldn't fathom how his perception of this woman before him had changed so much in such a short space of time.

'And Devil's Kiss? You trained him?'

Iseult flushed. 'With my father. We both did.'

Nadim felt on a more even keel here. 'How do you know that you haven't overtrained him? That he isn't peaking too early?'

Sheer pride straightened Iseult's back. 'Do *you* think he's peaking too early? Couldn't you tell just from riding him today that if anything his winning those races was just a sign of things to come?'

Her confidence astounded him, but he had to admit grudgingly to himself that he had formed that opinion. 'You're very confident.'

'Because I know horses, and I know Devil's Kiss. He's not yet shown half his potential. His lineage is pure thoroughbred; his father was Hawk Eye and his dam was Sheila's Wish, whose line goes back directly to Queen of Tara.'

Nadim knew Devil's Kiss's stellar lineage back to front, and Iseult was right. 'If what you say is true...you do know what you're saying?'

Iseult nodded. 'He could become something very special.'

'More than special—a world champion.'

Iseult nodded again, surprised to recognise that he was hearing her and taking her opinion on board. She'd chafed to think that he didn't rate her training skills. While she knew she had a long way to go, she'd always had the confidence instilled within her from her grandfather to trust her instincts. And she knew she was right when it came to Devil's Kiss.

The Sheikh stood from the desk then, and in a skittish move Iseult took a step back—even though feet separated them. She caught his dark look and cursed herself for reacting, hating that he might suspect she was so aware of him. She watched as he walked around the desk and sat down in the high-backed leather chair that had been her grandfather's.

He gestured her forward to take the seat on the other side. Too hot inside, and bemused, Iseult couldn't even feel insulted that he was clearly taking control. When she'd sat down, he flicked a hand over a sheaf of papers on the desk.

'The papers are signed, Iseult. I now own everything.' His dark look speared her. 'I now own *you.*'

Iseult's throat dried up. She was reacting to too many things at once. The fact that he'd just called her by her name, with that deep voice and sexy accent making it sound deliciously foreign and sensual, and also—

despite her assertion earlier that she wasn't part of the inventory—the fact she couldn't refute his claim that he owned her. She was as much a part of this place as the earth of the land and the stones of the house. She'd even been born in her parents' bedroom upstairs.

'So…?' she managed to croak out. 'What…?'

Nadim looked at the young woman opposite him. He didn't like to acknowledge how hearing how old she was had seemed to make his awareness of her increase thousandfold within him—as if he'd been denying it to himself when he'd believed her to be out of bounds.

And she still was. Yet, despite that assertion, he knew what he wanted with stunning clarity—and what he wanted was to keep this woman close, for such myriad reasons that he wasn't even going to investigate them now. He made a split-second decision.

'A chain of events has been set into motion. This will become my European base. It will need to be built up. As you may already know, I've acquired the land adjoining the stud down the road…'

Iseult nodded in acknowledgement. It had been the first sign of how determined he was to buy them out. He'd been so confident of acquiring their stud that he'd invested in the land around them before they'd even announced the sale. Her anger at his arrogance had surged from that point. But, in fairness, she could see now that it would have been directed at anyone who had stepped in to buy them out…

'I've already hired a new manager to come in and take over both facilities—the training grounds and the stud—'

Iseult gasped, pulled out of her straying thoughts. 'I thought you were going to allow my father to stay on.' Anger blurred her vision. For a second there she'd been distracted by this man's sheer charisma, when all along— 'If you think that you can come in here like this and just—'

He surged up from his seat to place both hands on the desk, and towered over Iseult in the chair. '*Stop* talking—right now.'

Her heart nearly jumped out of her chest, and along with shock at his quick anger Iseult also felt a dangerous thrill at being so close to that vibrant, tightly coiled energy.

He sat back down and raked a hand through his hair, impatience bouncing off him in waves. 'You are unbelievably impertinent. No one speaks to me like this— *no one*. The fact that you are even here, having this conversation with me, is because I recognise the role you have played here. That is *all*. Believe me, in any other instance you would be lucky to have me acknowledge your existence—never mind conduct a discourse like this.'

Iseult clamped her mouth shut on the words aching to trip off her tongue at his arrogance. In truth, he was intimidating her more than she cared to admit, and after seeing the evidence of his protective entourage she could well imagine that he wouldn't normally have cast someone like her a second glance. The thought surprisingly sank like a lead balloon in her belly.

'Your father *is* being kept on—exactly as I promised. But in an advisory capacity at first. I will *not* allow someone to take over the running of this place who has so obviously let it slip between his fingers. And, despite your noble defence of him, I'm not convinced that his weakest traits are behind him.'

Iseult could feel herself blanch. He meant her father's drinking. She couldn't meet the Sheikh's eyes for long, feeling as if he was looking right into her soul and seeing her own private fears laid bare. Because she wasn't entirely sure herself how her father would react.

'My newly appointed manager will start here tomorrow, early, and I expect you to give him a full rundown of everything. I know you still have some mares. The fact that you have a training facility here at the house is one of your great advantages, making this a fully sufficient stud, which is exactly what I want to expand upon. Then will come the task of acquiring new foals, yearlings, stallions and mares, and slowly building everything from the ground up again...'

Iseult nodded her head, a tiny spark of excitement spiking through her to think of them getting an overhaul and breeding once again. 'I can fill the new manager in when he comes...we'll have some time, though, won't we? The autumn yearling sales won't be starting for a few weeks.'

Nadim just looked at her, and Iseult felt something unspoken move between them. Instinctively she shivered.

'*He* will have plenty of time, yes. Along with your father. You, however, will have just the morning to acquaint him with everything you've dealt with. Because tomorrow early evening you'll be travelling to Merkazad with Devil's Kiss.'

CHAPTER THREE

ISEULT just looked at the Sheikh dumbly. She shook her head faintly. '*Merkazad?* What's Merkazad? I'll be needed here.'

His face tightened ominously, 'Merkazad is where I live—my country. It's a small independent sheikhdom in the southern region of Al-Omar. And, yes, you are coming.'

Fear made her heart stop. 'But *why*? Why would you need me to come there? You have a veritable industry in your own country.'

He arched his brow again. 'You've been checking me out?'

Iseult flushed, mortified. 'I just looked you up to see who our new owner was, that's all.' Except now all she could think of were those pictures of his glamorous women.

Nadim couldn't really believe he was still having this conversation. He *told* people what he wanted and they obeyed. It was simple and straightforward and had been all his life. But for the first time it wasn't. And it came in the shape of this redhaired, quick-tempered woman before him, who was still dressed in the clothes she'd worn when riding Devil's Kiss earlier.

He looked at her mouth, which was as lusciously full and sensuous as he'd suspected it would be when he'd first seen her, and felt a flash of desire in that moment so strong that he had to clench a fist against his thigh under the desk. He questioned his sanity at insisting she come to his country, but something compelling wouldn't allow him to backtrack.

He gritted out words through that unbidden and unwelcome wave of desire. 'You will be coming to Al-Omar, and then on to Merkazad. There will be no further discussion on this.'

As if his words had finally broken through her shock at his announcement, Iseult stood up jerkily from the chair and spun away into the room. She put out a hand, as if that could encompass everything.

'But I can't just leave here. This is my home. I've been working here for ever.' She could feel hysteria rising as it all hit her at once—the magnitude of what he was saying. 'My father—how will he cope without me? And the kids? I'm all they have. I can't just leave them behind—'

The Sheikh had stood too, his whole body taut with obvious anger that she persisted in defying him. '*Who,*' he barked out, frowning fiercely, 'are *the kids*? Don't tell me you have a brood of children up your sleeve that your father omitted to mention?'

Nadim didn't know why that sudden thought made his vision blur with incandescence—so much so that he barely saw Iseult shaking her head forcibly.

'No—*no*, of course I have no children. I'm talking about my brothers and sister. Since Mum died I'm all they've had.'

Nadim's vision cleared. He was surprised to find that he was so angry, and so *relieved*. He moved around the desk to the other side, further enraged at seeing how Iseult backed away. Her hair had all but unravelled from her ponytail, and long tendrils curled like dark flames around her slim shoulders.

He forced himself to keep his eyes on her face and ignore the banking desire within him, still astounded that she was having this effect on him. It had to be some arbitrary reaction because he'd not taken a new mistress in months. Sheer sexual frustration, that was all. A physical response to an attractive woman.

'You said they were all in college.'

'They are…' Iseult desperately tried to appeal to this man. 'But the twins are just eighteen years old. They've never lived away from home before.'

'Their home isn't going anywhere,' Sheikh Nadim pointed out curtly. 'I've been more than generous in allowing your family to remain here.'

'No,' said Iseult, feeling guilty again, knowing how different things would be if they'd been facing a takeover by the bank, 'but if I'm not here…they…'

Even as she said the words she could recognise how pathetic they sounded. She knew very well that Paddy Junior was fine and most likely not coming home until Christmas time, and the twins were in the same college, happily set up in on-campus accommodation with other schoolfriends who were doing the same course. Iseult had settled them in herself, just last week.

'When I was eighteen I'd already travelled the world on my own—*twice*.'

Iseult took in the arrogant look on the Sheikh's face.

Her blood boiled ominously again. 'You come from a very different part of the world—'

'Not so different. I was educated in England.' His voice was dry as toast. 'Not around a campfire in the desert, as you might imagine. And yet I took off as soon as I tasted my chance of independence. Your siblings are grown-ups and you are not their mother.'

Iseult flushed at having her prejudice pointed out to her and choked back the need to say, *But I have been their mother.* Ridiculously, she felt tears threaten. Her responsibility to her family was so ingrained she felt as though she truly *was* a mother being asked to turn her back on her children.

Before she could say anything, though, Sheikh Nadim continued bitingly, 'I know very well what it's like. I lost both my parents at a young age and had to take responsibility for not only my own younger brother but also for my country. It will do your siblings good to know that you won't always be here for them, and it will do your father good to step into his role more fully. *He* will be here if they need him.'

Somehow Iseult managed to swallow back her emotion, recognising on some level the merit in what Sheikh Nadim said, while also being intrigued at the glimpse into his own personal history, of which there had been very little on the internet. The unexpected empathy she felt blindsided her momentarily.

'But…what would I do in…in Merkazad?'

'You will become part of my staff. Initially you will work at the stables, and in time I may allow you to stay involved in Devil's Kiss's training—once I'm confident of your ability. My ambition is to race him as a three-year-old in the Prix de l'Arc next year, with a view to the Dubai World Cup the year after, so my main concern now is that he's not peaking too early.'

Despite the fact that her world was being upended around her, Iseult felt a quiver of excitement deep in her belly at knowing that she was being offered the chance to stay near Devil's Kiss. This man, after all, was the man who had thrown the racing fraternity into disarray just last year, and he had a growing reputation as a thoroughbred owner, breeder and trainer to be matched with the best in the world. But even so what he was saying was too huge to process. Still she resisted. 'What if I refuse to go?'

Sheikh Nadim strolled towards her then, and she had to fight every impulse to run. She stayed standing in front of him. He stopped just mere feet away and she looked up, her throat drying again in acknowledgement of his sheer height and powerful build. That too-beautiful face with its harsh lines. It made her think of the desert and wonder how he'd look in that environment.

Nadim reacted forcibly to something deep within him not to give Iseult any way out other than *his* way. 'It's quite simple, Iseult. If you refuse to go then you will be escorted off this property for good. If you refuse then I won't have you working for me in any capacity.'

'You can't do that,' she blustered, desperately scared that he *could*. 'My father would still be here.'

'I could arrange for that to be otherwise. Like I've said before, I'm still not convinced he will be an asset to this stud.'

Iseult had a horrible vision of her brothers and sister being told that they'd lost their home. She rushed to a quick defence. 'My father is a brilliant trainer. He's just been through a difficult time, that's *all*. He just couldn't—'

She stopped. She'd already said too much. Sheikh Nadim filled in the gap when he said with deceptive softness, '*Cope?* Is that the word you're looking for?'

Iseult's eyes felt gritty, but she refused to be too intimidated to look this man in the eye. Her voice quivered with passion. 'My father is a good man and he knows his business inside out. He taught me everything I know, and he will turn this stud around...with help. All he needs is a chance.'

Sheikh Nadim seemed to ignore her last words. 'Was he the one who taught you to be so wilful?'

Iseult bristled. 'Where I'm from women are encouraged to be independent and to have an opinion and not be scared of sharing it. I'm sorry if you're not used to that.'

Nadim smiled mockingly. 'I don't think you're sorry at all. I think you'll find that women in my country are encouraged to do exactly the same thing—' here his eyes ran her up and down and clearly found her lacking '—but they go about it in a rather more genteel way.'

Iseult's fists clenched, emotion surging easily again. What was it about this man? He seemed to have taken control of some inner emotional barometer she'd never been aware of before. She'd never felt so conscious of her tomboyish state as she did now, and deep down in the very centre of her anger was a secretly treacherous desire to be as genteel as those women Sheikh Nadim spoke of with such respect in his voice. She hated him even more for making her feel like that.

Every righteous bone in her body quivered. 'So my only option is to go and work for you, or face being thrown off this land that has been in my family for generations?'

Nadim's jaw hardened. He had to consciously *not*

give in to the compelling need to force this woman to bend to his will. 'I think you'll find that you're being offered an opportunity that many would give their right arm to experience.' This was said with not a little arrogance. 'And you do have a choice, Iseult. There's a whole world out there. I'm not stopping you from leaving to seek employment elsewhere. I'm sure with your experience and crude training ability you'll find a job soon enough—and who knows? You might even become a trainer of some recognition some day.'

Iseult opened her mouth with a hot response, but Sheikh Nadim put up a hand to stop her. Her mouth closed ineffectually.

'But if you come to my stables you'll have the chance to be taught by the best in the business. And if and when you do return here to work, it would be beneficial for you to know how I run my stables and stud. You would also have the chance to see Devil's Kiss mature into the greatness we both believe he has within him. Can you walk away from that?'

A sense of inevitability washed through Iseult. Of course she couldn't walk away from that. Devil's Kiss was the last in a long line of horses they had owned and bred themselves—the last of her grandfather's legacy. They'd had to sell all the others off just to survive.

She'd nurtured Devil's Kiss like her own baby, and the thought of not seeing him come to fruition after showing such promise was too painful to contemplate. It hurt to recognise the fact that if not for this man she could very well have been waving goodbye to Devil's Kiss the following day, only being allowed to follow his progress secondhand in the papers or on the internet.

She might also have been facing the prospect of leaving her house and home too—for good.

All she had to do was sacrifice her own desire to remain here, and that would keep her father, the kids and Mrs O'Brien safe and secure. How could she not do that? How could she deny Mrs O'Brien the chance to receive a wage again after months of working for just board and food?

Her fears had stemmed from hearing stories of other rich buyers coming and firing countless lifelong employees, only to instal their own hand-picked staff. That had been one of the reasons for Iseult's fierce antipathy to this buyout: the fear of the same happening. But it wasn't. Sheikh Nadim was, as he'd already pointed out, being more than generous, and if Iseult wasn't careful she would be the one to sabotage everything.

She lifted her gaze from somewhere to the left of Sheikh Nadim's shoulder and looked him in the eye. Some little stone of resistance within her made her ask, 'Why are you doing this? I mean, why aren't you just letting us all go?'

The Sheikh's dark eyes glittered dangerously, and Iseult had the feeling that not many people questioned anything he did. His jaw clenched, but he answered tightly, 'Because I know what it's like to have everything you know jeopardised. I'm aware this is a relatively small community, and I don't really want to start on the wrong footing by having your neighbours reluctant to do business with me out of loyalty to your father. I also don't see the merit in letting your father or housekeeper go when they know the lie of this land. As it is, retaining them is worth more to me than the money I'll be paying them.'

His face hardened then, and Iseult shivered.

'But, having said that, I'm also aware that it won't do too much damage in the long run to bring in new staff. So, Iseult, what's it to be? My patience is wearing very thin.'

Iseult knew she really didn't have a choice if she didn't want to risk her family's security or be cast out of her own home for ever. She was aware on some dim level that yet again it was falling to her to take responsibility, but that was eclipsed by her curiosity to know more about his personal history.

Iseult had been avoiding his eyes, but now looked at him. 'How long do you expect me to stay in Merkazad?'

His eyes flashed that warning that was already becoming familiar. 'You will stay for as long as I wish it.'

You will stay for as long as I wish it. His words were so arrogant...so implacable—so ridiculously autocratic in this modern environment. And yet in that moment Iseult felt uncharacteristically powerless to defy him. Mentally she took a deep breath, feeling as if she was stepping into a deep, dark void. 'Very well. I'll travel to Al-Omar with you and Devil's Kiss tomorrow.'

Sheikh Nadim smiled a mocking smile, and an infuriating glint of triumph lit his eyes. 'Oh, you won't be travelling with me. I'll be leaving as soon as the new manager gets here in the morning. You'll travel with the horse. And I'll expect him to arrive in as good condition as he is right now.'

With that, as if he hadn't just whirled through Iseult's world like an angry tornado, ripping everything apart in its path, he flicked a glance at his expensive-looking watch and said, 'If you'll excuse me, I've got a function to attend in Dublin this evening, and a helicopter waiting to take me back to my hotel. I've made arrangements for Devil's Kiss's travel, and a plane will be ready and waiting. One of my own vets will meet you in the morning and travel with you. I trust you'll have everything you need ready to travel tomorrow?'

Iseult cursed the fact that she couldn't turn around and say that she had no current passport—after all, she'd never been further than England—but all she could do was nod her head and say, 'I'll be ready.'

Late the following morning, as Nadim's plane took off from Dublin Airport, he looked out of the window. But the rolling green fields and the city disappearing underneath couldn't distract him from the one face and one body that he couldn't get out of his mind. It was as if her image had been burnt there with a brand.

Iseult O'Sullivan. A slip of a girl. He could remember the tremor that had run through her body when he'd stood so close behind her in the dining room—how his blood had boiled and he'd wanted to knock the plates out of her arms and snake an arm around her waist and pull her back against him.

His body tightened, and his mouth compressed with anger—at himself. And that anger surged when he recalled how he'd blithely told her things that he'd never discussed even with close aides. The fact that he'd lost his parents as a teenager was common knowledge if you went looking for it, but not something he ever mentioned—*or* the fact that he knew how it felt to have everything he'd taken for granted ripped asunder... And yet with her the words had tripped off his tongue as if he'd been injected with some kind of truth serum.

He should be leaving her here. It made sense on many levels. But what had he done? Ensured that she would be a constant presence and a thorn in his side by insisting that she come to Merkazad with the horse.

Why had he done it?

Her image, the way she'd sat so imperiously on the horse when he'd first seen her blazed into his imagination in an eloquent answer.

He thought of the way she'd stood before him so defiantly the day before, and how he'd had to struggle to remember his train of thought when his mind had melted in a haze of lust at imagining revealing her breasts, to see if she hid them as he suspected she did. He shook his head now, as if that could dislodge her image from the gnarled heat in his blood.

He reassured himself that he'd been right to insist that she come to Merkazad. He did want to ensure a smooth transition for Devil's Kiss, and the horse was clearly attached to her. She was also wilful and independent, and had obviously grown far too used to running the business with disastrous consequences. The girl was a liability, and could do with being taught the proper way of things. He could no more leave a loose cannon like her here than he could blithely allow her father to retain complete control.

Nadim felt himself relax. He was merely protecting his new venture by keeping Iseult O'Sullivan where he could see her. He had full confidence that when he touched down on his own familiar soil—*home*—and saw her in his environment, the spell she'd cast over him would dissipate like the mirage of an oasis in the desert.

He ruthlessly ignored the *frisson* of something that felt awfully like erotic anticipation when he thought of seeing her at his own stables, against the backdrop of his own rocky and austere land.

He was used to being in control of his desire for women, that was all, and she'd taken him by surprise. *That was all.* He'd learnt the most tragic of lessons not so long ago. Emotions and women were a fatal mix. Since then his life had been about logic and clear reason.

He refused to believe that his life was deviating in any way from the clear and controlled lines he'd grown used to.

Iseult blinked and breathed in the warm and very foreign air. They'd arrived at a small airfield in Al-Omar just a short time before, and while the vet was checking Devil's Kiss in the specially modified hold of the private jet Iseult had stepped out onto the tarmac, already too hot in her slim parka jacket.

It was night, so she couldn't see much, but she felt the residue of a very hot day settle around her shoulders like a warm cloak. The sky was a dark indigo colour, and a crescent moon hung suspended on its back, as if knocked from the sideways perch she'd grown used to seeing it take all her life. Stars glittered so close and clear she felt as if she could reach out and touch one.

Just then she heard a noise, and saw a couple of sleek dark Jeeps driving across the tarmac to greet them—one with a horsebox attached. They stopped, and Iseult's heart stopped too. Would *he* be here to meet her? It scared her slightly, how her heart leapt at that thought and her throat dried in anticipation.

But when the Jeeps came to a stop and she didn't see him emerge she immediately felt silly. Of course he wouldn't come to meet her. She was just an employee now. Some official-looking men got out of the vehicle without the horsebox and she looked to them.

Nadim hesitated before he got out of his Jeep. Iseult O'Sullivan stood on the tarmac looking unbelievably vulnerable, and even from here he could see the shadows of fatigue under her huge eyes. Her hair was back in that untidy ponytail.

She'd been cool and contained that morning when he'd come to the farm, studiously avoiding his eyes and concentrating on the new manager. Her reluctance to leave her home had been tangible. Something twisted in Nadim's gut now, and he cursed the impulse which had led him first of all to bring her here, and now to come and collect her himself. The last thing he needed was to be feeling inordinately protective over a new employee.

He'd told himself that it made complete sense for him to meet Iseult and Devil's Kiss himself. But his head groom Jamilah's eloquent silence had spoken volumes when he'd told her what he was doing. She hadn't needed to spell out that he'd never done this before—especially when *she* was usually the one to meet new horses and bring them to the stables.

Iseult was watching the uniformed men approach her and starting to feel very alone and very conscious of the fact that she was in a foreign land with not one person she knew anywhere near. What if they didn't speak English? What if they weren't expecting her? But just then she felt a prickling on the back of her neck, and heard the sound of a door opening from the other Jeep.

Her head whipped round and her heart stuttered to a stop as she saw the impossibly tall and broad figure of Sheikh Nadim uncoil from the vehicle. He was dressed all in black, and looked so ridiculously gorgeous and exotic that Iseult felt weakness invade her limbs. She told herself it wasn't abject relief at seeing him there.

He strode over to where she stood, and Iseult was rendered speechless. At his brusque, 'I trust you had a pleasant flight?' she just nodded helplessly.

He gestured then to the men in uniform, who had stopped a respectful distance away. 'These men are from Immigration in Al-Omar and Merkazad. They'll check through your documents and issue you with the work visa that I've organised.'

Iseult's head was spinning as she murmured something that she hoped was coherent. This wasn't what she'd been expecting at all, and being faced with Sheikh Nadim like this was making treacherous butterflies erupt in her belly. It was very disturbing to know that this man had completely upended her life in the space of thirty-six hours, and what she felt for him had morphed from intense antipathy and mistrust to something much more nebulous and scary.

In no time at all the smiling men had handed Iseult back her passport, which was now covered with various official-looking stamps. Sheikh Nadim was with the vet and leading Devil's Kiss out of the hold, down a ramp.

He looked at Iseult as she approached. 'He fared well through the journey?'

Iseult looked to the vet for confirmation. He nodded his head. 'Yes, he was fine.'

'That's good news,' Sheikh Nadim said. 'Sometimes if a horse does not weather its first air journey well, it's an indication of problems.'

Iseult was trying to ignore the persistent feeling of relief—and also the way Nadim's big graceful hands, smoothing over Devil's Kiss's flanks, was making her feel hot inside.

Together they installed Devil's Kiss in the most luxurious horsebox Iseult had ever seen, and after saying goodnight to the vet Sheikh Nadim made sure Iseult's luggage was installed before they got into the Jeep.

It was only as they were driving out of the airfield that Iseult noticed two other similar Jeeps come into position—one before them and one behind them. She guessed that they must be his bodyguards. It was only then that she saw all the Jeeps had ceremonial flags attached on either side of the bonnets, reminding her of the status of the man beside her.

Once they were on a well-lit and sleek-looking motorway, Iseult said nervously, 'I wasn't expecting to see you at the airfield.'

Sheikh Nadim flicked her a cursory glance and said coolly, 'I had a meeting with the Sultan of Al-Omar, but he got called away on sudden business so I decided to return home tonight. I have a meeting in Merkazad in the morning that I don't want to miss.'

Iseult's hands twisted in her lap. Of course he hadn't come to meet her out of anything other than pure practical necessity.

She was acutely aware of the Sheikh's huge rangy body beside hers in the luxury Jeep, and was so tense she nearly jumped out of her skin when he said, 'You'll have time to rest and settle in once we get to

my stables. I won't expect you to start to work
straight away.'

Iseult looked at Nadim, taking in his harsh but beautiful profile. Being taken out of her comfort zone so
spectacularly was making her feel intensely vulnerable.
'It has been a bit of a whirlwind… This isn't exactly
what I was expecting.'

He inclined his head. 'My head groom is called
Jamilah. She'll show you around in the morning and tell
you how things run. It'll be up to her as to how she sees
fit to use you.'

Iseult was taking this information in, and her silence
must have sent a message to Sheikh Nadim, who sent
her a mocking glance. 'You weren't expecting that I'd
employ a female head groom?'

Iseult flushed and said defensively, 'It's not that
common. Even in Ireland it's more usual to find stables
largely run by men.'

'You'll find that women are widely employed in all
kinds of jobs in Merkazad—although outside the main
towns and cities things are still more conservative and
traditional. If anything, we try to cling onto that. It's a
pity the more traditional nomadic Bedu way of life is
becoming a thing of the past. The Bedu warriors are the
ancestors of my people. Merkazad has always been a
defensive stronghold.'

Despite her tiredness, Iseult was suddenly fascinated
to know more. But she felt too shy to ask, and instead
just asked how far they were from Merkazad.

'Our journey won't take long. Ordinarily we would
fly my horses into B'harani, the capital of Al-Omar, but
it adds a couple of hours onto the journey. Sometimes
we use that airfield, which is closer to the Merkazad

border. We're in the process of building an airstrip and a small airport in northern Merkazad, but it won't be ready for at least another year.'

'Oh…' Iseult fell silent and looked out at the impenetrable darkness outside, wondering what lay beyond. Was it desert? She'd seen them cross over the Arabian Sea as they'd flown in to land, so they weren't far from the coast. She'd read up on Merkazad last night on the internet, and had learnt that it was tiny—literally just about one hundred miles from north to south, and two hundred miles from east to west. It had a natural border of a mountain range within Al-Omar, and had been ruled by Sheikh Nadim's father before his death some twenty years before, when it had passed to Nadim.

The little information apart from that had told her how it had been fought over for many years by various rulers of Al-Omar, before Sheikh Nadim and the current Sultan of Al-Omar had reached a momentous peace agreement fifteen years ago. Iseult had realised that Nadim must have been only about twenty-one then, and had felt stunned to think of someone that young taking on such responsibility.

They were climbing into the mountains now, and Nadim explained to Iseult, 'Once we're through the mountains the altitude drops again. The country literally sits within them, almost like a plateau. It'll probably surprise you when you see it if you're expecting a desert. We have our own ecosystem, thanks to the geography, and we're the only region that experiences a monsoon. We've just come out of it, so the land is still relatively lush.'

Before long Iseult could feel that they were indeed driving down, and within the hour she finally saw lights ahead. She was reminded of footage she'd seen on TV of what it was like to approach Las Vegas in the desert at night.

There were no skyscrapers or buildings taller than two or three storeys, but everything glittered and looked very clean. It was late, so not many people were on the streets. A beautifully ornate mosque was floodlit against the night sky and stars. The architecture of the buildings was a mix between something very Arabic and also something much more European, and she recalled reading in its history of a brief invasion led by colonising Portuguese. The roads were wide and straight, with tall palm trees swaying gently in the night breeze.

Not long after driving through the intriguing city and into a more suburban area Sheikh Nadim turned onto a long winding road which eventually led to a white-walled compound where a lit-up sign read *al Saqr Stables*. The huge heavy gates opened slowly and the Jeeps filed in.

Iseult's eyes opened in wonder as the interior was revealed. A massive courtyard held all sorts of vehicles: horseboxes, Jeeps and cars. There was an enormous green grassy area, where a water fountain shot high in the air, falling down in a glittering cascade into an ornate pool.

Two wide driveways appeared to lead away from the courtyard, and while the bodyguards' Jeeps parked up, and Iseult saw huge burly men emerge, Nadim kept driving and took the right-hand fork.

'I'm taking you to the staff accommodation area, which is beside the main stables. One of the grooms will meet us there and take Devil's Kiss to his new box.'

Iseult was beginning to feel light-headed, and she wasn't sure if it was from fatigue, delayed shock, or just the effect of Sheikh Nadim. She realised that not once since she'd arrived had she thought of home or her family.

Meeting the new manager that morning, and seeing the way he'd listened so patiently to her father, had made her feel inordinately relieved. She'd been even more relieved to hear that he too was committed to a vision of keeping O'Sullivans from becoming a homogenous conveyor belt stud. It had driven home to Iseult how lucky they were to have been bought out by Sheikh Nadim.

The Jeep came to a halt and Iseult got out, seeing that they were in another huge courtyard, with modern-looking stables on one side and a long, low one-storeyed building on the other. The building was L-shaped and crumbling, but she guessed in a deliber-ately artful way. It had the same stamp of Arabic design she'd noticed already. She also noticed the fact that it was cooler here than it had been in Al-Omar, which had to be due to the higher altitude.

A sound came from behind them, and she turned to see Sheikh Nadim greet the most stunningly beautiful woman Iseult had ever seen. She was dressed casually in jeans and a shirt, and her hair was a sleek fall of midnight-black down her back.

Her eyes were huge and piercingly blue—which, along with her olive skin, made Iseult think she had to come from somewhere almost mythical. She turned to face Iseult and a warm smile lit up her face, making her even more beautiful. She held out a hand. 'Hi, I'm Jamilah, the head groom. Welcome to Merkazad and the al Saqr stables.'

Iseult shook her hand and glanced up at Sheikh Nadim, who was frowning down at Jamilah. 'I thought I told you not to wait up.'

Something pierced Iseult deep inside when she heard the obviously affectionate rebuke in his voice, and saw his concern. She looked back to Jamilah, who was still smiling. 'Of course I had to be up to meet Iseult—*and* this wonder horse you've been talking about. It was nothing. I just set my alarm for when I knew you'd be home.'

She walked around to where a stablehand had magically appeared to open the horsebox. Jamilah led Devil's Kiss out and gave him a thorough onceover, before saying with obvious appreciation, 'He really is a beauty. You've done a good job. I can see that you're going to be a welcome asset here, Iseult.'

Iseult blushed with pride. No one, apart from her father or grandfather, had ever complimented her before. And Sheikh Nadim had all but accused her of potentially ruining Devil's Kiss. 'Thank you.'

Iseult felt Sheikh Nadim's heavy gaze on her as she followed the stablehand who was now leading Devil's Kiss to his new home. It too was as luxurious as the horsebox had been.

She was trying desperately to ignore the fact that she felt so all over the place now that she'd noticed the special relationship between Jamilah and the Sheikh, and then Jamilah came alongside her and took her arm with friendly ease. She had Iseult's case in the other hand, and Iseult insisted on taking it from her.

'Come on—you must be exhausted after you've been so summarily dragged across the globe. I'll show you to your rooms and you can rest. There will be plenty of time to show you around tomorrow.'

Iseult tried weakly to joke. 'I'd hardly call private air travel being dragged across the globe.'

Out of the corner of her eye she could see Sheikh Nadim raise his hand in a gesture to Jamilah, who nodded silently back to him. Easy communication flowed between them. He wasn't even making any attempt to say goodnight to *her*, and Iseult hated the fact that she'd noticed. Clearly he'd gone above and beyond the call of duty in meeting Iseult to bring her and Devil's Kiss here, and now couldn't wait to be gone. Perhaps he hadn't even trusted that she would have taken care of Devil's Kiss on the journey, and that was why he'd met them himself.

The Jeep and horsebox disappeared out of the stables area, and Jamilah led Iseult over to the long L-shaped building. She could see now, as they drew closer, that it must have been the old stables, now converted.

Jamilah had a key, and opened a door in the furthest part of the building and led Iseult in, turning on lights which sent out a low warm glow. Iseult came in and put down her suitcase. The downstairs was open-plan, with a kitchen and sitting area furnished in cool white and neutral tones. Up some stone stairs there was a comfortable and pristine bedroom and bathroom, again furnished in whites and creams. It screamed understated luxury, and was a million miles from the kind of accommodation staff would have been used to at O'Sullivan's stables, even in the good times.

Jamilah was explaining. 'They're all pretty much the same in this block. I'm in the one at the other end— nearest the stables. That's where my office is too. We have bigger ones for couples, and we have proper houses too, for staff with families, not far from here. I hope this is suitable for you?'

Iseult whirled around, aghast that Jamilah might have taken her stunned silence to mean anything else. 'It's wonderful. I had no idea what to expect, but it certainly wasn't anything as luxurious as this…'

Jamilah quirked a smile, and once again Iseult was struck by her beauty. 'Nadim takes care of his staff very well. That's one of the reasons why he's so respected and gets so much out of his workers.'

'You…' Iseult bit her lip. 'You call him Nadim… Don't we have to call him Sheikh?'

Jamilah laughed—a beautiful tinkling sound. '*No!* He'd hate that.' She slanted a stern look at Iseult, but her mischievous eyes told her not to take her too seriously. 'Nadim insists on informality, but that's not to say that everyone doesn't know their place and respects him as the ruler and supreme leader of Merkazad… Don't worry—you'll see how it works.' Jamilah led Iseult over to a low window and pointed outside. 'From here you have a view of the castle, that's where Nadim lives.'

Iseult looked out, and shivered when she took in the sight. The castle was more like a fortress—too huge and imposing to be described as beautiful. It was like the man himself. Effortlessly intimidating. It was built on a rocky outcrop which she guessed would have a view out over Merkazad and, like the other buildings she'd seen on their journey to the stables, Iseult recognised the Arabic influence. The wide sweeping archways and ornately intricate designs of the trellised stone perimeter glowed white in the moonlight.

'It dates from the sixteenth century, and although it's been updated and modernised on the inside, the outside is still the same as when it was a defensive castle. It has some of the best examples of intact Islamic murals on the Arabian peninsula. Scholars come from all over the world to study them.' Jamilah straightened up and smiled. 'I'll take you there and show you around in the next few days, when you've got your bearings.'

Iseult felt shy. 'Are *you* from here?'

A shadow seemed to pass across Jamilah's face just for an instant, and then she answered easily. 'Partly. My mother was from here, but my father was French. I was born in France, but then we came back here. My father worked for Nadim's father. My parents died in the same air crash that killed Nadim's parents, and as I had no other family he took me into his.'

'I'm sorry. I didn't mean to pry.'

Jamilah waved a hand. 'Don't be silly. It was all a long time ago. I owe Nadim everything.' She moved to go downstairs, and then turned back abruptly. 'And, despite what you may have thought just now, Nadim is like my older brother. Nothing more.'

Iseult blushed beetroot-red and stammered, 'I didn't...didn't think...anything like that...'

But Jamilah was already disappearing back downstairs, with an enigmatic smile on her face. Iseult followed her, mortified to think she'd been so obvious in her assessment of their relationship. If Jamilah had seen her reaction, had Nadim? Her insides curdled at the thought.

Jamilah showed Iseult a few more practical things about the accommodation, like where the food was stocked, and then left her, telling her that she'd come by to get her after she'd had a long lie-in in the morning.

That night, as Iseult lay in the strange bed, all she could think about was the fact that Nadim and the stunningly beautiful head groom weren't in a relationship.

And her predominant feeling was one of something scarily like relief, when she had no earthly right or reason ever to imagine herself in any kind of a relationship with such a man.

CHAPTER FOUR

THE following morning Iseult was surprised to find that she'd slept right through, for about eleven hours. She could hear a hum of activity coming from outside, and after a quick shower and cup of coffee she went to investigate with something that felt suspiciously carefree in her chest. She'd never been in a situation where she wasn't automatically responsible for every little thing.

As soon as she opened her door she faltered on the doorstep. The sheer intense heat nearly knocked her sideways. She realised she'd have to go shopping at some stage. Her Irish wardrobe of long-sleeved T-shirts, jumpers and fleeces would be woefully too much for here.

There was an intense hive of activity before her. The quiet stables courtyard from last night had been transformed, and was now full of people all engaged in various activities. Iseult immediately felt guilty. At home she would have already been up for several hours and working.

Horses were being led to and from stalls—some by women in the long Muslim *abeyya*, with veils covering their hair. But others were in Western dress—jeans and

T-shirts—which negated her suspicion that they had to dress in a more conservative fashion.

There were also a couple of Western staff. To her relief she could see Jamilah in the distance, waving to her from the stable where Devil's Kiss had been installed last night. Iseult walked over, smiling shyly at the people she passed, noticing one very friendly-looking blond man, who grinned at her appreciatively as he got out of a Jeep.

When she reached Jamilah the woman was sending a mock-censorious look to the young blond man. 'Stevie, shouldn't you be down at the equine pool this morning, to cover for Abbas?'

He saluted cheekily and sauntered off. Jamilah said, with a touch of weariness in her tone, 'Stevie Bourne is an incorrigible flirt, and already has a string of broken hearts all over Merkazad. If he wasn't such a good groom I'd have let him go a thousand times.'

After checking on Devil's Kiss, and seeing that he appeared to be getting over the journey well, Jamilah took Iseult off on a tour in a golf buggy. She explained that it was the quickest way to get around the vast stables.

After just five minutes Iseult's mouth seemed to be welded open.

She'd seen some of the biggest stables and studs at home in Ireland, and they were impressive, but this— *this* was on another level altogether. At her own rough count she reckoned that she'd seen close to one hundred horses in training. Yearlings, colts, fillies and older. She'd spotted the magnificent Desert Rose, who had won at Longchamp the previous year, and who clearly, despite fevered media speculation, wasn't being retired to stud yet.

She was introduced to the head trainer, a quietly spoken Frenchman called Pierre, who had a select team underneath him. They had sand-based gallops, and also an extravagantly watered grass-based gallops too. Plus they had an impressive length of all-weather racetrack.

By the time Jamilah was heading back towards the main stables Iseult was feeling seriously overwhelmed, and felt even more so when she was led to a Jeep and told she was being taken to the stud, which was about two miles away. In the Jeep, Jamilah ascertained that Iseult didn't really have appropriate clothing for the heat, so they stopped off in Merkazad to get some clothes.

In the bright vibrancy of daylight Iseult could see that it was a bustling, heaving city. All the buildings were close together, and modern architecture nestled alongside ancient buildings teeming with history in a glorious mix. Women covered from head to toe, with beautiful flashing kohled eyes, passed her in the street, and dark men in *dishadashas*, with turbans on their heads.

Bedu nomads had set up in groups alongside the main road, erecting their tents into makeshift villages with beautiful dark-eyed children running back and forth.

Despite Iseult's protestations, Jamilah insisted that she would pay for the clothes, telling her she could put it against her first month's wages. Iseult had no choice but to accept.

The stud was as impressive as the stables, set in liberally watered and surprisingly lush grounds, with gorgeous stables to house all the stallions, mares and foals.

It was late afternoon by the time they got back to the main stables, and Iseult could see that Jamilah was anxious to get to her own work. She assured her she'd be fine now that she had an idea of where everything was, but had to quell the dart of loneliness when Jamilah disappeared.

After she'd checked on Devil's Kiss, and made herself something to eat, she found the communal common room that Jamilah had shown her earlier, where she could make a phone call to her father. To her intense relief he sounded fine, and even confided to Iseult, 'To be honest, love, this is the best solution. We could have lost everything. I know it's not ours any more, but our name is still on the gate and the new manager is a good man. I'm glad the stress of keeping the place going has been taken out of my hands...I'm looking forward to concentrating on training again.'

Iseult finally put the phone down after reminding her father that the twins were due home for a visit that weekend, to make sure that Murphy got his heart medication in his food, and that it was Mrs O'Brien's birthday tomorrow.

She nearly jumped three feet high when she heard a deep, drawling voice say from behind her, 'Still running operations from here?'

Her whole body exploded in a wave of heat as she turned slowly to face Sheikh Nadim. He was leaning nonchalantly against the wall near the door, dressed in a pristine dark suit and white shirt and tie. He looked so incongruously gorgeous against the plain background that she felt stunned, as if she might be imagining him. But when she blinked he didn't disappear.

Immediately Iseult felt self-conscious and stiff. 'I

was just checking in—letting my father know that I'm safe and well.'

'And are you? Well?'

Iseult nodded, suspicious of Nadim's concern. 'Yes… Jamilah has been very kind, showing me around today.'

'You rested well last night?'

Iseult nodded again, her mouth twisted. 'The rooms are more than comfortable. I thought I'd be lucky to get the corner of a stable beside Devil's Kiss.'

Sheikh Nadim tutted and stood away from the wall. Immediately Iseult felt threatened. 'Such an imagination. All my staff are taken care of, Iseult. I don't believe in the outdated view that stablehands are little better than skivvies.'

His obvious implication that that was all she was made Iseult's back straighten with innate pride. It was a long time since anyone had considered her just a stablehand. Her chin came up. 'You don't have to remind me of my place, Sheikh. I'm not exactly in a position to demand the right to keep training Devil's Kiss.'

When Iseult answered back, with that defiant little chin-tilt, Nadim had a split second of realising how inappropriate it had been to come here like this, on the pretext of seeing how she had settled in. He should have been content with the call he'd put in to Jamilah earlier, when he'd found that she was doing the grand tour with Iseult, even if at that moment Iseult had been in a changing room in a shop in town, trying on clothes. But when he'd driven through the main gate just a short while before he'd found himself instinctively turning towards the stables, unable to ignore the impulse to see her.

His jaw tightened and the self-recrimination running

through him made his voice harsh. 'No, you don't have that right. We've yet to see you work. There are staff who've been here for a year and haven't earned the right to work under Pierre. And I won't have you dragging Jamilah off on shopping errands again. She's far too busy and valuable to the running of this place.'

The unfairness of his accusation made Iseult gasp. 'I didn't even want to go shopping. Jamilah saw that my clothes weren't suitable and kindly insisted on taking me, and I'm glad she did. Who knows when I might have got out? I'm well aware I'm just here on sufferance, because you have some idea that I'd do more damage than good back at home.'

Nadim fought the intense urge he had to stride over and haul Iseult against his too hot body, and quell her words in a very carnal way. He couldn't believe she was so effortlessly making his blood pressure zoom skywards within just minutes of seeing her again. He'd followed some rebel impulse to see her for himself and now *this*. There were plenty of foreign staff at his stables, and he'd never concerned himself about how *they* were settling in.

Sexual tension was so immediate and taut between them it could have been cut with a knife, and any hope Nadim might have had that bringing Iseult O'Sullivan here would diminish her effect on him was laughable. Despite being busy all day today, he hadn't been able to get her out of his mind.

In two quick strides he stood right in front of her, and saw how her eyes widened and a dark flush stained those alabaster cheeks. His hands were clenched into fists at his sides to stop himself from reaching out to loosen her hair and see it spread across her shoulders.

Wanting Iseult was completely inappropriate and unwelcome. He didn't sleep with staff, and she was a world away from the type of woman he would normally go for...

He gritted out, 'It's *Nadim*. No one here calls me Sheikh. And you are as free as anyone else to explore Merkazad on your days off. Jamilah has all the information you'll need on getting around.'

So abruptly that Iseult swayed on her feet Nadim turned and was gone again, taking his intense forcefield of energy with him and leaving a vacuum behind. Iseult sank down into a chair behind her. For a second there she'd had the overwhelming feeling that he was going to kiss her. Even now her mouth tingled in anticipation. She touched it lightly with her fingers and it felt sensitive to the touch. Her skin prickled all over, and down lower between her legs a pulse throbbed disconcertingly.

As abruptly as Nadim had left, Iseult stood and fled back to her rooms, shutting herself inside. Remembering the intensity of Nadim's eyes just now, she prayed that he wouldn't feel he had to check up on her again. Because evidently when he came within three feet of her she turned into someone else. Someone who couldn't control her tongue and who was reduced to a mass of heated desires.

To Iseult's intense disappointment her prayers were answered, and for the next two weeks she saw no sign of Nadim. She settled into a routine at the stables, and heard Jamilah say in conversation with others that Nadim was in Europe.

As much as that should have comforted her, it

didn't. Despite everything, Iseult couldn't stop thinking about Nadim, and that hot intensity she'd felt between them the last time she'd seen him. Every minute of every day people referred to him in hushed, awed and reverent tones. But not one person had a bad word to say about him. And his knowledge and impeccable instinct when it came to horses was apparent all around her.

She wondered why it was that he was only just beginning to make a name for himself, when the stables and the stud had been in operation since his father's time. Jamilah had been uncharacteristically tight-lipped when Iseult had asked, and Iseult hadn't pursued it.

When Iseult had finished at the stables one day, after Nadim had been gone a fortnight, she walked over to the training grounds, where one of Pierre's assistants was supervising the exercising of Devil's Kiss. The assistant explained that Pierre had also gone to Europe for a few days.

One of the other trainers, a man called Alain, came over, looking seriously disgruntled. In the course of the conversation between the two men, it transpired that a yearling was proving difficult to break in.

Feeling curious, Iseult asked Alain, 'Can I have a look at him?'

The trainer shrugged nonchalantly. 'Be my guest. I was hoping to have good news for Pierre when he returned, and at least have the bit between his teeth, but it looks like only Nadim or Pierre will be able to tame this one.'

Iseult wandered over to a fenced-in area and saw the yearling. Her well-practised eye assessed him in an instant, and she felt a deep sense of satisfaction run through her. Also a deeply ingrained instinct. She could work with this yearling. She knew she could.

She took the bridle and bit off the fence, where Alain had left them after his fruitless attempt. She was barely aware of the small crowd gathering as she climbed up and sat on the fence, just watching the horse for a long time. When she felt the time was right she slid down and into the enclosure, slowly starting to walk around, going in ever-decreasing circles closer and closer to the horse. She was unaware of the alarmed look passing between Alain and the other trainer.

She was unaware of anything but the horse. She always got like this when she was breaking in a horse. It was a silent communication that hummed between them, and she had no idea where it came from. She gently crooned words that her grandfather had used to use—old Gaelic words.

She was close enough to the horse now to touch him, and he stood still. Recognising her. With infinite gentleness and patience Iseult put the bridle over his head and the bit into his mouth. It was only when she realised the whispers had ceased that she looked up and became aware that everyone had scattered.

There was just one person standing there now: Nadim, with his face as dark as thunder, hands on lean hips.

Iseult's heart went out of control, as if she'd received a shot of adrenalin. She gulped guiltily, taking in the fact that he looked gorgeous after an absence of over two weeks. He was wearing jeans, and a T-shirt that moulded across his chest and showed off his taut musculature and broad shoulders.

Iseult took the bridle off the yearling again and patted

him down, then walked back to the fence on shaky legs. The minute she had slipped out through the gate and closed it Nadim strode over and took her arm in a tight grip.

'Wait a second,' she protested. 'You're not even giving me a chance to—'

He silenced her with a thunderous look. 'Not a word. Jamilah's office *now*.' Nadim all but threw Iseult into his Jeep and drove the short distance to the main stables, tension crackling between them. Iseult was tight-lipped, with arms crossed.

When he drew to a halt Iseult jumped out and preceded him into Jamilah's office, aware of eyes everywhere taking this in. She knew very well that Nadim had a right to be angry with her for overstepping her mark—but *this* angry?

Jamilah was there too, but Nadim dismissed her with a curt instruction in guttural Arabic. She sent Iseult a questioning look as she walked out and quietly shut the door behind her.

Nadim raked a hand through his short hair and turned to face Iseult. She refused to be intimidated and waited for the explosion. But it didn't come. Nadim just said easily, 'Was it too much to expect that I might leave here for a couple of weeks and hope that you wouldn't get into trouble?'

But then she saw his flashing dark eyes, and the thin veneer of his civility became apparent. Iseult could sense that he was holding back with supreme control, and it made her quiver inwardly.

Even so, she hitched up her chin and crossed her arms defensively again. It was impossible for her not to react defensively with this man—he shook her right to her foundations. 'You're right. I shouldn't have gone into that enclosure. Why don't you just say what you've got to say and let me go?'

'Where did you get the nerve to think you could go near such a dangerous yearling and attempt something so foolhardy?'

Iseult saw a pulse throb in Nadim's temple and had to focus on his words. She frowned. '*Dangerous?* What are you talking about? No one said anything about him being dangerous...' She was genuinely confused now.

'The reason that yearling is on his own and apart from the others is that no one has been able to get near him. I'd left explicit instructions that no one was to attempt anything with him until either myself or Pierre got back. Only three weeks ago he kicked one of the trainers, who luckily escaped with just a cracked rib.'

Iseult was stunned at this information—and stunned to recognise how gullible she'd been. Clearly Alain and the other trainer had set the new girl up in spectacular style. 'I had no intention of doing anything in the first place. I was watching Devil's Kiss exercising and someone mentioned that they were having trouble with a yearling. I went to look at him, that was all.'

She stopped and looked away, and then back to Nadim. How could she explain this to him? 'But then, when I saw him, I just...saw that I might be able to handle him...and I did. I can't explain it. It's not something rational. If I'd had any idea he was considered so dangerous of course I wouldn't have gone in there. I'm not a complete idiot.'

Nadim folded his arms too, making Iseult feel hot in her belly when she saw his muscles bunch. Then he frowned suspiciously. 'No one encouraged you to try your hand at breaking him in?'

As much as Iseult knew that the trainers had been mischievous in deliberately misleading her, she wouldn't say anything. She'd walked into their trap. She was the newbie, and there under sufferance. She wouldn't do herself any favours by squealing.

So she shook her head miserably and said quietly, 'No.' And then more fiercely, looking directly at Nadim, 'It was purely my idea.'

Nadim dropped his arms and prowled close to Iseult, making her breath hitch. 'Apart from your arrogant boldness at thinking you could succeed where no one else had, no one in the training area is allowed to go in without adequate head protection, and that is non-negotiable. I've sacked trainers for not wearing proper protection.'

Iseult looked up at Nadim and dropped her arms. 'I was *not* being arrogant—I just saw the yearling and thought I might be able to help. And how would I know about wearing protection if no one thought to tell me?'

His blistering tone cut her off. 'Dammit, woman, do you have to argue with everything I say? You should be in the habit of wearing protective head gear no matter what. Horses are unpredictable. You had everyone mesmerised by your horse whisperer routine, so it's no wonder no one mentioned the hat. I promised your father I'd take care of you, but I can't do that if every time I turn my back you turn into a walking liability.'

To disguise the sharp pain which lanced her at the thought that his apparent concern was just born out of a sense of responsibility to her father, Iseult said cuttingly, 'Oh, so now you're best friends with my father, who you deemed unfit to run his own stud farm?'

In an instant Nadim had reached out to haul Iseult

into his body, his hands tight around her upper arms. Iseult opened her mouth in shock, and had the split-second realisation that Nadim was going to kiss her just a breath before he did. She recognised in that moment that since she'd laid eyes on this man she'd wanted this, with a wild singing in her blood. There was not even a moment of hesitation. Every cell in her body was fizzing and jumping.

Iseult had never been kissed before. And certainly not like this. Not with such intensity that it felt as if she were burning up from the inside out. Somehow she was vaguely aware that Nadim had rested back against something and had pulled her even closer, right into the cradle of his thighs, where she could feel the shockingly hard press of his arousal. It made wet heat explode between her legs.

His hands finally let go of her arms to snake around her back, and of their own volition Iseult's hands went to the back of Nadim's head, tangling in the surprisingly silky strands of his hair. The moment went on and on, suspending them in time and space. It was as if Iseult's world had gone from zero to a thousand on a sensual voltage scale that she had no control over.

Iseult's mouth opened, instinctively seeking more, and Nadim groaned deep in his throat, his tongue meshing with hers in a hot dance. She could feel her hair being pulled free of her ponytail and falling in a heavy weight down her back. Nadim tugged on it gently, to force her head back, and she sucked in a gasp when she felt his mouth and lips trail hot kisses down her jaw and neck, finding where the pulse beat out of control and sucking there for a moment.

One hand snaked up under her T-shirt and Iseult's

belly clenched in delicious anticipation when she felt him find and cup her breast. She groaned when she felt his impatience, and he snaked that hand around to open her tight sports bra, releasing her heavy breast into his hand.

With her eyes still shut tight, as if opening them might make the spell break, Iseult let Nadim guide her head back to him, and his mouth slanted hotly over hers again, tongue stabbing deep as that hand cupped and moulded her unfettered breast. Between his thumb and forefinger he caught the hard nipple and teased it, squeezing and pulling. Iseult's hands tightened around his skull—and in that moment she felt the shift in energy—as if they had both woken from the sensual spell at exactly the same time.

Iseult opened heavy-lidded eyes and looked into deep dark pools full of recrimination. She was breathing heavily, chest rising and falling, and Nadim still cupped her breast intimately.

With an abrupt move he put his hands on her arms again and physically moved her back. Iseult's legs felt so unsteady for a moment that she swayed and had to put out a hand to the back of a nearby chair.

Nadim's voice broke the taut silence. 'That shouldn't have happened.'

Iseult winced inwardly to hear Nadim say the words so curtly, and cursed herself. What had she expected— that he would take her in his arms and profess that he couldn't get her out of his head? That she was driving him mad with desire? And how had she gone from hating this man for taking a wrecking ball to her world less than three weeks ago to wanting him so badly right now that she shook all over?

'No, it shouldn't have happened,' she agreed faintly. She couldn't look up. Her shaking hands went behind her back to do up her bra, hiding her too voluptuous breasts from view once more. When she'd developed too early she'd got used to hiding her breasts, terrified that she'd get teased like other buxom girls at school. And then, with riding every day, it had been more practical to wear sports bras to contain them.

She saw his shoes come into her vision, and then a hand tipped her chin up. Even her skin there burned at his touch.

Nadim looked down into Iseult's eyes and had to hold back the wave of need spiralling through him again. It made a mockery of the trip he'd just taken to Europe in a bid to restore some sanity to his lust-hazed brain. It hadn't worked. Instead of forgetting about this witch he'd found himself waking in the night, aching all over with frustration. He hadn't stood a chance as soon as he'd seen her again. It galled him even more to acknowledge that he'd gone to such lengths to avoid her effect on him.

Iseult's mouth was swollen and pink and still moist. His body was taut, tight and aching with hot arousal. With unfulfilled need. But it had been a mistake to kiss her. Even if he had wanted Iseult on sight, and every moment between them had led to this explosion of lust, it couldn't happen again.

She was an employee. And a wayward, unpredictable one at that. He was the ruler of Merkazad and had a reputation to maintain. He was forgetting that far too often when he came within mere feet of this woman. But he was finding it hard to think right now, when she was so close. When her delicate natural scent wound around his body like a siren call. He had to resist her.

She was not a sophisticate, and here at his stables it was too close to home, too close to raw memories.

He stepped back now, dropping his hand, but saw how Iseult's chin stayed defiantly hitched, even though her big amber eyes were still dark and wary, full of swirling emotions. Seeing that made something hard solidify in his chest, and made it easy for him to regain some perspective.

'It won't happen again.'

He raked a hand through his hair, leaving it dishevelled. 'Despite your behaviour today at the training ground, I'm prepared to let you move there under Pierre's tutelage once he's back in a couple of days. Perhaps if you're properly supervised in the area you seem to naturally gravitate towards, you'll be less of a liability.'

Before Iseult could reply Nadim had coolly walked out of the room. She sank back down into a chair behind her because her legs gave way. She heard muted tones outside and guessed that he was talking to Jamilah. A few minutes later there was silence, and then the sound of a Jeep starting up and driving away.

Jamilah came in, and Iseult couldn't look at her. She was too ashamed, and hated to think that perhaps Jamilah would suspect Nadim was moving her to work with Pierre because she'd manipulated him on purpose.

She looked up to see Jamilah making something like tea; when she sent her a quick look to ask if she wanted some, Iseult just shook her head. 'Jamilah, I—'

The other woman turned around, and Iseult quailed at the stern look on her face. Her belly fell.

'I know what Pierre's guys are like. As soon as he leaves Merkazad they turn into pranksters. I know they probably set you up—they've done it before.'

Iseult started to protest. 'But I never said anything to Nadim—'

'I know you didn't.' Jamilah was still grim, but then she smiled mischievously. 'When Nadim told me what had happened I put two and two together. To be honest I'd love to have seen their faces when you got into that enclosure and did what they couldn't do. It'll serve them right. They also probably got the fright of their lives when they realised you weren't wearing a hard hat...' Jamilah sat down on a chair near Iseult and said, more seriously now, 'I don't know if you've heard anything yet about Nadim's wife?'

Iseult's heart stopped dead. She could feel herself pale, and her hands gripped the chair. Nadim was *married*? And he'd just kissed her like *that*?

Jamilah seemed to read her mind and shook her head. 'He's not married any more. His wife died nearly four years ago now. Sara was killed when she took one of the colts out to ride; she wasn't a natural horse-woman. It threw her and kicked her in the head. She wasn't wearing protective head gear and suffered massive brain trauma. She was three months pregnant at the time. She and the baby died.'

Iseult went cold all over. 'That's horrendous.'

Jamilah continued. 'Nadim nearly closed the whole stables and stud down...only in the past couple of years has he shown an interest again. That's why he went so berserk when he found you. He's obsessive about staff wearing head protection.'

Iseult bit her lip, something very dark gripping her at hearing the evidence of just how much he must have loved his wife. 'I had no idea.' She felt shaky all of a sudden. 'Has Nadim told you—?'

Jamilah quirked a brow. 'That he's moving you to Pierre? Yes. But anyone can see that training is where you should be. I told him that since you've been here you've put in more hours than anyone else, even though it's obvious how over-qualified you are…'

Iseult flushed, unaccustomed to being noticed for her work. She got up to go, protesting that Jamilah must have things to do. Jamilah stood too, and put a hand on Iseult's arm.

'I can see that there's something between you and Nadim.' Iseult blushed furiously, but Jamilah just continued gently, 'It was obvious from the moment he brought you here with Devil's Kiss himself.' She smiled a little wryly. 'And also while I was waiting outside just now there was an extremely long *silent* moment when you stopped shouting at each other. That's another thing—no one shouts at Nadim and gets away with it.'

Iseult blushed even harder.

Something tortured crossed Jamilah's beautiful face then, and she said, 'Just…be careful. The al Saqr men can be ruthless in their pursuit, and equally ruthless when they're finished with you. I'd hate to see you get hurt…'

Iseult frowned. 'What are you saying? Did you—?'

Jamilah shook her head. 'No, nothing has ever been between me and Nadim. I don't think about him like that. But his women didn't last long before Sara, and they don't last long now.'

Jamilah took a breath. 'He has a younger brother, Salman…' Her mouth twisted. 'Let's just say I've experienced their ruthlessness first-hand.'

Jamilah gave her a quick impetuous hug then, and Iseult felt tears prickle. She'd never had a close female friend before.

Feeling uncharacteristically emotional for the rest of the evening kept Iseult in her rooms. She sat by the window of her bedroom with her knees drawn up under her chin and looked at the harsh, imposing castle in the distance. She shivered. When Nadim had kissed her earlier she'd become something, *someone* else. Someone feminine and delicate. Sensual. And it was hard to acknowledge that part of herself. It was so alien.

That kiss had crystallised the feeling that had been born within her the very first moment she'd laid eyes on his image on the internet. It was the yearning of her long-buried femininity, wanting to unfurl like a flower and be allowed to breathe for the very first time.

Iseult grimaced. Well, not the very first time. She had explored what it was to be a desirable woman once before, but it had ended in such humiliation that she'd locked it away deep down inside, where she wouldn't have to look at it again.

That was why she found it so easy to brush off the effusive flirtations of someone like Stevie Bourne, the over-friendly groom she'd seen on her first day. She had a well-developed wall of protection around her. But Nadim… Iseult quivered deep inside. With Nadim she had no protection…

Thinking of this made the painful memory of her final year of school and the graduation dance surge back. As it had approached Iseult had fully expected not to be asked, as she'd always been too busy and too shy to flirt with the boys in her school. Losing her mum at a vulnerable age had made her feel awkward and self-conscious.

The other girls had long given up on asking her along to their weekly shopping trips, or including her in endless conversations full of gossip—not that Iseult had really minded; she'd had bigger concerns. But still…some of the girls had seemed to take it personally, and had jeered that she thought she was better than them. Iseult had learnt to ignore them, which she knew had probably made things worse.

But, to her absolute shock, as the dance had approached that last school year, the most handsome boy in the school had asked her out. She'd been too flattered and surprised to think logically about how unlikely it was, and hadn't been able to stop the flare of purely feminine excitement to think that perhaps life wasn't all about grief, work and responsibility.

The boy, Luke Gallagher, had told her he'd meet her in their local town's main square, under the clock, on the evening of the dance. Iseult's father had dropped her off, clearly delighted that his daughter was doing something for herself for a change.

With no spare money even then to splash out on a proper dress, Iseult had felt achingly self-conscious in an old dress of her mother's that she'd adjusted to fit her. She'd hoped that she'd achieved the 'vintage' look, but had an awful suspicion it just looked hideously out of date. When her little sister Nessa had told her she looked like a princess she hadn't had the heart to change.

Iseult had waited for a long time, with people walking past her and staring, before she'd had to face up to the fact that she was being spectacularly stood up. It would have been glaringly obvious what she was waiting for, as practically everyone knew everyone's business in the small town.

It had only been when it started to rain that she'd

finally stood up from the seat and started to walk the long three miles home. At least in the rain she'd been able to give in to tears of embarrassment and rage, taking her high-heeled shoes off to walk barefoot when they became too painful.

Luke and some of the girls from school had passed her by in a flashy sports car then, blaring the horn, laughing and swigging from bottles of alcohol. But Iseult had just kept her head high and ignored them.

Even when Luke Gallagher had bumped into her a year later in the local supermarket, and made a blushing, stumbling apology—saying something about a stupid dare—it hadn't done much to assuage the deep hurt or her lingering mortification.

Iseult's focus came back into the room. Clearly Nadim had found her passably attractive for a brief moment, but it was crystal-clear that he'd regretted kissing her almost as soon as he had. The fact that he didn't relish seducing an employee had been etched all over his face, and had made her feel cheap and grubby.

That treacherous yearning to be found desirable and feminine would just have to be pushed back down to where it belonged. She couldn't bear to be hurt like that again, so no way was she going to let Nadim know how he effortlessly connected with such a secret part of her.

CHAPTER FIVE

NADIM sat back in his chair in the informal dining area of his private suite at the castle. He held a glass of whisky in his hand and swirled the dark amber liquid around, but his body tightened with predictable inevitability when the colour of the liquid reminded him of Iseult's eyes, and the way she'd looked at him after he'd kissed her to within an inch of their lives.

Disgusted anew at his woeful lack of control, he swallowed back the liquid in one gulp, relishing the burn down his throat as if it could burn away the desire that still hummed through his body. Something caught his eye then, and familiar guilt gripped him like a vice when he saw the sweet face of his dead wife smiling out benignly from a photo on the table nearby.

The pervading lingering guilt he felt at having been responsible for not only her death but their unborn child's had prevented him from putting away reminders like photos. It was like an open wound—guilt mixed in with ineffectual anger. And it served as a reminder never to let another woman get close enough to be hurt by him again.

In a reflex move Nadim surged to his feet and put the photo face-down. His hand was shaking. He'd never done that before. But then he'd never had to deal with such desire on his doorstep before...he'd always made sure to keep his affairs discreet and far away from Merkazad. Which was why this growing obsession with Iseult was so unwelcome. She was a world apart from the women he took as lovers now, and every instinct told him that she could be exactly the type to get hurt...

Nadim's hand tightened around the glass as he recalled the sheer panic that had gripped him when he'd seen her in that enclosure with the wild yearling, as blasé as anything.

He'd seen red. He'd actually thought he might be ready to send Iseult home. Anything had to be better than having her torturous presence there, under his feet. But instead of telling her to pack her things he'd hauled her into his arms and kissed her, any resolve not to get involved dissolving in a wave of lust so strong he hadn't been able to fight it.

Just then his chief aide Hisham came into the room and bowed. 'Sir, the conference call you requested has been set up in your private office.'

Nadim turned. 'Thank you.' As he strode out behind Hisham it struck him as faintly ridiculous that he was allowing someone as unsophisticated as Iseult to get under his skin so easily.

Clearly he needed a new mistress, that was all. And when he went to B'harani in two weeks' time for the Sultan's birthday party he'd find someone eminently suitable there. Polished, mature, acquiescent, invulnerable...*not* someone who dressed like an eighteen-year-old boy, wore too-tight sports bras to hide her breasts, and yet had the temerity to talk back to him and kiss him like no woman had ever kissed him before.

* * *

Two days later Iseult was still feeling skittish, jumping two feet in the air whenever anyone looked sideways at her. She'd seen Nadim from a distance earlier that day, for the first time in the traditional Merkazadi dress. In theory he should have looked ridiculous in the long flowing cream robes, with the distinctive turban on his head, but it had made an ache of gigantic proportions settle low in her belly. He'd looked even more exotic and regal, showing some guests around the stables. Iseult had had to use every ounce of her ability to stay focused on the job and listen to what Pierre was saying.

She was walking Devil's Kiss back to his stables later that evening and that ache was still in her belly, even though she hadn't seen Nadim in hours. She felt wrung out. A curious tension was in the air, and she was glad to find the stableyard empty, all the other horses having been returned to their stalls. After hosing Devil's Kiss down with cool water, and making sure he was settled, she turned around to leave and nearly jumped out of her skin to see Stevie Bourne lounging against the stable door, watching her.

Iseult felt a little annoyed. Stevie had been becoming more and more persistent in the last few days. 'Stevie, you scared me half to death.'

Stevie came in and closed the stable door behind him. Immediately Iseult felt threatened. 'I was just leaving. What are you doing here?'

He came closer, his blue eyes glinting. Iseult knew that plenty of the other girls fancied him, but he held no appeal for her. She tried to step around him now. 'Stevie, look, I'm tired and I need to get some dinner—'

With surprising speed he blocked her, so that now

Iseult was trapped between him and Devil's Kiss. She knew that Devil's Kiss could get antagonistic in small spaces, with too many people around him. He was already moving impatiently, as if he'd had enough of these humans taking up his space.

Stevie backed Iseult into the corner and put an arm on either side of her head, trapping her. Iseult didn't feel threatened any more, she just felt exasperated. 'Stevie, stop it. I don't feel that way about you.'

He just smiled his most seductive smile, and Iseult felt faintly ill. 'Come on, Iseult, you don't know what you're missing. And I've missed you around here. It's not fair you got moved over to Pierre so quickly. There's a rumour, you know, that Nadim favours you.'

Iseult blushed and put up her hands to try and push Stevie away. 'That's ridiculous. Now, please *move back*.'

'Not until you kiss me.'

Iseult could feel Devil's Kiss move more impatiently now, and sensed that a kick could be coming their way any minute. But Stevie was immovable, and his strength sent a dart of panic through her as she blurted out, 'I'm not going to kiss you. Now, *move*.'

She leant forward, aiming to push him out of the way, but in a lightning-quick move he pulled her into him, pinioning her arms to her sides, and kissed her furiously, with little finesse.

Iseult couldn't breathe, and started to panic in earnest while still being very aware of Devil's Kiss beside them.

Suddenly through the wave of rising panic Iseult heard an arctic, 'What the *hell* is going on in here?'

Stevie moved back so abruptly that Iseult stumbled

against the back wall. She automatically wiped the back of her hand across her mouth. Nadim stood in the doorway of the stable, holding onto Devil's Kiss's head. He filled the doorway with his huge frame, and Iseult saw the rope belt around his waist, an ornately decorated curved dagger thrust into it. In her eyes at that moment he could have been an ancient warrior king.

She couldn't take her eyes off him.

Stevie blustered, 'Iseult called me in here. I thought she needed a hand with Devil's Kiss, but—'

Nadim cut him off ruthlessly. 'Get out of here *now*, Bourne. And don't let me see you at the stables for at least a week.'

Stevie scarpered like the coward he was, and Iseult stood shakily, aware that Devil's Kiss had calmed right down now that Nadim was here. She walked forward on jelly legs.

Before she could even get a word out Nadim said fatalistically, 'That's it. This time you've gone too far.'

Iseult's inner fire rose, even though she felt wobbly all over. 'I am *not* going to take the blame for that. Stevie is a pathological flirt and *he* followed *me* in here. He wouldn't leave when I asked him—'

Nadim folded his arms. 'So you thought you'd persuade him by kissing him? Give me a break. I know what I saw.'

'No, you don't. I did *not* welcome that kiss.'

Nadim arched a brow. Sarcasm dripped from his tone. 'You didn't welcome it in the same way that you didn't welcome my kiss the other day?'

Iseult's face flamed. She looked down at the ground and mumbled, 'That was different.'

Nadim had moved into the stable, and the air seemed

to contract around them. Iseult looked up warily and was aware that this was totally different from how it had been with Stevie. Devil's Kiss, the traitor, now stood as still as a placid statue.

'*How* different?'

Iseult looked up into Nadim's dark eyes, in awe of him dressed like this, and said huskily, 'Because I liked being kissed by you…'

Iseult couldn't even feel chagrined at her honesty. She simply couldn't lie when Nadim stood before her like this. All her good intentions, her very necessary intentions of protecting herself around this man, were dissolving like wispy ineffectual clouds. That deep secret inner part of her was unfurling like a bud in the sun. She tried desperately to cling onto how disposable she'd felt after he'd kissed her the other day, but she was fast losing any grip on reality.

Nadim came even closer and snaked out a hand. His thumb came to her lips and rubbed back and forth, and his eyes got even darker. Iseult pulsed deep inside in response. The air was thick and heavy around them.

Nadim spoke roughly, his eyes fixed on her mouth. 'I don't like the thought of another man's taste on your lips.'

Iseult tried to shake her head but it felt heavy. His thumb still rubbed her lips. 'Neither do I.'

Obeying some primal urge from deep within her, Iseult stepped right up to Nadim and went on tiptoe, reaching to pull his head down. Her heart kicked and a light sweat broke out all across her skin when with a muffled groan Nadim's head came down and his mouth covered hers with barely restrained violence.

Mouths opened on a breath, tongues tangling intimately, hotly. It felt as if Nadim was branding her, eradicating any evidence of the other man, and Iseult welcomed it.

Nadim's hands moved down her back to cup her bottom, pulling her up and into him, where she could feel the hard evidence of his arousal through the voluminous robe. Iseult's hips moved in a silent and eloquently feminine plea against him, her hands smoothing across his shoulders, revelling in their broad strength.

Nadim tore his head away and looked down at Iseult's face, at her flushed cheeks and her mouth that looked beestung with arousal. She hadn't looked like this after Stevie had kissed her just now, and Nadim felt an intense surge of masculine satisfaction run through him. Quick on its heels came anger, swift and bright, at the acknowledgement that blind rage had nearly had him ripping Stevie Bourne limb from limb.

She'd done it again. Reeled him in like a fish on a line. He put his hands on her shoulders and put her back from him. She opened her eyes with an effort. She looked stunned.

Once again Nadim's lack of control seared him inwardly. He watched as Iseult tried to compose herself, and even now, though he knew it was sheer madness, he just wanted to shut the door and throw her down onto the hay, where he could sate himself properly.

He followed an instinct too strong to ignore, not even thinking of the ramifications of his decision. His voice was grim. 'I want you to go back to your rooms right now and pack your things.'

CHAPTER SIX

ISEULT felt as if she'd just been punched in the gut. Ice trickled through her veins. 'You're sending me home?'

Nadim was grim, his features stark. 'The next best thing.'

Iseult struggled to comprehend. She still felt spaced out—dizzy. 'What do you mean…? Where are you sending me?'

'You're moving up to the castle. You've proved that I can't trust you to stay out of trouble. Perhaps you'll stay out of trouble if you've got less time to tempt the staff down here.'

Nadim turned as if to go, and Iseult reached out on a reflex to grab Nadim's robe. 'Now, wait just a minute.'

Slowly Nadim turned around to face Iseult again, but she refused to let him intimidate her. She kept a tight hold on the sleeve of his robe. 'Why should I be the one to be punished when Stevie came after me?'

Nadim arched a brow. 'And within mere minutes of kissing him you were throwing yourself at me?' His mouth twisted faintly. 'You've proved that your taste is not only indiscriminate but insatiable.'

The words *But you kissed me back* died on Iseult's

lips. She blanched to recall how she had stepped up to Nadim and pulled his head down, how she had pretty much begged him to kiss her. She let go of his robe. Self-doubt assailed her. *Had* he really kissed her back, as she'd believed he had? With the same level of passion? Or had it all been a figment of her twisted imagination? Had that awful yearning to be desired fabricated his response? The knowledge shamed her now.

She looked at Nadim steadily. He would *not* see what he was doing to her. 'If I move up to the castle what will people think?'

Nadim's jaw clenched. 'That is not for you to worry about.'

'But I will be working here. I have to face these people every day.'

Nadim came close to Iseult again, and as predictably as the sun rising in the morning she could feel her resolve dissolving again.

'No one questions what I do, or the decisions I make. I am the Sheikh, and that is something you would do well to remember. Leaving you here to your own devices is not something I'm prepared to do any more. Every day you will report for work as usual, and every evening you will return to the castle and your rooms there.'

'So I'm to be a virtual prisoner?'

Nadim quirked a mocking smile. 'Oh, I don't think you'll feel like a prisoner when you see your new rooms, Iseult. And you're free to leave at any moment. No one is stopping you.'

Iseult ignored the dart of alarm at the thought of that, and retorted caustically, 'No—only the fact that if

I do leave I risk jeopardising my entire family's future…'

He moved to the door and said coolly, 'I'll let Jamilah know, and she can bring you up once you've packed your things.'

Iseult stood in the imposing main courtyard of the castle, completely intimidated. The very stones beneath her feet oozed history. Holding onto her one suitcase, she felt as if she'd just travelled a thousand miles into some Arabian fantasy—not just up the long drive from the stables with Jamilah in a Jeep.

The walls were so high she couldn't see anything beyond them, and carved into the huge slabs of stones were Arabic letters, swirling and graceful. The place was reverent, hushed.

Jamilah came around the front of the Jeep. Taking Iseult by the arm, she led her into the castle.

As soon as they walked through the giant looming archway light exploded around Iseult and she realised they were in another courtyard, but smaller, with a warren of pathways snaking off in every direction. Huge tall columns extended down these paths as far as the eye could see. As opposed to the almost austere main courtyard this one was full of small trees and plants. A pond with a small burbling waterfall graced the centre and even as Iseult watched a small iridescent fish leapt high and then fell back into the water.

Jamilah drew her attention to a small figure hurrying towards them, covered from head to toe in the traditional *abeyya* and *burka*, with just the most beautiful and enormous dark eyes visible.

Her belly was twisted in knots as Jamilah introduced

the girl to Iseult. 'This is Lina. She'll be your personal maid while you're here, and show you to your rooms.' Iseult turned and gaped at Jamilah, who just smiled wryly. 'You're in another world now, Iseult.'

Iseult couldn't speak, and just watched helplessly as Jamilah looked at her watch and grimaced. 'I'd love to stay and help you settle in, but we've got a horse arriving any minute now. I'd better get back...' She gave Iseult a quick hug and said, 'You'll be fine. I'll see you tomorrow...' And then she was gone, her slim figure walking away quickly.

Still stunned at the evidence of the sheer grandeur around her, Iseult followed Lina down a dizzying maze of pathways and corridors. Some were covered and some were not, with the darkening dusky sky visible and lending an even more magical quality to the whole place.

Even though the castle was stunning, breathtaking, there was an air of a mausoleum about it. There should be the sounds of children running about, more hustle and bustle. Iseult's heart clenched when that made her think of what Jamilah had told her about Nadim's wife and baby. If his wife hadn't died presumably he'd have a small family by now.

They passed through a door in an ornately latticed wall and Lina came to a stop outside another door, halting Iseult's dangerously wandering thoughts. She opened it and gestured for Iseult to enter. Iseult walked in, her heart thumping, to see a room of such understated luxury that she simply couldn't believe it. Thick carpets felt like clouds of air. Everything was cream and dark gold. The sitting room they'd entered led into a bedroom the size of the dining room at Iseult's house at home, with a bed the size of her entire bedroom dominating the space.

The bathroom was pure opulence, with a sunken bath and an enormous shower. Open terrace doors led from the bedroom to yet another courtyard, and when Iseult stepped out she could see that it was bursting with a wild profusion of flowers. The scent was more heady than any perfume she'd ever smelt.

She turned back to see Lina watching her.

'There must be some mistake… This can't possibly be my room…'

The girl shook her head and took Iseult's case firmly out of her hand. She said in softly accented English, 'This is where you are to sleep. You are in the women's quarters. This is your room.'

Lina was opening the case and sorting through Iseult's clothes, and Iseult put out a hand, mortified to see this luxurious room tainted by her rags. 'No, please—you don't have to do that.'

But Lina ignored her and kept unpacking. A knock sounded on the main door, and Iseult went out to see another similarly clad girl entering with a silver tray covered in small plates and bowls of food. The smells were mouthwatering. Before Iseult knew it she'd been manoeuvred to the sitting room, where she was shown to a dining area. A low table was on the ground, and the girl was putting out the food, indicating that Iseult should sit down, cross-legged, on one of the huge silk cushions.

Another set of open doors led out to the courtyard from here, and, thoroughly bemused, Iseult could only sit and watch speechlessly as Lina and the other girl took their leave through them. Lina stopped at the door and said, 'I'll come back in an hour to run your bath.'

Iseult jumped up. This was going too far. *'No!'* She saw
the way the other girl seemed to flinch slightly and mod-
erated her tone. 'Sorry, I didn't mean it like that. All I mean
is that there's really no need. I can manage on my own.'
She gestured to the food. 'And thank you for this…but in
future can't I just go to the kitchen or something?'

Lina seemed to giggle, and held a hand up to her
mouth. She shook her head. 'No, Miss Iseult. This is
how it is here. You are a guest of the Sheikh. I've been
instructed to wake you at six in the morning…if you're
sure you won't require any further assistance?'

Iseult shook her head quickly and the girl left. The
reminder of her wake-up call brought her back to earth
a bit. She might be living in these spectacular rooms
now, but tomorrow she'd be back at the stables and
working hard, and she had no doubt at all that Nadim
wouldn't be paying her another visit.

She wondered where his rooms were within the vast
castle, and then chastised herself, sitting down again to
eat some of the deliciously prepared food. She tried to
focus instead on what she'd been doing that day with
Pierre, but every second moment the sheer opulence of
her surroundings would floor her again, and all her
mind could do was helplessly gravitate to the tall dark
man who was turning her upside down and inside out.

Nadim heard nothing. He knocked again. Still nothing.
Dammit—where was she? With a surge of something
hot within him that he labelled anger, and not something more sexually primal, Nadim opened Iseult's
door and went in. Silence greeted him, and he saw
the remnants of her dinner on the low table in the
sitting room.

With the carpet muffling his steps he walked into the vast bedroom—and stopped dead at the sight before him. One light threw out a halo of a dim glow. Iseult lay asleep on the bed, with just a short white towel wrapped around her body. One arm was flung up by her head, in a curiously childish gesture, the other across her belly. Her hair had been wrapped in another towel turban-style, but it had come loose and now a long skein of damp hair rippled across the pillow beside her, a stain of red against the pristine white cotton. Her skin was almost as pale as the sheets she lay on.

For a second sheer lust threatened to blind Nadim as his gaze dropped and he took in the swells of her breasts against the towel. And her endless legs. Her thigh muscles were toned and strong from years of riding, and all he could imagine now was how they might feel clamped around his waist as he drove into her welcoming heat again and again. How she would arch her back so that he could feel her breasts crushed against his chest.

In an effort to claw back his rapidly disappearing control Nadim looked around the room. Her jeans were hung tidily on the back of an ornately brocaded chair, with what looked like a fresh shirt and clean underwear. This evidence of her setting out her clothes so methodically for the next day made something in his chest feel weak.

He should be walking away, retracing his steps back out of her room. He should never have come here, and he should not come here again. He should not be wanting her this badly, with a raging fever in his blood. He should not have moved her here, to the castle. He should never have brought her here from Ireland.

And yet as his treacherous gaze settled once again on the woman on the bed he knew he would fight off an army if they came to take her away from here, from him. There was also that very unwelcome sense of protectiveness he'd had ever since he'd realised the size of the burden she'd been carrying for years in maintaining the O'Sullivan stud. Even now he could see that those purple shadows that had been under her eyes had faded away, and the angular thinness he'd first noticed was softening.

In that moment Iseult's long-lashed eyes fluttered open, and the breath left Nadim's body when he saw their dark amber glow settle on him.

Iseult lay very still on the bed. Was she awake or was she dreaming? She was lying on the softest bed she'd ever known, and in the dim seductive light Nadim was just standing there, watching her, dressed in a snowy white shirt and dark trousers, his beautiful harsh face set into shadows by the light. His tall lean body looked intimidatingly powerful and awe-inspiring.

She blinked, and as if a spell was broken Nadim took a step back and turned, walking swiftly out of her room. She heard the faintest click of the main door closing.

Reaction set in; her heart hammered painfully and she felt the most curious wrenching feeling. Her whole body tingled, as if Nadim had walked over to her and twitched the towel aside to look at her. The image was so audacious that Iseult had to question very seriously if she'd just experienced a hallucination.

To wake like that and see him there…it couldn't be possible. The fact that no words had been spoken seemed to make it even more dreamlike. Iseult sat up and felt seriously disorientated. The heavy damp length of her hair fell down her back. And yet all she could think of was how the persistent ache within her gnawed with renewed intensity...and all because her traitorous mind was now conjuring up three-dimensional apparitions.

She stood from the bed, and wobbled a little precariously before striding purposefully to the bathroom to dry her hair. This was ridiculous. She was twenty-three, she'd never been kissed properly until Nadim had kissed her for the first time, and she was a virgin. She was also hurtling headlong into a crush of monumental proportions on a man so out of her league at every possible level that it was ludicrous.

She winced as she ran the brush through her hair before drying it, and ignored the too-bright glitter of her eyes in the mirror. From now on she was here to work, and not to dream or moon or have hallucinations. *Work*—that would be her salvation, and in time she would request that she be sent home so that a few oceans and thousands of miles would be put between her and this dark nemesis of her vulnerable imaginings.

After a broken night of sleep, gritty-eyed, Iseult heaved a deep sigh when she saw delicate lines of pink usher in the dawn in the sky outside. Just then she heard the sound of a solitary voice calling people to prayer. She'd grown used to it since she'd arrived, coming at regular points in the day, but here in the castle it was much clearer.

Obeying an instinct to follow the sound, Iseult got out of bed and pulled on a short silk robe over her T-shirt and knickers, and on bare feet went out of her bedroom. Everything was still and hushed, and the slightly cool morning air made goosebumps pop up on her skin.

Still half asleep, she wandered down the long corridor, following the sound of the chant which was getting louder and clearer. She passed ornately decorated doors and other corridors which led down to mysterious passages, and then one in particular caught her eye. She investigated, and spotted old stone steps leading up to a higher level.

Climbing up, she went through a tiny door and emerged outside with a little gasp of delighted surprise. She could see that she was on one of the castle's open rooftop terraces, with a stunning view over Merkazad. She went over and stood by the wall, letting her hands rest on it.

Lights were winking off as the sun rose, and the small city glowed pearlescent against the blush stained sky. The distinctive minarets of the main mosque pierced the skyline, and that evocative and melodic chant against the stark silence of the morning made something deep within Iseult tug in a very primal way.

'It's the Muezzin, issuing the *adhan*.'

Iseult whirled around so fast she felt dizzy, and even dizzier to see Nadim leaning nonchalantly against a wall behind her in faded jeans and a crumpled T-shirt, as if he too had just stumbled out of bed and thrown them on. Dark stubble shadowed his jaw, making it look even harder. He looked as if he hadn't slept either, and liquid heat invaded Iseult's veins.

'I…didn't think anyone would be up.'

Hands in pockets, Nadim hitched his chin towards the city and pushed off from the wall to come and stand closer to Iseult. She couldn't take her eyes off him. He looked like a devilish angel, not the supreme ruler of a country. 'The whole city will be stirring now, and getting up to face another day.'

He wasn't looking at her, just facing out to the city, and Iseult followed his gaze, suddenly feeling very undressed and very vulnerable as she remembered last night. She longed to blurt it out—*Were you in my room last night or was I dreaming?*—but right now she felt certain that it had to have been a dream, a treacherous fantasy.

'Why did you come up here?'

Nadim's voice sounded harsh, and she sensed he was angry with her for disturbing his peace. Iseult could feel his eyes rake over her, and one of her hands gripped the robe tight at her breasts. Imposing a huge strength of will, she avoided looking at him, certain that his proximity would show him how affected she was by him.

Her voice was unbearably husky. 'I heard the chant and…I don't know…it seemed to call to me. It's beautiful.'

'Yes, it is.' Nadim's voice had softened perceptibly. 'And it *is* a call. It's meant to make you want to follow it, to express your devotion.'

Unable not to, Iseult snuck a glance up at Nadim, and the breath stalled in her throat when his dark gaze caught hers. He was looking at her so intently. She felt as if *he* was issuing some silent call, because right now if he'd taken her hand and asked her to follow him anywhere she would have said yes.

Iseult was in serious danger of drowning in those dark dark eyes, but from deep within her some self-preserving instinct kicked in: the memory of how he'd kissed her came back, and the obvious self-recrimination he'd shown. *Both times.* She heard herself saying, 'You must miss your wife…'

Immediately there was a reaction. Nadim's jaw tightened and those eyes flashed. But her question had had the desired effect; in that mere second she could feel the distance yawn between them, even though physically he hadn't moved an inch. And, conversely, Iseult regretted saying anything.

'I shouldn't be surprised you've heard.'

'I'm sorry… I can't imagine what it must have been like to lose her.'

'You're forgetting it wasn't just her…it was our baby too.' Nadim's face was tight with anger, his voice as harsh as she'd ever heard it.

Now Iseult felt about as low as it was possible to feel. Why on earth had she opened her big mouth? She flushed and moved back. 'I'm sorry, Nadim, I didn't mean…I didn't want to make you think of this…'

He laughed, and it sounded bitter. 'Don't worry. I don't need you to remind me of something that's seared into my brain.'

Finally he looked away for a moment, and Iseult felt the breath whoosh through her as if he'd held her suspended. Her heart squeezed at the bleak look crossing his face, even as a pain seemed to pierce right through it at the same time.

The assertion reverberating in her head tumbled out. 'You must have loved her a great deal.'

He slanted a look down at her, his face closed and stark. But then his mouth turned up in a cynical smile, and it sent a shot of trepidation through Iseult.

'That's just the thing. I didn't love my wife. It was an arranged marriage. But she loved me…she expected more from me than I could give.' He smiled mockingly, obviously seeing something on her face that she wasn't even aware of. 'Does that shock you, Iseult? Do you think we're barbarians here for arranging marriages like that? For not falling in love only to divorce two years later, like the Western world?'

Iseult shook her head. Her brain throbbed. He sounded so *hard*, and in that moment she felt a surge of sympathy for his wife having entered such a cold marriage. To have loved this cold, implacable man.

Nadim's mouth was a grim line now. 'This is normal here, Iseult. I am the Sheikh. I above anyone else am expected to make a good match, a practical match. It's not about falling in love.' He nearly sneered when he said those words. 'People get married every day, and it's for many reasons. Love rarely, if ever enters into it. To expect love is to expect too much.'

'But your wife did… Perhaps she just couldn't help herself.' Iseult had intended it to come out with a sarcastic edge, but she just sounded sad.

Nadim's eyes bored down into hers, and bitterness rang in his voice. 'She should have known better. Like I said, she expected too much. And don't think a day goes by when I'm not aware of what I couldn't give her—what I can't give any woman.'

It was almost as if he'd resigned himself to some kind of fate, and that bleakness reached out and touched Iseult like a cold hand. She shivered, and saw Nadim's eyes drop and take in her bare legs. When his eyes rose again her body temperature had risen with them.

Had he moved closer? Iseult felt as if he had, even

though the same space was still between them. He didn't move to touch her, but in that moment their eyes locked. Iseult felt as if Nadim was making some decision, staking some silent claim. As if he'd sent her some telepathic communication to say the subject of his wife was closed and the focus was back on her.

Something almost tangibly primal moved between them, and Iseult would have to have been made of ice not to notice it. The skin all over her body tingled, and she felt in great danger even as a treacherous lick of excitement kicked through her. She told herself fiercely that it had to be just her rampant imaginings—*had to be*.

The Muezzin's last chant was fading away on the morning air. And Nadim just said, 'Shouldn't you be getting ready for work?'

Iseult's hand still gripped her robe, and with a strangled reply of something inarticulate she forced her legs to move and fled. Nadim hadn't even touched her, but as she half stumbled back down the stairs and to her room she felt as though she'd been branded in some way…and, worse, as if she'd given him some tacit signal of acquiescence.

'I think you should take Iseult with you to the horse festival this weekend.'

Nadim looked at Pierre and bit back the urge to flatly refuse the suggestion, trying to block out the image of how she'd looked that morning, when she'd appeared like an apparition in front of him on the terrace.

'Why do you think that?'

The older Frenchman looked at Nadim. 'I've never seen anything like her talent, Nadim. She's truly extraordinary—light years ahead of some of the guys I've had working with me for years. I will admit that her technique is a little rudimentary and rough around the edges, but that's only from being largely self-taught. She told me her grandfather was her biggest influence, and I remember him well. He too had the same gift that put him above and beyond other trainers. Unfortunately he died when she was young, so she missed out on a lot of his teaching. But she has an expert eye—I think she could be very valuable to you if you see any pure-breeds in the mix up there.'

Pierre was referring to the annual Bedouin horse fair—the biggest gathering of native Arabian horses in Merkazad and Al-Omar each year. It was held high on a plateau in the northern mountains that bordered the two countries, and comprised buying and selling horses, and races and other social events.

It was also a chance for him to get out to the further reaches of his country and see his people.

Nadim made a non-committal response and welcomed the interruption of one of Pierre's staff asking a question. He was still reeling from his encounter with Iseult that morning. And still reeling from the fact that she'd managed to somehow get him to reveal far more than he ever would have intended about his wife and his marriage. Not many knew the bald facts, and he had to concede now that, despite coming from a culture of arranged marriages, most of his people would have harboured the fantasy that he had loved his wife.

Iseult had caught him off guard. *How* had she known to come to the one place in the whole castle that was his private space? When he was much younger he used to go up there and look out onto the view, contemplating the terrifying fact of his fate and the prospect of one day taking responsibility for an entire country.

No one had ever disturbed him there. It had been the one place he could escape from his brother, parents, obligations…his wife and the love he couldn't return, the awful guilt of that… But now something, *someone*, had superseded all of that.

He'd gone back to his room last night and hadn't been able to sleep a wink, with frustration coursing through his body. Eventually he'd gone out there to try and clear his head, get some perspective…and then *she'd* appeared in front of him like a taunt, in that flimsy half-robe, long legs bare, hair in a tousled tangle down her back. The seductive shape of her body had been more than clear, her face fresh and clear of any make-up, and those eyes— He cursed as his body tightened with annoying predictability.

As he'd looked in her eyes that morning a sense of inevitability had washed through him. He either sent Iseult home and forgot about her, moved on with a new mistress, or else he slaked this desire and got her out of his system once and for all. And he already knew what his only choice was…

CHAPTER SEVEN

THE following day Iseult was sitting in the back seat of one of the Jeeps which was following Nadim out of Merkazad and up into the mountains. Two of his body-guards sat in front, and a veritable retinue of vehicles snaked behind them, including a couple of empty horse-boxes. Nadim was in the vehicle just ahead of them, and he'd barely glanced at Iseult before they'd set off from the main courtyard of the castle. He'd been dressed in traditional dress again—a long cream *thobe*, with a gold-trimmed robe over it.

She was still getting her head around the fact that Nadim had asked her to accompany him on this trip. Iseult had been in too much shock early that morning as in her half-sleep she'd let Lina chatter and manoeuvre her around and pack her a bag. And then before she'd had time to draw breath they'd been getting into the vehicles and were on their way. She had no idea why Nadim would want her to go along on such an expedition.

They were driving through the rockiest terrain Iseult had ever seen. Every now and then she caught a tanta-lising flash of abundant green and colour, and was reminded of when Nadim had told her that they'd just had a monsoon. It was hard to believe, driving through such an inherently arid land.

They drove ever upwards, and finally came to a halt. One of the bodyguards stepped out and opened Iseult's door, and when she got out into the bright sunlight and searing heat she could see Nadim waiting just a few feet away. He was looking at her, but then looked away.

Instantly her body reacted with a disturbing rush of desire. She stiffened her shoulders and walked over to him, seeing that some of the vehicles had kept going and the rest of the convoy had stopped in a kind of lay-by.

Hesitant, she stood beside him and followed his gaze, gasping when she did so. The whole of Merkazad was laid out before them from this vantage point. She could see the city shimmer in the far distance, and way beyond that the craggy crests of more mountains. Amidst the aridity were huge pockets of oases, in green and colours so beautiful that Iseult wanted to rub her eyes. In the near distance a magnificent waterfall cascaded down a mountainside.

It was like a vision of that mythical place Shangri-La. She finally managed to tear her gaze away and looked up to the man beside her, who stood tall and proud. 'It's…spectacular. I had no idea.'

He looked down to the ground and gestured for her to look too. She saw a clump of the most beautiful flowers she'd ever seen. They were vibrant pink with four large pointy-tipped petals.

Nadim said, 'That's the desert rose—native to here. The land blooms with them for months after the rains, and then they fade away just before the rains come again next summer.' He looked at her then. 'This is one of the best vantage points to see Merkazad.'

Overcome with some nameless emotion, Iseult looked at the view again and said huskily, 'Thank you for showing me this.'

She'd always thought of herself as a home bird, but she had to admit that she hadn't felt homesick here at all. It was as if her heart had skipped a beat and gone on at a different rhythm, and she knew how easy it would be to be seduced by this land.

She felt a light yet burning touch on her bare elbow. She looked up to see Nadim's dark eyes staring down into hers, and in that moment everyone and all the vehicles around them disappeared. She knew it wasn't just the land she was in danger of being seduced by; it was this man. And she was quite sure he wasn't *trying* to seduce her!

'Come—you will travel the rest of the journey with me.'

And with just the slightest inclination of his head the man who had been sharing the back seat of his chauffeur-driven Jeep got out and took Iseult's place where she had been. She was guided into the back of Nadim's Jeep. She doubted very much that even if she had protested she would have been listened to.

She sat tensely in the plush confines of Nadim's Jeep, with his big body far too close for comfort, and blurted out, 'Why are you bringing me with you?'

He turned his head to look at her, and the breath shrivelled up in her throat. In his turban and traditional robes he looked so…exotic and other-worldly.

He quirked a small mocking smile. 'I'm bringing you along because I value your opinion, of course.'

Iseult all but snorted inelegantly, and partly to escape his dark penetrating gaze said, 'I doubt that. You probably just don't trust that I can be left to my own devices for a weekend.'

'You're right about that.'

Iseult turned to look at him again, full of chagrin and fire, but before she could speak he was saying, *'But* I also do happen to wonder what you'll make of the horses we'll see here. Most are not worth bothering about, but sometimes there are some fine pure-blood Arabians.'

Slightly mollified, but still feeling very confused and out of her comfort zone, Iseult nevertheless felt a spark of interest pique her. She asked him about the Arabian horses, and before she knew it she had twisted fully in the seat to face him. They were talking so intensely that she didn't even notice when they'd come to a halt.

The driver opened Iseult's door, and she got out to see the most magical sight laid out before her. They were high in the mountains in an ancient-looking village—a cluster of buildings nestled around them. They all seemed to be made out of hard-packed red clay. Men, women and children had come to a standstill to see the Sheikh—*their* Sheikh—arrive.

One of the men, with a white skullcap on his head, darted forward to greet Nadim, who had come around to Iseult's side of the Jeep. Nadim gestured autocratically for Iseult to follow him, and with the bodyguards crowding around her and Nadim she had no choice.

With wide eyes she took in the scene: tall palm trees swayed in the light breeze, and beyond the village she could see that there was a flat lush greenness all around them, surrounded by craggy mountains. In the distance she could see a large area which had huge crowds milling around and tents erected.

Iseult caught up with Nadim. 'What is this place? Where are we?'

He cast her a quick glance. 'This is al Sahar, the tribal home of my ancestors. These are my people...literally. The al Saqrs are descended from the Bedouin warrior people who roamed this land for hundreds of years. It's a mountain oasis, fed from the springs that are abundant after the monsoons.'

Iseult could see that they were approaching some lavish-looking tents, and saw too that Lina was entering a small tent with Iseult's things. Nadim stopped and Iseult nearly ran into his back. She stepped back hurriedly, her face flushing.

He gestured to the small tent Lina had just disappeared into. 'That is your lodgings. I have business to discuss with village leaders and Bedouin visitors. Someone will bring you to the horse enclosure where the sales and races are going on. I'll meet you there later.'

And with that, and a flick of his robes, he was gone, taking his whole retinue with him, leaving Iseult standing there stupidly.

Lina popped her head out of the heavily draped velvet curtains. 'Miss Iseult...'

Iseult went in, and her eyes had to adjust to the dim light after the bright sunlight. And then her eyes widened. She'd walked into a scene straight out of *One Thousand and One Nights*. Richly embroidered carpets littered the floor in a haphazard clash of luxurious colour, and dominating the small space was a bed which seemed to be made entirely out of sumptuous velvet and silk cushions. Beautifully intricate chairs and a table were in another corner, and Lina was showing her where a softly draped curtain hid a changing and washing area.

Once again she felt like asking if they were in the right place, but Lina was already busy unpacking Iseult's things. Iseult couldn't have felt more out of place in her dusty jeans, T-shirt and scuffed riding boots.

Lina hurried to the opening of the tent and said to Iseult, 'Jamal is here now. He will take you to the horses…'

Almost glad to get away from the slightly oppressive feeling of being hemmed in by such opulence, Iseult hurried out to where a shy young man waited. He led her towards where the crowds were milling. She could see that it was mainly men, and they turned to look at her curiously as she came through. Many more tents had been erected nearby, although none as lavish as hers and what she assumed to be Nadim's. In clusters around the tents she saw women, busy preparing food and washing.

There were many enclosures. Some with horses, some with camels. In the distance she could see that a camel race was taking place. Jamal, her guide, seemed to be happy for her to wander around, so she did so for a couple of hours. Interspersed with the horses and camels were some women selling colourful pottery and jewellery. Iseult smiled apologetically, because she had no money, and vowed to come back and buy some things later or the following day.

Moving away, she came to a few enclosures that

held just one or two horses with serious-looking men discussing them. She could see instantly that these were a superior breed to the other horses and her heart quickened. All the modern thoroughbred horses around the world were supposedly descended from three Arabian stallions, and looking at these particular horses now Iseult could see why.

There was one in particular which caught her eye, on its own. She could sense that it was a little wild. She'd seen some of the men trot horses bareback around the enclosures, so Iseult didn't think much before she was about to climb over the fence and have a closer look at this stallion.

Just as she was about to lift her leg over she felt herself being pulled back. Knowing it couldn't be the shy Jamal, and knowing full well who it was just by the way his touch seemed to sear right through her, she swung back down to see Nadim glaring down at her.

'What do you think you're doing?'

Iseult squared up to him. 'I was just going to take a closer look at a horse—that's why you brought me here, isn't it?'

He seemed to look at her for a long time, and then a muscle twitched in his jaw. 'He's not saddled.'

'I was riding horses bareback before I learnt how to ride in a saddle.'

Another long moment passed, and then he said, 'Very well. But you don't go in there without a hat.'

Iseult all but rolled her eyes. None of the men trying out the other horses was wearing a hat. But remembering his wife's accident kept her quiet and suddenly subdued. In an instant Jamal returned and handed Iseult a hard hat. She slapped it on her head and tied it securely, and gave Nadim a look that had his eyes flashing dangerously.

Iseult took a box over to where the horse stood and, using it to gain height, vaulted easily onto its back. He was skittish, but soon calmed down, and she could feel the sleek power of his muscles move beneath her as she made him go into a light trot.

Nadim watched Iseult ride the stallion, and was aware of every other man watching her too. A hush had fallen over the crowd. He'd never seen someone ride a horse with such ease and effortless grace. Her long hair trailed down her back from under the hat like a living flame of colour. And the line of her back was as straight as a dancer's. Her whole carriage was that of a regal queen, and he was reminded of that first moment he'd seen her on Devil's Kiss in Ireland. One hand rested nonchalantly on her thigh, the other on the horses's reins.

She was his. The assertion ran through him, stunning him with its force. He could see that she was about to come to a halt, and had a moment of premonition before he realised that a horse race was about to start in the distance. Suddenly the loud crack of a starter pistol rent the air.

All Iseult knew was that she was about to dismount when a huge burst of sound made the horse rear into the air. With nothing but flimsy reins to hold onto she was thrown off like a rag doll. Landing on her back, she felt the wind knocked out of her, and she struggled to regain breath. Just in that instant a huge dark shape appeared, and she felt the hat being gently pulled off her head. Then hands were everywhere—probing her head, neck, shoulders and ribs with an expert touch.

She wanted to smack the hands away, but she was too weak and they were too insistent. Finally she managed to take in a big sucking breath of air. She struggled to sit up, but big hands kept her down. Suddenly the aches and pains she could feel starting to register were nothing compared to the fact that Nadim loomed above her, with his hands all over her.

Finally she managed to knock away his hands, protesting breathlessly, 'I'm fine. I've been thrown a million times before.'

Nadim was livid. Iseult could see that. 'Yes, but not on ground like this. It could break your back.'

She struggled to sit up, and Nadim helped her. Iseult looked into his grim face. His hands were still on her arms. Guilt flooded her. 'I'm sorry,' she said immediately, thinking of his wife.

Her expressive face must have given her away, because Nadim said grimly, 'This is completely different.'

Remorse flooded Iseult as she tried to stand awkwardly. Of course it was. Even if he hadn't loved his wife, he must have had great affection for her. Not to mention his unborn child. And she...she was nothing to this man but an irritation he couldn't seem to help himself from kissing when the mood took him.

This view was compounded when he lifted Iseult up into his arms before she knew what was happening, and strode out of the enclosure saying caustically, 'I swear your middle name is trouble.'

Ridiculously, tears threatened, and Iseult had to blink rapidly to ease the burn. Her throat was clogged. She couldn't even protest and ask to be put down, and it felt all too devastating to be held like this against

Nadim's broad and hard chest as he cut a swathe through the gawping crowd. The material of his *thobe* was silk and felt ridiculously flimsy. The heat from his body was making her skin tingle all over.

He brought her to his Jeep, which was nearby, and placed her in the back. Closing her door, he went around and got in the other side. Iseult tried to say something, and hated the way her voice sounded so thready. 'You don't have to do this. I can walk back. It's not far from here.'

She even put her hand on the handle of the door, and Nadim barked out, '*Woman*, will you just stay put!' He put an arm across her belly, stopping her from getting out, and Iseult could feel emotion welling again.

She was barely breathing, begging silently for Nadim to take his arm away as the Jeep started to move. Clenching her jaw to keep the emotion down, she resolutely looked out of the window to avoid more censure.

She heard a deep sigh and his arm was gone—but only for a hand to come to her chin and turn her face to his. Iseult heard him mutter something that sounded guttural and foreign. To her utter horror and chagrin, tears flooded her eyes. Nadim cursed again and took out a handkerchief, handing it to Iseult.

She took it warily and blew her nose.

'I'm sorry, I didn't mean to make you cry...are you hurt?'

Iseult shook her head and blinked back the tears, swallowing. 'No...just a bit bruised, I think. On my back.'

'Show me...' His voice was more gentle than she'd ever heard it, nearly undoing her again.

Iseult didn't know what was happening until Nadim had nudged her forward on the seat so that he could pull up her T-shirt to look. 'What are you doing?' she demanded. But he paid no heed, and his muttered words told her that she must have a few glorious bruises already blooming. Her bottom felt as if it had taken most of the impact, but the thought of him looking down there made her go hot all over.

Nadim set her back, and to her surprise he couldn't meet her eyes. He said stiffly, 'I should never have brought you here or let you get on that horse. I thought he looked too skittish.'

'I'm fine—honestly. I bruise easily, so it probably looks worse than it is. It's nothing a hot bath won't cure. And you wouldn't have known how skittish he was unless someone had got on his back.'

Nadim cast her a grim look. 'Yes, but it didn't have to be you. That's what those boys are there for. They're hardy and well able to handle horses like that.'

Iseult bit her tongue, knowing Nadim wouldn't welcome a heated defence right now. The Jeep came to a stop and Iseult could see Lina hovering anxiously. Had word reached her already? She opened the Jeep door and winced when she felt her back protest. Nadim was there, and she saw his face darken ominously. He rapped out instructions to Lina and helped Iseult from the Jeep.

When she was out, he said, 'Lina will take care of you and see to those bruises. You should rest this evening.'

And then he was handing her to Lina and stepping away abruptly. Iseult felt bereft, and wanted to protest that she'd be fine, not wanting to miss out on anything. There was an air of suppressed excitement around the camp as a group of black-clad giggling women went past, but she knew better now than to push Nadim, so just said meekly, 'All right.'

Lina wouldn't leave even when Iseult protested that she'd be fine. She drew her a bath, and when Iseult sank her aching body into it, it was like slipping into warm silk. Lina had added all sorts of oils, and even rose blossoms floated on the fragrant water. With her hair piled high onto her head she sank back, and had to admit that she'd never experienced something so deca-dently sensual.

Suddenly at the thought of that word *sensual* she felt ridiculous, and sat up as if to get out. Immediately a stern-eyed Lina was there. 'You stay in the bath, Miss Iseult. You need to let the healing oils work.'

Iseult sank back down hurriedly—as much because she'd never been naked before someone else as any-thing else. 'Okay,' she said sheepishly, but then added, 'But only if you stop calling me Miss Iseult...it's Iseult.'

Iseult could see from Lina's dark eyes that she was smiling, and wondered what she looked like. 'Okay, Miss Iseult.'

She left her alone again, and when Iseult was starting to feel like a prune, she reappeared, holding a large towel. Iseult got out and Lina wrapped her in the towel. After she'd dried herself Lina appeared again with a pot of ointment, and smoothed the cream into her tender back and buttocks. Then she draped a robe of some sort over a nearby chair and bade Iseult goodnight.

Iseult dropped the towel and drew on the robe. It was made of brushed silk, and felt far too delicate for someone like her. An edging of gold thread went around its whole perimeter. There was a long golden ribbon-like tie which ran just under her breasts, and she looked up from tying it to see herself reflected in a mirror in the washing area.

She was caught unawares, and stood transfixed by the unfamiliar person reflected back at her. In the mirror was a woman with a long graceful neck, highlighted by the hair piled high on her head. Her eyes were huge, her mouth full and pink. She looked pale, her skin almost luminous in the low lights. She looked very nearly... *beautiful*.

With a shaking hand Iseult reached up and undid her hair, so that it fell down her back and over her shoulders. With one hand on the tie under her breasts, and the other falling limply to her side, she couldn't stop looking. She'd been transformed into someone else. *The person she felt stirring within her when Nadim kissed her.*

The material fell in a diaphanous swirl of cream and gold to her feet, skimming over curves she'd never thought she had, making them look fuller, more alluring. The generous shape of her breasts she'd always fought to hide was accentuated by the deep V and empire line of the robe, with her cleavage a shadowy line between them.

She looked...she looked like— She heard a sound then, and the breath left her throat. Her skin tingled and the hairs stood up on the back of her neck. Hoping against hope it was just Lina, but knowing exactly who it was, she turned to see that Nadim had come to the entrance of the tent.

He was dressed in dark gold robes now, and Iseult

could see that the sun was setting outside, just beyond his turbaned head and broad shoulders. Every cell in her body reacted violently at seeing him there, and she was caught in such a vulnerable moment she could only look at him helplessly.

Nadim fought to remember why he'd come to Iseult's tent; perhaps it had been some bid to assure himself that he *could* resist her, and that he should keep trying to resist her—because she was an employee, and because he knew that beneath that spiky exterior she was vulnerable and had shouldered a heavy burden for a long time. She wasn't worldly, like the mistresses he was careful to take now—women who knew the score. No emotional involvement. He could end up hurting Iseult, just as he'd hurt his own wife...

Despite all those very good reasons he fought to try and say something, anything coherent, and not just stand there like a teenager transfixed by the first naked woman he'd ever seen.

And she wasn't even naked! But the delicate robe might as well have been see-through. The line of her cleavage still looked damp, the skin pale and silky-looking next to the material. And through the fall of the robe he could see those long long legs, and in between them the shadowy promise of a carnal satisfaction he'd never craved this badly before... It made his blood thrum and his body harden in rampant response.

'How is your back?' It was a miracle he'd found his voice. Nadim didn't dare even move one inch towards Iseult, knowing that if he did he wouldn't re-emerge from that tent until he'd had her. And the gut-clenching panic he'd felt when he'd seen that horse throw her like a rag-doll still made him feel very vulnerable. Too vulnerable.

Iseult blinked and suddenly felt cold. For a moment there— She mentally shook her head and was instantly self-conscious. She was practically naked! She crossed her arms to cover her breasts, unaware of how it pushed them forward, or of how the robe gaped slightly, showing a long length of leg. She was also unaware of how Nadim tensed, because he was cast in shadow.

'Fine... Lina gave me some ointment...'

Nadim just inclined his head. 'Good. Lina comes from a family of healers, so you're in good hands. But you'll probably be sore tomorrow.'

Iseult shook her head. 'Really. I'm fine. I'm sure you have to be somewhere...?'

He nodded once abruptly. 'Goodnight, then, Iseult.'

'Goodnight.'

Of course he had somewhere else to be, a voice mocked her. He left, and seemed to suck the energy of the space out with him. Iseult sagged, literally, against the chair, and a wave of humiliation washed through her to think of how she'd been mooning at herself in the mirror, believing that she was looking at someone different. Believing she might be beautiful. *Feminine*. Believing that perhaps he'd brought her here because of something elemental that had passed between them that morning on the terrace.

She was no different from the girl who had never been feminine—the girl her classmates had found it so easy to send up. And she would never be anything else. She would never be the kind of woman to have a man like Nadim. They were worlds and leagues apart, and clearly he just felt some misguided sense of responsibility towards her.

With an inarticulate sound of rage at herself, she tore off the robe, hearing it tear.

Tears pricked her eyes as she found and pulled on the pants and T-shirt she normally slept in. Castigating herself bitterly for her weakness, she crawled into the sumptuous bed, suddenly wishing she were back at home in Kildare and sliding between plain flannel sheets—not these silky decadent sheets that made her think of Nadim and want hot, forbidden things.

CHAPTER EIGHT

THE following day Iseult was up and dressed in her usual uniform of jeans and a shirt and riding boots. Ready and waiting to take on the day and ignore her disturbing growing feelings for Nadim. Without waiting for instruction she went back to the horse enclosure, to the same horse that had thrown her off the day before.

Determined to prove something to herself as much as anyone else, she put on a hat and got onto his back to conquer the fleeting fear that such a fall always engendered.

Nadim watched Iseult from a distance and shook his head ruefully. He knew she hadn't seen him yet as that telltale tension in her body whenever he came near hadn't come into her. At that moment he knew that any hope of control over this attraction was futile. He'd thought somewhat misguidedly that he might be able to wait until the Sultan of Al-Omar's birthday party next week, but even the prospect of looking at another woman was anathema to him now.

He grimaced at the thought of a day of meetings ahead, and celebrations in his honour tonight, but even with aides clamouring for his attention Nadim didn't move away until he saw that Iseult was safely off the horse.

That evening Iseult could feel the aches and pains from her fall the day before making themselves known again. She'd been aware of Nadim at a distance all day, but he'd made no attempt to come and talk to her, staying deep in discussion with the group of men who followed him around. She felt a little bereft to think that he undoubtedly regretted bringing her and had no further use for her.

Lina had served Iseult dinner in the tent, and had told her that she and some of the other women were due to perform a traditional Bedouin dance for Sheikh Nadim and his guests that night so she had to get ready. She was leaving now, and a sudden fear gripped Iseult that Nadim would materialise again and send her flimsy control to pieces. On an impulse she asked Lina if she could come and watch her get ready.

Lina hesitated for a moment, and then with sparkling eyes nodded, taking Iseult by the hand and leading her out to another small tent nearby. Once inside, Iseult could see about a dozen women. She smiled shyly at them and watched as Lina took off her *burka*, revealing a luxurious fall of black hair to her waist and an extraordinarily pretty face.

Lina giggled at Iseult's reaction and got ready, revealing that under her long *abeyya* she had been wearing jeans and a T-shirt. Fascinated, Iseult sat down cross-legged in a corner and watched as the girls and women took turns to get each other ready. Lina had disappeared behind a screen, and when she emerged again Iseult was shocked after having seen so little flesh bared up till now. She was dressed in silk and chiffon harem pants with ornate ankle bracelets, and her hair was plaited in a shining rope of black against her back.

A short-sleeved top exposed her belly and hips, and she had gold rings up her arms and a gold chain around her curvaceous waist. A veil was secured at the back of her head, which she pulled across her face above her nose, obscuring her features again.

One of the other girls giggled and said something to Lina, who looked at Iseult with a mischievous expression. Iseult saw her advance and knew that look. She started to protest even as Lina reached down and pulled her up with both hands. Before Iseult knew what was happening she was being administered to by a dozen women, all intent on getting her dressed exactly as they were.

Iseult protested again, but to no avail; they were determined, and as she had no idea what to expect she gave herself up to the experience, telling herself they were just having fun. Soon she was dressed exactly like the others, and Lina was fastening a gold chain around her waist. She felt all at once naked and exhilarated.

Lina stood back and clapped her hands. 'Miss Iseult, now you're one of us!'

Iseult smiled weakly, and mentally compared her own milk-bottle-white skin to the glorious olive of the girls around her. She felt completely exposed in the brief silk top. Her breasts were bigger than the other girls', and she was all but spilling from the low neckline. But there was something decadently sensual about the trousers sitting on her hips and the gold chain around her waist. A long veil was attached to her own hair, which Lina had coiled down her back, and she showed her how to cover her face from view.

For a brief moment she was transported back to the previous evening, when she'd caught sight of her reflection in the mirror. But there was no mirror or Nadim here to break the spell being woven around her as one of the other girls knelt at her feet and fastened ankle bracelets. She'd never experienced this girly camaraderie of dressing up and it was heady.

Thinking that they were just having fun before they went to perform, she was completely unprepared when Lina took her hand again. Suddenly they were all on the move.

'Wait, where are we going?' she asked.

Lina looked back. 'We're one dancer short… Just stay behind me and copy what I do—you'll be fine!'

Her cry of, *'But I've never danced in my life!'* got lost as the girls flitted like exotically beautiful ghosts through the inky twilight between the tents. Iseult desperately covered her face with the veil, and sent up a silent prayer that Nadim wouldn't recognise her. If he did…she shivered inwardly…he'd kill her for sure.

They stood at the back of a huge tent, where lots of men sat on cushions in groups around low tables piled high with food and drinks. Iseult's heart was thumping when she saw a long line of men at the top, with Nadim right in the centre, looking stern and austere in black robes. They made him look even more dark and gorgeous. *And dangerous.*

The beat of a drum started nearby—a seductive beat of another world. Iseult watched as the other girls started to move out amongst the tables, lifting their arms high and moving their veils back and forth, alternately revealing and hiding themselves, hips moving in a primal rhythm to the drums.

They went out two by two, and then Lina was moving and taking Iseult with her. Iseult had no choice but to follow, and concentrated desperately on copying Lina's movements—the small steps she took, the way her hips swayed with such effortless sensuality. She knew she was nowhere near emulating her.

They were dangerously close to the top of the room now, just feet away from Nadim, and Iseult had the veil clutched tight across her face above her nose. She could feel the warm evening air skate over her bared midriff, and knew it would take a miracle for him not to notice her pale skin.

Even so, despite her fear of being caught, Iseult couldn't help the way the beat of the drums seemed to ignite a fire in her blood, and following Lina was very mesmeric. As if determined to thwart her best efforts, though, she found herself darting a quick glance to the big dark presence just a few feet away.

Nadim sat with one leg propped up and an arm resting on his knee. And he was looking right at her with a dark, blistering gaze that tore strips off her skin. Iseult nearly stumbled, but somehow managed to keep going, ripping her eyes away from Nadim.

To her intense relief Lina was moving towards the back of the room, where the other girls were in a huddle, giggling. Iseult tried to reassure herself that Nadim hadn't known it was her; he couldn't really have noticed in the dimly lit tent. The drums were still beating, and with shock at what she'd just done setting in Iseult took a step outside to gulp in big breaths of air. She was shaking all over.

Just then, out of nowhere, came a movement so quick and overpowering it took her completely by surprise. She was being lifted off her feet against a wall of steel, with one arm just below her breasts and a big hand over her mouth. As if she weighed no more than a bag of sugar her captor strode away with her into the shadows.

CHAPTER NINE

ISEULT kicked her legs uselessly into thin air and tried to scream—but of course she couldn't get a sound out. The most terrifying thing was that she knew exactly who it was, because the wall of steel against her back felt incredibly familiar. She'd felt it that day in the dining room at home in Ireland. And suddenly it wasn't terror she was feeling but a wild excitement.

Iseult put her hands up to try and claw his hand down from her mouth but he was immovable. She saw that they were approaching a big tent, set apart from the others, with two tall lamps holding burning flames at its entrance. In scant seconds they were through the heavy drapes at the entrance and Iseult was summarily dropped to her feet.

She whirled around to face her captor, breathing harshly. Her heart thumped violently to see Nadim so tall and dark and intimidating. Any angry words she'd articulated in her head disappeared as she realised that she was half naked. Her body felt as if it was on fire under Nadim's still blistering gaze.

He bit out caustically, 'Were you born into this world with a mission in life to drive me completely insane?'

Iseult was coping with too many things at once—not least of which was the fact that her heaving breasts felt as if they were about to pop out of her top—so she just said shakily, 'You took me out of my world and into yours, so if I'm driving you mad you only have yourself to blame.'

He almost flinched, as if she'd hit a nerve. 'I knew it was a mistake to bring you here.'

Hurt and anger lanced Iseult at hearing his bitter words, seeing his undeniable reaction of regret. 'Well, then, why don't you just send me home and out of your hair once and for all?'

Iseult made as if to move around him to leave, but Nadim caught her by her bare upper arm. She stopped, still breathing raggedly. She wouldn't look up into that harsh, beautiful face.

His voice sounded guttural, hoarse. 'I can't let you go because to send you away would drive my insanity to another level entirely. You're in my blood now, Iseult.'

Slowly her head lifted, and she looked up at Nadim and stopped breathing when she saw the heated intensity in his eyes. 'Wh-what are you talking about?'

He brought her round so she stood in front of him again, and with his free hand tore the turban off his head and threw it into a corner. He suddenly looked much younger, and unbearably rakish. 'I want you. I've wanted you since the moment I saw you.'

Iseult's legs turned to jelly. She fought not to let herself be swept away by a rising tide of desire. 'I won't let you kiss me again just because you feel like it, only to cast me aside as if *I've* done something wrong.'

Nadim moved closer, both hands on her arms now.

Iseult was finding it hard to breathe or stay clear-headed. He shook his head, eyes burning down into hers. 'I've tried staying away from you but I can't any more. It's making me crazy. I'm not even going to ask how you ended up dancing with Lina. Every time I turn around you're doing the unexpected... When I saw you appear before me in that excuse of an outfit any control I may have had disappeared... I need to know now—do you want this too?'

Iseult looked up at Nadim. Just inches separated them from bodily contact. Their breaths were already mingling. Her breasts felt full and aching against the tight top, and she had the curious sensation of the real world slipping away. Here in this dim light, in the ornate and luxurious surroundings of Nadim's tent, they could have been transported back one hundred years in time to another world.

Nadim looked like a warrior king, his jaw tight, the planes of his face austerely gorgeous as he waited to hear her answer. Everything that had happened between them was crystallised in this moment. And Iseult knew what she was going to say with a bone-deep feeling of rightness.

Yes.

It rose from deep within her, with an inexorable flooding of heat into her body. She was no more capable of denying she wanted him, than she was of surviving another second without breathing.

'Yes...' she said faintly, huskily. 'I want this too...'

With a perceptible tremor in his hands that surprised Iseult, and comforted her on some very vulnerable level, Nadim pulled her closer until their bodies were touching. Suddenly Jamilah's warning words came back to her: *The al Saqr men can be ruthless in their pursuit, and equally ruthless when they're finished with you.*

But in that moment Nadim's head was lowering, that unbearably sensuous mouth was coming closer and closer, and it was very easy for Iseult to block the words out.

When Nadim's mouth settled over hers it felt as though time had slowed down to a drip-drip of sensual delight. He kissed her with such languorous intent, exploring softly, teasing, tasting, biting down gently on her full lower lip, before coming back to settle over her mouth again with a hint of barely leashed passion.

That tipped Iseult over the precarious edge she'd been clinging onto even unbeknown to herself, and with a faint moan she leant closer into him, her arms climbing up to twine around his neck.

And as if Nadim hadn't entirely trusted her words, but had been waiting for a tacit signal, he drew her even closer, so that the space now between their beating hearts was non-existent. His tongue made a bold foray into Iseult's mouth and she welcomed it, welcomed him, her tongue shyly touching and tasting.

Passion quickly blazed up around them. Iseult was barely aware of Nadim flicking away the veil from the back of her head. His hands were on her bare hips, pulling her in even closer, where she was dimly aware of something hard digging into her belly. Belated realisation of what it must be had her pulling back for a moment to look down. Nadim followed her gaze to where his ornate dagger was still tucked into his rope belt.

He quirked a sexy smile. 'I don't think we'll need that.'

Mouth dry, Iseult watched as he pulled it out. About to throw it aside, he seemed to reconsider. He pulled it from its scabard and with one hand turned Iseult so that her back faced him. She shivered slightly, but with anticipation, not fear. She felt him pull her hair aside, so that it hung over one shoulder, and then he pulled the back of her top taut. The cold edge of the blade touched against her skin for the tiniest moment, and then suddenly the tightness of her top was released and air whistled over her naked back.

With a sucked-in breath of shock and excitement Iseult brought her hands to her breasts, holding the top in place. She heard the dull thud of the knife falling somewhere, and then Nadim's big hands were smoothing the rent sides of the short top apart, and she felt his breath feathering before he started to press kisses from her neck down her spine.

Iseult's head fell forward, her heart thumping wildly as she felt Nadim's hands settle on her hips, fingers curving around to her soft belly as his mouth travelled back up to her neck and shoulder, nudging the ripped side of her top down over one shoulder.

She had no experience, but Iseult felt some deeply innate feminine instinct kick in at that moment. So when Nadim turned her around gently to face him again she looked up, straight into his eyes, and fell into two pools of dark sensual promise. Any hint of remaining doubt fled.

Staring deep into her eyes, mesmerising her, he let his hands come to the shoulders of her top and tug softly. Iseult's hands impeded the process, still welded as they were across her breasts.

'Trust me...' Nadim said, and with a slightly choked breath Iseult let her hands drop. The top gaped, and Nadim's eyes left hers to look down as the stiff silk material was finally pulled away and down her arms, baring her to his hot gaze.

Iseult trembled. Her breasts felt heavy and aching, her nipples tight and hard, prickling with sensation. The ruined top fell to the floor. Iseult saw Nadim's face flush, his jaw tighten. He reached out a dark hand and cupped the heavy weight of her breast. She had to bite back a moan and couldn't look down, knowing that she might collapse altogether if she saw the darkness of his skin against the paleness of hers.

'You're so beautiful...' he breathed, and before Iseult's inner demons had time to rise his thumb had found her nipple and brushed back and forth, teasing it to even further tingling tightness. This time she nearly did fall, and on a reflex put out her hands to his arms in an effort to stay standing.

The movement caused her breast to press into his hand fully, and even holding onto him couldn't keep Iseult upright any more. In an instant Nadim had bent and lifted her into his arms, and carried her over to a sumptuously clothed bed.

He laid her down as reverentially as if she were made of china and then stood back. All Iseult could do was look up, dry-mouthed, as Nadim started to disrobe. The heavy outer robe fell to the ground, the rope belt came off, and in a split second the dark *thobe* had disappeared.

Iseult's gaze fell to take in the magnificence of his broad chest, leanly muscled and olive skinned, two blunt dark nipples standing amongst a fine sprinkling of dark hair.

Her eyes dropped to the low slung waist of his undertrousers, loose, but not loose enough to disguise the

prominent bulge. Cheeks flaming, Iseult lifted her eyes
again and saw Nadim's riveted on her. Feeling self-
conscious, she brought up an arm over her breasts.

And then he was there, beside her, one hand removing her arm from her breasts, brushing against a
sensitive nipple. He stretched her arm up, over her head,
where his fingers interlaced with hers, holding her
captive.

He bent his head and feathered a kiss to her mouth.
'Don't hide yourself from me...'

A heated languor melted through Iseult's veins, and
yet at the same time she felt more energised than she'd
ever felt, with a dull, throbbing ache setting up in her
lower belly and between her legs.

With a slowness she was sure was meant to drive her
insane, Nadim traced his other hand and fingers around
her breast, moulding the fleshy contour before cupping
it and squeezing gently, so that the hard tip stood out
like an enticement.

With a wicked gleam in his eyes, still holding one
hand captive, he bent again and pressed hot open-
mouthed kisses all down her chest, between the valley
of her breasts, and then after a screaming second of
torture he licked around the aureole and dragged that
hot, tingling tip into his mouth.

Iseult's back arched as if she'd been electrocuted.
She'd never felt anything like it in her life, and she
squeezed her legs together reflexively to stem the tide
of liquid heat. Her fingers clasped Nadim's in a death
grip, and her other hand funnelled through his silky
hair, keeping his head and that wicked mouth in place.

He moved to the other breast, administering the
same torture, making Iseult gasp out loud and suck in

short breaths. He finally released her other hand and
drew back slightly, but only to look his fill. Iseult felt
wanton and uncontrollable. Her nipples were wet from
his mouth and tongue, his cheeks flushed, eyes glittering.

'Nadim...' she husked, not even knowing what she
was asking for.

Nadim had to pause for a moment. For the first time
in his life he felt out of control with a woman. Heat and
lust had morphed together, clouding his brain in a
searing heat haze, and all he wanted to do was bury
himself so far and deep into Iseult's slick body that he
knew if he didn't impose some control he'd hurt her.

But it was near impossible to regain that control. Her
breasts were like two succulent fruits, her back still
slightly arched. When he'd felt that spasmodic response
as he'd closed his mouth around one hard, tight nipple
and sucked it deep, he'd damn near exploded. She was
biting her lip now, her eyes glazed, dark golden pools
of desire...her hair was spread out around her in
glorious disarray.

Smoothing his hands down the sides of her body, out
over the gentle swell of her hips, he snagged on the ties
of her skimpy harem pants. With little more than a tug
they were gone, falling away in a diaphanous cloud by
the bed, taking her panties with them.

Now she lay there with nothing except the gold chain
around her waist and the gold ankle bracelets, and
Nadim did not have the spatial ability to even attempt
removing those. Feeling suddenly constricted, he stood
and dispensed with his own trousers. He saw Iseult's
gaze drop and her cheeks pale slightly when she saw
the sheer evidence of his arousal...

Iseult knew all about sex, even if she'd never had it. She'd watched stallions mount mares all her life, so she knew all about the earthy reality. But to see Nadim fully naked and fully aroused intimidated her more than she cared to admit. Any thought of telling him she was a virgin fled her mind. They'd gone too far now, and even as she balked at his physicality she knew she didn't want to turn back. If he knew she was a virgin…

Nadim came down on the bed alongside Iseult, scattering her thoughts. He lay on his side and with a possessive arm pulled her into him. She breathed in the musky scent of their arousal. She could feel his erection pressing against her and it made her want to move her hips. Any trepidation fled.

Tentatively she trailed a shy hand up over his lean waist and torso, watching how his belly was sucked in on a short breath. Her fingers found a hard blunt nipple, and acting on pure instinct she bent down and found it with her mouth, kissing it before biting and nipping gently, savouring the salty taste of his skin, running a hand down his back to the indent just above his firm buttocks.

Nadim fisted a hand in her hair and pulled her head back up. Pressed torso to torso, length to length, they touched everywhere. With an enigmatic look that Iseult couldn't decipher Nadim covered her mouth with his in a searing kiss and pulled her even closer, his arms wrapped around her so tight that her breasts were flattened against his chest. She didn't even know where he ended and she began.

An urgency was building between her legs and in her belly, a tightening coil of tension, and Iseult moved restlessly, unwittingly causing stars and spots to explode behind Nadim's eyes as he fought to retain control.

Nadim's hands smoothed down her back, down to her bottom, pulling her into him even more. Instinctively Iseult opened her legs, feeling Nadim's heated erection sliding between them. Hearts were thumping out of control, and Iseult felt a light sweat break out all over her skin. She'd never been so intent on one thing: reaching an elusive peak with this man.

In an effortless move Nadim shifted them so that Iseult was flat on her back and he lay between her legs. She could feel the potent strength of him between her thighs, but still he didn't move. He just bent his head and found her mouth again, drugging her with his kisses.

She heard the faint sound of foil ripping, and there was a moment when Nadim pulled back. She opened her eyes with a faint mewl of despair. She needed something right now that only he could give her. She wrapped her hands around his biceps, feeling them bunch and move under silky-smooth skin.

Her legs moved further apart even as her thighs gripped his lean waist, and she felt him move down slightly. He touched her intimately with one finger, drawing it slowly up the desire-drenched folds of her sex, finding where the evidence of her arousal was a hard swell of nerve-endings and rubbing her there.

Iseult's back arched again. Pressing herself into his hand, she couldn't breathe, couldn't think straight. Her hands gripped his arms so tight that she thought she'd leave him with permanent marks.

'Nadim...' she said hoarsely, desperately. *'Please...'*

'What?' he asked, all innocence wrapped up in the

devil, and he continued to tease her with his finger,
which was moving inside her now, where she felt slick
and hot.

'I could tease you and watch you all night, but not
any more... I can't wait...'

Before Iseult knew what was happening, or had
sucked in a breath, Nadim was pushing himself into her.
Filling her, stretching her...impossibly. She gasped for
a moment, and jerked her hips as if to move away from
his penetration, but even as she did she could feel a
glorious friction.

Nadim frowned down at her. 'Iseult...are you...?'

Iseult somehow knew the discomfort would be
fleeting. She reached up and pulled his head down,
pulling him closer, and wrapped her legs around his
waist.

'Don't stop. Please don't stop, Nadim...' She saw
him wage what looked to be an intense inner battle,
before he made an inarticulate sound and said gut-
turally, 'Relax...this might hurt for a moment...'

Iseult looked up into his eyes, telling him silently
that she trusted him implicitly, and in that moment she
did. She could feel him flex his bottom, and then he
thrust in, making her breath catch at the searing,
burning pain.

Immediately his mouth was on hers, kissing her,
drugging her as she felt him go deeper. And the pain
was fading magically, and as he started to pull out again
she felt that delicious friction. Loath to let him go, she
moved her hips with him, but then he came back, thrusting in again, even deeper this time.

Iseult's legs were locked around his waist, her chest
arched up to his and her head falling back as she strug-

gled to comprehend all the sensations running through her body and head.

Nadim brought a hand around her back, arching her up even more, and thrust again, deeper, a little harder. Iseult moaned. She felt his breath feather over her hot skin and gasped out loud when he took a nipple deep into his mouth, swirling his tongue around it, biting gently as he took up a remorseless rhythm, driving in and out of her body.

The intensity of sensation was overwhelming. Iseult could only cling onto Nadim. He was her anchor, the centre of her universe, and he was threatening to topple her over an edge she'd never known before. But with him looking down into her eyes she was fearless.

His strokes got longer, deeper and faster, and Iseult felt her muscles clenching. She was rushing headlong into something she could only guess at, and in that moment everything exploded around her, and a carnal pleasure she'd never even imagined existed pulsed through her even as Nadim still moved in and out.

Iseult could feel her muscles spasm along his hard length, but she couldn't articulate anything, knowing that she must look shocked. She felt shocked. What she'd just experienced had reformed all her cells into a new configuration, and this man's stamp was all over them.

As she watched Nadim's eyes closed tight, his head was flung back, the veins of his neck stood out. And with one final powerful thrust he stilled, and the only sound that could be heard was their laboured breathing.

Iseult was still floating in a limbo land of half-consciousness when she felt herself being lifted out of the bed by strong arms. She murmured something and felt Nadim's breath close to her ear. His deep husky voice sent a frisson of remembered ecstasy through her. 'Shh, I've run you a bath…you must be sore.'

Iseult shook her head with an effort, not even able to lift it from where it lay on Nadim's shoulder. She sounded drunk. 'No…not sore…happy.'

She only started coming back up through the layers of satedness when she felt Nadim lower her into a warm, fragrant bath and felt the water close over her languid body. His arms were leaving, pulling away, and instinctively she made a sound of protest, catching his arm, finally opening her heavy eyes.

She was in a bathing area much like her own, but far bigger and more opulent. Nadim's arm was under her hand, and she saw that he'd put on a robe. She felt completely disorientated, and if an alien had appeared in that moment with the news that they'd arrived on another planet she wouldn't have been surprised.

Nadim pressed a kiss to her mouth, and a chain reaction started in Iseult's blood. She wanted to ask Nadim to get into the bath with her, but something in his closed expression forbade it. He looked cool and composed, austere again. Not like the man who'd told her with such a tortured expression that he wanted her. And who had then made love to her…had initiated her into womanhood.

She took her hand from his arm, something inside her contracting protectively amongst the feelings of opiate languour.

Nadim stood up and towered over Iseult in the bath. 'I've left a robe on the chair for you. I'll be outside when you're ready…'

Iseult watched him walk out, and felt alternately as if he'd just slapped her across the face and as if he'd just given her the greatest gift. She sank down in the water, wanting to hide away, feeling hideously self-conscious all of a sudden. Deeply embedded doubts and fears started to rise up to the surface.

Had she initiated this? Had she somehow twisted things again so that she could justify it to herself because Nadim had really wanted her? Had she thrown herself at him like some out-of-control groupie?

Her belly quivered when she remembered how he'd lifted her up and carried her to his tent like a marauding pirate. A tiny trickle of confidence returned. He'd told her he'd wanted her from the moment he'd seen her…so that tension in Ireland hadn't been her imagination…but why was he being so aloof now?

Iseult's brain started to throb with questions and insecurities and attempts to reassure herself. Sitting up to wash herself perfunctorily, she stopped for a moment when she saw faint bruises flowering across her skin, redness from where Nadim's stubble had grazed her delicate skin. Heat bloomed low again, and Iseult avoided touching that part of herself which still tingled and stung slightly.

Nadim stood at the heavily draped curtains at the entrance to his tent. Hard to believe that only an hour or so had passed, when the entire world seemed to have shifted on its axis. Sounds of revelry came faintly from the tent he'd left earlier. But all he could remember was the sheer blind lust that had galvanised him.

When he'd first spotted Iseult in the tent, dressed in that excuse of an outfit, he hadn't recognised her. But he hadn't been able to look away. She'd been more inherently voluptuous than the other girls, and her movements had been gauche and untutored. It had been odd, as the girls who danced that dance would have learnt it from their own mothers at a young age.

His eye had been drawn to the unknown woman and his body had stirred in response. Nadim's first feeling had been intense relief—*Iseult hasn't bewitched me completely.* But almost in the same instant, she'd come closer, and he'd had the sinking realisation that it could be none other than her. The perfect pale alabaster of her skin had glowed with luminescence in the dim light. And her eyes, flashing dark gold above that veil, had given her away completely.

And then had come the burning acrid jealousy because every other man there would be looking at her and coveting her charms. It had taken all his control and self-restraint to wait until she'd disappeared at the back of the tent to go and get her. And the minute he'd pulled her into his body he'd known that there was only one possible outcome to that scenario.

The knowledge sliced through his brain and body as if he'd been blocking it out: *she'd been a virgin.* And yet she'd made love to him with such passionate abandon that if he hadn't felt her body's initial resistance he might not even have known.

He'd only ever slept with one other virgin: his wife. Nadim's brain seized there. Yet another comparison thrown up to mock him and make his belly roil with guilt as he had to acknowledge the vast differences between the two women...

He realised then that the splashing of the bath had stopped, and he heard a soft footfall behind him. Feeling intense trepidation, he slowly turned around to face Iseult.

CHAPTER TEN

ISEULT steeled herself for whatever was coming, even though she had no idea what that might be. She belted the robe around her waist tightly. Between her legs she could feel tenderness, and the memory of how it had felt to have Nadim surge so forcefully into her body made her feel weak with desire all over again.

Slowly he turned around, his face unreadable, his long robe concealing his body. He came into the tent, the drapes falling closed again behind him.

'Why didn't you tell me you were innocent?'

The simple question blindsided Iseult for a moment, but she recovered. 'Would you have slept with me if you'd known?'

No way, was Nadim's quick and instinctive response—along with a rogue voice saying, *Liar, you wouldn't have been able not to.*

As Iseult watched, she could see Nadim battle with something, but eventually he said, 'Probably not, no.'

Iseult ducked her head, ashamed of having been duplicitous on any level, and had to admit, 'I think I knew that…but I didn't want you…not to sleep with me.'

She lifted her chin again, feeling something defiant

move through her. She knew if she had the moment again she'd act in the same way. She'd wanted Nadim and he'd wanted her.

Nadim had moved closer and Iseult could feel heat rising. His smell wound round her again, and that musky tang of *sex*.

'You know this changes everything.'

Iseult could only look at Nadim. 'What do you mean?' She had a sudden horrifying vision of Nadim telling her that because he'd been her first lover some ancient desert law decreed that they should be married.

As if reading her mind, he quirked a hard smile and said mockingly, 'You can stop that overactive imagination right there. This may be a country with indelible ties to ancient customs, but those customs don't apply to women I decide to take as my mistresses…'

For a long second his words didn't sink in. *Mistresses.* There was something so inherently insulting about that word and title. As archaic as the laws he'd just spoken of. And yet Iseult had to mock herself. Nadim was hardly the kind of man who'd have something as trite as a *girlfriend* or a *partner*. He was of the modern world and yet *not* of the modern world.

She tried to comprehend. 'You're saying that just because we've slept together now I'm your mistress?'

He moved closer, and Iseult's hands tightened on her belt. Her breath hitched unsteadily. 'Precisely that's what I'm saying. Sleeping with you once is not enough. Not by a long shot. You're innocent, Iseult. I can teach you…help you explore your sensuality.'

Iseult's brain melted, and the part of her that rebelled was drowned out. How could he know what he said? How could he know that with those few words he was taking out one of her innermost vulnerabilities, looking at it in the light and saying, *Let me help you with this.*

She shook her head and felt her hair move across one shoulder, saw how Nadim's eyes flicked there momentarily and how his eyes grew darker. Her heart thumped in response. 'I...don't know how I feel about that.'

In a cataclysmic second he was close enough to snake a hand around her waist and pull her into his body. Their robes were so flimsy she could already feel the potent burgeoning strength of him, and at that moment the thought of being denied another chance to sleep with this man was anathema to Iseult.

His eyes blazed down into hers, mesmeric. 'I'm offering you all I can give, Iseult. You will be my mistress and we will explore this attraction for as long as we both feel it.'

How could she think when he was so close? When it felt as if a mythical kingdom lay just beyond the tent, calling to her seductively to give in? When this man had woken her from a deep dark and cold sleep and shown her an enticing taste of what it was to be a desirable woman? Iseult couldn't believe that there was anything more to this than sheer random carnal attraction. But one thing she did know: if anyone had the ability to make her feel beautiful it was going to be this man, and *now*. Nadim was making it perfectly clear to Iseult this would only last for a very finite time.

Feeling as if she was stepping out over a cliff-edge and into a void of nothing, Iseult just said shakily, 'Okay...'

An expression crossed Nadim's face—one that made Iseult tense instinctively; it had looked like cynicism. She had a sudden flash of understanding that she'd just joined the leagues of other women who'd never said no to him, and for a second wished that she could be stronger. But, feeling her tension, Nadim pulled her even closer, and now his expression was full of only one thing: desire.

Taking Iseult's hand in his, he led her back to the bed, which was still rumpled. He lay down and pulled her down to lie alongside him, the movement causing her gown to slide aside so that one breast was exposed.

Immediately embarrassed, Iseult went to cover up again, but Nadim stopped her hand, pulling the robe further apart and down her arm, making Iseult's pulse throb between her legs when she saw how he looked at her. Her breast flowered under his gaze, swelling and tightening, the tip becoming an aching hard point.

Before he touched her, though, Nadim asked innocuously, 'Are you hungry?'

Iseult's throat dried. She was, but not for food. As if reading her mind, Nadim chuckled darkly and said, 'You are learning fast, my sweet Iseult…time for food later, I think…'

Feeling desperately wanton, Iseult couldn't move as Nadim bent and cupped her breast and brought that tingling peak into his mouth where he sucked hard. Iseult gasped. Her hand tightened on the bedclothes. And then he pushed her back and opened her robe fully, spreading it apart, baring her to his gaze.

With a dark look of intent he started to press kisses down over her flat belly to where dark red curls hid the secret place of her desire. She felt Nadim's hands spread her legs apart and said shakily, through the fire building at her core, 'Nadim?'

He looked up at her, all dark and awe-inspiring, and

said, 'This time is going to be all about you and your pleasure. I will show you another way to fall off the edge…'

As Iseult watched he started to press teasing hot kisses up her inner thighs, and then she felt his breath feather between her legs as he showed her exactly what he meant.

The following early evening Iseult looked around at where men were taking down tents, packing up. Lina had already left with Iseult's baggage, and now she waited for Nadim by his Jeep. For their return to Merkazad, there was no question of how she was travelling. She was with Nadim. As effectively as if she had a sign around her neck that proclaimed, *I slept with Nadim and am now his property!*

But even that thought couldn't dampen the ardour in her veins as she saw Nadim in the distance, with his head inclined towards an old and gnarled man who leant on a stick, listening patiently. He'd awoken a hunger within her that she feared might never be quenched.

Even the memory of Lina's reaction to her arrival back at her own tent early that afternoon couldn't quench the heat. The teasing, warmly affectionate banter was gone, and Lina had morphed into someone who wouldn't meet Iseult's eyes. She'd acted with such an obsequious manner that Iseult had felt a little ill. When she'd asked Lina if something was wrong, Lina had replied evasively that nothing was wrong, but clearly things were different now. Iseult had become part of Nadim's retinue and therefore had to be treated accordingly.

Even so…Iseult couldn't feel regret or remorse for

the decision she'd taken. She watched Nadim stride towards her, with his cream robes billowing out around him, and felt weak with longing.

As they made the journey back down the mountains and into the Merkazadi plateau again, Nadim spent most of his time on a cellphone, speaking in a dizzying array of languages. One minute French, the next Spanish, back to English, and then something unmistakably Arabic.

Iseult tried to relax and look at the scenery but it was impossible. Her body seemed to be vibrating at a higher frequency, and Nadim would periodically reach for her hand, touching her, seeking her eyes, setting off a chain reaction of heat waves through her body and over her skin.

Nadim had made love to Iseult over and over again, but each time without seeking his own release. He was letting her body get used to the pleasure he could so effortlessly evoke, and even though she'd begged him to take her he'd held back, showing her how pleasure could come in many different ways. It had left her feeling sated and restless all at the same time.

'What are you thinking of?'

Iseult whirled around, face flushing. She'd been so engrossed that she hadn't even heard him terminate his conversation. 'No…nothing…' she stuttered ineffectually, as she feared what she had been thinking about must be engraved all over her face.

Nadim smiled that seductive, mocking smile and took her hand, taking it to his mouth where he pressed a kiss against her inner palm. Iseult squirmed and blushed and tried to pull her hand away. '*Don't*…the driver…'

She looked to the front, but the driver was looking resolutely forward. Nadim let her hand go and drawled softly, 'We're as good as alone. Asad doesn't speak English.'

Iseult blushed more. 'That may be, but he wouldn't have to speak English to know what's going on.'

A familiarly autocratic look crossed Nadim's face, and Iseult cut in before he could speak. 'I know, I know—you're the Sheikh and no one questions what you do. But what about me? I have to work—'

'You don't have to work any more…'

Iseult's mouth opened and closed. As much as she hated the thought of gossip, she wasn't going to hide away either. Fire built in her belly and she rounded fully on Nadim. 'I am not going to be locked up in that castle like some concubine. I want to keep working with Devil's Kiss. And I want to help Jamilah in the stables.'

Nadim shrugged, nonchalantly picking a bit of non-existent lint off his regal cuff. 'I have no problem with you working—as long as you're in my bed when I want you…'

He came close then, and Iseult saw that his nonchalance was just a thin veneer. She'd angered him again with her outspokenness. 'You're my mistress now, Iseult, in my bed until I say so…'

Rebellion quivered in Iseult's belly. 'What about me? Don't I have any say in this?'

He shook his head, and again reality chaffed. No other woman had ever questioned his intentions. 'Not really, *habiba*.'

Distracted for a second, Iseult asked, 'What does that mean? *Habiba?*' He'd called her that a few times over the past night.

Nadim's mouth twisted for a moment. Something dark crossed his face, and then with clear reluctance he said, 'It means *beloved*…but it's just a figure of speech.' He put a finger under Iseult's chin, and his voice was hard. 'I know how your first lover can inspire feelings… Don't fall in love with me, Iseult. I *won't* be responsible for your heart.'

The sharp pain that gripped her chest made her lash out without thinking about what she was saying. 'I can take care of myself. I wouldn't be foolish enough to give my heart to someone who didn't even love his own wife.'

Nadim's eyes flashed in angry response and his hand tightened on her chin. Immediately Iseult felt contrite. But before she could say anything he just replied, 'Good. Then we both know where we stand.'

Iseult jerked her chin away from Nadim's finger, going cold inside at the evidence of his implacable stance. 'And, anyway, who's to say you won't fall in love with *me*?'

Something about her was so endearingly vulnerable, like a lion cub standing up to a much bigger opponent, that Nadim had to curb his reflex to haul her into him, crush her against his chest and kiss her into oblivion, until they were both going up in flames and it would be the easiest thing in the world to slip out of his robes and open her jeans and pull them down… He cursed the driver just inches away. He might not understand English, but Iseult was right. He already had a damn good idea what was going on. His whole retinue did after he'd carried Iseult into his tent last night like some ancient warrior.

The lack of his usual control made him say starkly

now, 'I won't fall in love, Iseult. You can be assured of that. Love serves no purpose in my life.'

As she looked at him he could see something much more vulnerable cross over her face, and she said quietly, 'But you'll marry again some day…'

'Yes, of course,' he dismissed easily with a hand. 'But this time I'll make sure that my chosen bride is under no illusions that there will be love.' His face was no less harsh, but not as closed as he said, 'The present, Iseult, is all I'm interested in, and *you* are the present. When we get back to Merkazad you'll see that Lina will have moved your things to a room closer to mine.'

Iseult's mouth twisted. 'Out of the women's quarters and into the harem?'

Nadim smiled. 'Something like that.'

Iseult shivered, and wondered what it was about this man—how he could hold her in such thrall when he could be so cold and cruel. She wondered if his aversion to the notion of falling in love had become hardened by the very tragic and weighty expectations of his wife. She could understand that as a ruling monarch the luxury of falling in love wouldn't be an acceptable reason for marriage. He would have to marry strategically and well.

Nadim's phone rang again at that moment and he answered it curtly, releasing Iseult from his intense gaze. She welcomed the brief respite, but cast him a quick, surreptitious glance and felt weak all over again just looking at his regal profile—that strong jaw, that olive skin—and remembering how he'd so easily brought her to ecstasy countless times with just his hands…his mouth.

Was she being the biggest fool on earth to indulge in such folly? Two voices warred in her head with con-

tradictory answers… She knew that unless she was to
walk away completely, and go home and risk the
security he now gave her family, she had no choice but
to stay. And, if she was being completely honest, she
knew she couldn't leave. This man was taking her on a
sensual journey and she simply didn't have the will to
deny herself. Not when she'd resigned herself to a fate
of never exploring it.

Jamilah and Nadim needn't have warned Iseult to be
careful; she wouldn't be falling for him. No way.

It was very hard to cling to that assertion, though, some
hours after they'd arrived back at the castle and Iseult
heard the door of her bedroom open and close quietly.
Her new bedroom was even more sumptuous than the
last one, but none of that captivated her now. What captivated her was the tall, broad figure that darkened her
doorway, long flowing robes barely concealing his
powerful physique.

In a few long strides he was by her bed and the robe
was gone. Iseult's throat dried at the stunningly perfect
musculature of Nadim's body as he stood tall and proud.
He reached down and twitched back the sheets. Iseult lay
there in just pants and a T-shirt. Nadim grimaced. 'I
need to see about getting you some more alluring night-
wear.'

Instantly Iseult was defensive, reaching down for
the sheet again. But Nadim came down beside her and
stopped her hands. She rounded on him. 'I'm not some
doll you can just dress up for your pleasure only. I
happen to be very comfortable as I am.'

With his hands holding her captive, and far more
naked than her, Nadim bent down and covered her

mouth with his, kissing her deeply and so thoroughly that by the time he'd finished she was dizzy with lust.

He growled at her, 'You could be dressed in a coarse sack and you'd still turn me on…but you need to know the sensuality of silk and lace too…and I can do that for you…'

Rendered defenceless just by his kiss, Iseult said unthinkingly, 'I don't need silk or lace. I just need you…'

Nadim released her hands and pulled at her T-shirt until she lifted her arms and it was gone. Sitting back for a moment, he looked his fill at her beautiful full breasts, with their hard rosy tips. She lay back like a courtesan of old, hands above her head, hair spread out around her in glorious abandon, and Nadim had to wonder in that moment if he'd been mistaken—if she hadn't been as innocent as he'd believed.

But just as he thought that she bit her lip and brought her hands down to cover her breasts, and something exultant moved through him. To disguise it, he bent forward and took her hands away, and before lavishing attention on each generous mound of flesh he said, 'And no more unflattering sports bras…'

Iseult sucked in a breath and closed her eyes when she felt Nadim's mouth on her. Hot, wet, and sucking her into some parallel universe of pleasure. With an economy and deftness of movement he'd taken off her knickers, sliding them down her legs, and then he was right beside her, the whole length of his naked body next to hers.

Iseult instinctively closed a hand around him in an intimate caress, loving the feel of his steely strength covered with such silk. 'Please, Nadim…' she said between drugging kisses. 'I want you to make love to me…like you did before.'

Nadim pulled back for a moment. His hand smoothed down over her contracting belly and sought the juncture of her thighs, where she felt so wet she was embarrassed. 'You're not tender any more?'

Iseult was struck at his concern. This was why he'd held back? She shook her head and moaned softly when she felt him penetrate her with a finger, moving her hips towards him in wanton abandonment.

She barely heard the foil wrapper, or saw him smooth the protection over his erection. He didn't lie her flat on her back; he pulled her in close to his body, face to face. She felt him lift her leg so that it lay over his hip, opening her to him intimately.

And then he shifted down slightly, and she felt the blunt head of him at her slick entrance, and then with a surge of power his mouth found hers and his body penetrated hers so fully that stars danced before her eyes.

Her hands were clasped around his neck, hips locked with his. Nadim was buried inside her, and in that moment, before he started moving again, Iseult knew that whatever assurances she'd given herself earlier about not falling for him were lies, lies, lies.

Nadim started to move, slowly and powerfully, in and out. His mouth moved down her jaw and neck and Iseult couldn't think any more. He cupped her breast, and as he thrust again he took it into his mouth, sucking roughly, biting gently. Iseult's hand funnelled into his silky hair, holding him to her as her back arched into him even more, as her leg tightened around his hip, clasping him to her, while his powerful buttocks threatened to make her world explode.

And, feeling one long thrust deep inside her, Iseult couldn't hold back and did explode—and it was far more earth-shattering than anything she'd known before.

When Iseult woke the next morning to the alarm clock on her phone, she knew she was alone in the bed—on her front, spreadeagled in abandon. She immediately felt self-conscious and grabbed for the sheet, pulling it over her and lying on her back.

Her whole body felt sated and lethargic, as if some soporific drug had been injected into her veins. When she and Nadim had recovered last night, after making love *again*, Nadim had cradled her against him as her breath had finally returned to normal after the tumult. But then he'd extricated himself from her embrace, picked up his robe and left the room as quietly as he'd entered.

Iseult had heard the term *wham-bam, thank you, ma'am* before, but never really had a context for it. Now she did.

And yet, she had to ask herself angrily, what had she expected? She could be under no illusions. Nadim had been brutally clear and honest from the very start. What *had* she expected? Tender words of love? Hours of cuddling and hand-holding?

Despite the unwelcome realisation that perhaps this was how his wife had felt, Iseult felt her treacherous heart give a little lurch in longing, and suddenly she knew with a terrible misgiving that Nadim had the potential to destroy her.

That evening Iseult ached all over: from tension and from work. She'd held her head high all day, but it was clear in the way that everyone treated her now that they all knew about her new status in Nadim's life...and bed. People walked on eggshells around her, and she could only hope and pray that if she resolutely got on with the job as normal they'd soon forget about it...

To her intense relief Jamilah had treated her no differently. She'd given Iseult an enigmatic look, but then Iseult had noticed that the other woman had been distracted and slightly strained-looking herself. When she went looking for her at the end of the day, to see if anything was wrong, Jamilah had gone out somewhere.

Taking advantage of Jamilah's empty office, Iseult called home to speak to her brothers and sister and father, as it had been a few days. Putting down the phone on the conversation, she took a deep breath—just as Jamilah's door opened with a bang and Nadim stood there, glowering.

Immediately Iseult's protective instincts kicked in, and her back stiffened even as another part of her melted inside to see him dressed in a stunning suit and tie, every inch of him the urbane businessman again.

'Why aren't you up at the castle waiting for me?'

Iseult stood up, quivering from head to toe at his autocratic tone. 'I wasn't aware of any schedule I had to follow—perhaps there's some *Mistress to the Sheikh* guidebook I need to study?'

Nadim came in and closed the door behind him, instantly threatening. 'Still as impudent as ever. So much for hoping that passion might tame that tongue of yours.'

Iseult's shoulders straightened. 'I'm not some animal that can be *tamed*, Sheikh. Just because I've stupidly agreed to sleep with you it does not mean that

I've become lobotomised in the process. Strange as this might sound, it wasn't my life's ambition to become the mistress of a sheikh.'

To Iseult's utter surprise, Nadim threw his head back and laughed uproariously. He came even closer, eyes sparkling, and pulled a resisting Iseult into him.

She struggled and said, feeling curiously emotional all of a sudden, 'Don't laugh at me.'

Suddenly all mirth was gone as Nadim looked down into her eyes and said, almost musingly, 'I think that's why you're so good with thoroughbreds…you can sense their struggle against being tamed and they can sense your empathy…'

It was the first time anyone had articulated what Iseult had always felt instinctively.

And then he said huskily, all arrogance and autocracy gone, 'I thought we'd moved on from Sheikh? And you weren't stupid to agree to sleep with me…I think that was a very wise decision… In any case, you weren't going to be allowed to refuse.'

'I wasn't?' Iseult asked shakily, mesmerised by the tension in his body and his glittering gaze.

Nadim shook his head. 'No. I wouldn't have rested until I had you exactly where I wanted you.'

He pulled at the band holding her hair up in its habitual ponytail and she felt her hair fall down around her shoulders, saw how his eyes followed the movement. He was so close now she could feel the latent strength in his body, could feel him stir against her, and she had to fight not to squirm against him.

He looked down at her again and quirked his mouth. 'I don't think Jamilah would appreciate us making love on her desk, do you?'

Iseult shook her head faintly, a gush of liquid heat rushing to her groin at the sudden image of Nadim stripping and spreading her back on the desk to move between her legs and take her.

'Well, if we don't make a move soon, that's exactly what's going to happen. We're having dinner together this evening in my rooms, and I've bought you some gifts…'

Nadim watched a wary look cross Iseult's face as he took her hand to lead her from the room. He could still remember the hot irritation that had surged through him at finding she hadn't returned to her rooms. Through all his intensive meetings today he hadn't been able to concentrate—helplessly distracted when images of their night together last night had inserted themselves with dismaying frequency into his mind.

The hunger to see her again had been so powerful that when she hadn't been waiting meekly for him he'd seen red and come racing down to the stables—only to find her in Jamilah's office, evidently calling home.

Iseult let Nadim lead her out of the office and into his Jeep, parked just outside. All the way up to the castle silence hung around them like a cloak.

Once at the entrance to the castle he said, 'Hisham will come for you in an hour…'

She turned to go and he called her back, his face unreadable but his eyes so black she felt breathless. 'I'd like you to wear the gold dress…'

Before she could protest that she didn't have a gold dress he'd turned to walk away, and it was only when she walked into her room and saw Lina amidst what looked like an explosion of glittering paper and bags and boxes that she recalled what he had said about getting her gifts. Lina's face was uncovered, even though she still wore the veil, and she too seemed to be mesmerised enough to forget her new distance. Her eyes sparkled.

'Look, Miss Iseult! All this for you!'

Iseult felt a little stunned and weak. She sat on the bed, and then had to jump up when she realised she'd sat on a pair of shoes. She picked them up. They were gorgeous. Dark green suede, with diamanté details on one side. Heels so high they looked lethal.

Lina was in officious mode, and had obviously been given instructions. She herded Iseult to the bathroom now, where Iseult saw a full bath, complete with floating rose petals and lighted candles. Iseult resisted, feeling as though she could only tarnish such a seductive picture. Somehow in the desert it had been easier to take—as if she had matched the rugged terrain.

But Lina, for all her petiteness and delicacy, was surprisingly strong, and had Iseult stripped and in the bath before she quite knew how it had happened. Lying in the bath, feeling totally unlike herself, Iseult could hear the rustle of paper outside, and the clang of hangers as Lina hung things up. Every now and then there'd be a silence, and then just a long deep sigh as Lina obviously came across something too beautiful to resist sighing over.

But this was no fairytale. She was the Sheikh of al Saqr's mistress and he was just kitting her out.

If anything Iseult should be feeling insulted…angry… But when she walked back into her bedroom in just a towel, and saw Lina standing at the mirror holding up a vision of a golden dress, anger was all too elusive.

CHAPTER ELEVEN

LINA turned and held out the dress with reverent hands. It was a tunic made in what looked like pure gold, with intricate embroidery around the hem in deep iridescent silver. When Lina brought it closer, the colour shimmered in the light, showing a whole range of different shades of gold running through it.

On the bed lay a couple of wisps of underwear, also gold in colour. Iseult felt sweaty, and fear prickled over her skin. 'Lina, I can't wear this... I'll wear my jeans...'

But Lina whipped the towel off Iseult so fast that she yelped, and had no choice but to get into the underwear if she wanted to cover up. The bra looked minuscule, but it fitted like a glove. The pants were cut like French knickers. Lina handed her a pair of slim-fitting trousers in the same material as the dress and she put them on, followed by the dress.

It whispered down over her body and hips, cut with a daringly low V-neck, so that a tiny hint of lace from the bra could be seen in her shadowy cleavage.

'It's pure Indian silk, Miss Iseult.'

Lina sat her down and started to dry her hair, taking

it back on one side and holding it in place with an ornate, antique-looking comb, leaving the rest to fall over her shoulder. Then she put some kohl on her eyes, and mascara, making Iseult look almost as mysterious as the women she'd seen in the streets that day she'd gone out with Jamilah to buy clothes. After a moment Lina stood back to admire her handiwork and said, 'You are lovely, Miss Iseult.'

Iseult grimaced at her reflection. The truth was she almost didn't recognise herself, and this whole experience was so close to a dream she'd buried deep within her that she wasn't sure if she could stand without trembling all over.

Lina had disappeared, and now returned holding out a pair of kitten-heeled gold sandals. Iseult got up shakily and put them on, all fingers and thumbs on the delicate clasps until Lina bent down to help her.

Just then there was a knock on the outer door and Lina said, 'That'll be Hisham. He'll escort you to Sheikh Nadim's rooms.'

Iseult's cheeks burned. Did absolutely everyone know what was going on? Lina all but pushed her out through the door, and Iseult followed the slightly wizened man who led the way.

By the time they'd reached Nadim's room, which they'd climbed up another level to reach, Iseult's heart was thumping and she was dry-mouthed with fear. All she could imagine was that either Nadim wouldn't be there—it had all been some huge mistake—or that he'd take one look and laugh at her efforts to try and be…beautiful.

But Hisham was knocking, and the door was opening, and…there was Nadim. All Iseult's doubts fled in a flood of heat. He was dressed formally in a white shirt and black trousers, shirt open at the neck. He'd obviously not long showered, as his hair was still damp and curling slightly.

He said something indecipherable to Hisham, who melted away, and then he was reaching out a hand for Iseult and drawing her into his rooms. With her hand in his, she could only gape at the sheer magnificence of his suite. Gold and cream brocade, abundant fresh flowers...doors open and leading out onto a private patio that overlooked the entire complex, and the lights of Merkazad glittering in the distance against the dusky sky.

He let her go briefly, but Iseult hardly noticed she was so mesmerised by the view. Eventually she turned around and saw Nadim pouring a honey-coloured sparkling drink into two crystal glasses. She walked back in and Nadim handed her a glass. 'A toast,' he said.

Iseult held her glass up to his and Nadim said throatily, 'To you, Iseult. You are beautiful tonight.'

Immediately, despite his words, Iseult felt self-conscious and awkward. She blushed and took a sip of the sparkling liquid, nearly coughing when the bubbles fizzed effervescently down her throat. Nadim smiled and quirked a brow. 'Have you had champagne before?'

A little of Iseult's fire returned. 'Of course. I'm not a complete hick.' She smiled then too. 'But I'd wager that the champagne I've tasted isn't exactly of the same vintage as this.'

Nadim was transfixed by the smile curving Iseult's generous mouth. In truth he'd been transfixed since he'd seen her at his door with Hisham. He'd expected her to be lovely in the gold dress he'd picked out...but she was so much more than that. The material skimmed her curves, clung to the lush line of her breasts, her small waist, the surprisingly womanly flare of her hips.

Her hair shone like a glowing red flame against the gold and, just as he'd suspected they would, her eyes looked even tawnier. She walked away now, to look at something, and Nadim heard her ask, 'Is this your wife?'

Iseult knew she shouldn't have asked as soon as the words came out of her mouth and tension came into the room. She looked from the framed picture to Nadim warily, and then back again. The dark woman was incredibly pretty, and she was gazing up at a younger, softer-looking Nadim so adoringly that Iseult felt a physical pain pierce her heart.

'Yes,' he said briefly, curtly. 'That's Sara. I'm sorry. I should have put it away.'

Iseult disguised the dart of hurt. Despite everything he'd said, he had to have had *some* feelings for his wife—or else why would he keep such a memento close by? She turned away from it and said, 'Don't be ridiculous, Nadim, she was your wife. It'd be strange if you didn't have pictures around.'

He looked incredibly harsh in the luxuriant gold light of the many dim lamps, but he just said, 'The only ridiculous thing is how far away you are from me. Come over here.'

Iseult firmly shut the door on the pain that seeing the picture of his wife had engendered and walked over, saying lightly, 'You're so bossy. Has anyone ever told you that?'

He smiled then, a genuine smile, as if something had relaxed inside him, and reached for her hand as soon as she was close enough. 'No. Only you have the sheer audacity to insult the Sheikh of Merkazad.'

'Good thing, too, I'd say. It must be unbearable with all that bowing and scraping going on.'

They smiled at each other, and Iseult felt an alien lightness unfurling inside her. Just then a discreet knock sounded at the door, and Nadim emitted a brief instruction in Arabic.

In an instant the room seemed to be full of a stream of staff, entering carrying steaming plates of the most mouthwatering food. Nadim led her back out to the terrace, where a table had been set with candles flickering gently in the warm breeze.

With speed and economy of movement, plates and platters were laid out, and Hisham stood patiently by, asking if they needed anything else.

Nadim shook his head, and as the man turned to go Iseult said, *'Shukran.'*

When he'd left she turned to Nadim and saw the expression on his face. 'What?' she asked nervously.

'You've been learning Arabic?'

Iseult shrugged, feeling self-conscious again. 'Jamilah has been teaching me a few words.'

It was crazy for Nadim to feel suddenly jealous of Jamilah teaching Iseult Arabic, but he did. Feeling uncharacteristically out of control, he pulled out a chair for Iseult to sit down. When she moved her scent wrapped around him like a caress. He sat down opposite Iseult and poured them both some wine. He held up his glass, 'Well, if you'll permit me, perhaps this evening I can teach you a little about traditional Merkazadi food...'

A couple of hours later Iseult protested, putting up a hand. 'Please, no more food. I've never eaten so much in my life.'

Nadim reluctantly put down a plump and succulent date. Watching Iseult taste and eat the array of dishes and then feast on the dates had him so tightly wound that he had to exert some control over his rogue hormones.

Iseult sat back and let a delicious languour invade her veins. She'd never thought eating dinner had erotic possibilities, but she knew after sharing dinner with Nadim this evening she'd never sit at another table with him and not blush.

He'd dismissed the use of knives and forks and had fed her himself. Balls of mashed rice infused with delicate spices. Morsels of Kingfish that broke apart on his fingers so she had to stick out her tongue to catch them. Wine…and dates…fat dates…oozing with illicit sticky sweetness, washed down with strong, tart coffee called *khawa*.

He sat back and looked at her for a long moment, and then said, 'I thought you were too thin when I first met you.'

Iseult attempted humour to deflect the intensity that seemed to drench the air around them. 'So you're just trying to fatten me up?'

He sat forward. 'It must have been hard for you, covering for your father and trying to keep things going.'

Iseult blinked, shocked out of the languid desire that had been sneaking through her veins. Instant shame came back—the shame of her father's illness that they'd all done their best to cover up. Iseult's mouth twisted, and she played with her empty coffee cup. 'It wasn't that bad really…'

Nadim caught her eye and raised a brow. 'I know

how hard Jamilah works, and she has a whole team under her. I know how hard it is to run even moderate-sized stables. And then to have to deal with an alcoholic parent…'

Iseult was defensive. 'My father never got abusive or angry. He just…tried to drown his sorrows—literally.' Iseult shrugged minutely and looked out to the glittering view of Merkazad in the far distance, with the distinctive minaret of the mosque standing out. 'As for keeping things going…I never really had time to think about it.'

That bare explanation hid the sheer toil she'd endured on a daily basis, sometimes skipping school to work at home. Saying anything that might be construed as wanting sympathy had always been anathema to her.

Wanting to divert Nadim's intense regard, she remembered something he'd said in Ireland. She looked back at him. 'What did you mean when you said you knew what it was like to have everything you know jeopardised?'

Nadim was quiet for a long moment, and then stood from his chair, taking his glass of wine with him, and went to stand against the stone balustrade of the private balcony.

He spoke so quietly at first that Iseult had to strain to hear, and then silently she got up too and went to stand with her back to the view, just looking at Nadim's proud profile.

'It happened a couple of times. We'd always had an uneasy alliance with Al-Omar. We'd been gifted our independence many years before, but when the current Sultan's great-grandfather took control he wanted Merkazad back under his control. He never managed to attack, but the intention went down the line. When I was twelve we were attacked by the Sultan's father and taken by surprise as we hadn't had to defend ourselves for many years…'

Iseult was mesmerised, leaning on one elbow to listen. What Nadim spoke of was utterly fantastical.

'Salman and I were woken in the middle of the night by my mother and told to get out of bed and sneak down through secret passages, but we were caught.'

'What happened?'

'We were held prisoner in an ancient jail in the basement of the castle.'

Iseult gasped. 'But you were the ruling family. Isn't there some sort of protocol for that?'

Nadim's mouth twisted. He flicked her a glance. 'Not in this world.'

Shakily Iseult asked, 'How long were you kept prisoner for?'

Almost carelessly Nadim said, 'Nearly three months. I think it affected my brother much more profoundly. For some reason our captors used to delight in tormenting him. They would take him out of the jail for hours on end, and when they returned him he wouldn't say a word. I tried to make them take me…but they'd just beat me back.'

He continued briskly, 'We were lucky. Our Bedu neighbours came to help us. Our invaders had grown complacent, thinking that we would just rot away in the dungeon…but we had powerful friends who were more interested in keeping us a sovereign state. And my father was a well-loved ruler. They attacked one night and we were freed. But everything was gone…the stables and stud were ransacked…they'd shot all the horses. The castle was looted of all but the murals on the walls…'

Iseult shook her head, trying to understand how it must have felt, first of all to be incarcerated and then to come out to find everything changed or gone.

He turned to face her, twirling the glass of wine between his long fingers. 'And then my parents died in a plane crash when I was sixteen and Salman twelve. Instantly we were under threat again, but this time we were more prepared as my father had enlisted warriors to keep watch over every strategic weak point in the border, so the ruler of Al-Omar couldn't attack again.'

'The Sultan's father died while I was in school in England, with Salman, and for the first time we knew we might be safe. Advisors ran the country while I finished my education, until I reached the age of twenty-one and could legally take over as Sheikh and ruler…'

Iseult realised something then. 'Jamilah must have been so young when her parents died.'

'Yes, she was only six. She stayed here and went to school in Merkazad. I made sure she was cared for by members of our extended family.'

'But now there's peace? You said that you're friends with the current Sultan?'

Nadim nodded. 'We went to school together in England.' He smiled. 'At first we hated each other, and used to get into fights at every opportunity. But then we discovered a mutual interest in peace and living in a democratic and progressive society and were bonded by our ideals. After his father died we vowed to forge an iron-clad alliance that would stand for many genera-tions to come…'

Hearing this made Iseult feel humbled. From such an early age he'd been aware of responsibility and duty.

In many ways they were similar, and yet…*not*. Iseult's responsibilities had been confined to a much narrower world. And when she thought of that she was reminded of the great yawning chasm between Nadim's life and hers. Some day he would find a suitable bride and marry again, go on to have heirs to continue his legacy, and she— Her mind halted when Nadim put down his wine glass on the table and reached for her.

As if pulled by a magnet stronger than she could resist, she went into his arms and shook with emotion— emotion that he was effortlessly arousing.

Nadim trailed a finger down the silky smoothness of Iseult's cheek. He felt slightly shell shocked. He'd just blithely spilled his entire life's secrets to a woman when he'd never felt the desire to do so before. Lovers had tried to get him to tell what they thought were fantastic exotic tales, but he'd seen the manipulative glitter in their eyes, as if they'd thought it would inspire more intimacy.

The only other woman who had known everything had been his wife, Sara. And that was because she'd come from here and had lived through everything they had as the daughter of one of his father's closest allies. He felt bitterness rise when he thought of it; it was one of the reasons she'd been deemed so *perfect* for him.

But Iseult… What was it about this woman and the effortless feeling of kinship she evoked within him? She was looking down…away. And he jealously wanted her eyes on him… He tipped up her chin with a finger and felt her clench her jaw slightly. What he saw in her eyes was something serious and deep. It sent tendrils of trepidation through him, even amidst a heady sweet feeling he'd never experienced before.

To drive away the regret that he'd said anything at

all, and the fleeting panic because he recognised the look in her eyes, he bent his head and kissed her soft mouth, willing passion to come and obliterate any intellectual thought.

Hours later—her beautiful golden dress, underwear and hair-comb long gone—Iseult lay sprawled in inelegant abandon over Nadim's equally naked body. She was pressing little kisses over his chest. His skin was still dewed with moisture and it tasted tangy and musky.

Within seconds of Nadim kissing her out on the balcony everything had been forgotten as intense desire had taken over, obliterating anything but sating their physical needs. She had a strong suspicion that he regretted telling her all he had, but she was too lethargic right now to let that thought bother her.

Iseult put her cheek onto Nadim's chest and felt his heart beating, strong and steadily. She'd never felt so deeply sated in all her life, as if she was drunk and yet never more sober…a heady mix.

Idly, she trailed her hand across Nadim's chest, and then lifted her head and propped her chin on her hand. His eyes were like two dark pools, making her heart kick all over again and fresh tendrils of desire coil through her.

'Do you know,' she mused, 'I've seen you in jeans and a T-shirt…and a suit and tie…and your traditional robes…' She smiled and started to trail her free hand down Nadim's chest, and lower, watching how his eyes darkened even more.

'But I think I like you naked best of all…' Her hand wrapped around him in an intimate caress, and she exulted when she felt him harden and swell under her touch.

He brought his hands to her arms and with an easy strength flipped them, so that Iseult was under him. He hovered over her and between her legs, where his hair-roughened thighs made her move her hips.

In an unconsciously sensual move Iseult bent one leg and ran her foot down the back of Nadim's leg, the soft silky skin of her inner thigh against his hip.

With a growl, he caught that leg and held it. He bent his head to hers and said, 'Remember what I said, Iseult...don't fall in love with me.'

Iseult tried to stem the instant gush of pain, and in that second knew that it was already too late. Somewhere it had happened; it could have even been just now out on the balcony, when he'd told her so dispassionately about his turbulent history, or it could have been in that tent in the desert when he'd first made love to her, or it could have been that moment she'd first seen him in Ireland, but somewhere along the way she'd fallen irrevocably in love.

She knew she couldn't deny it, and that vulnerability made her say defiantly, 'As long as you don't fall in love with me.'

He smiled, and to Iseult's eyes in that moment he looked incredibly sad. He didn't need to say it, but it was written all over his face: *I won't*. And then his mouth met hers, and she twined her hands around his neck, feeling alternately angry with him and absurdly tender, and irritated that all he had to do was kiss her to scramble any rational thought.

CHAPTER TWELVE

'I'D LIKE you to come to the Sultan of Al-Omar's birthday celebrations with me.'

Iseult just looked at Nadim. He was leaning nonchalantly against the door of Devil's Kiss's stable, looking far too gorgeous for his own good in faded jeans and a T-shirt. Earlier she'd watched him break in a new yearling, and it had been sheer poetry in motion.

She stood now, keeping a hand on Devil's Kiss, as if he could keep her rooted in reality. The thought of leaving the cocoon of Merkazad was slightly threatening. 'But…where is it? When?'

Nadim hid the dart of irritation that she wasn't more enthralled at the prospect. 'It starts tomorrow night in B'harani, for family and close friends, and then the main celebration is on Saturday night, when the *crème de la crème* of world society will come to fawn and ogle, and women will vie with one another for the Sultan's favour.'

Iseult felt an equal mix of horror at the thought of such an event and a wild surge of excitement. She gave a little wry smile, hiding her trepidation. 'Do I have a choice?'

Nadim smiled too, and it was the smile of a wolf. 'Of course not. I was merely allowing you the illusion of choice. If you say no then I'll instruct Lina to do whatever is necessary to render you helpless, and merely carry you there over my shoulder.'

A warm pool of desire settled in Iseult's belly. A little breathlessly she said, 'Well, in that case, I'd love to join you…'

But then she bit her lip as all joking fled and old insecurities rose. It was one thing dressing up for Nadim in his own private rooms, but another thing entirely in public. 'But, Nadim…I'm not…I've never been to anything fancier than a family wedding. I won't know what to do or say…'

'Nonsense,' Nadim declared arrogantly. 'You'll be with me. That's all you need to worry about.'

But the following evening it felt as if Iseult had a lot to worry about. Lina had travelled ahead to B'harani with some of Nadim's retinue early that afternoon, and now she and Nadim were getting into a helicopter which was going to fly them to the same airfield in Al-Omar that she'd flown into just a few weeks before.

Feeling more and more apprehensive and tense, Iseult was silent for the journey, taking in the mountainous landscape below them, looking when Nadim pointed out various things. At the airfield a small private plane was waiting, and the disparity between how she'd flown in and her position now didn't escape her, highlighting the impossible chasm between Nadim's world and hers, and also the tenuous nature of their relationship. Just when would he lose interest? After this weekend? In a week? A month?

After they'd boarded, and were sitting in plush seats, Nadim opened a laptop and became engrossed in whatever he was doing, so Iseult just looked out of the window, glad he wasn't scrambling her brain. The flight was a relatively short thirty minutes, and she sucked in a deep breath when she saw the intricate glittering web of B'harani laid out below as they came in to land. She could make out soaring skyscrapers which glinted in the setting sun, and she could see the Arabian ocean in the distance, like a flat sheet of dark blue.

She turned to Nadim, who had put the laptop away and was watching her. 'I didn't realise B'harani was so big...it's a proper city.'

She winced inwardly, hating that she sounded so gauche. But Nadim just nodded. 'Yes, it's got a population of nearly a million. It's a thriving metropolis. Tourism is a huge industry here for the Sultan, along with the oil fields out in the desert... He too has stables and runs a stud.'

Iseult smiled. 'Ah...competition?'

Nadim looked comically affronted. 'No competition at all. He knows who the superior horseman is.'

Iseult thought privately that from what she'd seen very few horse-breeders and trainers would be superior to Nadim.

Just then the plane touched down with a minute bump and they landed.

On disembarking, Iseult saw three limos waiting, all with tinted windows. The air was hot, acrid, and she could taste the salt from the sea. Dusk was turning the sky a bruised colour, and the skyscrapers in the distance made her feel as if she'd travelled to another planet. Merkazad was a world away. But

Iseult had a feeling that this place wouldn't lay claim to her the same way that Merkazad had from the moment she'd seen it.

After speeding along a sleek highway that cut right through the towering skyscrapers they turned a corner and drove up what looked like a private road. Right in the centre of the city, a huge, imposing fortress loomed from behind giant walls. It was stunning, soaring and breathtaking.

Nadim said, 'This is the Hussein Palace. Sultan Sadiq's ancestral home.'

Iseult looked at him aghast. 'We're staying here?'

Nadim nodded, obviously amused by Iseult's awe. She made a face at him and looked out of the window again, to see that they were driving into a huge court-yard where what seemed like hundreds of staff in pristine white uniforms waited to greet them.

Nadim was dressed formally in his robes, and Lina had left out a smart trouser suit for Iseult that morning. She was grateful now, as a flurry of activity burst around them and they were summarily ushered into the entrance of the palace.

A huge archway dominated the entrance, and then staff were leading Nadim and Iseult further into the stunning complex, through another open-air courtyard and into a blissfully cool atrium with more soaring ceilings.

Iseult gasped with delight when she saw a multi-coloured bird fly in and out again. One of the staff, a smiling girl who wore a long white *abeyya* but no veil, stopped outside a door and indicated for Iseult to enter.

Nadim sent her a look, and she saw that he was being shown through another door just down the hall. Iseult went in and her eyes widened. The opulence she'd grown used to at Nadim's castle should have inured her to luxury, but it hadn't.

The room was massive, dressed in cool, peaceful whites. There was an enormous four-poster bed, and a bathroom with a marble sunken bath which looked big enough for a rugby team. Floor-to-ceiling French doors led out to a private garden, complete with lush grass and blooming trees. She heard a door open and saw Nadim step out just a few feet away.

'It's a double suite…our rooms are adjoining.'

'Oh…' Iseult said faintly, the stunning surroundings paling into insignificance as she took in Nadim, his skin so exotically dark against the cream of his robes.

He arched a brow. 'I think a bath before dinner would be nice.'

Iseult said immediately, 'I showered just before we left…' Then she saw the look in his eye and remembered the huge bath and blushed. 'Oh…'

Nadim held out a hand. 'Yes, *oh*. Come here, Iseult…'

A couple of hours later Iseult blushed again in the mirror, as Lina did up her dress at the back, just thinking about what had taken place in Nadim's bath. She'd barely made it out in time to come and meet Lina in her room, and she blushed even harder now, when Lina said, 'You're so flushed, Miss Iseult. Is it the heat?'

Iseult made some strangled reply and meekly followed Lina away from the mirror to sit down, so she could do her hair. After what seemed like an age of pulling and curling, with something that looked like an instrument of torture, Lina stood back and gestured for Iseult to look in the mirror.

Immediate fear gripped Iseult's insides as she approached the reflective glass as if she were walking the plank. *How* had she forgotten this for a moment? How could she be putting herself back in this position again? To be publicly humiliated? Because no matter what Lina had done, no matter how expensive the dress was, she was still tomboy Iseult O'Sullivan from a farm in Ireland.

She stopped in front of the mirror and for a moment couldn't look. And then she did. For a wild moment she didn't recognise the girl in front of her. She wore a long, fitted satin strapless dress in a dark greeny-blue, with an ostrich feather detail over one shoulder. Her skin looked very white, and her breasts swelled enticingly over the bodice. Long glittering green earrings swung against her neck, and Lina had somehow curled her impossibly straight hair and lifted it up and away into a loose chignon. Amidst the glossy red waves a diamanté comb sparkled.

Iseult felt tears burn the back of her eyes, a lump tighten her throat. Just then a knock came to the interconnecting door, and before Iseult could compose herself Nadim strolled in with proprietorial ease.

In an instant he'd politely dismissed Lina, and all Iseult could do was look at him through the mirror. He came to stand behind her, stunning in a black tuxedo. His jaw was tight, and she saw a muscle clench.

He noticed the sheen in her eyes and turned her around, frowning. 'What's wrong?'

Iseult shook her head and looked down, desperately trying to stem the flood of incipient tears, mortified. 'No…nothing…I just—I don't think I can do this. I'm not made for this kind of thing.'

He tipped up her chin. 'You're made for me, Iseult, and you will walk by my side. You are beautiful...do you not see how beautiful you are?'

'I'm not beautiful. Really, I'm not. We'll go into that room and you'll see...and you'll be embarrassed.'

Nadim thought cynically for a moment that Iseult was just fishing for a compliment, but then he saw the genuine distress in her eyes. The genuine disbelief. He shook his head. 'Someone has obviously made you feel that you aren't beautiful. Who was it? Your father?'

Iseult shook her head fiercely. 'No. It was just...' She sucked in a shuddering breath and tried to regain control, sure he wouldn't want to hear of her schoolgirl humiliation. 'I've never been the girly type. I'm not used to this. I'm more at home in a stables or in a field...'

Nadim turned Iseult back to face the mirror, and with his hands on her shoulders bent his head and pressed a heart-meltingly sweet kiss to her cheek. 'You can't hide in the stables for ever,' he said. 'You are beautiful...stunning.' He kissed her jaw. 'Here...' Then he kissed where her neck met her shoulder. 'And here...and everywhere. You will be the envy of every other woman.'

His eyes compelled hers to his in the mirror, until a very fledgling feeling started to burgeon within her— a feeling that felt scarily like *belief*. Nadim turned her around again and said, 'I have something for you.'

He handed her an ornate red box with gold edging. Iseult opened it to reveal a pure gold bottle nestled in white velvet. She looked up at Nadim. 'What is it?'

He quirked a smile. 'Al-Omar is famous for its perfume. It's one I had specially commissioned for you.'

Iseult's heart clenched at the sheer seduction of Nadim, and she wished he wasn't charming her so easily. If he was more perfunctory she could cope; she could pack ice around her heart.

She put the box down with a shaking hand and opened the bottle, taking a tentative sniff before spraying a tiny bit on her wrist. It smelled like an intoxicating mix of delicate roses, together with musk and a hint of tantalising spices.

And as if reading her mind, Nadim said dryly, 'I think it captures your personality. There's amber in there too, because it reminded me of your eyes...'

Speechless, Iseult let Nadim take the bottle out of her hand and spray a tiny bit on her neck, before rubbing it in with a finger. Then he held out her arm and found the delicate skin at her inner elbow and rubbed there. Then he sprayed another bit just above her cleavage. By the time he was finished Iseult was breathing unevenly and her legs were weak.

Nadim put down the perfume and took her hand to lead her out. At the door Iseult stopped him and said huskily, 'Thank you for the perfume... You didn't have to get me anything, but I love it...'

Nadim fought not to let the artlessness of her words grip him tight, like a vice. It only reminded him again of how different she was from other women, and of what a risk he was taking with her. But even so...he knew he couldn't stop.

He just tugged her along and said, 'We'll be late for dinner.'

A couple of hours later Iseult was still in awe of the splendour around them. So much for a gathering for close family and friends. She smiled wryly. There had to be at least two hundred people there, and one or two A-list actors even she recognised.

She'd met Sultan Sadiq Ibn Kamal Hussein before dinner. He was a man cut from the same cloth as Nadim. Tall, handsome and powerfully built. He was also dressed in a tuxedo, and his unusual light blue eyes stood out. He wore an air of jaded cynicism, though, and his forbidding looks to approaching women made Iseult feel sorry for them.

When he'd bent low and taken her hand to press a kiss to the back of it Nadim had pulled her close with a possessive arm that had sent a thrill through her. She'd had to tell herself not to read anything into it. Nadim was no different from this man in many ways.

She saw the tall, debonair Sultan in the distance now, surrounded by a fawning crowd, and wondered if he too had a mistress.

Just then Iseult noticed someone else approaching them, and exclaimed happily, 'Jamilah!' She looked at Nadim. 'I didn't know Jamilah would be here. We could have come together.'

Nadim frowned and said, 'I didn't know she was planning on coming...'

They embraced when Jamilah reached them; she looked even more stunning than usual in a dark royal blue dress that fell in a swirl of silk from just above her bust. Her glossy black hair was tied up in an elaborate chignon, but her face was pale and strained-looking.

Instantly Iseult felt concerned. 'Jamilah, what is it?'

Jamilah smiled tightly. 'Nothing at all.'

But as Iseult watched Jamilah saw something or someone behind them, and went even more pale.

Iseult turned around and saw a very tall, strikingly handsome man approaching. A jolt of recognition went through her, even though she'd never seen him before in her life.

She sensed Nadim tense beside her too, and when the other man arrived—so like Nadim in many ways but so different—Nadim said, 'Iseult, I'd like you to meet my brother Salman…'

Iseult shook his hand, but even she could see that he wasn't interested in her or Nadim. He had eyes only for Jamilah, who muttered something about finding someone and fled across the room. Salman watched her go, and Iseult thought she'd never seen anyone look so haunted in all her life. She'd heard gossip around the stables that he was known internationally as the Playboy Sheikh, and rarely came home, but now she could only think of what he and Nadim had been through as young boys.

With the bare minimum of conversation Salman went to leave too, but Nadim stopped him for a moment and said fiercely, 'Don't you think you should leave her alone?'

Salman looked at Nadim, his dark eyes flashing a warning that Iseult knew well as she'd seen it before. 'Stay out of this, Nadim.'

And then he was gone. Iseult took a deep breath and felt shaky all of a sudden. For a moment there she'd had a vision of how she was going to be reacting in the future, when Nadim had dumped her for his next mistress, or even a wife. At the thought of not being able to be a part of that, she felt a physical pain grip her belly.

Iseult's melancholic mood after witnessing Nadim's exchange with his brother and Jamilah's obvious distress had lingered through the rest of the evening and into the night, even when Nadim had made love to her with an almost fierce abandon, taking them both to a level of ecstasy that had left her shattered.

That melancholy rose again now, as she stood at the wall of the garden outside their rooms and looked out over the stunning city of B'harani in the distance, just beyond the huge walls of the palace.

But all she could see ahead of her was inevitable self-destruction if she continued on this path with Nadim.

She was also very afraid that the longer she indulged herself in this fairytale world of beautiful clothes and a personal maid and being made over on a daily basis, the more deluded she would become in thinking she *was* that kind of person.

Iseult knew herself well enough to believe that while she was sensible enough not to get sucked into that world immediately, it would be headier and more seductive than even she might be able to resist if it went on for much longer. And the mere thought of seeing Nadim take another mistress, or even a wife, nearly made her double over with pain.

A sound came from behind her, and she had a split second of composing herself before she felt a naked body at her back and strong, familiar arms snake around her waist. Iseult closed her eyes and leant back into Nadim, a sudden lump tightening her throat despite her best efforts.

Luckily he couldn't see her face, and when he started to kiss the sensitive back of her neck and said huskily, 'Come back to bed…' Iseult let him take her by the hand and lead her inside. Weakly she told herself that she would give herself this weekend here in B'harani to indulge every aspect of this fairytale moment in time, but that as soon as they were back in Merkazad she had to end this affair.

CHAPTER THIRTEEN

'WE NEED to talk.'

The four words guaranteed to strike fear into the hearts of men everywhere and make them feel weak at the knees—for all the wrong reasons.

Iseult was looking at herself in her bathroom mirror. She tried again. 'Look, Nadim, we need to talk…about *us*.'

She winced and made a face at her reflection. No matter how she said it, it still sounded like dialogue from a bad daytime soap opera.

Just then Lina appeared behind her, and Iseult started.

'Sheikh Nadim is waiting for you.'

Iseult ignored Lina's expressive look at her clothes, and took a deep breath and turned around. She made her way from her room up to Nadim's palatial suite. He was expecting her for dinner. They'd returned from B'harani the day before yesterday, and this was the first moment she would have alone with him since their return.

The second night of Sultan Sadiq's festivities had been as lavish and decadent as Nadim had said it would be. Lina had dressed Iseult in another full-length couture gown, this time in a deep red. And Nadim had presented her with a stunning set of ruby necklace and earrings to wear with it, not listening to her protests for a second. Weakly, Iseult had given herself up to the headiness of it all, guiltily relishing her finite time.

There had been close to a thousand guests, and a world-famous iconic rock band who, despite being in their twilight years, had strutted their stuff like men half their ages. Women on stilts in dresses made entirely of fresh flowers had moved among the guests. Enormous and intricate ice fountains had melted as the evening wore on into pools full of rare multi-coloured fish. Trays of vintage champagne had abounded, and belly dancers had flitted through the guests like exotic birds of prey, reminding Iseult hotly of her own brief foray into that world, and what had happened...

There had also been a charity auction in aid of hundreds of different charities, which had precipitated a spending frenzy that had escalated into the millions. Nadim had contributed some of the most exorbitant sums, clearly in league with Sadiq to up the ante by encouraging competition among the wealthy who hadn't seemed to know when to stop.

He had confided dryly to Iseult at one stage, 'Sadiq likes to lull his monied guests into a false sense of security by putting on a lavish show and then doing his darnedest to extract as much out of them as possible. When they leave after the weekend they're invariably stumped as to how he managed to get them to part with so much money *again*.'

Iseult had tried to sound upbeat, even though with each passing moment she'd grown more melancholic.

'A regular modern-day Robin Hood, with you as his wing man...'

Nadim had shrugged negligently. 'It's not many people in this world who can command a crowd full of some of the most powerful titans of industry, and Sadiq makes the most of it.' He'd winked at Iseult. '*With* a little help from me.'

Iseult was nearing Nadim's door now, and her mind emptied. As much as she knew it would be easy enough to indulge in another night of the dream...perhaps even another couple of weeks...she knew she couldn't. She had to take responsibility for her actions.

Her stomach churning, she knocked lightly and then went in, having a flash of *déjà vu* to when she'd gone into the study at home to have her first discussion with Nadim.

He looked up, smiling, when she walked in, but his smile quickly faded when he saw that she hadn't changed out of her jeans and shirt—the clothes she'd been working in. She closed the door behind her, but didn't move into the room.

He frowned. 'Why haven't you changed?'

Iseult welcomed his censorial tone, allowing her hackles to rise. 'So as your mistress I have to dress to a code? I can't just come up here and be comfortable in jeans?'

Iseult saw how Nadim's body tensed. His eyes narrowed on her. 'What's going on, Iseult?'

Iseult bit her lip and then dived in. 'What's going on is that this affair is over.' She finished in a rush, 'I don't want to be your mistress any more.'

For a long moment Nadim said nothing, and Iseult wondered if she'd imagined saying the words. But then she saw that dangerous look come into Nadim's eyes, and how he literally seemed to shut himself away. Her heart broke. It was starting already.

He put his hands in his pockets and rocked back on his heels. 'What's this about, Iseult? You want more? You want to extract some kind of commitment? You saw something at the weekend and you want a slice of that world permanently? I thought you were different, but perhaps I was naïve to think you wouldn't be swayed by what you've seen.'

Iseult felt sick at his obvious cynicism, and raised a hand in a slashing movement. '*No*. How can you think that?'

Nadim said almost musingly, 'I don't know, Iseult, it's a very seductive world. Are you telling me that out of all the women there last weekend you're the only one who could walk away from it all and *not* want it?'

His voice turned slightly sneering now. 'Or perhaps I've got it wrong. Perhaps you fancy your chances with Sultan Sadiq? I can assure you that we're quite matched when it comes to our fortunes…'

Before Iseult could answer the door opened abruptly, jostling her forward. It was staff arriving with dinner. One look from Nadim made them all melt away instantly.

He looked at her again, dark eyes spearing right through her. 'So is that it? You want more?'

I want you! Iseult wanted to shout, but didn't. Instead she said, 'I want to go home, Nadim. I don't want to see you any more.' For a split second Iseult thought she might bluff her way out of this—confirm his cynicism and protect herself in the process. Her mouth twisted. 'You see, you are partly right. I'm afraid that I'm going to get too used to all of this.' She looked around the room and gestured with a hand. 'And then one day, when you've grown weary of me, I'll be sent back to the stables.'

But then she looked back at him, and knew she couldn't bluff her way out of this by pretending to have grown spoilt. The look of haughty cynicism on Nadim's face was too much to bear.

Defeat laced her voice as she said, 'But it's not the trappings that concern me, Nadim. I've enjoyed every minute of it, but none of it matters really. I'm afraid that it's *you* I want, and you I know I can't have.'

Nadim frowned and tried to understand. He wanted to command Iseult to come closer. She stood near the door in those dusty jeans and shirt, looking as if she was about to bolt like a skittish horse. But he couldn't. Something held him back—some instinct.

'You're my mistress. You have my undivided attention.' He couldn't stop his voice sounding harsh, curt.

Iseult's body flinched slightly, and she hugged her arms around her belly in a classic unconscious gesture of defence. 'For now. But what happens when you lose interest? Obviously you've thought this through, and you'll be able to deal with seeing me every day while you take a new mistress. But I won't be able to deal with that.'

Nadim was growing impatient now. He put out a hand, silently instructing Iseult to come to him, even though an ominous sense of foreboding warned him to be careful. 'You're thinking about something in the future, Iseult. I've no plans to end this any time soon. Come here.'

She shook her head, her bright hair glinting deep russet in the lights. 'No. This is as far as I can go.'

Nadim dropped his hand, and his sense of foreboding increased just before Iseult hitched up her chin and said with quiet dignity, 'I'm afraid that I've done the exact thing you were so intent that I shouldn't do, Nadim: I've fallen in love with you.'

For a second her words didn't register. Everything was muffled, as if coming from far away, and Nadim actually had the very disturbing sensation for the first time in his life that he might faint. With a supreme act of will he stayed standing and felt anger rise. Anger at himself, for not trusting his instincts all along, and irrational anger at Iseult, for letting her emotions get involved. Anger that she was ruining this. And anger that she'd allowed him the power to hurt her. He'd learnt nothing.

'I don't believe you. You just want something from me. What is it? Commitment? An allowance? The promise of security for your family at home?'

She shook her head sadly. 'The only thing I want from you, Nadim, is the one thing I know you can't give me. Your love.'

An intense unnamed emotion rising up within him made Nadim lash out. He was barely aware of what he was saying any more—only aware that he had to push Iseult and her words back...far, far away. Everything he'd constructed around himself since Sara had died was being comprehensively threatened.

His voice was faintly scathing. 'What would you know about love?'

Iseult went very still before him, and immediately after he'd said the words he wished them unsaid. She paled in the dim light and turned away, her back looking too delicate. Nadim even reached out a hand, but dropped it when she turned back. Instead of the fire he'd expected, *wanted*, to see in her eyes, they looked dead now. And that was far worse.

Something within him was intensely moved by her innate dignity, compounded when she hitched her chin and looked him straight in the eye, unflinchingly. 'More than you, it would appear. I lost the two people I loved most in the world before I was thirteen and my world fell apart. I know about feeling so responsible for the people you love most that you can't sleep at night. I know about struggling so hard to make ends meet that it consumes you to the point where you forget you have choices in your life—but you don't care because you're doing it for someone you love.'

Nadim opened his mouth, but Iseult unwrapped her arms from her middle and cut him off with a slashing gesture of her hand. She moved a bit closer. Fire was returning to her eyes, faint colour to her cheeks. But Nadim didn't feel comforted. He felt as if he was watching something very precious break in front of his eyes.

The fierce look on her face forbade Nadim from speaking.

'I've fallen in love with you and I wish to God that I hadn't—believe me.' She smiled, but it was tight. 'Don't worry, you were perfectly clear all along the way, so I have no one to blame but myself. But I know it'll destroy me to continue to indulge in this dream world only to have it ripped away when you've had enough of this affair… I've lost too much already, Nadim. I can't wait passively by just to lose you too…'

The words died away into a heavy tense silence. Iseult felt numb. She couldn't believe she'd just said all she had, but his obvious horror at her declaration and the shameful surge of hope he'd dampened had sent a white-hot surge of anger through her: anger at herself for being so stupid. At no point had she intended this outpouring of her innermost feelings, and yet she knew now, facing him across this room, that she couldn't have contained it.

'That's why I want to go home, Nadim,' she said. 'To keep me here would be the worst form of cruelty, and I know you won't do that.'

She challenged him across the room with her eyes. Nadim looked as if a lorry had just run into him. His face had leached of colour, his eyes were like two stark pools of black in his face.

In a harsh voice she'd never heard before he said, 'I don't want you to leave, Iseult. I want you to stay and be my mistress. I can't promise how long our liaison will last, but I can promise that you will be looked after—no matter what.' He continued, 'But if you insist that you cannot divorce your feelings from our physical relationship, then I will have to let you go.'

Iseult wasn't sure how she was still standing. She couldn't feel her legs any more, and her heart felt as if it was tearing in two. Somehow she managed to find her voice. 'Then I have to go.'

She turned to leave. As she put her hand on the door handle she heard from behind her, 'You won't even stay for Devil's Kiss?'

Iseult's torn heart clenched hard, and she closed her eyes for a moment. Her deluded brain could almost believe for a second that she'd heard something desperate in Nadim's voice, but it had to be her imagination. She couldn't bear to turn around and see the coldly arrogant look that would be on his face.

Realisation struck home hard: Nadim had somehow managed to eclipse even Devil's Kiss. And, no, she couldn't even stay for him.

Not able to say another word, Iseult just let her silence speak her answer and left the room, closing the door softly behind her.

Nadim stood looking at the door, speechless and motionless for a long moment. In a blinding flash he realised that no matter what he'd just said Iseult had got to him on an emotional level he'd never experienced before. He turned around and, seeing something, went over to the small table where the photo of his wife sat in a frame. Her sweetly smiling face cut him straight to the quick and mocked him for the revelation—almost as if she was saying, *Now you know what it feels like.*

In a quick flash of anger so intense that it made his vision blur Nadim took the picture and threw it violently against a wall, where it shattered and fell to the ground.

CHAPTER FOURTEEN

ISEULT'S alarm went off and she stretched out a hand to turn it off, snuggling back under her warm duvet for another minute. The contrast between where she was now and where she'd been up until just a few days ago couldn't be more pronounced. It was winter in Ireland and it was dark outside—and freezing. With sickening inevitability she couldn't help her thoughts gravitating to the tall, dark, hard man who had turned her life around and upside down.

Missing Nadim was a physical ache—especially at night in bed. After their last conversation things had happened with scary swiftness; Nadim had obviously been eager to see the back of her and get on with his life. Jamilah had come to Iseult, and the two women had shared a look that spoke volumes. It had been Jamilah who had escorted Iseult to the plane in Al-Omar, driving her herself, after Iseult had said an emotional farewell to Devil's Kiss. Both women had been tearful saying goodbye, and Iseult had extracted a promise from Jamilah that she'd visit Ireland soon.

Iseult had left a note for Nadim in her room with a simple message:

Nadim, thank you for making me feel beautiful.
It means more than you could ever know… With
my love, always, Iseult.

Chagrin burned her now to think of it. Even then she
hadn't been able to drum up the necessary self-defence
to protect herself. She'd gushed again. She might as
well have ripped her own heart out and handed it to him
on a platter along with a knife and fork.

And then, guiltily, she'd seen the exquisite small
golden bottle of perfume that Nadim had gifted her, and
hadn't been able to leave it behind, so now she tortured
herself every day with the scent that reminded her of
him indelibly.

Resolutely she threw back the warm cover and sat up
to put her feet on the cold wooden floor. It was over. The
fairytale had come to an end. She'd been greeted at
home by Mrs O'Brien's joyful tears, her father's bone-
crushing hug, Murphy's slobbering tongue, and a farm
and stud that had been comprehensively turned around
in the short time she'd been gone. But they still needed
her here. She was being kept busy from six a.m. until
ten p.m., and that was the way she would get through
this dark tunnel.

That evening, with darkness falling rapidly under a
threatening sky, Iseult stood looking at the gallops,
wrapped up against the cold in jeans and a polo neck
and a thick parka jacket, with her favourite flat cap on
her head. The last colt had just been returned to the
stables for the evening by one of the new stablehands.

She was just realising that she was standing in exactly the same spot where Nadim had stood when she'd

first laid eyes on him when she heard the low rumble of a powerful engine behind her.

Not expecting any visitors that evening, Iseult turned to see who it was—and her blood stopped in her veins when she saw a silver Jeep with tinted windows. And then the door opened and a familiar tall, dark figure got out. It was only the sound of the door shutting that made Iseult move jerkily away from the fence.

She thought she might be hallucinating, and spoke as much to convince herself that she wasn't as to acknowledge him. 'Nadim.'

He was dressed in dark jeans and a jumper, a worn black leather jacket. And he looked so exotic against the grey leaden skies that Iseult couldn't take another step in case she fell down.

For a wild and exhilarating second she thought that he might have actually come for *her*—and then stomach-churning realisation hit her like a punch in the gut when she remembered how cold he'd been, how quickly he'd got her out of Merkazad. How he hadn't even said goodbye.

She walked forward and stumbled slightly, heart palpitating now with humiliation that for a second she'd thought— Ruthlessly she focused her wayward mind. 'You're here to see my father…or…or Peter the manager…? Well, Peter's gone home, but my father is up in the house. If you want to come up…'

Panic was rising through Iseult in waves—panic that he'd seen something of her helpless yearning reaction. He was standing there so implacably, looking so hard and stern, with dark stubble lining his jaw.

She'd never thought for a moment that she'd have to face him again so soon. This cruelty knew no bounds, and if she'd had the co-ordination she'd have marched over to him and hit him. Panic taking complete control now, Iseult whirled away and started to walk up the drive, not even feeling her legs move.

'Iseult, wait.'

Iseult stopped, breathing hard, but didn't turn around. She couldn't.

'I haven't come here to see your father or Peter. I've come to see you.'

Damn that exhilaration. It was snaking through her veins again. Still, resolutely, Iseult wouldn't turn around, terrified he'd see her reaction.

'I don't want to see you. I think you'd have to agree that we both know where we stand.' Her voice became bitter. 'I made my feelings quite clear.'

For a long moment there was silence. Iseult nearly started walking again, and then she heard from behind her, 'Ever since I laid eyes on you I've felt a pull stronger than anything I've ever felt before. My parents had an arranged marriage, and although they didn't love each other they had great affection and respect for one another. That's all I ever wanted and hoped for in a marriage, and no one ever came along to shake that assertion. Not even my wife. Sara was a good, kind, beautiful woman...but she knew she didn't have all of me. She went on the horse that day even though she was pregnant, even though she was terrified of them, because she wanted to impress me.'

Iseult was rooted to the spot, his words causing an ache in her chest. She was barely breathing.

'Sara died because she wanted me to fall in love with her. My respect and loyalty and affection weren't enough. Yet from the moment *we* met you reached right down inside me to a place Sara never could have touched. And the guilt of realising that has nearly killed me.'

Slowly, Iseult turned around to face Nadim. He stood there with an expression she'd never seen on his face. Vulnerability.

'What are you saying…?'

He grimaced. 'I'm saying that I almost let my guilt rule my life. I almost let my guilt convince me that I didn't love you… Every time I was telling you not to fall in love with me I was telling myself not to fall in love with you, because I thought I didn't deserve it. When we slept together I felt guilty, because Sara had never enjoyed making love. I felt guilty because you were so vibrant and brave and beautiful. I had no right to indulge in falling in love when I hadn't been able to fall in love with my own wife…and it had killed her and our baby.'

On a wave of immense love and compassion Iseult half walked and half ran to Nadim, raising shaking hands to his face. 'You weren't to blame for your feelings. If it was an arranged marriage there was every chance Sara wouldn't have loved you either… You never asked her to get on that horse. And she took her own life in her hands—and her unborn child's. Not you.'

Nadim raised a hand and put it over one of Iseult's, and pressed a kiss to her palm. His stubbled jaw tickled her skin, and she could see now that he looked tired, with lines around his mouth. His skin was slightly grey under his tan.

Hoarsely he said, 'I know that now. I think I've finally begun to forgive myself for Sara's death. The minute you walked into my life I think the healing started, and the minute you walked away from me I wanted you back. But I was stubborn, convinced you wouldn't have the guts to go. I thought you wouldn't be able to leave the luxury behind, no matter what you said.'

He quirked a wry smile. 'I should have known you better. Of course you went. And all I could manage was three days before going so crazy that I had to come after you. Guilt or no guilt.'

He pulled Iseult's cap off her head and sent it sailing in the wind, over the fence. 'Hey!' Iseult protested half-heartedly, her head spinning. 'I liked that cap.'

Nadim put his hands around Iseult's face and looked down into her eyes with such intensity that she felt as if she were drowning.

'Iseult, will you come back to Merkazad and marry me and be my wife?'

Her heart flip-flopped. Tears filled her eyes, but as much as she wanted to shout out *Yes!* she bit her lip. 'Don't you have to marry someone *suitable*?'

'*You* are the only suitable wife for me. I want you…no one else.'

Iseult clung onto the anchor of intensity in Nadim's eyes and face as he waited. Shakily she finally said, 'Then, yes…I'll marry you…even though I've no idea what that will make me.'

'What it will make you, *habiba*, is my beloved wife. You will be my Sheikha, by my side through thick and thin. Best friends. Lovers for ever.'

Iseult smiled tremulously. 'I like the sound of that… But you might have to coach me in some of the social situations—it's not my area of expertise. And I do have a chronic lack of self-esteem sometimes, but it's getting much better.'

A familiarly arrogant look crossed Nadim's face. 'You are beautiful, and I will tell you a thousand times a day until you believe it down to the depths of your being. And you will be with me in every situation. That's all you need to worry about.'

Finally, as if she'd been holding back, still protecting some vulnerable part of herself, Iseult pulled Nadim's head down to hers and pressed her mouth to his with a desperate fervour matched only by his own. He lifted her up and Iseult wrapped her legs around his waist. Her arms wound around his neck, and she knew that they would never let each other go again.

Six months later...

Iseult stood at the fence at al Saqr Stables, watching the new trainer with Devil's Kiss. He was getting closer and closer to being ready for the prestigious event at Longchamp later that year. Her pride in the horse was matched only by her pride in her beautiful husband, who arrived at that moment and snaked his arms around her waist, pulling her against him with possessive familiarity.

Iseult tipped back her head and Nadim pressed a kiss against her cheek. 'Where did you disappear off to this afternoon?'

Iseult savoured the moment, turning around in Nadim's arms so she could look up into his eyes. 'I had to go into town to see Dr Nadirah.'

Immediately Iseult felt tension come into Nadim's body. His arms tightened. 'Is there something wrong?'

She smiled and shook her head, and took his hand and placed it on her still-flat belly. And then she said, with a distinct wobble in her voice, 'Nothing. But about eight months from now we may well be suffering from periodic bouts of sleep-deprivation and a serious over-load of love and joy…'

Nadim just looked down at her for a long, intense moment, and she saw everything in his expression. The poignant loss of his first baby, the residue of guilt, the fear of history repeating itself…

She put a hand to his jaw, caressing it. 'We deserve this, Nadim. *You* deserve this. And everything is going to be fine. I promise.'

He pulled her up against him and kissed her so passionately that some approaching staff did a quick detour in the other direction. With Iseult's feet still dangling off the ground, Nadim finally stopped kissing her and threw back his head. He laughed out loud. A shout of pure joy.

And Iseult was right. Everything *was* fine.

* * * * *

INNOCENT IN THE SHEIKH'S HAREM

Marguerite Kaye

Born and educated in Scotland, **Marguerite Kaye** originally qualified as a lawyer but chose not to practise – a decision which was a relief both to her and the Scottish legal establishment. While carving out a successful career in IT, she occupied herself with her twin passions of studying history and reading, picking up a first-class honours and a Master's degree along the way.

The course of her life changed dramatically when she found her soul mate. After an idyllic year out, spent travelling round the Mediterranean, Marguerite decided to take the plunge and pursue her life-long ambition to write for a living – a dream she had cherished ever since winning a national poetry competition at the age of nine.

Just like one of her fictional heroines, Marguerite's fantasy has become reality. She has published history and travel articles, as well as short stories, but romances are her passion. Marguerite describes Georgette Heyer and Doris Day as her biggest early influences, and her partner as her inspiration.

Author Note
Innocent in the Sheikh's Harem

I was thrilled to be asked to contribute to the *Summer Sheikhs* anthology. And also a bit daunted, since the Arabian world of the early nineteenth century is (if you'll pardon the pun) very much virgin territory. As for tents, my experience is confined to nights spent under canvas accompanied by those twin stalwarts of the Scottish summer, rain and midges. Not the most romantic and glamorous of backdrops, however breathtaking the scenery.

Then my lovely editor pointed me in the direction of the intrepid Lady Hester Stanhope and I was instantly captivated by the exotic, intoxicating and above all utterly 'other' world in which she had travelled. It made me wonder, what would it be like for a classic English rose to be stranded in such a place, completely overwhelmed by the alien customs and culture, and wholly in the power of the autocratic ruler of the kingdom in which she found herself. Which is exactly the fate that befalls my heroine, Lady Celia, who finds herself in the behind-closed-doors sensual world of the harem, in thrall to an imperious, powerful sheikh who is so revered as to be thought flawless. Could she possibly be the one to capture the heart of this moody and magnificent prince?

I hope you enjoy immersing yourself in the intensely sensual world I have conjured as much as I have enjoyed creating it.

Nearly two hundred years separates my protagonists from the other couples in this anthology, but one thing binds them irrevocably together: the magic and the overwhelming power of true love.

For Joan (Johanna), who taught me to read,
inspired me to read lots, and who was there that
day on the beach in Cyprus when Kit and Clarissa
first popped into my head. Thank you, and love.

CHAPTER ONE

Summer, 1818

'OH, GEORGE, do come and see!' In her excitement, Lady Celia Cleveden leaned precariously over the side of the dhow in which they had just completed the last leg of their journey down the northern part of the Red Sea. The crew lowered the lateen sail which towered high above their heads and steered the little craft skilfully through the mass of other dhows, feluccas and caiques, all jostling for space in the busy harbour. Celia clung to the low wooden side of the boat with one gloved hand, the other holding her hat firmly in place, watching with wide-eyed wonder as they approached the shore.

She was dressed with her usual elegance in a gown of pale green sprigged muslin, one of several which she had had made especially for the trip, with long sleeves and a high neckline which in London would have been quite out of place but which here, in the East, she had been reliably informed, was absolutely essential. A straw hat with a long veil, also essential, covered her distinctive copper hair, but her tall, slender figure and youthful creamy complexion still attracted much attention from the fishermen, boatmen and passengers of the other craft currently vying for space in the busy port.

'George, come and see,' Celia called over her shoulder to the man sheltering under the scant cover provided by a tattered tented roof over the stern. 'There's a donkey on that boat with a positively outraged expression. He looks exactly like my uncle when a parliamentary vote has gone against him in the House,' she said with amusement.

George Cleveden, her husband of some three months, made no move to join her, and clearly was in no mood to be amused. He too was dressed with his usual elegance, in a cutaway coat of dark blue superfine teamed with a striped waistcoat from which a selection of elegant fobs dangled, and buckskin breeches worn with top boots. Sadly, though his outfit would indeed have been perfect for a coach journey from his mother's house in Bath to his own lodgings in London, or even for the ride from his London lodgings to his small country estate in Richmond, it was very far from ideal for a trip down the Red Sea in the blazing heat of summer. The starched points of his neck cloth had wilted many hours ago. His head ached from the heat of the sun, and there was a very distinctive rim of sweat marking the band of his beaver hat.

George eyed his young bride, looking confoundedly cool as a cucumber, with something akin to resentment. 'Blast this infernal heat! Do come away from there, Celia, you're making a show of yourself. Remember you are a British diplomat's wife.'

As if she needed reminding! Celia, however, continued to marvel at the spectacle unfolding before her eyes, choosing to ignore her husband. It was something at which she had become surprisingly adept during the short period of their marriage. The wedding had taken place on the very day upon which they had set out for the long journey to Cairo, and George's new diplomatic posting. George, the collected, organised undersecretary who worked for Celia's father, Lord Armstrong, at the Foreign Office, had proved to be a rather less than intrepid traveller. This left Celia, who was no more experienced than he when it came to traversing the globe, to manage as best she could the challenging task of getting them—along with their mountain of baggage—from London to Egypt via Gibraltar, Malta, Athens, and an unplanned stop in Rhodes, when their scheduled ship had failed to arrive, and much of their luggage had disappeared. For this, and for a plethora of other minor mishaps which were the result of Celia's naïve but plucky determination to get them in one piece to their destination, George blamed his wife. Damp sheets or no sheets at all, poor wine and much poorer food, insect bites and insect stings, nausea-inducing pitching seas and seas that were becalmed—George had borne none of these with the equanimity Celia had so much admired in the man she had married.

She put much of it down to the tribulations of travel, and maintained an optimistic outlook which she had intended to be reassuring, but which seemed to have rather a contrary effect. 'How can you be so damned jaunty?' George had demanded during one particularly uncomfortable crossing, memorable for its weevil-infested ship's biscuits and brandy-infested ship's captain. But what was the point in lying abed and bemoaning one's fate? Far better to be up on deck, watching hopefully for land and admiring a school of porpoises with comically smiling faces swimming alongside them.

But George could not be so easily distracted, and eventually Celia had learned to keep her fascination for all things strange and colourful to herself. Foreign climes, or at least Eastern foreign climes, clearly did not agree with George's constitution. This was rather a pity, since fate had brought them here, to a clime so foreign Celia had never even heard of it and had been forced to ask one of the consuls in Cairo to point it out on a rather large and complicated map kept under lock and key in his office.

'A'Qadiz.' Celia said the word experimentally under her breath. Impossibly exotic, it conjured up visions of closed courtyards and colourful silks, of spices and perfumes, the heat of the desert and something darker and more exciting she could not put into words. She and her next sister, Cassandra, had read the Arabian tales, *One Thousand and One Nights*, in French, sharing an edited version with their three younger sisters, for some of the stories hinted at distinctly decadent pleasures. Now here she was in Arabia, and it looked even more fantastic than she had imagined. Watching from the dhow as the dots on the harbour became people and donkeys and horses and camels, as the distant buzz became a babble of voices, Celia wondered how on earth she would be able to convey to Cassie even a tenth part of what it actually felt like.

If only Cassie were here with her, how much more fun it would be. As quickly as the very unwifely thought flashed through her mind, Celia tried hard to suppress it—an act rather more difficult than it should be, for though she had been married for exactly three months,

one week and two days, she did not feel at all like a
wife. Or at least not at all as she had expected to feel
as a wife.

The match was of her father's making, but at four-
and-twenty, and the eldest of five motherless girls—two
of whom were already of marriageable age—Celia had
seen the sense in his proposal. George Cleveden was
Lord Armstrong's protégé. He was well thought of, and
great things were expected of him.

'With a hostess like you at his side, he can't fail,'
Papa had said bracingly when he'd first put forward the
idea. 'You've cut your teeth in diplomatic circles as my
hostess, and a damned fine fist you've made of it. You
can hold your own with the best of them, my girl, and
let's face it, Celia, it's not as if you've your sister's
looks. You take after my side rather than your mother's,
I'm afraid. You're passable enough, but you'll never be
a toast, and it's not as if you're getting any younger.'

Celia bore her father's casual assassination of her appearance with equanimity. She neither resented nor
envied Cassie her beauty, and was content to be known
as the clever one of the five Armstrong girls. Elegance,
wit and charm were her accomplishments—assets
which stood her in excellent stead as her father's hostess
and which would stand George in equally excellent
stead as he rose through the diplomatic ranks, as surely
he would if only he managed to shine in this posting.
Which of course he would—if only he could accustom
himself to being away from England.

George, it seemed, was the type of man who needed
the reassurance of the familiar in order to function
properly. It had been his idea to postpone the consum-
mation of their vows. 'Until we are settled in Cairo,' he

had said on their wedding night. 'There will be enough for us to endure on our journey without having to contend with that as well.'

Even at the time his words had struck her as somewhat ambiguous. Though lacking a mother's guidance, Celia was not entirely unprepared for her marital duties. 'As with so many things in life,' her stately Aunt Sophia had informed her, 'it is an act from which the gentleman derives satisfaction and the lady endures the consequences.' Pressed for practical details, Aunt Sophia had resorted to obscure biblical references, leaving Celia with the vague impression that she was to undergo some sort of stamina test, during which it was vital that she neither move nor complain.

Slightly relieved, though somewhat surprised, given Aunt Sophia's certainty that gentlemen were unfailingly eager to indulge in this one-sided game, Celia had agreed to her husband's proposed abstinence, spending her first night as a married woman alone. However, as the nights passed and George showed no inclination to change his mind, she could not help wondering if she had been wrong—for surely the more one postponed something, the more difficult it became to succeed? And she wanted to succeed as a wife, eventually as a mother too. She liked and admired George. In time she expected to love him, and to be loved in return. But love was built on sharing a life together, and surely sharing a bed must play a part in that? Lying alone in the various bunks, pallets and hammocks which had marked their progress across the globe, Celia had swung between fretting that she should do something about the situation, and convincing herself that George knew best and it would all come right in the end.

But after a week in Cairo, with George restored almost to his pleasant and agreeable self, he had still shown no interest in joining his new wife in her bed. Plucking up all her courage, Celia had tried, extremely reluctantly, with much stumbling, blushing and almost as many vague biblical references as Aunt Sophia, to broach the subject—a particularly difficult task, given her lack of any certain knowledge of what the subject actually entailed.

George had been mortally offended.

He was trying to be considerate, to give her time to adjust to married life.

They barely knew each other.

It was highly unnatural of Celia to show such a morbid interest in these things which all the world knew only women of a certain class enjoyed.

And finally, he was doing her a favour by restraining himself from imposing what he knew she would find unpleasant upon her, and she had thrown that favour in his face!

Celia had retired, confused, mortified, hurt and a little resentful. Was she so unattractive? Was there something wrong with her? Certainly George had implied that there was.

Or was there something wrong with George? Not her first unwifely thought, but the most shocking. She banished it. Or tried to. In the absence of any other woman to consult—for she could not quite bring herself to confide such intimate matters to the forbidding Lady Wincester, the wife of the Consul General of Cairo—she had resolved to write to Aunt Sophia. But it was such an awesome task, and putting her fears into words seemed to make them more real, and perhaps George was right—it was just a matter of time. So she had instead written colourful descriptions of all she had seen and all she had done, and made no reference at all to the fact that her husband continued to spurn her company after dark.

When this special assignment on which they were now engaged had come up, it had been with immense relief that Celia had turned her attentions to preparations for the trip. She had accompanied George against the express wishes of the Consul General. A'Qadiz was no place for a gently bred woman, apparently, but on this matter George had stood firm, and refused to go without her. Impressed by what he took to be a newlywed husband's devotion to his wife, Lord Wincester had most reluctantly agreed. Under no such illusion, Celia had prepared to resume her role as chief nurse, comforter and courier with an air of sanguinity she'd been very far from feeling.

The scenery through which they had sailed was enchanting. The deep waters were clear enough for her to watch the shoals of rainbow-coloured fish just by hanging over the back of the boat. Reefs with coral all the shades of sunset and sunrise could be seen just below the surface, shimmering like tiny mystical cities teeming with life. Along the shoreline were palm, orange, lemon and fig trees, olive groves and a myriad of plants with scents so heady that it was, as she had said to George at dusk one night, like being inside a huge vat of perfume.

'It's playing havoc with my hay fever,' he'd sniffed, putting paid to the eulogy she had been about to deliver.

The port of A'Qadiz in which they had now arrived looked impossibly crowded, swarming with people swathed in long robes. The women were all veiled, some with light gauze such as Celia's own veil, others draped in heavier material, with only slits for their eyes. A stack of enormous terracotta urns stood on the quayside, waiting to be loaded for transport north. Through the open doors of the warehouses could be glimpsed bales of silks in a rainbow of colours, and hundreds more of the large urns.

As the dhow pulled alongside, it was the noise which struck Celia next. The strange, ululating sound of the Arabic language, with everyone talking and gesturing all at once. The high-pitched braying of donkeys, the rumbling of carts on the rough stony ground, the low-pitched bleating of the camels which reminded Celia of the rumbling noise her father made when he was working up to an important announcement. Picking up her skirts and leaping lightly to the shore, careful to make sure her veil remained in place, she couldn't help thinking that the camels themselves, with their thick lips and flaring nostrils, looked rather like Aunt Sophia.

She turned to share this mischievous thought with George, but he was clambering awkwardly to the shore with the assistance of two of the crew, cursing under his breath and frowning heavily in a way that did not bode well for his temper. She made a mental note to share it instead with Cassie, in her next letter.

Rummaging in her reticule for a little bottle of lavender water, Celia tipped a few drops onto her handkerchief and handed it to her husband. 'If you wipe it on your brow it will cool your skin.'

'For God's sake, not now! Are you determined to show me up, Celia?' George batted the scrap of lace away.

It fluttered to the ground, where four semi-naked

children contested for the honour of retrieving it and handing it back. Laughing at their antics, Celia thanked them all solemnly in turn. By the time she looked up George was disappearing into the crowd, following the trail of their baggage, which was being carried on the heads of the crew of the dhow, ushered on its way by a man dressed in flowing black robes.

Struggling through the small forest of children's hands clutching at her dress, her gloved hands, her long veil, Celia made slow progress. The colours dazzled her. In the relentlessly glaring light of the sun, everything seemed brighter, more starkly outlined. Then there were the smells. Sweet perfumes and incense, spices that tickled her nose, the dusty dryness of the heat, the strong musty smell of the camels and donkeys all combined to emphasise the incredible foreignness of the place, the far-awayness, the overwhelmingly exotic feel of it.

Except, she realised, stopping amid her small entourage of children to try and locate the train of her luggage with her husband in its wake, it was really she who was the foreigner here. She could no longer see George. *Had he forgotten all about her?* Panic and a spurt of temper made Celia instinctively push back her veil in order to obtain a better view.

A startled hiss came from the people in her immediate vicinity. The children all turned their heads away, covering their eyes. Fumbling for her veil with shaky fingers, she managed to catch the gauzy material in a hat pin and grew flustered. *Where was George?*

Anxious now for a glimpse of her husband, she cast a frantic look around the crowds. The docks were set into the shade of a low outcrop, and many of the storehouses and animal pens were built into the rock itself.

Celia's eyes were drawn to the top of the hill, where a lone figure sat astride a magnificent white horse. A man dressed in traditional robes, and if anything even more magnificent than the beast which bore him.

Outlined against the blazing blue of the azure sky, dazzling in his white robes, he looked like a deity surveying his subjects from the heavens. There was something about him—an aura of authority, a touch-me-not glaze—which dazzled and at the same time made her want to reach out, just to see if he was real. He both compelled and intimidated, like the golden images of the pharaohs she had seen in Cairo. And, like the slaves in the murals she had seen on the walls of the temple the day she had finally persuaded George into taking a sightseeing trip, Celia had an absurd desire to throw herself to her knees at this stranger's feet. He seemed to command adoration.

Where on earth had that come from? Celia gave herself a little mental shake. He was just a man. An extremely striking man, but a mere mortal all the same.

He was dressed entirely in white, save for the gold which edged his *bisht*, the lightweight cloak he wore over the long, loose tunic which all the men here favoured. There was gold too, in the *igal* which held his headdress in place. The pure white of his *ghutra* fluttered like a summons in the light breeze. It fell in soft folds, and must be made of silk rather than cotton, she noted abstractedly. Underneath it, the man's face showed in stark relief. His skin seemed to gleam, as if the sun had burnished it. It was a strong face, the clean lines of his cheeks, his nose, his jaw, contrasting sharply with the soft, sensual curve of his mouth.

His eyes were heavy-lidded—a little like hers. She

could not see their colour, but Celia was suddenly acutely aware that his piercing gaze was trained directly on her. She was not properly veiled. He should not be looking at her thus. Yet he showed no sign of looking away. Heat began to seep through her, starting from somewhere in her stomach. *It was the hot sun!* It must be, for it was most unlike her to feel so unsettled.

'My lady?' Celia turned to find the man who had taken charge of their bags standing before her, his hands pressed respectfully together as if he was praying.

Reminded by his averted eyes to pull her veil back into place, Celia dragged her gaze away from the god on the hilltop and returned the gesture with a slight bow.

'I am Bakri. I have been sent by my master, His Highness the Prince of A'Qadiz, to escort you to his palace. I must apologise. We were not expecting a woman.'

'My husband does not travel well. He needs me to take care of him.'

Bakri raised a brow, but swallowed whatever words he was about to say. 'You must come,' he said instead. 'We must leave soon—before night falls.'

Sheikh Ramiz al-Muhana, Prince of A'Qadiz, watched her go, a frown drawing his dark brows together. The man with the weak face could only be the English diplomat, but what in the name of the gods did he think he was doing, bringing a woman companion? His wife? His mistress? Surely he would not dare?

Ramiz watched as the woman followed Bakri to where the Englishman waited impatiently by the camels and mules which would form their small caravan. She was tall and willowy. In the East, where curves were seen as the apex of womanly beauty, she would be deemed unattractive, but Ramiz, who had spent much of his adult life in the great cities of the West, completing his education and later acting as his father's emissary, was not so biased. She moved with the grace of a dancer. In her pale green dress, with her veil covering her face, she made him think of Guinevere, the queen from Arthurian legend. Regal, ethereal, temptingly untouchable. Definitely not a mistress, he decided, yet she had not the demeanour of a wife either.

Ramiz watched in disgust as her husband chastised her. The Englishman was a fool—the type of man who blamed everyone but himself for his faults. He should not have let her out of his sight. The woman was not responding, but Ramiz could see the tension in her from the way she stood a little straighter. Her cool exterior was belied by that flame of hair which he had glimpsed when she had thrown back her veil. She would be magnificent when angry. Or roused. Despite her married state, Ramiz was certain her passions slumbered still. He wondered what it would take to awaken them.

Her husband was not just a fool, but obviously inept. It was one of the things which Ramiz found incomprehensible—this reticence the English had regarding the arts of love. No wonder so many of their women looked uptight. Like buds frozen into permanent furls by frost, or simply withered through lack of the sun, he thought, as he watched the Englishman struggle to mount one of the camels. The woman was organising the loading of their baggage onto the mules. She made short work of seating herself on the high platform which formed the camel's saddle, arranging her full skirts with elegant modesty, for all the world as if she rode one every day. Unlike her husband, who was clutching nervously at the pommel, making the animal dance playfully, the woman sat with her back straight, holding the reins at precisely the correct angle, swaying in tune to the undulating movement of the beast.

Ramiz cursed under his breath. *What did he think he was doing, looking upon another man's woman in such a way?* Even if the man appeared to be an incompetent fool, honour forbade it. The Englishman was his guest, after all, and here at his invitation.

Ramiz was under no illusions. The English, like the French, were waiting in Cairo like vultures, ready to prey upon any sign of weakness as the Sultan of the once-great Ottoman empire struggled to retain his control over the trade routes. Already the ruthless Mehmet Ali had taken Egypt. A'Qadiz, with its port on the Red Sea, could prove a valuable link to the riches of India. Ramiz was in no doubt about the benefits to his country that playing such a role might bring, but nor was he blind to the disadvantages. Westerners were desperate to plunder the artefacts of the old world, and A'Qadiz was a treasure trove of antiquities. Ramiz had no intention of allowing them to be hauled off and displayed in private museums by greedy aristocrats with no understanding of their provenance or their cultural value, any more than he intended handing control of his country over to some conquering imperialist. As Prince al-Muhana he could trace his lineage back far beyond anything English or French dukes and lords could dream of.

Examine what is said, not he who speaks. His father's words, and wise as ever. The Englishman deserved a fair hearing. Ramiz smiled to himself as he turned his horse away from the harbour. Three days it took to travel across the desert to his palace in the ancient capital city of Balyrma. Three days—in which time he could observe, study and plan.

Six camels and four mules formed their caravan as they wound their way up the hill from the port of A'Qadiz into the desert, for Prince Ramiz had assigned them three guards in addition to Bakri, their guide. The guards were surly men, armed with alarming curved swords at their waists and long slim daggers strapped to their chests, who eyed Celia with something akin to disgust and muttered darkly amongst themselves. Their presence was alarming, rather than reassuring to her. George, too, seemed uncomfortable with them, and stuck close to Bakri at the head of the train.

This part of the desert was much rougher underfoot than Celia had anticipated—not really sand at all, more like hard dried mud covered with rock and dust—and it wasn't flat either. After the first steep climb from the sea, the land continued to rise. In the distance she could see mountains, sharp and craggy, ochre against the startling blue of the sky, which was deepening to a velvety hue as the sun sank. The sense of space, of the desert unfolding for miles, beyond anything she could ever have imagined, was slightly intimidating. Compared to such vastness, she could not but be aware of her own insignificance. She was awestruck, and for a moment completely overwhelmed by the journey they had travelled and the task ahead of them in this land as shrouded in mystery as the people were shrouded in their robes.

However, as the caravan made its way east over the

desert plain and she became more accustomed to the terrain as well as to the undulating movement of the camel, Celia's mood slowly lifted. She amused herself by picturing Cassie's face when she read of her account of her ride on the ship of the desert, and revived her flagging optimism by reminding herself of the very high esteem in which George, as a diplomat, was held. This mission would be a success, and when it was, George would stop fretting about his career and turn his mind to making an equal success of his marriage. She was sure of it!

They came to a halt in the shelter of an escarpment, the terracotta-coloured stone glittering with agates, as if it were chipped with diamonds. Above them, the sky was littered with a carpet of stars, not star-shaped at all, but huge round bursts of light. 'You feel as if you could just reach out and touch them,' Celia said to George, as they watched the men put up the tent.

'I'd like to reach out and touch my four-poster just at the minute,' George said sarcastically. 'Doesn't look like very luxurious accommodation, does it?'

In truth, the tent did look more like a lean-to, for it had only three sides, with a curtain placed down the middle to form two rooms. The walls were woven from some sort of wool, Celia thought, feeling the rough texture between her fingers. 'It must be goat's hair, for I don't think they have many sheep here. I'm pretty sure that was goat we had for dinner, too,' she said. 'You should have tried some, George, it was delicious.'

'Barbaric manners—eating with their hands like that. I was surprised at you.'

'It is their custom,' she replied patiently. 'You're supposed to use the bread like a spoon. I simply copied what they did, as *you* must do if you are not to starve. Now, where shall I put this carpet for you?'

'I'll never sleep like this, with the guards snoring their heads off next door,' George grumbled, but he allowed Celia to clear the rocks from a space large enough to accommodate him and very soon, despite his protestations, he was soundly asleep.

Celia sat outside the tent, looking up at the stars for a long time. She was not in the least sleepy. Such a vast space this desert was. Such beauty even in its apparent barrenness. When it rained, Bakri said, it was a carpet of colour. She thought of all the little seeds sleeping just below the surface, ready to burst into life. *Promise is a cloud; fulfilment is rain,* Bakri had said.

She was obviously expected to share the same room as George, but she couldn't bear the idea of their first night together to be *this* night, even if her husband was fully dressed and already sleeping. Celia took her carpet and found herself a quiet spot a short distance away, tucked up behind a large boulder. 'Promise is a cloud; fulfilment is rain,' she murmured to herself. Perhaps that was how she should think of her marriage. Not barren, just waiting for the rain. She fell asleep wondering what form such a rain would take if it were to be powerful enough to fix what she was beginning to think might be unfixable.

Above her, still and silent, Ramiz watched for a long time over the dark shape of the sleeping Englishwoman who could not bring herself to stay in the tent beside her husband. Then, as the cold of the true night began to descend, he made his way back to his own small camp some short distance away, wrapped himself in his carpet, and settled down to sleep next to his camel.

CHAPTER TWO

THEY came just before dawn. Celia was awoken by the sound of camel hooves. She sat up, cramped from her sleeping position, and peered out over the rock at the cloud of dust moving frighteningly fast towards the tent. A glint of wicked steel drew her attention. Whoever these men were, they were not friends.

There was still time. A few moments, no more, but enough. She must warn the guard. She must save George. It did not occur to Celia that it should be the other way round. She scrambled to her feet, and had taken one step from behind the rock when a large hand covered her mouth and a strong arm circled her waist. She struggled, but the hold on her tightened.

'Keep still and don't scream.'

His voice was low, but the note of command in it was perfectly apparent. Celia obeyed unhesitatingly, too frightened even to register that he spoke English.

The hand was removed from her mouth. She was twisted around to face him, though still held tight in his embrace. 'You!' she exclaimed in astonishment, for it was the man she had seen yesterday on the hill.

'Get back behind the rock. Don't move. No matter

what happens, do not come out until I tell you. Do you understand?'

'But my husband…'

'What they will do to him is nothing to what you will suffer if they find you. Now, do as I bid you.'

He was already dragging her back towards her sleeping place. Behind her she could hear shouts. 'Please. Help him—save my husband.'

Ramiz nodded grimly and, wresting a glittering scimitar from its sheath at his waist and a small curved dagger from a silver holder in the same belt, he gave a terrifying cry as he leapt, sure-footed as a lion, over the short distance to the tent, calling out to the three hired guards to come to his aid.

But the guards were nowhere to be seen. Only Bakri stood between the English diplomat, cowering in the far corner of the tent, and his fate. Ramiz cursed furiously and turned his attention to the first of the four men, shouting to Bakri to see if the Englishman had a gun.

Whether he had or not, it was destined never to be used. Ramiz fought viciously, utilising all his skills with the scimitar, slicing it in bold arcs through the air while defending himself with his *khanjar* dagger. It was four to his one. Trapped in the circle of the men, he fought like a dervish, managing a disabling cut in the shoulder to one man before swirling around, his scimitar clanging against that of his enemy with a last-minute defensive move, the strength of which vibrated painfully up his arm.

Two down. Two to go. As Ramiz fought on, sweat and dust obscuring his vision, he became dimly aware of a cry coming from the corner of the tent. Turning towards it, he saw one of his own hired guards raising his dagger over Bakri. 'Help him! In the name of the gods, help him,' he cried out to the Englishman.

It all happened so fast after that. The Englishman moved, but instead of attempting to lend his assistance he pushed past Bakri and his attacker, making for the entrance of the tent. Bakri fell, clutching the dagger which had been plunged deep into his heart. Ramiz abandoned his attempts to slay the other two men and lunged forward. The Englishman was running away. Disgust slowed Ramiz's steps. Even as he reminded himself that the foreign coward was nevertheless his honoured guest, it was too late. One of the invaders raised his scimitar and sliced deep into the Englishman's belly.

A piercing scream rent the air. The woman abandoned her hiding place and, running full tilt towards them, distracted everyone. They would kill her as they had killed her husband. He realised it was what they had come for, these men of Malik, the ruler of the neighbouring principality, for it could only be he who would have contemplated such a dastardly plot. Fuelled by fury, Ramiz launched himself at the two men. They had already reached the woman, yanking her hair back and pressing a lethal dagger to her throat. A well-aimed kick sent the first one flying, unconscious, his dagger soaring through the air in the opposite direction. The sight of Ramiz, his face taut with rage, his scimitar arching down towards his head, sent the other man prostrate to the ground in the time-old attitude of abasement.

'Please, Lord. Please, Your Highness, I beg of you to spare me,' the man muttered, over and over.

Ramiz yanked him up by the hair. 'You have a message for me from your prince?'

'Please, do not. I beg of you. I…'

Ramiz twisted his hold, making the man scream. 'What does Malik have to say?'

'To invite strangers into our house is to risk disaster.'

Ramiz dropped his hold and turned the man onto his back with the toe of his boot. 'Tell Malik that I invite who I choose into my house. Tell Malik he will live to regret this day's work. Now, go—while you still have your life—and take your sleeping friend with you.'

Needing no further encouragement, the man scurried over to his unconscious comrade and roughly bundled him onto a camel, before mounting one himself and galloping off in a cloud of dust.

Ramiz knelt over the body of the fallen diplomat, but there was nothing he could do. As he got slowly to his feet, the Englishwoman staggered towards him. Instinctively Ramiz stood in front of the body, shielding it from her gaze.

'George?' Her voice was no more than a whisper.

Ramiz shook his head. 'It is best you don't look.'

'The guards?'

'Traitors.'

'And Bakri?'

Ramiz shook his head again. Bakri, who had been his servant since he was a boy, was dead. He swallowed hard.

'You saved my life. I'm sorry I didn't listen to you. But I heard George, you see. My husband. I thought— I thought…' Celia began to shake. Her knees seemed to be turning to jelly. The ground was moving. 'I'm a widow,' she said, a touch of hysteria in her voice. 'I'm a widow, and I've never really been a wife.' As she began to fall, Ramiz caught her in his arms. The feel of them, securing her to the solid, reassuring bulk of his body, was the last thing Celia remembered.

She was climbing through a tunnel. Slowly up through the thick darkness she went, fighting the urge to curl up and stay where she was, safe, unnoticed. A slit of light lay ahead. She was afraid to reach it. Something horrible waited for her there.

'George!' She sat up with a start. 'George!' Celia struggled to her feet, clutching her head as the ground rolled and tipped like the deck of a ship in a storm. She was in the tent. *How had she got there?* It didn't matter. She staggered out into the open air.

The blaze of the sun dazzled her eyes, temporarily blinding her. When her vision cleared, she clutched at the tent rope for support. The blood had dried dark on the ground, and she remembered, in a rush, what had happened. The men arriving in a cloud of dust like something from the Bible. The man from yesterday. *Who was he? And what was he doing here?* Then the fighting. The cries. And George running. Running away. Even though he had a gun. Even though he used to practice shooting at Manson's every week. He had been running away. He hadn't even looked for her.

No! She mustn't think that way. He had just panicked, he would have come back for her.

A clunking sound coming from the back of the tent distracted her. Celia made her way cautiously, already knowing in her heart what she would find. Sure enough, the stranger was there, his gold-edged cloak discarded on a rock. His headdress was tied back from his face, which glistened with sweat from his exertions. He was smoothing sand over a distinctive mound of desert earth. He must have found a shovel with the supplies their traitorous guards had left when they'd fled.

He was facing away from her. The thin white of his tunic clung to his back with sweat, outlining the breadth of his shoulders. He looked strong. A capable man. Capable of saving her life. A man who knew how to take care of things. Who didn't run away. *Stop!*

He put down the shovel and wiped the sweat from his brow. She must have moved, or made a noise, or maybe he just sensed her, for he turned around. 'You should stay in the tent, out of the sun.'

He spoke English with an accent, his voice curling round the words like a husky caress. His eyes were a strange colour, like bronze tinged with gold, the irises dark. He walked with a fluid grace. Celia could not imagine that such a man was regularly employed in manual labour. It struck her then that she was quite alone with him, and she shivered. *Fear?* Yes, but not as much as there should be. She was too shocked, too numb to feel anything much at the moment.

He stopped just in front of her, was watching her with concern. She didn't like the way he looked at her. It made her feel weak. She didn't like feeling weak. She was normally the one who took care of things. Celia straightened her back, tilting her head up to meet the stranger's eyes, forgetting all about protocol and hats and veils.

'Who are you?' Her voice came out with only the tiniest of wobbles.

'Sheikh Ramiz al-Muhana,' he said, bowing before her with a hint of a smile, lending a fleeting softness to the hard, rocky planes of his face. It lightened his eyes to amber, as if the sun shone from them. Everything about him gleamed. She remembered thinking yesterday of the ancient pharaohs. He had that air about him. Of command.

'Sheikh Ramiz...' Celia repeated stupidly, then realisation dawned. 'You mean Prince Ramiz of A'Qadiz?'

He nodded.

'We were on our way to visit you in Balyrma. George is—was...' She drew a shaky breath, determined not to lose control. 'I don't understand. What are you doing here? What happened this morning? Who were those men? Why did they attack us?'

Her voice rose with each question. Her face was pale. Her eyes, with their heavy lids which gave her that sensual, sleepy look, were dark with a fear she was determined not to show. She had courage, this Englishwoman, unlike her coward of a husband. 'Later. First you must say your farewells, then we will leave this place.'

'Farewells?'

Her lip was beginning to tremble, but she clenched it firmly between her teeth. Big eyes—the green of moss or unpolished jade, he thought—turned pleadingly towards him. Ramiz took Celia's arm and gently led her towards the graves.

Two graves, Celia noticed. And another two at a distance. Prince Ramiz had obviously laboured long and hard as she lay unconscious. Such labour had spared her much. She could not but be grateful.

They stood together, she and the Prince of A'Qadiz, in silent contemplation. Sadness welled up inside Celia. Poor George. A tear splashed down her cheek, then another. 'I'm so sorry,' she whispered. 'I'm so sorry.'

They should never have married. George hadn't really wanted a wife, and she—she'd wanted more from her husband than he'd been prepared to give. It was as well he had not, for were she standing here a real wife, with three months of real marriage behind her, the pain would be unendurable.

Overcome with remorse, Celia clenched her eyes tight shut and prayed hard for the husband she knew now she could never have loved, no matter how hard she'd tried. 'I'm sorry,' she whispered again.

'He is at peace now. He walks with his god.' Ramiz broke the silence. 'As does Bakri, who was my servant, and my brother's, and my father's before that.'

Celia roused herself from the stupor which threatened to envelop her. 'I'm sorry—I didn't realise. It must be a great blow for you to lose him.'

'He died an honourable death.' Ramiz closed his eyes and spoke a prayer in his native language. His voice was low, and the strange words had a simple beauty in their cadence that soothed. 'Now, go back to the tent. I will finish here.'

An honourable death. The unspoken criticism hung like a weight from Celia's heart as she made her way slowly back to the tent. Though common sense told her she could not have saved George, that to have disobeyed Ramiz when he'd told her to hide would almost certainly have resulted in her own death, it did not prevent her from being racked with guilt for having survived.

George was dead. She was a widow. George was dead—and in such a horrible way that it was as if she had dreamt it, or imagined it as a tale from *One Thousand and One Nights*. If only it had been. If only she could wake up.

But she could not. All she could do was behave with what dignity she could muster. With the dignity her father and Aunt Sophia would expect of her. With the dignity which others would expect of George's wife, a representative of His Majesty's government, she reminded herself strictly.

Thus, when Ramiz joined her half an hour later, though she longed to sink onto the carpeted floor, to curl up under the comfort of a blanket and cry, Celia forced herself to her feet. 'I must beg your pardon, Your Highness, if I have offended you by appearing rude,' she said, turning towards Ramiz, remembering belatedly to avert her eyes from his face. 'I must thank you for saving my life, and for the trouble you took with—with my husband.' She swept him a deep curtsy. 'I realise I haven't even introduced myself. I am Lady Celia Cleveden.'

'I think we are long past the need for such formalities,' Ramiz replied. 'Come, we must leave this place if we are to find another shelter before dark. I don't want to risk spending the night here.'

'But what about—? We can't just...'

'There is nothing more we can do. I have already formed the animals into a caravan,' Ramiz said impatiently.

She had not the will to argue. Questions tussled for prominence in her mind, but she had not the strength to form them. And she had absolutely no desire at all to remain here, in the presence of the dead, at the scene of such horror, so she followed the Prince obediently to where her camel was tethered, and when it dropped to its knees at Ramiz's barked command Celia climbed wearily onto the high wooden platform which served as a saddle. Vaguely she noticed that the beast Prince Ramiz mounted was as white as his horse yesterday had been. That its saddle cloth was silk, intricately embroidered with gold, and that the tack was similarly intricately tasselled and trimmed with threads of gold.

He mounted with the ease of long practice, and took up the halters of the leading camel in the caravan, as well as a halter attached to Celia's own camel. Under any other circumstances she would have been furious to have her mount's control taken from her. Now she was simply relieved. It was one less thing to worry about.

They rode for about two hours. When the sun began its spectacularly fast slide down towards the horizon, striping the sky with gold and crimson, they stopped and made camp. Unbelievably, Celia had dozed for part of the way. Distance and rest had already started the healing process. As she fulfilled each of Ramiz's curt instructions her mind sorted and sieved through the events, forming questions which she was determined he would answer.

They sat by a small fire, eating a simple meal which Celia prepared from their supplies. A new moon was rising. *Hilal.* The crescent moon. The sign of new beginnings.

'Do you know what happened this morning? Why it happened, Your Highness?' Celia asked when they had finished their food. 'How did you come to be there?'

'Ramiz. You may call me Ramiz while we are in private. I was following you. I wanted to see what kind of man your government had sent to talk to me. I wanted to run the rule over him before our official meeting. I had not anticipated him bringing his wife. If I had known you were coming I would certainly have made alternative arrangements for your journey to my citadel.'

'Just because I am a woman it does not mean I need to be wrapped in cotton wool. I am perfectly capable of dealing with the hardships of a trip across the desert.'

'From what I saw, you are far more capable than your husband was,' Ramiz said dryly, 'but that is beside the point. In my country we take care of our women. We cherish them, and we put their comfort before our own. Their lives before our own. Unlike your husband.'

Celia shifted uncomfortably on the carpet. The narrow skirts of her robe made kneeling difficult. 'George was just—George was not—he was…'

'Running away,' Ramiz said contemptuously. 'Was he armed?'

'He had a gun,' Celia admitted reluctantly.

'He could have saved himself and the life of my honoured servant.'

'Your Highness—Ramiz—my husband was a good man. It is just that this was all—and the attack—it was terrifying. He acted on—on instinct.'

'A man whose instincts are to abandon his wife in order to save his own skin is not worth saving. Nature has bestowed upon women their beauty for man to appreciate. To man has been granted the strength to provide and protect them. To break such rules is to go against the natural way of things, the formula civilisations such as mine have been following very successfully for many thousands of years. Your husband was a coward and therefore not, in my eyes, worthy to be called a man. I am sorry to be so harsh, but I speak only the truth.'

Though all her instincts told her to defend George,

Celia found she could not. To a man like Ramiz, what George had done was indefensible. And in a small corner of her own mind she agreed. She turned her attention to obtaining answers to the rest of the questions she knew would be asked of her when she returned to Cairo. Nothing could bring George back, but she could brief the Consul General, provide at least some information about this principality of which they knew next to nothing. In a tiny way it would mean that George had not died in vain. 'You knew the men who attacked us today, didn't you?' she asked. 'Who were they?'

Ramiz threw his head back to look up at the stars, suspended like lanterns so close above them. 'Until two years ago my elder brother Asad was the ruler of A'Qadiz. This kingdom and those surrounding it are lands of many tribes, many factions, and my brother embroiled us in many battles. He believed that the sword was mightier than the tongue. It was to cost him his life.'

'What happened to him?'

Ramiz shook his head slowly. 'He was killed in a pointless, ultimately futile skirmish. I don't share his philosophy. I believe most men are reasonable, and reasonable men want peace. Peace is what I have been working tirelessly to achieve, but not all my neighbours agree with me. Nor do all accept my strategy of negotiating with foreign powers such as the British. Today was a warning, and I must act swiftly or everything I have begun to achieve will crumble into dust. It is unfortunate that you have been caught up in this, but there is nothing I can do about it for now. It is another two days' journey to Balyrma. We must start at first light.'

'Balyrma!' Celia exclaimed. 'But surely—I mean, I had assumed you would take me back to Cairo.'

'There can be no question of that. I must return home urgently.'

'Can you not provide me with another escort?'

Ramiz indicated with two spread arms the vast empty expanse of the desert night. 'You think I have magic powers? You think I can summon an escort for you by sheer force of will?'

'I'm afraid I was not briefed, and my husband chose not to share the details of this mission with me. I can be of little use to you in that regard.'

'It is of no matter. It would not be appropriate to hold such discussions with a woman in any event,' Ramiz said dismissively.

She already knew that. George had said as much, and it wasn't really so very different from the way things were back home in England. 'If that is the case, surely it would make more sense for me to go back to Egypt. It is but a day's travel to the port and...'

'I have spoken. You would do well to remember that in this country my word is law.'

Celia was taken aback by the abrupt change of tone. Ramiz had removed his headdress. His hair was black, surprisingly close cut, emphasising the shape of his head, the strength in his neck and shoulders. Now he ran his fingers through it, making a small lick stand up endearingly on his forehead, and Celia realised he was younger than she had thought, perhaps only two or three and thirty. But his looks belied his maturity. He spoke with the voice of authority, the voice of a man used to being obeyed without question. A man, she reminded herself, who held the power of life and death over her.

Celia, however, was not a woman to whom unquestioning obedience came naturally. 'Is it because of the attack this morning?' she asked carefully. 'Are you worried they may return?' She had not thought of this until now—how vulnerable they were, only the two of them. Nervously, she peered out into the inky black of the desert, but she could see nothing beyond the vague contours of the hills.

She was immensely relieved when Ramiz shook his head decidedly. 'They would not dare return now they know of my presence here.' His mouth thinned. 'It is a stain on my honour, and on that of A'Qadiz, that they came at all.'

'You saved my life.' Without thinking, Celia laid her hand over his. 'You could not have known that your own men would turn traitor.'

Her hand was cool. Her fingers were long, that same lovely creamy colour as her face. Women with such colouring so often turned an ugly red in the sun, or freckled, yet she looked to be flawless. Ramiz wondered how flawless. Then he reminded himself that he should not be wondering. He removed her hand deliberately. 'You will come to Balyrma with me, and that is an end to it.'

'For how long?'

Ramiz shrugged. 'Until I decide what is to be done with you.'

Celia frowned. It seemed she had no option. Would it not be best to accept her fate rather than estrange her host by arguing? Though she did not know the details of George's mission, she knew much depended upon it. In any case, even if she was granted her wish to return to Cairo immediately, as George's widow she would not be permitted to stay. She would be sent home. Was that what she really wanted? The answer to that question was obvious.

'Where will I stay in Balyrma?'

'In the palace, as my guest.'

'I don't think that would be good idea,' Celia said uncertainly. 'As an unaccompanied woman it would not be appropriate for me to stay in your palace, especially as you are clearly going to be occupied by urgent matters of state.'

Ramiz laughed harshly. 'You may talk like a man, but you are a woman, are you not, Lady Celia? You need not worry about your virtue. You will be housed in the women's quarters, to which no man but me is permitted entry.' He turned towards her. In the firelight, his eyes seemed to glow like amber.

'Do you mean I am to stay in a harem?' Celia's eyes widened in shock. Images from *One Thousand and One Nights*, of scantily clad concubines oiling themselves and lolling about on velvet cushions sprang to her mind. 'You expect me to form part of your harem? You're not serious. You can't be serious.' Her voice had a panicky edge to it. 'I am not—you expect me to…'

It was that word—*harem*. Ramiz saw immediately what she was thinking. He had encountered the same misunderstanding time and again during his travels as his father's emissary. Europeans imagined a harem to be some sort of exclusive bordello. It angered him to have such inaccurate assumptions made, so he no longer tried to explain. If their fevered imaginations wanted to conjure up scores of nubile women in a perpetual state of arousal waiting for their lord and master to take them to his bed, let them!

'The harem is the place for women in the palace, so that is where you will stay.'

'Your Highness—Ramiz—I am flattered that you should consider adding me to your collection of wives, but…'

'My wife! You over-estimate your value. A sheikh may only marry an Arab princess of royal blood. It is the custom. A Western woman, even a titled one, could not aspire to such an exalted position. At best perhaps she could serve as a concubine.'

Celia gave an outraged gasp. 'You expect me to be your concubine? I absolutely will not! How dare you? How dare you suggest such an outrageous, indecent…?'

He moved so suddenly she had no chance of escape. He seemed to uncoil, to pounce, so that one minute she was sitting next to him, the next she was being dragged helplessly to her feet, held in arms so strong it would be pointless to struggle. Tall as she was, Ramiz topped her by several inches. She was pressed against him, thigh to thigh, chest to chest. His breath was on her face. She could smell him, warm and overpoweringly male. She had never been held thus. She had never been so close to a man before. Not like this, held in such a way as to make her unbearably conscious of her own powerlessness. She should be afraid, and she was, but she was also—something else.

'What do you think you're doing?' Her voice was annoyingly breathless. 'Let me go.'

'You think me a savage, don't you, Lady Celia?' Ramiz said, his voice low and tight with anger.

'I do not! You are obviously educated, your English is flawless, and…'

His grip on her tightened. 'You think the ability to speak a simple language like yours is a measure of being civilised? I also speak French, Greek, German, Italian and at least four variations of my own language. Does that make me more civilised than you—or less? I have travelled widely too, Lady Celia,' Ramiz said with a vicious look. 'Far more widely than you or your pathetic husband. But still all of that means nothing to you, does it? Because I respect the traditions of my own country, and those traditions include keeping a harem. So I can never be anything other than a savage in your eyes, can I?'

Her temper, rarely roused, saved Celia from fear. 'I don't for one moment think of you as a savage! Your country is older by far than mine. I would not be so arrogant. I think it is you who are the one making assumptions about me.'

He had thought her slender, but even through the ridiculous constraints of her English corsetry he could feel her curves. The swell of her breasts pressed against his chest. The dip of her waist made the gentle undulation of her bottom even sweeter. She smelled of lavender and soap, and faintly of that enticing tang of female. The idea of her as his concubine, thrown at her out of anger, was shockingly appealing. Such a vision it commanded, of her creamy skin spread delectably before him, of her delightful mouth at his command, of her long fingers touching him, doing his bidding. Of her submission. He wanted her. Badly. Blood rushed to his groin, making him hard.

Celia struggled to free herself. 'I won't be your—your love-slave, no matter what you do to me. Anyway, they're bound to come looking for me when they hear nothing from George, and if they find me in your harem—'

'Enough!' Ramiz pushed Celia contemptuously away from him. 'I am a sheikh and a man of honour. I would never take a woman against her will. It is an insult that you think me capable of such an act.'

Realising just how foolishly she had leapt to all the wrong conclusions, Celia felt her cheeks burn. 'I'm— I'm sorry,' she stuttered. 'I'm not thinking straight. It's just, with everything that's happened…' A sudden wave of exhaustion hit her with such violence that she staggered. The horror of the day's events came back to her. George was dead, and she was alone in the desert with a man who seemed to think the world should do his bidding. This world was his world; he had good reason for making such an assumption.

Noticing how pale she had become, Ramiz eased Celia back down onto the carpet by the fire. 'You must rest now. We have a long day's travel ahead of us tomorrow. The camels are an excellent early warning of danger, and I will be here by the fire. You need have no fears.'

In the light of the stars her skin looked translucent and pale as the new moon. Her eyes were glazed, vulnerable, and no wonder. She had been through much today, and endured it with a stoicism and bravery that was impressive. His anger fled like a falcon released from its fetters. Ramiz covered her gently with a blanket, then placed himself at a short distance, laying his scimitar within easy reach, and prepared himself for a long night's vigil. He didn't think the assassins would strike again, but he was taking no chances.

CHAPTER THREE

CELIA slept heavily, waking the next morning just before dawn with a thumping headache and a brain which felt as if it was made of cotton rags. Ramiz was already up and about, readying their caravan, and a pot of sweet black coffee was bubbling appetisingly on the embers of the fire.

Ramiz seemed distracted, a heavy frown drawing his dark brows together under his *ghutra*, making him seem both more intimidating and older. As they wended their way inexorably east across the huge stretch of desert, following a trail which to Celia's untutored eyes made only fleeting appearances, she had ample time to observe him. Despite the fierce heat of the sun, which made the horizon flicker hazily and seared relentlessly through her thin dress and the veil which she kept in place to protect her from the dust, Ramiz sat bolt-upright in the saddle, on full alert. One hand sought the constant reassurance of the curved sabre in its silver sheath. His eyes—the only part of his face she could see, for he had pulled his headdress over the rest of his face—were slits of bronze, casting their keen gaze in front, to each side, to the rear of the caravan. On one occasion he stopped, pulling his white camel up so suddenly that the beast seemed to freeze in mid-trot. It would have been comical had it not been frightening. Celia pulled up beside him, peering anxiously where he pointed.

'Something moved,' he whispered, though she could see nothing, and could still see nothing when he relaxed. 'Just a rabbit,' he said, pointing at a tiny dot a few hundred yards away. 'If I had my falcon we could have had it for dinner.'

'Your falcon?'

'The wings for my heart,' Ramiz said. 'And a good provider too, out here.'

'You have an affinity with animals, I think. What happened to your beautiful horse? The one I saw you with the day we landed?'

'Stabled near the port. I think, from the way you hold your seat on a camel, that you like to ride?'

'Very much, and to hunt too. My father owns a string of racehorses and my sisters and I were thrown into the saddle almost before we could walk.'

'You have many sisters?'

'Four. I'm the oldest.'

'And your father? What does he do apart from race horses?'

'He is a statesman. Lord Armstrong—he is quite well-known in diplomatic circles.'

Ramiz's eyebrow lifted. 'You are Lord Armstrong's daughter?'

'You know him?'

'I met him once, in Madrid. He is a very influential man. Your marriage was of his making, then?'

'Why should you think so?' Celia asked, riled by his cool and annoyingly accurate assumption.

'It's obvious, having such a strategist as a father, and with such excellent family contacts—your uncle also serves in the British government, does he not?'

Celia nodded.

'Despite my own poor opinion of your husband, he must have been well thought of, and also very ambitious to have been given and accepted this mission. A most welcome addition to your father's sphere of influence, in other words. He would have been foolish not to recommend the match. Am I correct?'

Put like that, her marriage seemed a very cold affair indeed. But Papa had not put it like that. She could have said no—couldn't she? And George—he'd thought of her as more than some sort of useful social appendage, hadn't he? Celia found herself rather unwilling to answer this question.

'It is true my marriage had my father's approval, but the choice was mine. Just because such things are arranged in your country, you should not assume that we do things the same way.'

She could tell by the way Ramiz's eyes narrowed that she had made a mistake. It was not like her to speak so rashly. In fact she was known for her tact— one of the few virtues which George had openly admired in his wife. But there was something about Sheik Ramiz al-Muhana that put her constantly on the back foot. He was so sure of himself. And unfortunately so often right!

'I think it is you who are making assumptions, Lady Celia,' he said.

He was right. She was wrong. Yet she could not bring herself to apologise. 'Tell me, then, did your own wives have a say in the matter?'

'My wives? How many do you think I have?'

'I don't know, but I do know it is the custom here to have more than one.'

'Another lazy assumption. It may be the custom, but the reality is very much the choice of the individual. Some men have only one wife, others nine or ten—though that is very rare. Men provide their wives with the protection of their own household, they give them children and shelter, an established role. Women have a better life married than single. What is wrong with that?'

'What is *wrong* with it?' Celia bit her lip. She should not comment on things she did not understand, even things that just felt—wrong. Slanting a look at Ramiz from under her lashes, she wondered just for a moment how much of what he was saying he actually meant. The thought came to her that he was teasing, punishing her for her naïvety and a little for her English prejudice—which perhaps she deserved. 'I would not have liked to share my husband with another woman,' she said cautiously.

'I doubt your husband would have had either the capacity or the inclination.'

Once again, although Ramiz's words were shocking, he had merely voiced what Celia herself had begun to question. Entrenched loyalty and guilt, rather than faith in what she was saying, made her leap to George's defence. 'You are quite right, he wouldn't,' Celia said shortly. 'Because unlike you he believed in constancy.'

'He was so constant to you that he left you to die. If you were my wife...'

'I am very glad I am not.'

'If you were, at least you would know what it meant to be a wife.'

Celia bit her lip, torn between the desire to ask Ramiz what he meant and the knowledge that she would not like the answer.

'One of the differences between our cultures,' Ramiz continued, sparing her the indignity of asking him to elaborate, 'is that in mine we appreciate that women as well as men have needs. If you were my wife, they would have been generously satisfied. As George Cleveden's wife...' He shrugged.

She was extremely glad of her veil. Heat flushed Celia's skin, prickling uncomfortably on the back of her neck. *What did he know? How did he know?* Though her curiosity was certainly roused, embarrassment got the better of her. 'In my country, such things are not mentioned.'

'Which is why, in your country, so many women are unhappy,' Ramiz countered.

Were such things discussed in the harem? If that was where she was destined to go—not that she would for a minute actually allow Ramiz to... But if it was where she was going, would she be able to find out from the other women? Another wave of heat spread its fingers over Celia. 'We should not be discussing this,' she said primly.

'Between a man and a woman there is nothing more important to discuss.' Ramiz could see she was mortified, but somehow he couldn't stop himself. There was something about the too-cool Lady Celia that made him want to test her limits. And, though he should definitely not be thinking such thoughts, now that he had, in his imagination, placed her within his harem, he could not stop picturing her there. 'To take pleasure, one has also to give. In order to give, one must have knowledge. If you were to be my concubine,' Ramiz said outrageously, 'then I would first need to understand what gives you pleasure. And you would need to do the same for me.'

'But I am not going to be your concubine,' Celia said, the tension in her voice evident. 'You said so yourself.'

'True. But I wonder, Lady Celia, what bothers you more? The idea of being my concubine or the knowledge that, if you were, you would enjoy it?'

She was nonplussed by this question, as it had never occurred to her to think that this imperious sheikh, who could have any woman he wanted, might actually find her desirable. No one else ever had. Until George had asked her to marry him she had never been kissed. In fact, rather shamefully, no one had ever even tried to kiss her, whereas they seemed never to stop trying to kiss Cassie.

Men wanted to make love to Cassie. They wanted to make conversation with Celia. She was obviously lacking something. She was witty, she could be charming, she was educated and she was good company, but she wasn't desirable. It was not something which had bothered her until recently. Not until George had—or had not! Now, it was a curiously deflating feeling.

Was Ramiz toying with her? Celia peered through her dusty veil, trying to read his face, but with only his eyes visible, and those carefully hooded by his heavy lids, it was impossible. 'I think,' she finally said, after a long silence, 'that I have enough to cope with in real life without indulging in hypothetical and frankly ridiculous speculation.' She couldn't know for sure, but she sensed that he was smiling beneath his headdress. 'Can we change the subject, please? Tell me about

Balyrma. There is so little written about your country, I don't know very much about it at all beyond the name.'

They had been in the saddle for most of the day, riding through the heat of noon which, under less pressing circumstances, Ramiz would have avoided. Celia had made no complaint, sitting straight in the saddle, drinking water from the canteen only when it was offered, maintaining by some miracle a cool, collected appearance in clothes more fitted to a stroll in an English garden than a long trek across the merciless heat of the desert. Looking at her now, Ramiz felt a faint twinge of guilt. She might not have loved her husband, and in his view she was well rid of him, but she had endured a hugely traumatic time with remarkable courage, and deserved to be indulged a little.

So he told her of Balyrma, and became so engrossed and passionate when talking of his beloved city and its people, of their ancient traditions and its sometimes violent history, that he barely noticed the miles being eaten up. He discovered in Celia an attentive and intelligent listener, with a wide frame of reference, who surprised him with some of the astute observations she made. She was enthusiastic too, and eager to find links between A'Qadiz and the ancient Egypt of the pharaohs whose tombs she had explored. Her enthusiasm was infectious. In his anxiety to defend a point she disputed, enjoying the cut and thrust of their debate, Ramiz almost forgot she was a woman.

'You may be right about the true purpose of the Sphinx,' Celia said triumphantly, 'but the fact is you will never be able to prove it, for nothing like that was written down.' The sun was sinking. Ahead, she could see what looked like a small copse of trees. Thinking she must be mistaken, Celia pushed back her veil and shaded her eyes with her hand. It certainly looked like greenery.

'It is an oasis,' Ramiz explained, 'where water comes up from the ground and provides succour for plants, animals and weary travellers alike. We will stop here for the night. You will be able to bathe, if you wish.'

'Bathe!' Celia breathed the word ecstatically.

It was the first time Ramiz had seen her smile. It changed her completely, warming her complexion, softening the clean lines of her face with the curve of her full bottom lip, highlighting the slanting shape of her eyes, giving him the most tantalising glimpse of the sensual woman hidden beneath her cool exterior. There was something incredibly alluring about her. Unawakened. He remembered now that it was how she had first struck him. Perhaps it was the implied challenge in that which aroused him. Yet again he reminded himself that he should not be thinking such things.

They had reached the oasis. It was small—a watering place, no more—not big enough to encourage permanent settlement. But it was a well-known stop and Ramiz was surprised to find they were the only ones there. His camel dropped obediently to its knees and he dismounted, going immediately to assist Celia, who clambered stiffly down. Ramiz put his hands around her waist and lifted her clear of the pommel. She was light as a feather. He set her to her feet and reluctantly let her go.

'I will see to the animals. The bathing pool is over there, away from the well.'

Ramiz lifted her portmanteau down from the mule and handed it to her. Needing no further encouragement, Celia headed in the direction he had indicated. Underfoot, the sand of the oasis was much softer than the rough track they had followed, much more like the gently undulating desert she had imagined. The trees she had seen were palms, growing high in clusters by the drinking well, around which also grew little patches of green scrub. The bathing pool was an ellipse of vibrant blue set into the sand, no more than ten feet across, backing into a high wall of rock. Water trickled out from a fissure a couple of feet above the level of the pool. Over the years it had worn a track, so that now it formed a tiny waterfall.

Celia longed to stand beneath it. A quick check assured her that she was screened by the palm trees. In minutes, she had discarded her dusty layers of dress, petticoats, stays and stockings, and stood, for the first time in her adult life, shockingly naked, outdoors. It was a fantastically liberating experience. She stretched her arms above her head, tilting her face to look up at the first twinkle of the stars. A scatter of pins and her hair fell in a heavy sweep down her back.

She stepped into the warm pool. The sand sloped gently down, soft and firm underfoot. The water caressed her skin like velvet. At the deepest point, in the middle, it came up to her waist. She sank down to her knees, sighing with contentment as it worked its balmy magic on her aching limbs and dusty skin, before lying flat on her back, floating, her hair trailing out behind her. She soaped herself thoroughly, then washed her hair, rinsing it under the crystal-clear waterfall, relishing the contrasting icy cold of the water trickling over her shoulders before it merged with the warmer water of the pool. The crescent moon was reflected on the surface. In its pale light her skin seemed milky, other-worldly, as if she were a statue come to life.

She had never really looked at her body before—had taken for granted her unblemished skin, her slim figure, well-suited to the fashion for high-wasted narrow dresses, but otherwise unexceptional. Now, released from the fetters of her corsets and the bounds of polite society, she explored her shape. Standing under the waterfall, she watched the paths each drop made, down her arms to nestle in the crook of her elbow, between the valley of her breasts, along the curve of her ribcage to the dip and swell of her stomach. So familiar, and yet so new. She lay on her back again, floating weightlessly, gazing up at the stars. How would her body look to someone else. Too skinny? Too tall? Too pale? Her breasts were not small, but they were hardly voluptuous. Was this good or bad? What would a man think? Ramiz, for example…

'I was beginning to fear you had drowned.'

Celia started up out of the water, then sank quickly to her knees under it. 'How long have you been there?'

'You looked like Ophelia, with your hair trailing out behind you like that. Only unmistakably alive, I'm relieved to say.'

The look on his face was also unmistakable. He liked what he saw. The knowledge was shocking, but it gave her a little rush of pleasure all the same. Ramiz was barefooted, and without his headdress or his cloak. Even as she noticed this he began to unbuckle the belt around his waist, which held his knife and scimitar. Then he tugged at the little pearl buttons at the neck of his robe, giving her a glimpse of smooth skin, lightly tanned. It was only as he made to pull the *thoub* over his head that Celia realised he intended to join her. 'You can't come in,' she yelped. 'Not while I'm still here.'

'Then come out,' Ramiz said.

'I can't. I haven't anything on.'

'I couldn't help but be aware of that,' he said with a crooked smile. 'I'll look away, I promise.'

Still crouched below the water, Celia considered her options. She didn't even have a towel. The idea of boldly standing up and walking past him naked was horrifying, even if he did keep his eyes closed, but not nearly as alarming as the idea of waiting for him to take off his clothes and join her before she made her escape.

'Celia?'

Ramiz sounded impatient. Bored, even. He had probably seen hundreds of women without their clothes. And she was getting cold. And feeling a little foolish.

'Close your eyes,' she instructed, and as soon as he did so Celia took a deep breath and stood up. Wrapping her arms protectively round herself, she splashed her way out of the pool with as much grace as she could muster, trying to persuade herself that she was fully clothed and not dripping wet and stark naked.

Her clothes were in the shade of the palms to Ramiz's right. She just had to walk past him as quickly as she could. The sand was hot under her feet. She caught her toe on a stone and stumbled, only just retaining her balance. Glancing up she saw that Ramiz had kept his word. His lashes fanned dark on his cheeks. It was the strangest experience, standing there without her clothes, knowing all he had to do was to open his eyes. She felt exposed, and just the tiniest bit excited.

Celia paused. What if...? Then she panicked, and headed quickly for the shelter of the palm trees.

He felt rather than heard her hesitate, so intensely conscious was he of her tantalising presence. He didn't need to look. He could imagine her all too clearly as he heard the soft sigh of the water yielding her up, the shiver of the sand as it cradled her feet. Her retreating form, so tall and slender, would glimmer in the moonlight, her hips swaying like a call to pleasure. Her hair, dripping down over her shoulders, would be clinging lovingly to the pouting tips of her breasts. As her footsteps retreated quickly over the sand, he imagined her disappearing into the fringe of palms like a nymph into a forest.

The urge to follow her there, to enter the forbidden garden of such delights, was so strong that Ramiz took a step forward before he managed to stop himself. He opened his eyes. She was safely out of sight. She should be safely out of mind. As the widow of a British diplomat sent to discuss a treaty, and the daughter of an eminent statesman with influence across Europe, she was definitely not for him. Never before had it been so difficult to make his body do his mind's bidding, but he managed it. Honour. His god. He managed it, but only just.

A few yards away Celia dressed hurriedly in a clean nightdress. It was cotton, with long sleeves and a high neck, and in combination with her pantaloons and a shawl was, she decided, perfectly decent for a night in the open—for Ramiz had, to her relief, left the tent behind. She could not bear the thought of sleeping in her stays again, and banished the image of Aunt Sophia's shocked face by reminding herself that Ramiz had already seen her almost nude anyway.

Don't think about that! But she couldn't help it. He found her attractive. There had been no mistaking that look on his face. It was dangerous, not something she had taken into account at all, but it was also exciting.

It was not until she was making her way back across the sand to the fire, carrying her portmanteau, and saw Ramiz standing under the waterfall that she realised something quite astonishing. The attraction was mutual. At least she thought it must be attraction she was feeling—this sort of fizzing in her blood at the sight of him, this little kick of something in her stomach. The way her eyes were drawn to him. She hadn't felt it before. Ever. But she wanted to look. No, more than look—to devour him with her eyes.

He had his back to her, was leaning his hands against the rock and allowing the spray to trickle over his head, to find a path down his shoulders, his spine, to where she could just see the curve of his buttocks emerging from the pool. His skin gleamed, smooth and biscuit-coloured in the moonlight, stretched tight over the bunched muscles of his shoulders. She wondered how it would feel to touch. Then she realised she was spying on him, and decided that she didn't want him to catch her in the act, so she forced herself to walk back to their camp without once looking back.

By the time Ramiz joined her, dressed once more in a *thoub*—a clean one, she noticed—his hair damp, smoothed like a cap sleekly to his skull, Celia had the makings of a meal ready, and a composed expression on her face.

She fell asleep almost as soon as she had eaten, curled up in a blanket by the fire. She slept deeply at first, but then the dreams came. Strange dreams, in which she chased George through labyrinthine buildings, up stairs with no end, through rooms whose walls suddenly closed in on her, across endless passageways with too many doors. And always he was behind the one she couldn't open, or had only just closed. It was George, she knew it was George, but in the way of dreams he took many forms. All of them aloof from her. All of them despising her. In her dream she grew smaller. Frailer. More frantic with every attempt to find him, until finally she opened a door which proved to be in the outside wall of a high tower and she fell, fell, fell, waking with a startled cry just before she landed.

Strong arms held her when she was about to sit up in fright. A hand smoothed the tangle of her hair back from her face. 'A dream. It was just a dream.' A voice, soothing as the softest of cashmere in her ear. 'Go back to sleep, Celia. You're safe now.'

'I tried,' she mumbled. 'I really tried.' Her cheek rested on something hard and warm and infinitely comforting. Vaguely, she registered a slow, regular bump. Like a heart beating. 'Safe,' she mumbled.

A kiss on her brow. A fluttering kiss, cool lips. 'Safe,' the voice said, pulling her closer.

The nightmare faded into the distance, like a black beast retreating with its tail between its legs. She knew it wouldn't dare come back. Celia slept the rest of the night dreamlessly.

She woke feeling much refreshed. Curled up under her blanket by the fire, she could see by the sky that it was not yet morning. The air was cool on her face. She had been dreaming of George. It came back to her now—

the running, the never quite catching. She tried to picture her husband, but his image was blurry, like an old painting covered with the patina of age. The months of her marriage felt unreal, like a spell from which she had been freed, a play she had not meant to attend. Just as she had never quite seen herself as a wife, now she could not believe in herself as a widow. She was just Celia, neither Armstrong nor Cleveden, for none of these names meant anything here. Here she was alone in this desert wilderness, her fate in the hands of the man who lay sleeping on the other side of the fire. She was free to be whoever it was she chose to be, and no one in the real world would ever know. It was an intoxicating feeling.

As she crept carefully past Ramiz, heading for the washing pool with her clothes, she remembered something else. Could it really have been Ramiz who had held her so gently? It seemed so improbable. She must have imagined it. If she had cried out, which she thought she must have, it seemed much more likely that he would have woken her and bade her be quiet. But the arms that had held her had seemed so real, and she had felt so incredibly safe enfolded in them. Was Sheikh Ramiz al-Muhana capable of such tenderness?

Returning properly dressed, complete with the stays whose constraints she was starting to loathe, and a fresh pair of silk stockings she wished fervently to do without, Celia decided simply to pretend that nothing had happened and set about making morning coffee while Ramiz refilled their canteens. When he asked her how she had slept, she told him very well, and no more was said.

* * *

She had expected Balyrma to be a walled city, perhaps built into the mountains which were rising like huge sand dunes in the distance, but as Celia looked down on the capital of A'Qadiz from the vantage point to which Ramiz had led them, her first impression was of lush green, so vibrant and vivid that it looked as if the city had been mistakenly painted into the middle of a desert canvas. It was much larger than she had expected too. A patchwork of fields were laid out, stretching across the plain on either side of the well-formed track they were following, neatly bordered with what looked like cypress trees.

'The mountains on either side protect us from the worst of the sun in the summer, and they provide the water which makes all this possible,' Ramiz explained. 'If you look closely, you can also see that they protect us from invasion. See the little turret there?'

Celia peered in the direction he pointed. 'Are you under threat of invasion?'

'Not for more than five hundred years,' Ramiz said proudly, 'but it is a wise man who is vigilant. There are many who envy us our wealth, and some who would mistake my own desire for ongoing peace as a weakness. As you saw to your cost.'

They made their way with their caravan strung out behind them along the increasingly wide road towards the city. With her veil firmly in place, Celia rode behind Ramiz, and had ample opportunity to observe how he was received by his people. She knew he was a prince, of course, but over the last two days she had put his status to the back of her mind. It was impossible to do so now, as every one of the multitude of people with their mules, camels, horses and trundling carts who passed them on the approach to the city fell to their knees in front of Ramiz, uttering prayers and good wishes, keeping their heads bowed.

Once again Celia thought of the pharaohs, who had taken their status as gods for granted just as Ramiz seemed to be doing. She realised how much latitude he had bestowed upon her, and wondered how many hundreds of social solecisms she had committed. It appalled her, for she was used to thinking of herself as up to snuff on every occasion, and now here she was, entering a magnificent city in the wake of its prince with absolutely no idea how she should behave when she got there. Nerves fluttered like a shoal of tiny creatures in her stomach, making her feel slightly nauseous. She felt an absurdly childish inclination to turn her camel round and flee.

What would her father think of her? Lily-livered, he would say. Highly unusual as the circumstances were, Lord Armstrong would expect his daughter to think and to act like a statesman. Celia sat up straight in the saddle. Whatever lay ahead, she was ready to face it.

What lay ahead was a startlingly beautiful city. Once they had passed through the fields, groves of lemon, orange and fig trees and terraced olive bushes, they entered the city of Balyrma itself. It was walled after all, she realised as they passed through a majestic portal, their path still bordered with devotedly kneeling citizens, into a city straight out of *One Thousand and One Nights*. Terracotta dwellings with slits for windows and turreted roofs, blank walls with keyhole-shaped doors behind which she imagined cloistered courtyards, fountains tinkling at every corner. Through narrow alleyways she caught a glimpse of a souk selling cloth, colours bright as jewels. From another came the heady scent of spices. As they progressed towards the centre of the city the buildings became more ornate; tiled walls patterned with mosaic, elaborate high shutters on the windows worked with intricate patterns of wrought iron.

The palace stood in the exact centre of the town. A high wall, too high to see over, with two beautiful slender towers marking each of the corners. The wall was pristine white, with a flowing border of blue and gold tiles along the middle, leading to the huge central entranceway protected not just by a set of doors of gothic proportions, but also by a grille plated with silver and gold. It was the sort of fairytale palace that normally stood at the end of a drawbridge, Celia wanted to say to Ramiz, remembering just in time not to blurt out her thoughts. But then, as first the gate and then the doors were flung open to receive them, and she caught her first glimpse of the royal palace of Balyrma, Celia lost the ability to speak anyway—for Ramiz's home looked as if it had been conjured up by Scheherazade herself.

CHAPTER FOUR

THEY left the bedraggled caravan of animals and luggage outside. An army of white-robed servants appeared as if from nowhere, it seemed to Celia, and led them down a short covered passageway dotted with mysterious doors, each with a guard armed with a glittering scimitar. The stark white of their robes was relieved only by a discreet embroidered crest depicting a falcon and a new moon, which she had noticed embossed on the entrance gates too, and by the red and white check of their headdresses.

Following in Ramiz's wake, her head respectfully lowered, Celia felt more overwhelmed with every step she took. The huge courtyard they entered was perfectly symmetrical, the pillars and windows and doors which flanked it all mirroring each other, as did the mosaic design in blue and gold which formed the frieze around the walls, continued on the pillars which bounded the open space, and covered the floor of the courtyard itself. Two fountains played to each other. Risking a fleeting glance up, Celia saw another floor with a colonnaded balcony, and counted another two above that, all glittering white, trimmed with blue and gold.

Ramiz seemed to have forgotten her presence. Engaged deep in conversation with a man whose robes and bearing clearly proclaimed a higher status from the guards, Ramiz himself seemed to have metamorphosed as they entered his domain. His bearing now was remote and autocratic, that of a man who took his power for granted, as he did the obedience of others. She had no idea what he was saying, but even his voice sounded different—short, staccato sentences, none of the soft vowels and curling consonants she had grown used to.

She felt as if she didn't know him. She forced herself to accept that she didn't. What had happened over the last two days had been an oasis, an exotic interlude in the harsh, unyielding desert of reality. This was his real life. Suddenly she was a little afraid.

She hadn't taken his threat to make her his concubine seriously. She hadn't allowed herself to think about his harem. In fact, she had allowed herself to assume that it simply wouldn't happen, that when they arrived here he would change his mind and—and what?

She was alone. Worse, she was a woman alone, which meant she had neither the right nor the power to choose her own destiny. It wasn't a case of being forced to do Ramiz's bidding. She didn't have any other option.

Powerless. The full meaning of the word hit her like a sack of corn swung into her middle, so that she felt her breath whistling out, her stomach clenching. Celia began to panic, her fevered imagination conjuring up all sorts of hideous fates. It would be weeks—months, maybe—before she was missed. She pictured Cassie waiting anxiously every day for a letter which did not come, trying to reassure Caroline and Cordelia and poor little Cressida, and at the same time attempting to persuade Papa to take some sort of action. But what could he do, so far away in London? Nothing. And in the meantime she, Celia, would probably have been cast out into the desert and left to die.

Fortunately at this point Celia's common sense intervened. If Ramiz had wanted her dead he would not have saved her life. If he'd wanted harm to come to her, he'd have left her on her own at the site of the massacre. She couldn't claim to truly know the autocratic Prince standing a few yards away, oblivious to her presence, but she knew enough about the man to believe in his integrity and honour, and she knew enough of his hard-won and volatile peace to understand that he wouldn't risk upsetting the British government by slaughtering the daughter of one of their foremost statesmen. She was acting like a hysterical female when dignity and calm were what was required. She was in a royal palace, for goodness' sake! She was a citizen of one of the world's great powers. Ramiz wouldn't dare lock her in a harem and expect her to do his bidding.

Nodding to herself with renewed resolve, Celia looked up, but Ramiz was gone. She stood quite alone in the courtyard, with only the tinkling fountains for company. She had no idea which of the doorways he had gone through. Though the doors were all open, each was draped in heavy brocade and gauzy lace to keep out the fierce heat of the day. The keyhole-shaped windows of the salons, with their gold-plated iron grilles, stared out blankly at her.

'Hello?' she called out tentatively, feeling horribly self-conscious as she listened to her voice echo up through the courtyard. There was no answer. This is ridiculous, she thought, deciding simply to select a doorway and walk through it.

She was picking up her skirts and making for the nearest one when a voice halted her. Two men were approaching. Huge men with bellies so large they looked like cushions, dressed not in robes but in wide black pleated breeches and shiny black boots. Each had a vicious curved dagger held in the sash which marked where the waistband had once been. Under their black turbans each had a black beard and long black moustaches.

Like two of Ali Baba's forty thieves, Celia thought a little hysterically as the men stopped in front of her. Then they bowed, indicating that she follow them, and with her heart in her mouth she did, through a myriad of doors and cool dark passageways, until they came to another large wooden door set in another white-tiled wall. One of the men produced a large key and pulled the door wide. Celia stepped through into a courtyard almost a mirror image of the one she had left. She thought at first she was back where she had started. Then the door behind her closed, leaving the guards on the other side, and she realised where she was.

Just as Ramiz had told her she would be, she was in his harem.

It was everything she had expected, and yet nothing like it. For a start she was quite alone aside from the two maidservants who tended to her, bringing delicious foods, exotic fruits she had never seen before, fragrant meats cooked in delicious spices, cooling sherbets and tea served sweet and flavoured with mint.

Adila and Fatima were shy at first, giggling over Celia's clothes, astonished at the layers of undergarments she wore, and utterly confounded by her stays. In turn Celia, who allowed her dresser to look after her hair for grand occasions, but otherwise was used to managing for herself, found their care for her embarrassing—waving them away when they first attempted to bathe her, submitting only when she saw that she had offended them.

By nature modest, Celia had never shared such intimacies as bathing, even with her sisters, but within the seclusion of the harem it seemed less shocking, and she very quickly began to enjoy the pampering of baths strewn with rose petals and orange blossom, having oils scented with musk and amber gently massaged into her skin and preparations for her hair and for her face, which left her whole body glowing and more relaxed than she had ever known.

The harem itself covered three floors, its upper terraces reached by tiled staircases which zigzagged up through the towers, marking the four corners of the courtyards. These upper rooms were empty, echoing, as if they had not been used for some time. The lower rooms, which led one into another in a square around the terrace, were opulently decorated, with rich carpets on the floors and low divans draped with lace, velvet and silk, the jewel colours of blue and gold and emerald and crimson reflected in the long mirrors which hung on the walls. The only windows looked out onto the courtyard, and the only exit was the one through which she had entered, but once Celia had recovered from the shock of her incarceration and accepted there was nothing she could do save wait for Ramiz to return, she found it astonishingly easy to surrender to the magical world of the harem. She had nothing to do save surrender her body to the ministering of Adila and Fatima, and surrender her mind to the healing process.

As the days melded one into another Celia quickly lost all track of time, so strangely did the tranquil seclusion of the harem play on her senses. She had never been so much alone, never had so much peace to simply be. As the eldest, and having lost her mother not long after her youngest sister Cressida was born, it was second nature to Celia to put others first, to be always thinking ahead and taking responsibility for what happened next. Indulgence and inactivity such as had now been forced on her were quite alien. Those who knew her as always busy, always planning, managing at least ten things at once, would say without hesitation that such a life as she was now experiencing would have her beside herself with boredom or screaming for release. Celia would have said so herself. But right now it was the antidote she required to recover not just from the trauma of losing her husband, but from the trauma of realising she wished she had never married him in the first place. If Ramiz had intended this as a punishment, he had been mistaken.

Almost without her noticing a full month passed, marked by the changing of the moon, whose growth from flickering crescent to glowing whole reflected the healing process taking place in Celia herself.

Then, just as she was beginning to wonder if she would be left forgotten here for ever, and her temper was beginning to recover enough to resent Ramiz's extended and unexplained absence, the man himself appeared without warning.

It was evening. Dinner had arrived—a much more elaborate meal than usual, which required an additional servant to bring it. Out of habit Celia was dressed in an evening gown after the daily ritual of her bath and massage. She stared in consternation at the plethora of little dishes in their gold salvers, wondrously appetising but far too much for just one, set out on a low table in the largest of the salons, around which banks of tasselled and embroidered cushions were strewn.

'I can't eat all this,' she said helplessly to Adila, miming that they should take some of it back, but the maid only smiled behind her hand and backed out, shaking her head.

The door to the outside world opened. Not just the usual tiny crack, barely enough to allow the staff to slip in and out, it was flung wide open. Ramiz strode in, resplendent in a robe of opulent red.

She had forgotten how incredibly handsome he was. She had forgotten how tall he was too. He looked a little tired, though, with a tiny fan of lines crinkling around his eyes. He wore no headdress, no belt, and his full robe was more like a caftan with wide sleeves, flowing loosely down to his feet which were clad in slippers of soft leather studded with jewels. The robe was open at the neck, but for all his dress was obviously informal he looked even more regal, more intimidating than she remembered.

She was nervous. Her mouth was dry. Her heart was bumping a fraction too hard against her breast. Celia dropped a curtsy. 'Your Highness.'

'Ramiz,' he said. 'While we are alone, I am Ramiz.'

Alone. She decided not to think about that. Having imagined this moment many times over the last few days, she decided to act as if it were any other social occasion, and to treat Ramiz as if he were an honoured guest and she the hostess. And not, definitely not, worry about being alone with him in his harem.

'Are you hungry? Dinner is here. I wondered why there was so much of it. Now I see you were expected.'

'You would have preferred some warning?' Ramiz asked, picking up immediately on her unspoken criticism.

'It is your palace. It is not for me to dictate where you are, and when,' Celia said tactfully, preceding him into the salon in which the food was laid out, waiting until he had disposed himself gracefully on a large cushion before she sat down opposite him.

'I've been away. I've only just got back,' Ramiz explained unexpectedly. 'I told you I had urgent business to attend to.' He lifted the cover from a dish of partridges stuffed with dates and pine nuts and sniffed appreciatively.

'You mean only just got back as in today?'

'An hour ago.'

Celia was flattered, and then alarmed, and then nervous again. She poured Ramiz a glass of pale green sherbet and pushed a selection of dishes towards him. 'May I ask if your business was successful?' she said. 'I presume it was to do with the other prince—Malik, I think his name was?'

Ramiz looked surprised. 'Yes.'

'Did you—were you—did you have to fight with him?'

'Not this time.'

'What, then?'

'You really want to know?'

Celia nodded. 'I really do.'

It was not the custom to discuss such matters with a

woman. It was not in his nature to discuss such matters with anyone. But it had been a difficult few days, and there was something about this woman which encouraged the sharing of confidences. 'My council all urged swift and brutal retribution—as usual, since I inherited most of them from my brother.'

'But you ignored them?'

'Yes. I don't want to follow that path until there are no other options left.'

'So tell me—what did you do? How do you go about negotiating a deal with a man who wields power through fear? Come to that, how do you set about persuading your own people to accept such an alien approach?'

Ramiz smiled. 'You forget I am a prince too. I don't have to persuade my people of anything. They do as I bid.'

'Yes, that's what you say, but I'll wager that you try all the same,' Celia said, with a perception which surprised him. 'You don't really want to rule in splendid isolation, do you?'

'Splendid isolation? That is exactly how it feels sometimes. You can have no idea how wearing it is, trying to break the ingrained prejudice of years,' Ramiz said wearily. 'Sometimes I think— But that is another matter. With Prince Malik…'

He went on to tell her about the events of the last few days, spurred on by her intelligent interest into revealing far more of his innermost thoughts than he had ever done. It was a relief to unburden himself, and refreshing too, for this woman who talked and thought like a man had a knack for encouraging without toadying, and her shocking lack of deference lent her opinions a credibility he would not otherwise have conceded.

By the time the meal was over the weight of responsibility which was beginning to feel like a sack upon his back had eased a little for the first time since he had so unexpectedly come to power. This woman understood the cares of governing. She would have made an excellent diplomatic wife. George Cleveden had chosen well. But George Cleveden was dead, and Ramiz could not regret it, for the woman who was now his widow deserved better. Much better. Not that it was any of his business.

'Are you comfortable here in my harem?' Ramiz settled himself back against the cushions. The lamps with their coloured glass shades reflected the light in rainbow patterns onto the mirrors and the tiled white of the salon.

Celia thought she recognised that teasing note in his voice, but she could not be sure. 'Extremely,' she said cautiously. 'Your servants have looked after me very well, but I was surprised to find myself the only occupant.'

'I moved my brother's wives and children to their own palace. Those who wished were returned to their families.'

'And you haven't had time to—to stock up on wives for yourself?'

Ramiz burst out laughing. 'That's one way of putting it.'

'You led me to believe you had many wives.'

'No, you made that assumption yourself.'

Celia bit her lip. 'I suppose you get tired of people like me making such assumptions. You wanted to teach me a lesson, didn't you?'

Ramiz held up his hands. 'I confess. Tell me, what did you expect when you came here? A scene from *One Thousand and One Nights*?'

She blushed. 'Something like that.'

'And now?'

'Now I don't know what to think,' she said, opting for honesty. 'In one way, there's something almost liberating in being so cut off from the world and unable to do anything about it. I feel rested. Cured. Better. I've never had so much time to think. It's like I've been able to sort out my mind, make sense of things.'

'You had problems in your marriage, I think?'

After so many days of silence, so many hours spent scrutinising and questioning, it was a huge relief to speak her thoughts. 'I wasn't exactly unhappy, but I think I would have become so, and I know George already was.' A tear trembled on her lashes. Celia brushed it away. 'He was—he did not want—I think he wanted a companion rather than a wife. How did you guess?' She had not meant to ask, but here in the tranquil security of the harem, with the soft light casting ghostly shadows onto the walls, such an intimate topic seemed natural.

He had been conversing with her like a man, admiring her intelligence and strong opinions. Now he saw in that look stripped of its poise, in the vulnerable trembling of her lip, that she was all woman. He remembered her body, glinting pale and alluring in the moonlight by the oasis—an image which had crept unbidden into his dreams these last five nights, so unwanted, so dishonourable that he had banished its memory in the daylight. Now here it was again, and here in the rooms of the palace set aside for sensual pleasure, rooms he had never himself used, his resistance was beginning to falter.

He wanted her. There was every reason for him to deny himself, but he had done so much denying since his brother died he was sick of it. He wanted her. He wanted to teach her. He wanted her to know pleasure. And he wanted her knowing to be his doing.

Ramiz got to his feet. 'I guessed because you have the look of a woman starved of attention. Come with me,' he said, reaching out a hand to pull her to her feet, placing a finger over her mouth to stop her speaking. He led her out of the salon to the courtyard, where the fountains made their sweet music in the jasmine-scented air. 'Look up there.' The deep sapphire of the night sky was framed high above their heads. 'In my culture, we believe that love has wings—wings which can take you all the way up there to the stars, where the heavenly pleasures of the body are worshipped. It is a voluptuous journey. A journey which leaves its mark upon a woman in her eyes, in the way she walks, the way she learns to nourish and to relish her body, knowing that it is a temple of delights. I look at you and I see a woman who has not yet learned to fly. I look at you and I want to help you experience what it feels like to soar in the high clouds.'

His voice shivered seductively in her ear. They were standing by the fountain, his hands on her arms, stroking feathery light up and down her bare skin. She could feel the brush of velvet from his sleeves. He smelt of lemon-scented soap and night-scented man. She pictured herself flying. His presence, the scent of him, the feel of him, the husky sound of him, gave her a fleeting image of what that might be like. Of what he might do to her to make it happen.

She wanted it. Whatever it was, she wanted it, and she knew she would never find a more able tutor. His confidence was intoxicating. His aura of power equally so. His casual mastery, which could intimidate and anger, was here, under the secret stars fascinating, beguiling, and incredibly persuasive.

'Don't you want to know what it's like to fly, Celia?' Ramiz spoke into her ear. His lips whispered over her skin.

'I don't know if I can,' she said, which was the truth.

His laugh, like a throaty purr, so filled with assurance, made her stomach clench in anticipation. 'Trust me—you can.'

His tongue traced the shell of her ear. His fingers trailed up her arms to the nape of her neck, circling delightful spirals which whirled little pulses into life. Her heart was beating fast. Faster. She was hot and cold all at the same time. His mouth traced the line of her jaw, and she ached, ached for him to kiss her lips, but instead he moved down her throat. His velvet-soft mouth gave kisses that made her arch back in his arms like a bow, so that she could see the sky now, the stars glinting and beckoning and calling to her as his mouth reached the hollow of her neck, and her skin seemed to reach out to greet him, wanting more than the flickering kisses he gave her.

'Ramiz,' Celia whispered, 'Ramiz, please…I want to.'

He scooped her up into his arms, heading for the nearest salon, which happened to be the one in which she slept. The low divan, with its scattering of pillows and silk covers, took up centre place in the room. It was the strangest bed she had ever encountered, for it was round, with neither head nor footboard. Ramiz set her to her feet before it, gazing deep into her eyes, his own glowing amber in the shadowed light with something fierce she didn't recognise and wasn't sure she liked.

She lowered her lids, but he tilted her chin up, forcing

her to look at him again. 'You must not be ashamed of your body; you must learn to enjoy it. That is the first lesson you must learn or you will never leave the ground.'

Then his lips covered hers, fitting so perfectly that she stopped breathing. How could mouths fit like that? But they did. Warmth flooded through her. She stood pliant, unsure what to do, confused by the urgent need to kiss him back, so at odds with what she had been told. Ramiz snaked his arms around her back to pull her close. She could feel the solid hardness of his body pressed into her own softness. She had not thought of herself as soft before. Or curved. She had never encountered such blatant masculinity so close at hand. She was melting, and in the melting she succumbed to temptation and kissed him back.

Her lips were petal-soft against his, beguilingly untutored. Ramiz pressed his mouth against hers, tasting her delicately. He felt rather than heard her sigh. If he had not known better he would have said she had never been kissed. Certainly she had not been taught to kiss back. Her inexperience inflamed him. A primal instinct which surprised him to possess, to own, sent the blood surging to his shaft. His kiss hardened too, his mouth easing hers open, his tongue finding hers, coaxing at first, then forgetting to coax and instead demanding. She tasted of heat and promised ecstasy. An ecstasy he could not wholly indulge.

To give is to receive. Tonight he would give, and the giving would have to suffice. Ramiz tore his mouth away. 'Wait,' he said, breathing heavily. 'Tonight you must allow me to wait upon you.' Then slowly, tantalisingly slowly, he began his controlled onslaught on Celia's senses.

His hands tangled in her hair, pulling out the con-straining pins, his fingers combing through the rich copper mass of curls until it was spread over her shoulders, trailing down her back, curling over the pearly white of her bosom. He turned her around to unfasten her dress, his fingers trailing over her skin as he slipped it down over her shoulders to pool at her feet. She could feel his mouth on her neck again, on the knot of her spine. His breath was warm on her skin, but she shivered all the same. He unlaced her stays, pulling her close against him, her back to his chest, her skin against the velvet of his robe. She could feel the hard length of him nestling into the curve of her bottom. So other. So male.

She shivered again, but now she was hot, with fingers of heat creeping surreptitiously over her skin like the fingers of dawn through the mists of morning. Ramiz wrapped his arms around her, pulling her hard against him, nudging his erection into the soft mound of her buttocks. His hands stroked up from her waist to the curves of her breasts, through the soft fabric of her chemise, stroking so that her skin prickled. Her nipples hardened. He weighed her breasts in his hands, his thumbs scraping the tips, making them pucker, making her stomach clench, and between her legs something that felt like another unfurling bud seemed to clench too.

He turned her round, kissing her swiftly on the lips before he pulled her chemise over her head, leaving her clad only in her lace-trimmed pantaloons, for she had given up on wearing stockings. Instinctively Celia tried to cover herself, but Ramiz pulled her hands away from her breasts. 'How can you expect others to enjoy what you cannot admire yourself?' he said. 'You are beautiful.'

Celia blushed. 'I'm not. I know I'm not. My sister Cassie is beautiful. I'm too thin. I don't—men don't—I'm just not.'

'Look at me.'

She obeyed reluctantly.

Ramiz wound a thick tress of hair around his hands. 'The colour of desire. A reflection of the flames which can burn inside you if only you'll let them.' He cupped her head to look deep into her eyes. 'You have a mouth made to frame kisses. The way your lids hide your eyes, they speak of secrets if only a man knows where to look.' His palms grazed down her shoulders, shaping her breasts. 'Your skin is like alabaster, like cream, to be touched and tasted.' He bent his head and took her nipple between his lips, his tongue flicking over the tip, his mouth sucking slowly, then hard, tugging until she moaned, for it felt as if he had set up a path of flames, like a fuse, burning its way from the painful ache of it down through the pooling heat in her belly towards the curling, tensing heat between her legs.

She fell back onto the divan. Ramiz knelt between her legs, his hands spanning her waist as he kissed her breasts, tugging sensations she had never imagined from her, so that she writhed with them, clutching at the silk of the sheets, then at the velvet of his robe, then at the satin of his hair, wanting more and more of what he gave, at the same time vaguely conscious that this must be wrong—for surely she should not be feeling these things? Surely she should not be wanting in this way, even if she didn't know what it was she wanted? Except to fly, as Ramiz had promised.

He was licking his way down her stomach now, tugging her pantaloons over her legs, gently removing her hands when she would have covered herself, whispering to her in a mixture of his own language and hers that she was beautiful, beautiful, beautiful, until almost she believed him. 'Legs made to wrap themselves around a man,' he said to her as he kissed the crook of her knees, carefully pushing them apart to taste the skin on the inside of her thigh.

She was shocked. She was unbearably tense. She shouldn't be letting him do what he was doing, whatever it was he was doing, but she couldn't bear to stop him because she wanted him to do more of it. And when he did, his mouth just feather-touching the place between her legs where the aching was becoming a pulse, she jerked with both shock and pleasure, relieved that he held her down, released from fighting it when his hands stroked her thighs into position and his tongue eased its way onto her, into her, licking, causing such a fluttering sensation within her that she cried out, because it wasn't too much, it wasn't enough.

She felt them then, her wings budding, like the rippling on a pond when a feather lands. She stilled and shut her eyes tight and then she saw them too, pink-tipped wings, pushing their way out as Ramiz circled his tongue to help them on their way, circling so they could push up more, licking to encourage them, soft so as not to frighten, then harder as her wings grew, and pushed, and trembled with their unfurling, lifting her up so that she gasped with the sudden swoop of them, lifting her up again as they bunched tight, readying themselves. And then with one final burst she toppled, thinking to fall, and her wings opened and she flew, soaring and bucking and diving and swooping and soaring again, crying out with the sheer unexpected delight of it, crying out again until she glided and floated slowly, slowly, sleepily back down to earth, exhausted and sated and filled with the glitter of the stars she had touched.

Past experience had taught him the satisfaction of giving pleasure, but always it had been a prelude to receiving. Now, Ramiz gazed at Celia spread out on the divan before him, her perfect skin flushed with satisfaction, her lips, her nipples, her sex all swollen with his attentions, and felt a new kind of satisfaction. He had done this. He had given her this. Blood surged into his groin, swelling his already hard shaft, though he knew he would do nothing about it. He wanted to, but he did not need to. This was enough—this knowing that he had made his mark, that he had been the first if not to have her, then to pleasure her. He had given her something no one else had. She would not forget him.

As he would not forget this picture she made. Unwilling to tempt his self-control, Ramiz got to his feet and pulled the silk sheet over her. 'Sleep now,' he whispered.

Celia's eyes fluttered open. 'Ramiz, I…'

'Tomorrow we must talk of the future. For the moment, rest,' he said.

Then he was gone. Were it not for the cushions scattered across the floor, the rumpled state of the sheets, the faint tingling she felt all over her body, she could almost have persuaded herself it was a dream.

CHAPTER FIVE

CELIA awoke the next morning restless and confused, and rather appalled by herself. What she had felt last night had been shocking in many more ways than one. She'd had no idea that women such as herself could experience such raw emotion. Surely it was rather base to have done so? Was not such stuff the domain of courtesans? So she had always believed. Aunt Sophia had said so herself—women endured while men enjoyed. But last night—last night... Celia's face burned at the memory of her own abandonment. Then the heat focused lower as she remembered more.

Stop! She sat up in bed, burying her face in her hands, screwing her eyes tight shut in an effort to obliterate the image of Ramiz like some erotic god in his scarlet robe. It would be scarlet, of course. The colour of sin and shame. What he had done—no! *She had encouraged him. She had to admit it.* Her toes curled into the soft silk of her sheets. She had wanted him. And when he had gone she had wanted him again.

It must be the influence of this place. This harem, these rooms, built as a monument to the pleasures of the flesh. All that bathing and oiling of her body which went on—how could she help it if her mind was filled with indecent thoughts? This was a profane place. What she had experienced was temporal, bounded by the locked door to the rest of the palace, swathed in this secret sanctum by the velvets and silks and lace which screened the doorways, fuelled by her own fevered imaginings from that dratted book, *One Thousand and One Nights*. She was inhabiting a fantasy, that was all. A fantasy in which she might have acted as shamefully as a concubine, but that didn't mean she *was* one. She was still Celia.

Except, she thought, gazing distractedly at herself in the mirror once she had dressed in a white muslin gown trimmed with primrose yellow ribbons, she didn't actually know who Celia was any more. She tried to see herself with fresh eyes. She tried to see the Celia Ramiz saw. Did she look different? She wasn't sure. She felt different—more conscious of her body under the layers of her clothes, of the way the different textures felt against her newly sensitised skin when she walked, sat, stretched. Did she believe herself beautiful? Celia stared. No. Cassie was beautiful.

What, then, did Ramiz see? The beautifying effect of the harem? Perhaps some of its sensuality had rubbed off on her last night, but she could detect no trace of it now. 'What he saw last night, Celia Armstrong, was an available woman,' she said, sticking her tongue out at her reflection, failing to notice that she had reverted to her maiden name, because something else had just occurred to her. If last night had just been about her being available, why had Ramiz not simply taken his own pleasure?

* * *

At that precise moment Ramiz was busily engaged in sensitive matters of state, not pleasure. He sighed as he read over the terms of the draft treaty his trusted man of business, Akil, had prepared. Though A'Qadiz was the largest of the principalities involved, and the most powerful, it was a complex and delicate matter, with the disparate customs and rights of so many tribes to take into account.

'Sometimes I can understand my brother's preference for war,' he said, rubbing his tired eyes with the back of his hand. 'At least it is simple.'

Akil, who had known Ramiz since they were childhood friends, smiled thinly. Even in those days Ramiz had been a peacemaker, intervening with their father when his elder brother Asad went too far for their tutor or the families of his bullied victims to turn a blind eye, even if Asad was the royal heir. 'Simple, yes, but not necessarily effective. Don't give up, Ramiz. Your pact with Prince Malik has brought us a huge step forward.'

'If it holds,' Ramiz said wearily. 'What updates do you have regarding the new mines?'

Gold was the main source of A'Qadiz's riches, second only to the plentiful supplies of water which allowed the population not only to live well, but to trade key crops such as dates, figs and lemons. 'Good news,' Akil replied brightly. 'The richest seam yet, and it looks as if your hunch to test for silver to the south has paid off too.'

'Excellent. Let us hope that word of the find does not spread too quickly. For the moment the British and the French are content to bide their time in Egypt, scavenging whatever precious remnants of the past they can lay

their hands on. They think us a paltry little country to
whom they will throw a few stray crumbs by agreeing
to use our port to open up a trade route to the riches of
India, but if they find out the extent of the gold and
silver we have buried in our land, especially in the
mines so near to the coast, they will not be able to resist
trying to get their hands on it.'

'The Englishman who was killed—did you find
his papers?'

'His name was Cleveden. Yes, I did, but there was
nothing in them I didn't already know.'

'What of the woman?' Akil asked diffidently. All of
Balyrma had heard of the woman's arrival, but like
everyone else he was in the dark as to Ramiz's intentions. Despite their long-standing friendship, Ramiz
did not confide in him, nor did he take kindly to having
his decisions questioned.

'What of her?' Ramiz asked tersely.

'She is still here, I presume?'

'Of course she is.'

'What do you intend to do with her, may I ask?'

A vision of Celia spread naked on the divan last
night flashed into Ramiz's head. He had been unable to
sleep for thinking of her, unable to prevent himself from
imagining what it would have been like if he had taken
her as he had wanted to—plunged his shaft into the soft,
sweet depths he had prepared with such delightful
relish. What he wanted to do with her was just that.

But, as so often, what he wanted and what he could
have were very divergent paths. This time the honourable path was the least palatable. Fortunately he had
committed to it before the events of last night. If he had
not— But he would not think of that. It was decided.

'I wrote to the British Consul General in Cairo, informing him of what happened,' Ramiz explained. 'I did it as soon as we got here, for I couldn't risk the likes of Malik using it against me by trying to implicate me. I expect they'll send someone to collect her—in fact I'm surprised they haven't done so already. Until then she is safe enough here.'

'In your harem?'

'Of course.'

'Your—until now—empty harem, Ramiz?'

'What is that supposed to mean?'

Akil shook his head. 'You know very well what it means. The Council of Elders have asked me to urge you again to consider their list of suitable wives. It is a year since you came out of mourning for Asad, and they are anxious for your rule to be cemented. Also, the people would welcome a royal wedding. It has been a difficult and unsettling time.'

'Thanks largely to my brother,' Ramiz said sharply. 'It was Asad, not I, who embroiled us in shedding blood. If it were not for me—'

Akil held up his hand. 'Ramiz, no one knows better than I the pain and hardship of the journey which has brought us to peace, but you must understand the people, the council, they do not have your vision. To them, to fight is to prosper. They have not yet seen the benefits your hard-won peace will bring them.'

Ramiz got to his feet and began to prowl restlessly around the room. Aside from the large mahogany desk at which he had been seated opposite Akil, it was lined with bookcases, all of them full, an eclectic selection of works, from the ancient scriptures of his country to Greek and Latin classics and a wide range of modern

French and English literature. Much as he respected his heritage, his travels had taught him to respect the culture of all the great civilisations. If only his people were so open-minded.

'So my taking a wife would make everyone happy, would it, Akil?' Ramiz said, resuming his seat.

'If you were to marry one of the princesses the council have suggested, maybe Prince Malik's daughter, it would cement the peace, make us stronger, and make our people more secure. Even if you chose a princess from one of our own tribes—Sheikh Farid's daughter, for example—it would buy you much support. A royal wedding would go a long way to making your people feel—feel…'

'Spit it out, for the love of the gods,' Ramiz said impatiently.

'It would make them feel more secure, Highness. When you have sons, the dynasty will be settled. Without them there is only your cousin, and he is…'

'Weak.'

'Yes,' Akil agreed with relief.

Ramiz frowned. 'Why just one wife, then? If my marriage would cement the pact with Malik, why not do the same with our other neighbours? Why not two wives, or four, or ten?'

'You jest, I think, Highness.' Akil eyed his friend nervously. He looked calm, but Akil was not fooled. Ramiz drummed his fingers on the blotting pad, his mouth held in much too firm a line. Ramiz preferred to wield words rather than a sword, but when roused he had a temper which put his brother's into the shade as a lion's roar would drown out a kitten.

'You can leave off this "Highness" nonsense, old

friend. I know you only use it when you want something.'

Akil smiled. 'Ramiz, listen, the council has compiled a list of ten princesses. I have verified it myself. Each one would make an excellent match. You must marry—you know that—for the sake of A'Qadiz.'

'Everything I do is for the sake of A'Qadiz, it has been so all my life, Akil, *you* know that. I never fail to do my duty.'

Akil nodded. 'But this is a pleasant duty, Ramiz. You are a man. All men need a wife to tend to their needs. The women on the council's list, they are not just princesses, daughters of our neighbouring princes and most influential tribes, they are beautiful virgins. Not such an onerous duty as duties go, is it now?'

Ramiz opened his mouth to speak, then closed it again. What was the point in trying to explain what he didn't really understand himself? Akil spoke good sense, he always did, and he spoke it without all the shilly-shallying and obeisance that the council used. He knew he should marry. He knew his marriage would be first and foremost for the good of his country and his dynasty. It was the way of things, had been the way of things for centuries, but the very idea of entering into such a cold bargain repelled him.

Perhaps Akil was right. Perhaps he had spent too long in the West. But he didn't like the idea of himself as some sort of stud stallion, any more than he liked the idea of his wives as brood mares, vying in his harem for his attentions. He didn't want that. He didn't know what he wanted, but it wasn't that.

Ramiz got to his feet again. 'Put these amendments to the treaty before the council. Tell them I'll consider their list of princesses when it is all signed, and the agreement with the British is settled too.'

Akil smiled and bowed. 'A very wise decision, Highness. Your wisdom is only matched by the magnificence of your...'

'Enough,' Ramiz said wryly. 'Go now, before I change my mind. And have the Englishwoman brought to me.'

Celia followed the servant through a maze of corridors guarded by countless sentries, each wearing a white robe with the new moon and falcon crest. She wore no veil, but kept her eyes on the ground, wondering what on earth Ramiz was going to say to her, wondering how on earth she was going to face him after last night without turning the same colour as the guards' checked *keffiyey* headdresses.

The room she was shown into was a library—the first salon she had seen furnished in a Western manner. Ramiz was sitting behind a large desk made of mahogany inlaid with pearl and teak. He was wearing a robe of dark blue, but no headdress, and rose to greet her when she entered the room.

'*Sabah el kheer,*' Celia pronounced carefully, using one of the phrases she had managed to learn from Fatima.

'Good morning, Lady Celia,' Ramiz said, 'I trust you are well?'

What did he mean by that? 'Yes,' she managed faintly. 'And you, Your Highness?' *Your Highness! After last night!* Celia bit her lip and stared fixedly at the carpet. Silk, it was woven with an intricate pattern of vibrant and beautiful colours. It must have cost a fortune.

'It is Ramiz, and I am very well.'

Celia jumped at the proximity of his voice. He took her hand. How had he moved so quietly? Slippers, she saw, for her eyes were still fixed firmly on the floor.

'I wanted to talk to you. Perhaps you should sit down?'

'Yes.' She allowed herself to be ushered into a chair facing the desk. To her relief Ramiz resumed his seat opposite, putting a solid expanse of inlaid wood between them. 'You have a lot of books,' she said, raising her eyes to cast them around the room.

'I do. You may read any that you wish. I have regular packages sent from London and Paris.'

'Thank you. Although I don't expect I will be here long enough to read many of them.'

Silence ensued. Ramiz drummed his fingers on the blotting pad. Celia risked a glance at him from under her lashes. He was leaning back in his chair, looking quite relaxed, as if last night had not happened. Or perhaps it was because it meant nothing to him. She wondered what the etiquette was for such occasions, but, having no experience of them whatsoever, found herself at a complete loss. She thought of some of the women of the *ton* who were reputed to have *affaires*. She'd always been surprised, for the couples betrayed no sign of affection—except poor Caro Lamb over Lord Byron, of course, but one didn't want to take any leaves out of *her* book!

Perhaps the best thing to do was pretend it hadn't happened after all. Celia sneaked another look at Ramiz, caught his eye unexpectedly and blushed furiously.

'You will be wondering what I intend to do with you,' Ramiz said.

'I beg your pardon?' Now Celia did look up, her eyes flashing outrage.

'I've written to your Consul General,' Ramiz continued blandly, 'to let him know that you're safe.'

'Lord Wincester. Papa was at school with him,' Celia said irrelevently.

Ramiz raised an eyebrow. 'You are well connected indeed.'

'So I'll be going back soon?'

'In a few days, I expect. As soon as they send someone.'

'Oh.' She should be relieved. 'They'll send me back to England.'

'Don't you want to go back? To see your family? I think you mentioned sisters.'

'Yes, naturally I miss them—Cassie in particular. But—oh, it's nothing. Just that I was expecting to be here in the East for a couple of years, that's all. I was looking forward to seeing it, to learning something new, and now I shall have to go home to do—well, I don't actually know what I'll do, to be honest.'

'What did you do before?'

'Playing hostess for Papa took up much of my time. I looked after the London house, of course, and then there were my sisters. But Cassie, the next in age to me, is coming out next Season, under my Aunt Sophia's chaperonage, and now that he has me off his hands Papa intends to marry again, he told me so himself.'

'So you are worried there will be no place for you when you return?'

'A little.' Celia shrugged. 'I'm being selfish, thinking of myself. I like to be busy, you see, and I'm used to taking charge, having done so since our mother died. It would be too awkward to stay at home if Papa has a new wife, I'd be forever treading on her toes without meaning to, and anyway I'll be expected to go into mourning.'

'But you will marry again, surely?' The moment he said it, Ramiz realised he disliked the idea intensely.

Celia pursed her lips. 'I don't think so. I don't think I'm very good at being a wife.'

'Now you are feeling sorry for yourself,' Ramiz said with a twisted smile. 'You hardly had the chance to find out one way or another.'

'True, but— Oh, never mind my worries. I am very sure they are extremely trivial compared to yours. The main thing is I shall no longer be your problem.'

'No.' Strange as it was, he had not thought of her simply quitting his life. Their paths would be unlikely ever to cross again.

'And in the mean time,' Celia said bracingly, 'if there is anything I can do to help you, or—' She broke off, seeing his sceptical expression. 'You're going to tell me that business is men's work, aren't you?'

'I don't have to now that you've said it for me.'

'Papa said I had a brain worthy of a man. He often talked things over with me—not so much to get my opinion as to clear his own mind. He said it helped.'

'You're suggesting I confide the business of my kingdom in you?'

Celia could not help laughing at the shocked expression on Ramiz's face. 'The very idea of it—a mere woman giving her opinions. Too much time spent in the West, your people would say. It has infected him. We must lock him up until he is cured.'

Her eyes twinkled with merriment. Her smile was infectious. 'I think Akil would agree with you,' Ramiz said.

'Who is Akil?'

'He is what your father would call my under-secretary, I suppose, but Akil is much more than that. We have known one another since childhood. He is my other hand.'

'And what did you say to shock him?'

Ramiz steepled his fingers under his chin, gazing thoughtfully at the woman across the desk. In the bright light of day her hair was a deep copper, burnished with darker shades of chestnut. When she laughed, it accentuated the upward slant of her lids, making it look as if her eyes were smiling. She had dared to tease him and to question him, and now she wanted to advise him, and she seemed completely unaware of all the rules she was breaking by doing so. She talked like a man, with the assurance of one accustomed to being attended to, but she had a way of listening, of making him feel she really heard what he said, that made him want to know what she thought, that took away any element of condescension or patronage.

'Akil wants me to marry.'

'And has he a list of worthy brides lined up?'

'How did you know that?'

Celia shrugged. 'Papa told me they did the same for our Prince of Wales. Not that I'm advocating Prinny's marriage as a good example,' she said hurriedly, thinking of the lengths to which the Regent had gone to have his wife exiled, and the string of high-profile mistresses whom he courted blatantly in her absence.

'Your Prince George is a man who—you will forgive me for saying so—indulges in all the benefits of power while carrying none of its responsibilities,' Ramiz said thoughtfully.

'You are quite right. I would not dream of comparing you to such a man. In fact I think you are rather the opposite, for it seems to me that you put duty before all else. Many people envy princes and kings for having the world at their command, but I've never been one of them. It seems to me that it is rather the opposite.'

'You mean A'Qadiz has me at its command?'

'Yes, that's exactly what I mean. Ruling can be a very lonely business, I imagine. I would think you'd be pleased to have a wife to share it with you.'

'If—when—I take a wife, it will not be to reign by my side. That is not the way here.'

'But surely...' Celia bit her lip, realising she had been on the verge of overstepping the mark. Her previous exposure to royalty had led her to surmise that they were a selfish, conceited and not particularly intelligent race, decorative rather than useful, who relied upon others to actually get things done. Ramiz was different in every way. His authority was so ingrained that he thought nothing of it until it was challenged, but though the power he held was absolute, he wielded it for the general good, rather than for his own. Which did not mean that he took criticism, even well meant criticism, easily. 'I beg your pardon. It is not my business. I have no right to express an opinion.'

'What were you going to say? Go on. I promise I won't call the *siaf*.'

'*Siaf?*'

Ramiz grinned. 'The executioner.'

'Good God, I sincerely hope not. I'm very attached to my head.'

'It's a very clever head—for a woman.'

'From you, Your Highness, that is a great compliment indeed. If you must know, I was thinking that, since you are a prince and can do no wrong, there is no reason for you to stick to something just because that's how it's always been.'

'Tradition plays a very important part here. It is what binds many of the tribes together.'

'I understand that, and I'm not suggesting you turn A'Qadiz into a miniature England, but there are some things you could do which surely everyone would see were for the greater good. Like having your wife play more than the role of a brood mare.'

The fact that he agreed with her, that her words were almost an exact repetition of his own thoughts, was disconcerting. He wasn't sure that he liked it. 'A woman's first duty is to her children.'

'A wife's first duty is to her husband,' Celia said tartly. 'I fail to see how she can perform that fully when you lock her away from the world in a harem.'

'I've told you before, it is to protect her.' She was right, he knew that, but he didn't like being forced into defending something he had himself criticised. It put him in the wrong. Ramiz was not used to being in the wrong. 'Not all women are as—as *capable* as you, Lady Celia,' he threw at her exasperatedly. 'You forget that a wife's role is also to be a woman. Women, in case you have forgotten, are supposed to be the gentle sex. We have a saying here: a good woman is one who listens with stitched lips.'

'And we have a saying in England. The road to success is more easily travelled with a woman to mark the route!'

Ramiz threw his head back and laughed. 'Admit it— you made that up.'

He looked so much younger when he smiled. 'Yes,' Celia conceded, 'but that doesn't mean it isn't true.'

'I'm afraid it is a road I will have to travel alone, albeit with a few beautiful princesses in tow.' He did not quite manage to keep the bitterness from his voice.

'Why shouldn't you choose a wife you can like— grow to love, even? You're the Prince. You can do as you wish.'

'What I wish just now is to end this topic of discussion.'

'Ramiz, when you said I was a *capable* woman, what did you mean?'

A faint flush, just the tiniest trace of colour, kissed her cheeks. Her heavy lids veiled her eyes. 'You are not submissive. You speak your mind.'

'I thought—at least I used to think—that was a good thing. It's how I've been brought up—to think for myself, but not to...to trample on the opinion of others. I hope I don't do that.'

'That's not what I meant, and you don't. You listen. You're a very good listener.'

'But what did you mean, then? Did you mean that I'm intimidating?'

'Not to me!'

'But I could be to other men?'

He saw it then. She didn't mean other men. She meant one in particular. Her dead husband. 'A man who is threatened by a woman is not worthy of being called a man, Celia,' Ramiz said gently. 'Below the capable veneer you present to the world, you are every inch a woman. Did I not tell you last night? You are beautiful.'

She shivered as Ramiz lifted her hand to his mouth and kissed her palm. It felt shockingly more intimate than being kissed on the back of her hand. His lips were warm. Instinctively her fingers curled, forming a little hollow for him. She felt his tongue licking over the pad of her thumb and closed her eyes as the muscles in her belly clenched in response. 'Am I? Do you really think so?' she said, her voice sounding as if she were parched.

Ramiz laughed huskily, his breath caressing her fingers. 'Did I not prove that to you last night too? The point is not what I think, but what you think. Until you believe in your own beauty you will never be able to enjoy it. And if you can't enjoy it…'

Celia tugged her hand away, blushing furiously. 'That sort of enjoyment is what your women learn in the harem.'

'As you did.'

'We are not in the harem now.'

Ramiz pushed himself back in his chair, running his hand through his close-cropped hair. 'No, we're not. You're right. You may select some books to take back with you. I have more business to attend to.'

'Ramiz?'

'Well?'

'I meant it when I offered to help. If there is anything I can do—I'm used to being busy. Being waited on hand and foot, having nothing more to do than decide which scent to pour into my bath, is all very well for a few days, but—is there nothing?'

'You're bored?'

She nodded.

'Would you like to see the city?'

Celia's eyes lit up. 'I'd love that.'

'I can't spare the time today, and I would not trust

you with another escort, but I will take you tomorrow. I could arrange for you to pay a visit to Akil's wife instead, if you wish. Yasmina speaks good English. You will still be spending the day in another harem, of course, but at least it won't be this one.'

Celia smiled with pleasure. 'That would be lovely. Thank you.'

'One last thing. Delightful as it was, last night was a mistake. It won't happen again. Ever.'

He was gone through the heavily draped doorway before she could answer him. Which is just as well, Celia thought, inspecting the shelves of the library, because I have no idea whether that is a good thing or not!

Deciding it was best not to even attempt to make sense of that, she instead busied herself in preparation for her outing to visit Akil's wife. It would be good to spend time with another woman. It would also be good to spend time away from the deeply unsettling presence of one particular man.

CHAPTER SIX

YASMINA, a rather beautiful woman with eyes the colour of bitter chocolate and skin like toasted almonds, welcomed Celia warmly, pouring tea from a silver samovar into delicate crystal glasses in silver holders, speaking in careful English with a slight French accent.

The harem itself was a smaller version of the one occupied by Celia in the royal palace, a series of salons built around a courtyard with a fountain and lemon trees, but there the resemblance ended. The entrance was a gilded gate, not a door, and though it was guarded it was not locked. The rooms themselves were populated with Yasmina and Akil's four children, Yasmina's mother, Akil's widowed sister and her two children.

'I expect you think all harems are full of sultry slave girls,' Yasmina said, offering Celia a selection of delicately sugared pastries stuffed with sultanas and apricots. 'The fact is that most are like this. We all have our own salons, so we can be private when we wish to, but we eat and work together, we read and sew together, and as you can see we don't have to worry about being veiled.'

'But don't you mind being confined to one place like this?'

Yasmina laughed. 'We're not. The gate isn't locked. It's just symbolic. It marks a border that we can cross only if we are covered. You will find it is the same in all households in the city. In the desert it is different. Women can wander more freely with their tribes.'

'The door to the harem at the palace is locked.'

Yasmina nodded. 'That was Ramiz's brother Asad's doing. Are there still eunuchs?'

'Two of them.'

'Akil says that Ramiz doesn't know what to do with them. There used to be about ten, but the rest of them were happy to return to Turkey, where they came from, when Asad died. Akil says that Asad kept slaves there too.' Yasmina pulled her cushion closer to Celia's and lowered her voice conspiratorially. 'Concubines, from the East. They say they knew things which would make a man faint with delight.'

'What sort of things?' Celia asked, as much fascinated as shocked.

Yasmina pouted. 'I don't know. I asked Akil, but he wouldn't tell me. I don't think he knew either, though he wouldn't admit it. You know how men are—they like to think they know everything. Anyway, when Asad died Ramiz sent all the women home with dowries, and the wives went back to their families. We all assumed it was because Ramiz was going to take a wife, but he shows no sign of doing so. You should be honoured. You are the first woman to be permitted to enter Ramiz's harem. You will be the envy of every woman in the region.'

'But it's not like that. There is no question of me becoming…'

'His wife? Goodness, no,' Yasmina said with a shocked gasp. 'Of course not. A woman like you would not be permitted to marry Ramiz.' She placed the large tray with the glasses and samovar out of reach and beckoned to her two youngest children, a boy of three and a girl of two. 'This is my son, Samir, and my daughter, Farida.'

The little girl clung shyly to her mother's arm, but Samir was bolder, and reached out to touch Celia's hair. Smiling, she took him onto her lap and allowed him to play with her pearls, at which point Farida overcame her fear of the strange woman in the funny dress and demanded a turn. Laughing, Celia balanced the two children on her lap and taught them to play a clapping game which she'd used to play with her sisters, after which Samir insisted she accompany them on a grand tour of the courtyard to meet the other children. Rejoining Yasmina half an hour later, Celia was rather tousled, and extremely grateful for the cool drink of sherbet which her hostess handed her.

'You are very good with children,' Yasmina said, taking a sip of her own drink. 'I hope you have the opportunity to have some of your own one day.'

'That's unlikely now. I doubt I will marry again.' Celia bit her lip. 'Yasmina, when you said a woman like me could never marry Ramiz, did you mean because I am from the West?'

'Well, that is certainly an issue—it is expected he will marry a princess of Arabic blood—but it is not the main problem. It is because you were married.'

'But my husband is dead.'

Yasmina looked at her in surprise. 'That is not the point. You are not a virgin. Ramiz is a prince of royal blood. His first wife must be his and only his. His seed must be the only seed planted in her garden.' Celia blushed, but Yasmina continued, seemingly oblivious of having said anything untoward. 'His second wife now, or his third, if *she* were widowed it would not matter so much, but a first wife like me is the most important,' she said proudly. 'It is she who bears the heir. Not that I expect Akil to take another wife. Unless he tires of me—but that would be unlikely, for I am most skilled.'

Celia was fascinated and appalled. 'You mean there are—there are things that women can do to…?'

'Keep her man?' Yasmina nodded, smiling coyly. 'Naturally. One of the advantages of sharing a harem with other women is the sharing of such secrets. Wait here.'

Left alone, Celia cooled her wrists and temples in the fountain. What had possessed her to ask such a thing? To have such an intimate conversation with a woman who was a complete stranger? It was this place—the heat, the exotic strangeness of it all. The way the walls of the harem seemed to tempt curiosity about such sensuous matters out into the open. It was because she wanted to know. Not to experience, just to know. And if she didn't find out here, then she never would.

Yasmina returned with a small parcel wrapped in silk. 'Take these. They are charm pamphlets. You won't be able to read the spells of course, but the pictures explain themselves.'

Celia took the package with some trepidation. She should not even be contemplating looking at such material, but it would be rude to refuse. 'Thank you,' she said. 'Shukran.'

'It is nothing. You must come and say goodbye to the children now. Akil is waiting to escort you back to the palace. I hope you will come again before you go back to England.'

'I would love to. I've had a lovely time here; you are blessed in your family.'

Yasmina smiled. 'I hope you too will be blessed one day.' She pressed her visitor's hand. 'You must not grow too fond of Ramiz, Lady Celia. He is a very attractive man, and he has an air about him, no? Potent, I think that is the word. But he is not for you—and you, I think, are a type who loves only once. Forgive me for speaking so, but I have the gift. I don't think you loved your husband, but I think you could easily love Ramiz if you let yourself. He is well named. Ramiz means honoured and respected. He may indulge himself with you—he is a man and you are a woman—but he would never do anything which goes against the traditions of A'Qadiz. You will be hurt if you expect too much of him. Don't let that happen.'

'You're wrong, Yasmina, I promise you.'

Yasmina shook her head. 'I have the gift. I am never wrong in these matters.'

Celia returned to the palace in a thoughtful mood, having thoroughly enjoyed the time spent with Yasmina and her family. She had been surprised to discover that Yasmina's eldest daughter attended school every day. A different school from her brother, but she was, contrary to what Celia had been told by the Consul in Cairo, receiving an education.

Seeing a harem as a family enclosure rather than a bordello had been a revelation which made her look at Ramiz and his kingdom in a completely new light. Not that she agreed with everything Yasmina had said, mind you. Offering a home to her mother and her sister-in-law was one thing—indeed, it was in many ways exactly as things were done in larger families at home, right down to the disgraced, divorced aunt Celia had discovered lived in seclusion on the second floor of the harem. Every family had its skeletons. But as to Yasmina's acceptance of the possibility of sharing her husband with another woman simply because Akil had grown tired of her—no! Absolutely not. All Celia's instincts rebelled at the very thought. She knew, as everyone did, that the Prince Regent had married twice, though poor Maria Fitzherbert's wedding was not legal. She knew that many couples, Prinny included, tacitly consented to each other's *affaires* once an heir had been secured. She did not approve, though she knew she would be deemed prudish to say so. But the idea of living in apparent harmony with what must surely be one's rivals—no!

'That,' Celia said decisively, 'I could never do. As well put a notice in the *Morning Post* that my husband finds me lacking.'

'*Afwan*, Lady Celia?'

'Nothing, Adila,' Celia said, smiling at the maidservant and shaking her head, realising she had spoken out loud. 'It's nothing.'

They had run her a bath. Wishing to be alone with her thoughts, Celia dismissed Adila and Fatima, insisting that she could undress herself. She had come to enjoy their gentle ministrations, the daily oiling, massage and bathing ritual, and would miss it when she went home.

Home. The word sat like a stone on her chest. She didn't want to go home yet. 'So much more to learn,' she told herself as she stripped off her stockings and unlaced her stays. 'I've hardly seen any of the city.'

She'd never used to talk to herself. It was a habit she'd acquired here from being so much alone, and now it felt quite natural. Draped in a loose silk robe, she padded barefoot through to the bathing room. White-tiled, it was decorated as all the salons, with a blue and gold mosaic frieze, the bath sunk into the floor, surrounded by four pillars, with a small fountain bubbling icy cold water at one end. The walls above the waist-height frieze were covered in tiles like mirrors, and above the bath the ceiling arched dark blue, painted with a galaxy of silver stars.

Celia climbed up the shallow step and sank down into the soothing water. Tonight it was scented with cinnamon and orange blossom. The bath was deep, unlike the copper tub they used at home, and she did not need to hunch up, but lay stretched full-length, her head resting on the tiles, gazing up at the stars twinkling in the ceiling, her mind floating, randomly sifting through images of A'Qadiz like a colourful collage. The sunrise over the mountains of the desert. The way the sand changed colour during the day, from toffee to the creamy yellow of fresh-churned butter, to white-gold. Her first glimpse of Balyrma, the astonishing green of the fields, the jumble of fortress-like houses, the tiled walls with their keyhole-shaped doors, the minarets and the sparkling fountains, like a child's drawing of a fairytale land.

And Ramiz. She could not think of A'Qadiz without Ramiz. Her first glimpse of him at his most god-like, watching her from the hilltop above the port. Ramiz the warrior, his scimitar glinting like a vicious halo above his head. Ramiz the man, naked in the moonlit water of the oasis.

She had never met anyone like him, and was not likely to again. Every time she saw him she learned something new. He was intelligent. Amusing. Sophisticated. Intimidating. Arrogant. Above all fascinating. Last night when he had confided in her she had glimpsed a vulnerability in him, though it had been quickly cloaked. There were layers to him that no one was allowed to see. He kept himself apart, wearing his princely personality like a costume. No doubt about it—he was the very epitome of a magnificent and omnipotent ruler, but she liked the man beneath even more.

Celia smiled softly. His eyes—the way they changed colour with his moods as the desert sand did with the heat. The way that little lick of hair stood up like a question mark when he'd been running his hands through it. His lids were heavy, the same shape as her own, and, like her, he used them when he didn't want anyone to know what he was thinking. She liked that she knew he was doing it because she did it too.

And his mouth. Celia touched her fingers to her own mouth, remembering. Kisses like honey. Darker kisses—exotic, crimsoning kisses, filled with promise. She closed her eyes. The way his mouth fitted so exactly to hers. The way his tongue and his lips spoke to her without words, telling her what to do now, and next, and next. Her fingers fluttered down her throat to the soft flesh of her breasts. She traced their shape, made liquid by the lapping water of the bath, trying to recapture the magic of Ramiz's touch as he'd cupped them, grazing her nipples as he had with his palm, his thumb—like this. Like this…

Her breath came shallow and quick. Her heart fluttered like a bird against the bars of a cage. Warmth seeped through her, as if her blood was heating, trickling to the place just below her belly, where it built so slowly she barely noticed it. Last night Ramiz had said she was beautiful. He'd made her feel beautiful. The way he'd traced the lines of her body, as if he would sculpt her, or draw her a picture of herself. Below the water line her nipples puckered and hardened, needles of feeling, bursts of intensity, feeding the pooling beat of arousal lower down, as tributaries would feed a river.

Celia moaned softly. She traced the path of feeling down, cupping the point where it gathered like a delta. Beneath her palm she could feel herself—a tiny flutter like a whispered cry of need. Tentatively she touched it with her fingertip. Her stomach clenched. The thing inside her, like last night, bunched. The river was dammed, readying itself for the wall to burst. She touched herself again and moaned, imagining it was Ramiz, wishing it was Ramiz, aching for it to be Ramiz.

She moaned again, turning her head restlessly on the hard-tiled edge of the bath. Something moved on the periphery of her vision. She snapped her eyes open, and it was as if she had conjured him. He was standing in the doorway of the bathing chamber, frozen to the spot, dressed in a robe of pale blue, his face set into rigid planes.

'I came to find you to talk about tomorrow. I thought you would be having dinner.'

His voice was harsh, as if he were angry. Celia swallowed. She shook her head, licked her lips. Her mouth was dry. She tried to sit up, remembered her nakedness, and slumped back under the water.

She looked like Venus rising from the waves, her glorious hair tumbling down the side of the bath, damp curls clinging lovingly to her face. The flush of arousal coloured her cheeks and darkened her eyes. He had never seen anything so lovely. Never witnessed anything so intimate as the way she touched herself. Never been so aroused.

He should have left, he knew that, but he hadn't been able to tear himself away, and now he was here he could think of nothing, nothing, nothing but finishing her journey, of travelling with her, just this once. His hands stroking her flesh. Her hands, with their long delicate fingers, touching his skin. His mouth on hers. Her breathy moans of pleasure saying *his* name, wanting *his* caress.

Ramiz was beyond resistance. Beyond anything save the need to hold her, to taste her, to take her to the heights of pleasure and this time soar with her. He strode over to the bath, kneeling down on the top step, careless of his silk robe trailing in the puddles of scented water. For a long moment he simply gazed at her, damp and pink and creamy white, the fire of her hair reflected in the fire of her eyes, the sweetness of her breath like a whisper on his cheek.

'Celia.' He pulled her towards him, his hands slipping on her shoulders, feeling the delicate blades sharp beneath her flesh as he wrapped his arm more firmly around her, the long sleeve of his caftan trailing in the water.

'Ramiz.' Sleepy with arousal, the word wrapped itself around him as Celia's arms twined around his neck, and he was lost.

Water slopped wildly over the sides of the bath onto the shallow step, forming pools on the tiled floor as he pulled her up, kissing her wildly. No slow build, no delicate preliminaries, passion burst like a ripe fig as they kissed, hands slipping and gripping and sliding, the silk of his robe clinging to their skin, their lips, their tongues, kissing as if they would meld.

She had no thought of resisting, was too far gone in her own imagined lovemaking to refuse her dream made flesh and blood in the magnificent form of Ramiz. They were standing together on the tiled floor by the bath, wet skin, fevered lips, kissing and licking, licking and kissing.

'Celia, Celia, Celia.' Ramiz said her name like an incantation, punctuating it with kisses to her lids, her ears, her throat, his hands urgent upon her, raising torrents of feeling where before there had been only feeble tributaries. His mouth found her breast, his lips fastening greedily round her nipple. The delicious tugging produced such a rush of heat that she moaned, slumping in his embrace, arching her back so that her breasts implored him for more. His attentions moved to the other nipple. She moaned again, saying *his* name now, over and over, a plea for completion, of wanting and desperate need.

Her hands plucked at the silk of his robe, wanting to touch flesh. She struggled ineffectually with the buttons at his neck, eager now, desperate for the feel of his flesh upon hers for the first time. She wanted to touch him. To see him. To savour him. She wanted to give him what he was giving her. She wrenched at a button and it flew through the air to land with a click on the tiles.

Ramiz laughed—a low, husky noise which gave her goosebumps. She watched, fascinated, as he yanked the other buttons free and then, taking the neck of his caftan between his hands, simply tore it apart, casting it aside onto the floor to stand naked before her for the first time.

The word *magnificent* did not do his body justice. Celia gazed at him in awe—the golden skin stretched taut over the muscles of his shoulders and chest, the rippling ridges of his abdomen, like the contours of the desert sands of which he was prince. The sheen of water like a glaze cast each dip and rise into relief. Where she was curved he was sharper lines. Where she was soft he was...

She reached out her hand tentatively. Ramiz took her by the wrist, encouraging her. Where her skin was soft, like cashmere, his was smoother, like silk stretched on a tambour frame. She could feel the hardness of his muscles underneath. Ramiz pulled her closer. He guided her wrist lower. The concave stomach. Down. Her eyes followed the same path. Down. To the curving length of him, solid, intimidatingly large. She could not imagine how—where— surely it would hurt?

'Ramiz, I...'

'Touch me. There is nothing to be frightened of.'

'I'm not frightened.' But she was, just a bit, and her voice gave her away. She was afraid of her ignorance. Afraid of failing. Afraid that Ramiz would find her lacking.

He scooped her up, holding her high against his chest, pushing his way impatiently out of the bathing chamber to the next salon, where he kicked a heap of cushions together onto the carpet and sank down onto them. Satin and silk and velvet—she could feel them all on her back, her bottom, her thighs. Satin and silk and velvet on her mouth as Ramiz kissed her.

'To touch is to learn,' Ramiz whispered, trailing his fingers over her hip.

He leaned over her, his mouth following where his fingers had led, feathering kisses like whispers, speaking softly of the pleasure to come. She felt her skin tighten as her flesh seemed to swell under his caress. He kissed the crease at the top of her thigh, pulling her onto her side, positioning himself opposite her so that they lay like two crescents curved into each other.

Ramiz dipped his hand between her legs, lightly stroking his way through the moist folds of her flesh. 'Touch me, Celia. Do as I do. Make me feel as you do. Like this.' With his other hand he placed hers onto his shaft, wrapping her fingers round its length and gently guiding her. Satin and silk and velvet.

Her touch was entirely inexperienced and entirely delightful. He thought fleetingly of the man who had been her husband, a man who had obviously taken no interest at all in his wife's pleasure, and then he banished the thought, for he did not want to think of Celia as a wife, or having belonged to anyone else. He did not want to think at all, for to do so would be to stop, and he could not stop. Not now.

He slipped his fingers gently inside her, easing into the swelling heat of her, enjoying the way she clenched around him, the little gasp of pleasure emanating from her. 'This is what you are doing to me,' he said. 'When I do this, and you touch me like that, this is what it feels like.' Slowly he pulled out of her clinging moistness, only to ease back in again.

What he was doing was a prelude. Finally she understood. Her own fingers clasped around the part of him which was designed to meld them together. She stroked him, wondering at the slight curve on the satiny skin, at the astonishing hardness of him, tracing a line up to the tip of him, softer, rounded, velvety. He was watching her. She gasped as he pushed his fingers inside her again, closing her eyes at the peculiar smarting of this pleasure, more insistent, the edges rougher than last night. Then he did it again, and she stroked him in the same rhythm, and saw the pleasure she was giving him etched on his face, in the way his eyes darkened, the way he bit his lip to stop himself from crying out.

It was the same for him. It was really the same. What she was feeling—this mounting tension, this jagged excitement, this feeling of wanting it done, over, of wanting it to last for ever, this wanting to soar and wanting to cling—he was feeling it too as she stroked him and he stroked her. Then he slid upwards, touching her where he had touched her yesterday, and she felt herself began to slip, but forced herself to cling on. Her thumb caressed the tip of his shaft, and Ramiz gasped. Inside her, he worked magic of his own. It was like being pushed inexorably towards something deep and dark, and as she stroked him and circled him she could see he felt the same. His eyes were closed. A dark flush stained his cheeks. He gripped his lower lip with his teeth. His breathing was fast, uneven. Like her own. Her heart was thumping. Her body was cold, cold—freezing except for where Ramiz touched her and she touched Ramiz. She felt him thicken in her hand, felt herself swelling under his hand, heard him say her name, like a plea, for the first time asking something of her, but before she had time to wonder what he wanted the jagged swelling pressure in her burst through, like water coursing through a dam, and she cried out. Ramiz cried out too, spilling his pleasure over her hand as she melted into his.

He was right. To give was to receive. More than last night. More than she had thought possible. Enough to make her wonder what *more* would feel like. Enough to make her realise that she should heed Yasmina's warning. This was a fantasy formed in a harem and being played out free from the disapproval of the outside world. Nothing more. It could never—must never—be anything more.

Celia sat up, pulling a tasselled cushion onto her lap to cover herself.

Ramiz opened his eyes, reluctantly pulling himself back down from the heights to which her touch had sent him. He had not meant this to happen. *It should not have happened! What was he thinking?* He got quickly to his feet, pulling his torn robe around him. 'This was a mistake.'

'A mistake?' she repeated stupidly.

'It was wrong,' Ramiz said tersely. At least he had not risked any consequences! At least his sense of honour had not wholly deserted him.

His robe was soaking wet from the bathwater, but he didn't seem to notice. It clung to him, making him look like one of those naked statues, strategically draped for modesty's sake. Feeling at a distinct disadvantage, Celia hugged her cushion defensively. With his clothing, Ramiz had donned his mask. She hardly recognised the man who had moaned his pleasure at her touch only moments before.

'What do you mean, it was a mistake?'

'You are here under my protection. I should not have

allowed myself—this should not have happened. No matter how much the provocation,' he added.

'Provocation!' Celia's face burned with a mixture of shame and anger. 'I thought I was alone.'

'This is my harem.' He was being unfair, but it was true in a way. If she had not been—if he had not seen her in the bath like that... 'My harem,' Ramiz repeated firmly. 'I am free to walk in here any time I wish.'

'That's preposterous. It may be your harem, but as you've just pointed out I am a guest here. I am entitled to some privacy.'

'And I am entitled to expect my guests to behave more decorously.'

'You're being quite ridiculous.'

'You call *me* ridiculous? You forget yourself, Lady Celia. You forget who you are talking to.'

She knew he had a temper, but she had not before experienced it. His face was pale with anger, his mouth set in a thin line, his hands clenched at his sides. She had overstepped the mark as far as he was concerned, but as far as she was concerned so had he. Her own formidable temper was normally kept firmly under wraps, but his heady change of mood from euphoria to accusation sent it spinning out of her control before she could rein it in.

Regardless of her naked state, she flung the cushion away and got to her feet, her hair flying out like battle colours behind her. 'I don't care who you are—you are being ridiculous. I was taking a bath in the privacy of a bathing chamber. The fact that it happens to be in your harem is completely irrelevant. It is not my fault that you fell victim to your own base desires. I won't be branded some sort of siren just to satisfy your honour, be you prince, sheikh, or simply a man.'

He flinched as if she had struck him. As she had—with the truth of the matter. He had been unable to control himself. No matter that he had not taken her, he had wanted to. 'You are right.'

Celia's temper fled as quickly as it had arrived. There was an embroidered cover on one of the divans under the window. She snatched it up, wrapping it around her shoulders. 'Ramiz, you were not the only one to lose control,' she said painfully. 'I did not provoke you deliberately, but I didn't stop you either.' She reached out to touch his arm. 'You are not the only one to blame.'

He shrugged himself free of her hand. 'You are a woman. I should not have allowed you to submit.'

'Submit?' Celia stared at him in confusion. 'Why must you persist in the belief that I don't have a mind of my own just because I'm a woman? I make my own choices, even if they do turn out to be foolish ones.'

Ramiz sighed heavily. 'I am pleased you think this way, even if it is misguided. I hope this—this event—will not colour the view of my country that you take back to England.'

Realisation dawned, cold and savage. 'You're worried that I'll make things difficult for you through my father?'

'We are at a delicate stage of negotiations with your people.'

'I won't be crying ravishment, if that's what you're worried about.' She glared at him, determined not to allow the hurt she felt to show.

It was the last thing he'd been thinking of, but it *should* have been the first. He could not forgive himself. He could not allow himself to think about why he had done what he did. Or how Celia felt. And definitely not how he felt. It was a relief at least that his actions had not offended her. He must ensure he gave her no further cause.

'Tomorrow, if you still wish, I will take you out to see something of Balyrma.'

'Is that my compensation for keeping my mouth shut? If so, I'd rather stay here.'

'I thought you wished to see the city. If you have changed your mind…'

'I'm sorry, Ramiz, I shouldn't have said that.' Celia attempted a weak smile. 'All this—everything here—it's all so strange to me. I feel like I'm in a dream half the time. I'd love to see Balyrma, and if you have the time to escort me I'd be honoured. I'm sure I couldn't have a more knowledgeable guide. Akil told me you've written a history of Balyrma's origins.'

Ramiz shrugged. 'It is nothing. The work of an enthusiastic amateur rather than a scholar. I will have you brought to me in the morning.' He turned to leave.

'Ramiz.' Difficult as it was to speak of such things, she could not square it with her conscience to allow him to think he had forced her, any more than she had been able to accept that she had enticed him. 'Ramiz, I meant what I said. It was as much my fault as yours. You are not responsible for my actions, no matter how accustomed you may be to thinking you are.'

'It does you credit that you say so.'

'I say so because it's the truth.'

Ramiz smiled like a god descending from the heavens to join the mere mortals. It transformed him. 'It is not just me who is accustomed to shouldering the blame, is it? I think you must be a very protective sister.'

He kissed her cheek. 'You are certainly a most unusual woman.'

Leaving her to ponder the meaning of this rather enigmatic statement, Ramiz left.

CHAPTER SEVEN

NEXT morning Celia dressed for the promised sight-seeing trip in a lemon-figured muslin walking dress with a double flounce along the hem, trimmed with knots of gold ribbon. Gold ribbon was also threaded through the high neckline and the edges of the tight-fitting sleeves, which were fastened with a row of tiny pearl buttons. Adila had found a way for her to attach the gauzy veil of blond lace to the back of her head, rather as Spanish ladies wore their mantilla, obviating the need for a hat, much to Celia's relief. She wore the veil back over her hair while still inside the palace, and carried her gloves as she followed in the wake of the guard. Despite giving herself a severe talking to, play-ing over last night's conversation several times in her head, she was extremely nervous about meeting Ramiz again, and quite unable to decide how she felt about anything that had happened. In fact, in the bright light of day, released from the harem's sultry ambience, she found it difficult to believe it had happened at all!

Ramiz was in his library, dressed all in white as she had first seen him, complete with headdress and cloak. 'In desert prince mode,' Celia muttered to herself as he nodded a distant good morning from behind his desk and turned back to complete his conversation with Akil, leaving her standing like an unwanted caller at the doorway.

Though she herself had come to think of the harem as a separate place, ruled by the senses rather than the mind, and though she herself had made every effort to put last night's events firmly to the back of her mind, Celia couldn't help resenting the fact that Ramiz seemed so successfully to have done the same. She eyed him from beneath her lids as she wandered over to browse the bookshelves. How she envied him his detachment. How she wished she shared it. She wasn't used to this feeling of constantly being on the back foot. The Lady Celia Armstrong she knew was used to feeling in charge. In control. Calm. Cool. Sophisticated. Not like some country miss in her first Season, having constantly to consult a book of etiquette and even then always on the verge of a fatal *faux pas*.

But she was not that Lady Celia Armstrong, and she knew she never would be again. She could not forget what she had experienced in Ramiz's arms, under Ramiz's tutelage, and she was very much afraid that what he had taught her had spoiled her for ever for any other man—as this place, this whole experience of the exotic world of A'Qadiz, would spoil her even for her beloved England, if she let it.

It was a paradox, she thought, picking up a volume bound in soft blue leather which was on the table with a stack of books recently come from England. A paradox, because here in this kingdom, where women were veiled and segregated, where she spent much of her time behind the locked door of a harem guarded by two eunuchs, she had never been so free.

Celia opened the book. *Emma, a Novel in Three Volumes by the Author of Pride and Prejudice.* She'd really enjoyed *Pride and Prejudice.* They had read it together, she and her sisters, assigning themselves roles from the sisters in the story. She had been Elizabeth, of course, and Cassie had been Jane, the beauty of the family. Smiling to herself at the memory of Caroline and Cordelia squabbling over who was to be the flighty Lydia, Celia felt a pang of homesickness. She wondered what they were all doing now. She didn't even know what time it was back home—later or earlier? Was it sunny or raining? It was strawberry season. Cressida loved strawberries, though they brought Caroline out in a rash when she ate too many, as she always did, no matter how many times she was reminded. Cordelia preferred the strawberry jam they all made together from Mama's treasured receipt book. It had become an annual rite, taking over the kitchen for the day, filling the big country house with the sweetly cloying scent of jam as it bubbled in the vast copper pot. Cassie had charge of the receipt book now. It would be up to her to order the extra sugar, to take Celia's role as Jam-Maker-in-Chief, no doubt ceding her own role of Measurer-in-Chief to Caroline. Celia could already imagine the argument that would induce between the youngest two of her sisters. Poor Cassie, whose gentle temperament made her loath to intervene in any dispute, would wring her hands and implore them to share and tell them that one role was just as good as another, and they would ignore her completely, and Caroline would get involved, and without Celia to knock sense into all of them the whole jam-making would turn into a complete fiasco…

'Of course it will not,' she chastised herself. 'I just want to think so because it makes me feel indispensable.'

'What does?'

Celia jumped, dropping volume one of *Emma* on to the thickly carpeted floor—so thickly carpeted she had not heard Ramiz approach. Now he was standing uncomfortably close. Why did she always forget how tall he was, and how very good-looking? She took a step back. 'I beg your pardon?'

'You said, *"I just want to think so because it makes me feel indispensable."'*

'Oh. I must have been talking out loud. I hadn't realised. I was thinking of my sisters. It's nothing.'

'You miss them?'

'Yes, of course I do. Though I'm sure they're all fine without me,' Celia said, surprised to find her voice a bit shaky.

'But there's a part of you which hopes they are not, hmm?'

She smiled, trying surreptitiously to blink away the tears which had gathered in her eyes. 'I know it's a dreadful thing to think. I'm afraid I must be a very controlling female.'

'It's not surprising. You took on the role of mother to your sisters at a very early age, yes? It is perfectly natural that you should worry about how they are coping without you. It is something mothers do, even when their children have families of their own. A very feminine trait.'

Celia sniffed. 'Thank you. I think that might even qualify as a compliment.'

'If you wish to write to them, I will see your letter is safely delivered.'

'You're very kind.'

'I should have thought of it earlier. Your people will wish to be reassured that you are safe and well. They will not want to take my word for it. You must write tonight.'

'I see.' He wasn't thinking of her, but of his own reputation. Of his country's interests. 'If you are too busy for our outing today, perhaps we should postpone it.'

'There is no need. I have taken care of business for today, and Akil has it all in hand. Besides, I wish you to see something of Balyrma while you are here.'

'So that I can report back on how wonderful it is?'

Ramiz's eyes narrowed. 'Because I think it will interest you. If I was mistaken…'

'No, you're not,' Celia said hastily. 'I do want to see it. I was a bit disconcerted, that was all—seeing this book, if you must know. My sisters and I read another by the same author.'

'*Pride and Prejudice?* I read it myself, and enjoyed it. A very amusing account of your English manners. The author must be a very perceptive man.'

'You think it is written by a man?'

'The wit is acerbic, none of the characters are sympathetic, and there is none of the sentimental romanticism endemic in female writers. Of a certainty it is a man.'

'Of a certainty? If you say it is so, then it must be so, Highness.'

Ramiz looked startled, and then he smiled, showing gleaming white teeth and menacing amber eyes. 'You are learning, Lady Celia. I am granting you the honour of my company without escort and in public. You must treat me with respect and deference in front of my people, for if you do not I will be forced to confine you to the harem for the duration of your stay. I hope I have made myself clear?'

She met his gaze defiantly for all of ten seconds, then surrendered. In truth, when he looked at her like that she had no wish to defy him. And he *was* honouring her with his presence after all, and she *did* want his company, more than she cared to admit to herself. Celia drew her veil over her face, and her gloves over her fingers. 'Yes, Highness,' she said meekly, following in Ramiz's wake as he led the way across the courtyard. Which meant he did not see her pout cheekily at him as they went through the passageway and out of the gate into the city.

The heat was so intense it knocked the breath out of her—like walking into an oasthouse after the hops had been roasted. In the cool of the palace she had forgotten how fierce the sun could be, even this early in the day.

She had also forgotten the reverence in which Ramiz was held. People dropped to their knees as he passed. They did not look at him, but Celia could feel their eyes on her, curious rather than threatening. She was conscious of how strange she must look in her tight-fitting dress, and acutely aware, as she watched Ramiz nod and smile to his people, of just how big an honour he was actually conferring on her in being her guide for the day.

It was not yet nine o'clock, but Balyrma was a hive of activity. Ramiz led the way through the dusty streets away from the tiled houses and minarets of the more affluent quarter to the more crowded area nearer the city gates. 'I thought you'd like to see the souks,' he said over his shoulder. 'Each sector of the city is named for different artisans, and each has their own market. This alleyway here is populated by leather workers; down here is where the potters are, and the tile-makers. Come closer. I'm getting a sore neck talking to you like this.'

'I thought I was to follow in your wake to show you respect.'

'You can show respect just as well by doing as you are bid.'

Celia caught up with him. 'You have the makings of a frightful tyrant, you know,' she said with a smile. 'Highness,' she added as a deliberate afterthought.

'And *you* have the makings of a most subversive citizen.'

'I'm sorry if I seem flippant sometimes. It's just that you can be rather intimidating, and I'm not used to being intimidated.'

They had stopped momentarily, allowing the small retinue of children they had collected in their wake to swarm around her, reaching out to stroke the fabric of her dress. She smiled at them all abstractedly through her veil.

'They are not used to seeing clothing such as yours.'

'I wish I did not have to wear it. It's completely unsuited to this climate, and I feel as if I'm being baked alive.'

'You should have said so before. We can get you some fabrics at the souk. I will have the maids make up some traditional outfits if you really want to go native.'

'I would *love* to go native.'

'You never look hot. In fact you always look extremely elegant.'

'Thank you.'

'You are welcome. Do not look so sceptical, I mean it,' Ramiz said with a wry smile.

They set off again at a slower pace, stopping off at a stall selling sugared almonds, dried dates, long sticks of some sort of sticky toffee packed with sultanas and raisins, and all sorts of other sweet delights which had the children staring in wide-eyed wonder. Ramiz selected an assortment which he handed out before they moved on, walking companionably side by side, Ramiz having forgotten all about his desire for protocol.

'I don't know what it is about you that makes me speak my mind,' Celia said thoughtfully as they approached the fabric district. 'I assure you, every time you goad me into saying something outrageous I wish I had bitten my tongue out.'

'Before I have it cut out, you mean,' Ramiz said.

She could tell by the way his eyes gleamed, the way his mouth firmed into an upward curve that wasn't quite a smile, that he was teasing. 'Yasmina told me you rule with a hand of iron in a velvet glove. She also told me one of the first things you did when you came to power was to completely overhaul the legal system. You don't even have an executioner any more, do you?'

'There is no need. When people have enough to eat, somewhere for their family to live, a way to earn a living, they have no need to turn to crime. And when the punishment for transgression is to lose all that— banishment—I find it is incentive enough.'

'That is a very progressive way of thinking. Far more humane than we are in England, where a starving man who steals a sheep to feed his family can be hanged.'

'If you read Scheherazade's stories more closely you would see she shares my views.'

'And your people?' Celia asked.

'Some of the tribes prefer the old ways. For them, violence—wars, punishment, whatever—is a way of life. I spend a lot of my time trying to prevent them overturning my treaties. I am due to visit the head of one of the tribes later this week, as a matter of fact. They occupy land on the border of A'Qadiz, where the oasis is disputed territory. It is supposed to be shared. I will spend two days reminding him of this, and he will spend two days trying to extract as much gold as he can from me as compensation for what he claims to be his exclusive rights.'

'You bribe him not to fight?'

'Don't look so shocked. It's a tactic your government uses all the time. And for me it's cheaper in the long run than allowing him to start a full-scale war.'

'Can't you just have him—this head man—replaced with someone who believes in what you're trying to do?'

Ramiz laughed. 'That really would start a war. Enough of this talk. They are my problems, not yours. Come, the fabric district is just here. Take your time. Choose as much as you like.'

'Oh, but I don't have any money with me.'

'I will pay.'

'Absolutely not. I cannot allow you to buy my clothes. It wouldn't be proper.'

'It would not be proper for me to allow you to pay.'

'Then I won't have anything.'

Ramiz stared at her in consternation. 'You honestly think I am concerned about the price of a few yards of material?'

'It's the principle of it,' Celia said firmly. 'In England only a—a courtesan allows a man who is not her husband to buy her clothes.'

'We are not in England,' Ramiz pointed out. 'In A'Qadiz it is for the master of the harem to provide them. You are in my harem, I will pay for these, and that is an end to it.'

Celia was not at all convinced, but looking at Ramiz's face, at his mouth setting in a firm line, she decided not to antagonise him further. The day was young, and she wanted to make the most of it. She wanted Ramiz to enjoy himself, and if that meant breaking one of her own rules to keep his dignity intact, then so be it. 'Thank you, Highness,' she said with a graceful curtsy. 'In that case I will be most honoured.'

Ramiz grinned. 'You don't fool me with that meek and mild act. And you can stop calling me Highness. No one can understand what you're saying.'

'Thank you, Ramiz, then. I trust the royal coffers are sufficiently full, for I intend to make the most of these wonderful fabrics.'

If anyone had told him that he could enjoy the experience of shopping for silks in a souk, Ramiz would have laughed in his face. Though he enjoyed looking at a well-dressed woman as much as the next man, he had little interest in what that dress comprised of nor in any of the frills and furbelows which accessorised it. But Celia's child-like enthusiasm was enchanting, and for the next hour he watched entranced as she threw herself with unwonted zeal into the business of choosing colours and textures and trimmings.

Celia, who had never before seen such a display of colourful silks, rich velvets and delicate gauzy fabrics she could not even name, went from stall to stall in the souk with a rapt expression on her face. She removed her gloves to plunge her fingers into the thick nap of a crimson velvet, to rub a shawl of the softest cashmere against her cheek, to stroke silks and satins and fine net and coarse damask, turning the purchase of cloth into a wholly sensual experience she could never have imagined. In her excitement she forgot all about deference and reserve. She forgot to put her gloves back on and she forgot to replace her veil, but she was so charming, able to make her wishes clear despite the language barrier, and careful to praise even the plainest of fabrics displayed to her, equally careful to spread her purchases over as many stalls as possible, that rather than cause offence she was treated with real hospitality and warmth. They drank several glasses of tea, and Ramiz found himself playing second fiddle for the first time since he had come to power.

'Thank you for that,' Celia said to him as they left a shop specialising in *passementerie*—elaborate braiding made from gold and silver thread. 'I hope you weren't bored.'

'It was an education. Have you had enough?'

'More than. Do you have to go back to the palace?'

Ramiz shook his head. 'I have arranged a special treat for you.' He led the way through the maze of alleys and terracotta buildings with their stalls opening out from the ground floors, back to a large square where a palace guard was waiting with two snowy white camels. 'A short ride—half an hour, no more. Can you manage it in that dress?' Ramiz asked when Celia looked at him enquiringly.

'Where are we going?'

He smiled and shook his head. 'It's a surprise.'

They left Balyrma by a different gate than the one through which they had entered the city. This one led through an olive grove to the south, to a narrow track, only just discernible, wending its way towards the mountains. Ramiz told her a little more of Balyrma's history as the camels made their stately way along the path. As before, Celia's intelligent questions and thirst for knowledge made him relax his guard, drawing him out, making him laugh, extracting things from deep in the recesses of his mind—childhood memories and ancient legends he had forgotten until now. He liked her. It was a strange thing to say of a woman, but there it was. She was excellent company and he liked her.

The mountains seemed to rear up out of the sand like a child's model or an artist's impression, without foothills or any other preliminaries, more like monuments than natural phenomena. There was no path that Celia could see, and her heart sank at the thought of having to climb, until she realised that Ramiz was leading them to what looked like a large fissure in the rock. A cave?

It was not a cave but a narrow passageway, curving in an 'S' shape only wide enough to allow them to pass through in single file. Enchanted, Celia saw that the rock was carved with strange symbols, and little niches contained carved idols scattered at regular intervals. Craning her neck, she could just see the sky, the brilliant blue colour of approaching noon, though here between the rocks it felt cool. Then they turned the final bend and she gasped with astonishment, for they were standing in a large open square and before her lay a ruined city, built into the rock itself.

'The ancient city of Katra,' Ramiz said. 'We don't know how old it is exactly, but we estimate about two thousand years.'

The city was compact, and despite its great age in a remarkable state of preservation. 'I've never seen anything so wonderful,' Celia said as she wandered through the buildings. 'It's marvelous. I can't believe I've never even heard of it.'

'That is because we have been at pains to keep its existence a secret,' Ramiz explained. 'It is well known that the British and French stripped Egypt of many of its ancient treasures during the wars with Napoleon, and it is well known that your Consul General continues to send artefacts collected by his friends from all over Egypt and the Levant to his own little museum in England, as Lord Elgin did with the Parthenon marbles. I don't want that happening to Katra.'

'No, and I can see why. It's beautiful, and quite eerie too. I feel as if the people have just stepped out this morning and will come back any time. But if you don't want anyone to know about it, why have you brought me?'

Why? Because it was special, and he wanted to share it with her. He realised he couldn't say that. He knew he shouldn't have thought it. He hadn't until this moment. 'Because to understand Balyrma's history one must understand Katra's. I knew it would interest you.'

'You've no idea how much. It's one of the most marvellous things I've ever seen. Thank you.'

Celia had pushed back her veil again. She smiled up at him, her eyes alight with excitement that made them glitter like diamond-chipped jade. Her mouth made the most delightful curve—soft and full. The taste of her, sweet and flowery, came back to him like a punch in the stomach. Her lips like petals on his own. Blossoming as she had blossomed under his touch. Bloomed. Ripened. *What was he thinking?*

'It is past noon,' Ramiz said brusquely, looking up at the sun high overhead. 'I have arranged for shade and food. This way.'

For a fraction of a second she thought he had been going to kiss her. Her heart had begun to beat hard and fast, changing its tempo so suddenly she felt dizzy. Now he was striding ahead of her to where the camels were tethered, leading the way on foot back through the passageway so quickly she had to run to keep up.

As they emerged into the blaze of the sun she saw that a tent had been set up directly under an overhanging ledge. Like the one they had abandoned in the desert it was a square in shape, constructed from wool woven from camel or goat, supported by large wooden props tied with rope, but there the resemblance ended. Thick-piled carpets covered the sand. The walls were hung with tapestries depicting scenes from ancient mythology. Tasselled cushions embroidered with silks, embellished with seed pearls and semi-precious stones, were strewn across the carpet around a low table, upon which a selection of gold dishes were covered. The appetising aroma of spit-roasted goat filled the air, making Celia's mouth water.

Damask hangings created a small room to one side, where a pitcher of rose-scented water stood on a marble washstand. Celia rinsed the dust and sand from her face and hands, tidying her hair in the gilt mirror which had been thoughtfully provided, before she sat down to eat with Ramiz.

The food was delicate, packed with the exotic flavours she had come to relish. A lime and mint sherbet quenched her thirst. Aside from the usual selection of spiced meats and palate-cleansing fruits there was something called a *pastille*—a parcel of flaky pastry stuffed with pigeon, almonds and dates. Unlike at home, where it was the custom to partake only of those dishes within reach—even if one's favourite dish was at the other end of the table—she had discovered that it was expected of her to try a little of everything here. It was a practice she enjoyed, and she said so to Ramiz.

'Every meal is like a picnic, and if I don't like something I can just leave it because I've only taken a little bit. At home, especially at dinner parties, it is expected that you eat whatever is put on your plate. I can't tell you the number of times I've had to chew my way through a perfectly inedible piece of over-cooked meat or, worse, under-cooked fish.'

'It is your habit to drown everything in sauces, which I don't like,' Ramiz said. 'It makes me wonder why. Is the food so awful that it can't be eaten on its own?'

Celia giggled. 'You're probably right. I'm afraid that cooking is not high on the list of British accomplishments.'

She dipped her hands into a little fingerbowl in which jasmine petals floated. He watched her, thinking again what a strange mix she was. He could not understand his attraction to her. No doubt she was thinking the same thing. He could not understand why she had allowed him such liberties. He was the first to stir her, he knew that. Perhaps that was why she stirred him so?

As now.

He wanted to kiss her. He had to kiss her. Taking her by surprise, he reached down and pulled her to her feet, pressing her close, satisfyingly close, so that he could smell her scent and hear her breathing. He smiled at the look in her big green eyes.

'What are you doing?' Celia said breathlessly, though she knew full well what he was doing, and she knew full well that she wanted him to. His mouth was only inches from hers. His eyes were like cast bronze, glazed with heat. Her heart pounded wildly. Her mouth was dry. She was acutely conscious of him, the strength of him, the power in him coiled tight like a stalking tiger beneath the silk of his robe. To her shame, she could feel a wicked excitement rising, making her nipples peak painfully against her chemise.

Ramiz groaned—a grating sound—as if it were rasped out of him. Then he kissed her. A hungry kiss without restraint. The kiss of a man pushed beyond endurance. A kiss of surrender, an admission of need that shamed him even as it incited him to pursue that need to its conclusion. His wanting was so urgent and so immediate he felt he would explode with it. Blood rushed to his groin, making him so hard he ached with a painfully pulsing urge to cast off all restraints and thrust into her, to take her fast and hard and thoroughly, to mark her for ever as his. Her lips were swollen with his kisses. A long strand of copper hair trailed down her cheek.

'Last night,' he said raggedly, 'why did you not stop me?'

'I should have, but I somehow couldn't.' Celia bit her lip. 'It is the harem. There is something beguiling about it. Unreal. Otherworldly.'

'Unreal.' Ramiz nodded. 'Will you stop me now? Here?'

Celia veiled her eyes with her heavy lids. 'I think I won't have to,' she said eventually.

Ramiz sighed heavily. His smile was crooked. 'A very diplomatic answer.' He released her, tucking her hair back behind her ear and kissing the tip of her nose. 'We should get back.'

CHAPTER EIGHT

PEREGRINE FINCHLEY-BURKE was the fourth son of an earl. Peregrine's oldest brother, heir to the Earldom, was currently delighting the ladies of the *ton* with his illustrious person, and endowing the gaming tables at White's club with his father's guineas. Peregrine's second brother had chosen the army. Captain Finchley-Burke of the Thirteenth Hussars had been wounded at Waterloo—a bullet which grazed his cheek, leaving him romantically scarred but otherwise unhurt. Since returning to England he had been assisting his elder brother's attempts to gamble away his inheritance at the tables of White's. Peregrine's third brother was made of much sterner stuff, however. So imbued with moral rectitude was the Very Reverend Archdeacon Finchley-Burke that the Earl himself was wont to question his wife's fidelity on the few occasions when his son blessed him with his presence.

Which left Peregrine to serve his country by way of the East India Company. He had, in fact, been on his way to India when the vagaries of the weather had left him stranded in Lisbon long enough for the ambassador there to persuade him that by travelling to Cairo on his behalf to deliver some urgent papers he would be doing his country a great service. In fact, although the diplomatic bag entrusted to Peregrine *did* contain some documents pertaining to matters of the state, the consignment of port which accompanied it was the real matter of urgency. Of this fact, as of so many others, Peregrine remained in blissful ignorance.

It was serendipitous for the Consul General of Egypt, Lord Wincester, that Peregrine's arrival coincided with the need to send a messenger to A'Qadiz with a response to Sheikh al-Muhana's communication, informing him of the death of George Cleveden and the whereabouts of the Lady Celia, his widow. The Consul General had a small, overworked staff—a fact of which he was constantly reminding the Foreign Office—so the naïve and clearly biddable young gentleman who had just delivered his long-anticipated supplies of port was commandeered to act as emissary—a suggestion which much flattered the aforesaid young gentleman, who blessed his luck and began to dream of a glittering career in the diplomatic corps.

Thus was Peregrine's onward journey to India further postponed, and thus did he arrive, dusty, sunburned, saddle-sore and feeling considerably out of his depth, at the royal palace in Balyrma, in the company of the Prince's own guard.

Ramiz was informed of the arrival of this unexpected guest by Akil, immediately upon his return from Katra. It had been a silent ride back, giving him ample time to try to regret kissing Celia and ample time to wish that he had kissed her more. Assuming that the visitor had come to reclaim her, Ramiz found himself extremely reluctant to let her go—though he knew he should be relieved, and continued to tell himself so as he bathed and changed his robes.

Without success.

Ramiz arrived in the throne room, where it was the custom to receive foreign visitors, in a black mood. He wore a formal robe of dark blue silk, fastened with gold buttons embellished with sapphires. At Akil's insistence he wore a *bisht* over this, the jewelled cloak elaborately embroidered with his falcon and crescent insignia. It was a heavy garment, and consequently uncomfortably warm, as was the headdress and its gold-tasselled *igal*, which Akil had insisted upon too. With the famous Balyrman scimitar weighing down the belt at his waist, and the great seal of A'Qadiz weighing down the middle finger of his right hand, Ramiz strode into the throne room with Akil behind him, breathlessly attempting to keep up while avoiding the royal *bisht* which trailed along the tiles, and completing the briefing he had in turn received from Peregrine's escort, all at the same time.

'So this man Finchley-Burke is basically a junior secretary?' Ramiz said, throwing himself onto the throne. A large gilded and scrolled chair, it sat on a carpeted dais at the top of the room, which was some sixty feet long—a vast tiled space, with an ornate mosaic floor bordered on each side by ten pillars, lit by ten stained-glass windows, but otherwise empty of furnishings, forcing visitors to stand in exposed isolation in front of the seated monarch. 'What do you think, Akil? Are we to be insulted at this minion's lack of status, or impressed by the speed with which they have sent him to us?'

Akil took his place by Ramiz's side. 'I doubt they intend to insult you, Highness.'

'They certainly don't mean to flatter me either,' Ramiz replied acerbically. 'Nor Lady Celia, for that matter. Do they expect me to provide an escort across the desert for her? They take too much for granted!'

'Maybe they don't want her back.'

'What do you mean by that?' Ramiz asked sharply.

'Nothing, Highness. A jest, that's all,' Akil said hurriedly, wondering at his friend's mood.

'If you can't find anything sensible to say you will do better to hold your tongue. Go and fetch the Englishman. I've better things to do than sit and stew in this outfit.'

'Ramiz, is there something wrong?'

'Only that I seem unable to make myself clear today.'

Akil opened his mouth to remonstrate, caught the glitter in Ramiz's eye, and changed his mind.

Ushering the Englishman in from the ante-room where he had been pacing anxiously, Akil could not but feel sorry for him.

'How do I address him?' Peregrine asked, tugging at his sweat-soaked neckcloth.

'Highness. Leave your hat here, and your gloves. You must not shake hands, only bow like this.' Akil demonstrated gracefully. 'And do not meet his eyes.'

'What about this?' Peregrine said, pulling a sealed letter from the pocket of his cutaway coat. 'It's from the Consul General.'

'You may kneel at the foot of the dais and hold it out to him. Are you ready? Follow me. He is looking forward to meeting you,' Akil said, making a quick apology to the gods for the lie. 'Try not to look so terrified.'

Peregrine swallowed hard. 'Righty-ho.'

Akil rolled his eyes, nodded to the guard, who threw

open the double doors to the chamber, and stood back to watch as the Englishman made his scuttling way across the vast tiled expanse of floor towards the throne, with all the enthusiasm of a thief approaching an executioner.

Ramiz stood to receive his visitor. Though his manner was brusque, it was regally so, showing no sign of ill-temper nor any discourtesy. He took the letter, breaking the seal immediately, and quickly skimmed the contents, relaxing visibly as he did so. To Akil's surprise Ramiz then signalled for tea to be brought, and when it came, accompanied by cushions to sit on, he sat beside Peregrine—an honour of which the young man, awkwardly crouching, seemed unaware.

'So, you are not here to escort the Lady Celia back to Cairo?'

Peregrine eyed the sweet tea in its delicate glass with caution. 'No, Your Highness. That is—no. The Consul General extends his most profuse apologies, but he felt it better, in the circumstances, to summon Lady Celia's father to fetch her.'

'It is to my great sorrow that Mr Cleveden died so tragically while on the soil of A'Qadiz. Do you wish to take his body back with you?'

Peregrine looked appalled. 'Good Lord, no. That is—like a soldier, you know—buried where he fell kind of thing.' He took a cautious sip of tea. It was surprisingly refreshing. He took another, and allowed his ample derrière, aching from the wooden camel saddle, to sink a little more comfortably down onto the cushion. 'Didn't know the chap, of course, but gather he was destined for great things.'

A picture of George Cleveden fleeing the attack flashed into Ramiz's mind. 'Indeed,' he said non-committally.

'Despatch to Lord Armstrong went off in the old urgent bag just as soon as your own letter arrived,' Peregrine said, relaxing further. This prince was turning out to be a very nice chap—not at all the dragon he'd been led to expect. 'Frigate waiting off Alexandria, as a matter of fact. With a fair wind and a bit of luck her family will know she's all right and tight very soon.'

'You are acquainted with Lord Armstrong?'

'Good heavens, no. A bit above my touch. As is Lady Celia, if I'm honest. One of these frightfully clever females—type who has all the inside gen on who's doing what to whom—in a political way, if you know what I mean.' Peregrine tittered, caught Ramiz's stern glare, and lowered his eyes. 'Highness. Your Highness. Beg pardon. Didn't mean to—bit new to all this. Awfully sorry.'

Ramiz got swiftly to his feet. 'You will wish to see her?'

Peregrine, who had been hoping for the offer of some more substantial refreshment than tea before facing the Lady Celia, blinked, tried to get to his feet, slipped, and decided that remaining in obeisance on his knees, while lacking in dignity, was preferable to losing his head.

'Well?' Ramiz demanded impatiently.

'Yes—yes, of course. Highness. Your Highness.'

'Tomorrow, I think,' Ramiz said, much to Peregrine's relief. 'You must be tired after your journey. Akil will show you to the men's quarters now. There is a *hammam* there you can use.'

'*Hammam?*' Peregrine's eyes boggled. He could not decide whether to be honoured or revolted, for in his mind the word conjured up a fat exotic odalisque, rather like his nanny but in scantier clothing. Younger, of course, and he hoped not really too much like old Lalla Hughes who, now he came to think of it, had a bit of a moustache going.

'Steam bath,' Ramiz explained, trying not to smile, for Peregrine's thoughts were written plainly on his blistered countenance.

'Oh. Quite. Excellent…I suppose.'

'We dine late here, when the sun goes down. You will join me, I hope?'

'It will be an honour,' Peregrine said with a brave smile.

'If there's anything else you require, Akil will attend to your needs.' With a dismissive nod, Ramiz made for the doors, leaving Peregrine stranded on his knees on the floor of the vault-like chamber.

Back in the harem, Celia was unaware of the presence of her country's emissary. She lay on her stomach while Fatima rubbed scented oil into her skin. The girl's touch was gentle, but firm, easing the tension from her back and shoulders. Celia allowed her mind to drift, wholly accustomed now to the intimacy of her own nakedness, and to Fatima's capable fingers kneading her muscles. Strange how this could feel so pleasant, yet so impersonal. Strange how her body could react so differently to touch. Not just because of how it was done, but because of who was doing it. If Ramiz and not Fatima was delivering the massage, she would not be feeling so relaxed as to be upon the verge of falling asleep.

And of course as soon as his name popped into her mind, so too did his face, and his scent, and the feel of him, and she was wide awake. What was it about him that so obsessed her? Why Ramiz? Why now, at the age of four-and-twenty, was she being assaulted by these feelings? Such acute awareness of everything? Not just of Ramiz, but of colours and textures and taste. It was such a sensuous world, A'Qadiz, and Ramiz was at its epicentre, the very epitome of sensuality.

She was attracted to him—of that there was no doubt. She liked the way he looked. And the way he walked. And the way he talked. And the way he could be so arrogant one minute and so understanding the next. And the way he looked at her as if he saw something no one else saw. He made her feel beautiful. He said she *was* beautiful, and she believed him.

She was attracted to him, and he was attracted to her—a little. Probably because she was different. Infatuation, that was what it was. She was in thrall to him simply because he had been the first to kiss her. The first to touch her. The first to make her feel—*that!* The thing she couldn't put into words. Ecstasy. Carnal pleasure. *That!* She was beguiled.

But it felt like more than that. Ramiz made her laugh. They liked the same things. He knew things about her that she hadn't even known herself. And she knew him too, in a way others didn't. He'd let her see, even if briefly, how lonely, how isolated he felt.

Unreal. It was all unreal and meant nothing. Could never mean anything. She knew that. *She did.*

She was not an Arabian princess. In the eyes of his people her breeding meant nothing, for the blood which ran in her veins was English. No matter how many things she and Ramiz shared, no matter how similar their outlook on life might be, no matter even that they wanted the same things, she was not of his world and never could be.

Celia allowed herself to be helped from the divan into a warm bath. Sinking down into the fragrant water, she closed her eyes. Enchanted, beguiled, in thrall, under his spell. Whatever she was, it would not last.

In fact, according to Ramiz it was already over. Whatever it was. She wished it was not. She wished he would come to her again. Take her to the secret places he could conjure one more time. Continue with the fantasy for just a little longer, while she was here in his harem, locked away from the real world and the reality of the rather tedious life which awaited her as George's widow back in England.

She wished, though she mocked herself for doing so, that for one night she could live out her Arabian fantasy. Lying alone in the bath, she knew it was a dream. She thought of Ramiz—his kisses, his touch. She thought of him and the wanting came, and in the dark of the night she allowed herself to dream.

When Adila opened the harem door to one of the guards the next morning, Celia assumed Ramiz wished to see her, but the man who awaited her in a formal salon in the main body of the palace was a complete stranger. Dressed in a bottle-green cutaway coat, teamed with a rather alarming waistcoat embroidered with pink roses, he was about her own height, but considerably wider of girth. When he bowed, which he did with surprising grace given his apple shape, his fawn knit pantaloons stretched in a rather distressing manner, so that Celia dropped her own curtsy very rapidly, anxious to have him return to the upright in the hope of preventing what seemed to her an inevitable unravelling.

'Peregrine Finchley-Burke,' the young man said. 'At your service on behalf of His Majesty's government, Lady Celia.'

Realisation dawned. 'You have been sent to escort me home?'

Peregrine frowned. For a moment he could have sworn the lady was disappointed. 'No doubt you're eager to return to the bosom of your family,' he said cautiously.

'Indeed—though I have been very well treated here, I assure you. The palace is most luxurious.'

'Just so...just so.' Peregrine rubbed his hands together. 'Pleased to hear that, because the thing is I'm not actually here to take you back,' he said, flinching away instinctively as he delivered his ill tidings. To his relief, however, the tall, elegant woman in front of him did not break down into immediate hysterics, grab his hand, plea for mercy or even cry out in dismay. Instead her sleepy eyes widened and a smile trembled on her rather full mouth before she lowered her lids again and looked away into the distance, clasping her hands together.

'Not here to take me back?' Celia repeated faintly. 'You mean I am to stay here?'

'For the present. Thing is—dashed awkward all this. Forgot—should have said straight away have to pass on condolences. Terrible thing to happen. Consul General seemed to think very highly of your husband.'

'Thank you. You are very kind.' Celia rummaged for her handkerchief in her reticule and dabbed her eyes.

'And you, Lady Celia, it must have been a bit of an ordeal.'

'I was very fortunate that Sheikh al-Muhana was there,' Celia said with a watery smile. 'He saved my life, you know. Forgive my rudeness, Mr Finchley-Burke, please do sit down. Have you spoken with the Sheikh? How did he react when you informed him that I was to stay here?'

Peregrine waited for Celia to take a seat before he eased himself onto a divan opposite her. Having spent the previous evening balancing his bulk on a cushion, feeling like a seal stranded by the tide on a rock which was too small, he was relieved to find that he was not expected to conduct this particular interview on the floor. 'The Prince left this morning—visiting some outlying tribes or something. Won't be back for quite a few days, apparently. Said to pass on his *adieu* and hoped you would be comfortable until his return.'

What was that supposed to mean? Celia thought indignantly.

'Seems a decent enough chap,' Peregrine continued with a touch of condescension. 'Bit on his high horse at first, but suppose that was to be expected.'

Celia raised her brows delicately. 'He is Prince of A'Qadiz, and it is likely that he holds the balance of power in at least four of the neighbouring six principalities. He is also extremely intelligent, and wealthy beyond anything you can imagine. You underestimate him at your peril.'

'Oh, I don't, I assure you—not now I've seen the place for myself.'

'Why exactly are you here, Mr Finchley-Burke, if you are not to take me back? It seems very strange that you have come all this way simply to pass on a message.' *And, now she thought about it, if Ramiz was as indifferent to her presence as he wished her to believe, why had he not insisted that she leave with this rotund young man?*

'Thing is, Lord Wincester sent an urgent despatch back to Blighty—to your father. Thought Lord Armstrong should be the one to come and get you—best person to make the arrangements and what not, and also best person to complete the negotiations with the Prince, you know? Kill two birds with one stone, so to speak.'

'So I am to wait here until my father arrives?'

'Shouldn't be too long,' Peregrine said bracingly. 'Matter of a few weeks at most. Said yourself you're very comfortable here.' Peregrine opened his watch, wound it up, then closed it again. 'London time,' he said, à propos of nothing.

Celia raised her brows. 'Is there something else you wish to say to me, Mr Finchley-Burke?'

'Well.' Peregrine plucked a large kerchief from his pocket and mopped his brow. 'Well… You said it yourself, Lady Celia, this Sheikh al-Muhana could turn out to be quite an important man. A'Qadiz has the only decent port on the Red Sea. If we can do an exclusive deal with him and Mehmet Ali in Egypt it opens up a whole new trade route to India. Takes the journey time down from two years to only three months. Imagine that!' Peregrine eased forward confidentially. 'Thing is, don't want anyone else to steal our thunder, so to speak. Would be nice to know Sheikh al-Muhana isn't talking to the competition. That's where you come in.'

'Me? But Sheikh al-Muhana won't do business with a woman. And besides, I have not been briefed.'

'No, no. Of course not. Already said—your father coming out here provides a perfect opportunity. Obviously an opportunity borne out of tragedy, I hasten to add. Lord Armstrong is a skilled negotiator. If anyone can strike a deal with the Sheikh then he can.'

'So what exactly do you want *me* to do?'

'Ah. The Consul General said you'd understand because you're Lord Armstrong's daughter and you know what's what.'

Celia shook her head in bewilderment. 'Understand *what* is what?'

Peregrine swallowed nervously. 'He expects you to—to use your position to England's advantage.'

'My position!' Celia jumped up from her divan, forcing Peregrine to rise precipitately to his feet—an act which left him breathless and sweating. 'And precisely what position do you and the Consul General assume I occupy?'

'Well, I didn't mean to imply—' Peregrine broke off, blushing to the roots of his hair. 'I'm just supposed to tell you that your father would expect you to keep your eyes and ears open. You know—find out as much as you can of the situation here. Anything—no matter how trivial. We know so little of the man and his country, and you are in a unique position to...' he faltered under Celia's basilisk stare '...to—you know—glean what you can. Lord Wincester said to tell you that at least this way the whole damned mission won't have been a complete waste of time and money. Except,' Peregrine added contritely, 'wasn't supposed to say it in quite that way. Beg pardon.'

Celia dropped back onto the divan. The idea of trying to extract information by subterfuge from Ramiz was repugnant, and she was pretty certain it would also be completely unsuccessful. She doubted very much that he would give away anything he did not want her to know.

On the other hand, he *did* trust her. He had trusted

her with the secret of Katra. He had confided in her some of his troubles with regard to his neighbours too—had seemed glad of the opportunity to talk, in fact, within the cloistered confines of the harem.

No, she should not even be giving the idea thought. Even to pass on the little she already knew would be seen by Ramiz as a betrayal.

But if she refused, what would everyone think of her? What harm would it do poor George's memory that his widow had no loyalty to her country? Bad enough that his widow was relieved she was no longer his wife—surely she owed him this much in reparation? And, after all, Ramiz might never know. By the time he found out, if he ever did, she would be safe back in Cairo. In England, even.

'And if I do not agree with Lord Wincester's proposal, what then?' Celia enquired.

Judging by the startled look on Peregrine's face, this was not a possibility which had been considered. 'Why on earth wouldn't you? England, you know—empire and all that,' he said vaguely. He scratched his head. 'I suppose you could come back with me, but I'm not sure Sheikh al-Muhana would be too keen on the idea of you leaving without his say-so. Then there's the guards. You'd be kicking your heels in Cairo until your father arrived, and there's the issue of the treaty—because if you left against the Sheikh's wishes I don't doubt he'd be insulted, and your father would have come all this way for nothing and—well, you see how it is.' Peregrine spread his hands in a fatalistic way.

If she left it would ruin things, in other words, Celia thought. And, actually, the one thing she was sure of was that she didn't want to leave. She wasn't ready to say goodbye to A'Qadiz—not yet. Nor to Ramiz.

If she stayed she could agree to what Mr Finchley-Burke asked of her without actually acting upon it. In fact, Celia thought brightly, there was no need to make any decision right now, except to agree in principle to try and do as she was bid.

'Very well. I will stay until Papa arrives,' Celia said.

Peregrine executed as dignified a bow as he could manage. 'Excellent. That is excellent news,' he said with a relieved smile. 'Have to say didn't at all fancy having to run the gauntlet of those guards.'

Celia held out her hand. 'Goodbye Mr Finchley-Burke. And good luck with your posting in India.'

'What shall I tell Lord Wincester?'

'You may tell him that he can rely on me to do the right thing,' Celia replied. Which she would—whatever that meant.

Ramiz sent no word to Celia for the duration of his absence, though she learned from Yasmina that he was in regular contact with Akil. She spent another enjoyable day at Yasmina's house, eager to discover for herself what 'ordinary' life in Balyrma was like. Surprisingly like life at home was what she found, with much of the day given over to caring for the children—readying the bigger ones for school, teaching the smaller ones their letters, managing their meals, sewing their clothes, wiping their tears and telling them stories.

'Before Ramiz came to power, only my oldest son went to school,' Yasmina told Celia as the two women sat companionably embroidering a section each of a large forest scene stretched on a frame, while the younger children took their afternoon nap in a separate salon. 'There were no schools for girls. Most of them could not even read, for their mothers couldn't read so there was no one to teach them.'

'Because of course none of the men would,' Celia said sarcastically.

'Of course not,' Yasmina agreed. 'It is the way of things here, Celia. Things are changing, some things are changing very fast, but we must not let the wind carry us to places we do not want to go. Ramiz knows that.'

'I'm sorry, I didn't mean to sound rude. It is just that things are so different.'

'Just because it is different doesn't make it wrong,' Yasmina reminded her gently. 'There are many ways to skin a rabbit.'

Celia smiled. 'We say that too, only it is a cat, I don't know why. Tell me about the schools. What did Ramiz do?'

'Well, he was very clever. He knew unless they trusted the teachers the women would not allow their girls to attend school, so he brought in a teacher to teach the teachers, not the girls. The men didn't like it at first, and even now there are only three teachers and about a hundred girls, so my older daughter is very lucky to have a place, but it is a start, and Akil said Ramiz has big plans. One day everyone in A'Qadiz will be able to read and write. Of course many of our people think this is madness—they say it will change the old order for ever, because people will lose sight of their place and no one will want to do real work, which is why it is all going so slowly. That and the fact that Ramiz is stretched as thin as the finest lace, which is why Akil says he should take a wife.' Yasmina snipped the vermilion thread she had been using and selected a length of burgundy. 'Talking of Ramiz, did you look at those charm books I gave you?' she asked with a slanting smile.

Celia nodded, concentrating on her stitching. The books were filled with extremely explicit pictures showing men and women engaging in an astonishing variety of acts. 'Some of the things,' she whispered, 'I didn't think were physically possible.'

Yasmina giggled. 'I don't think they are. You are not supposed to take them literally. They are meant to inspire, not to instruct. Have they?'

'Have they what?'

'Inspired you?' Yasmina asked with a sly look. 'Don't pretend you haven't thought about it.'

Celia blushed. 'It just seems wrong to plan such things. Shouldn't they just happen—you know, naturally?'

'Of course—at first,' Yasmina agreed. 'And it certainly does not do for a woman to lead the way. Men like to think they do that. But later, when you know each other well, there is much to be said for something different.'

'Oh, well, then, I don't need to worry about it,' Celia said with relief.

'You and Ramiz have not...?'

'No. And we will not. I can't think why we're talking about this, I was just curious.'

'Curiosity killed the goat.'

'We say that too. Only it's a cat again.'

'Be careful, Celia. Remember what I said.'

'I know. He is not meant for me. As if I could forget it,' Celia muttered. Everyone seemed to have an opinion on the true nature of her relationship with Ramiz except her. And Ramiz, of course, who didn't have an opinion because as far as he was concerned there was no relationship. With a sigh, Celia resumed her sewing.

CHAPTER NINE

THE negotiations had stretched Ramiz's patience to the limit. Twice he had threatened to walk away, relenting only because of his determination not to let one of his own people destroy his hard work through ignorance and greed. An agreement had finally been reached and, following the twelve-hour feast ordered by the tribe's elders to celebrate their concord, Ramiz returned to Balyrma exhausted but well satisfied.

It had been a long few days in more than one way. He had found himself missing Celia. It was always a tedious business dealing with the tribes. They favoured a convoluted, highly formal bargaining process with which he was all too familiar, but he hadn't realised how alone it made him feel until now. It was not just the fact that he was one against many; it was also that, being the Prince, he had to appear inviolable and imperious. It was expected of him. Nothing must touch him, which meant there was no one to take his part except himself.

At night, alone in his tent in the middle of the desert, he'd found himself thinking of Celia. The scent of her, the feel of her petal-soft skin against his own. The taste of her mouth, succulent and honey-sweet. He'd wondered what she was doing. He'd wondered if she thought of him. He had cursed himself for wondering, for wasting precious time on such pointless and frustrating thoughts, though still he had indulged them. He had missed her.

He had not intended to seek her out immediately, but upon his return to the palace on the evening of his sixth day away, dusty and tense from the long ride back, that was what he did—without even stopping to change. She was sitting in the courtyard on a cushion, leaning against the fountain. She had been staring up at the stars framed by the square of the top floor of the building, her head thrown back, her long hair rippling loose down her back. When the door opened she turned, startled. Upon seeing him standing there a hand went to her breast.

For a few seconds she stared at him wordlessly. Her skin was ghostly pale in the twilight, her eyes glittering dark. As she got fluidly to her feet, he saw that she was dressed in clothes made from the materials they had bought at the market. Only a week ago, yet it seemed like months. She wore a long caftan slit to the thigh in mint-green silk. The sleeves and hem were weighted down with silver *passementerie* braiding. Loose *sarwal* pantaloons of a darker green, made of some gauzy material transparent enough for him to see the shape of her legs beneath, fluttered out around her. She was bare-footed. She seemed to float rather than walk. Her hair rippled like silk ruffled by a breeze. She looked so different. Exotic. An English rose in an Eastern garden.

Ramiz stood rooted to the spot. He hadn't expected

this. Hadn't anticipated the unsettling effect seeing her like this would have on him.

'You're back,' she said, stopping uncertainly before him.

'Only just now. I came to see how you were, since I did not have a chance to see you after the visit from your countryman. I half expected to hear from Akil that you had asked to return to Cairo with Mr Finchley-Burke.'

'Since my father has been summoned to complete the negotiations which brought my husband here in the first place, I thought it best to wait. Would you have allowed me to leave if I had asked it?'

Ramiz raised a brow. 'Is that what you would have preferred?'

Celia laughed. 'I should have known better than to expect a straight answer from such an accomplished statesman as yourself.'

'Or from such an accomplished diplomat's daughter as yourself,' Ramiz rejoined with a smile.

'Did your trip go well? You were away longer than you anticipated.'

Ramiz shrugged. 'It's done.'

'At a cost, I take it?'

Ramiz nodded. 'A cost worth paying, though.'

'Have you eaten?'

'I'm not hungry.'

He looked weary. There were little grooves of tiredness at the corners of his mouth. A frown furrowed his brow. Celia's heart contracted. Now he was back, now her heart was beating out its excitement at his presence, she could admit to herself how much she had missed him. Without thinking she reached out to smooth away the lines on his forehead. His skin was warm, gritty with sand under his headdress.

'You're all dusty,' she said inanely, for suddenly she could think of nothing to say, so overwhelmed was she by his presence.

'I should go and change.'

'Stay a while,' Celia said impulsively. 'Talk to me. I've—it's been lonely here without you.'

'You've missed me?'

There was the tiniest trace of a smile at the corner of his mouth. Celia managed a shrug. 'What do you think of my clothes?' she asked, executing a little twirl.

The soft material clung lovingly to her slender frame, hugging the curve of her breasts, the slope of her bottom. He saw the nakedness of her feet on the tiles, the soft flutter of her hair drifting out behind her as she twirled, heard the swish of her caftan as it floated out from her body then settled back down to caress her thighs. The scent of amber and musk drifted towards him, mingling with the warmer, fragrant smell that was Celia, and the whole combination went intoxicatingly to his head. Ramiz reached out to catch a long tress of hair, wrapping it like a bond of copper silk around his hand, pulling her towards him.

Under the caftan she wore only a wisp of silk. She might as well be naked. They were as close as they could be without touching. Heat rose between them. *Could he feel it too?* There was a smudge of dust on his right cheek. His left hand was wrapped in her hair, tugging her head back. The need to touch him was unbearable. Could he see her heart beating? Could he hear how shallow and fast was her breathing? Why was he here? Did she care as long as he was?

'Did you miss me?' Ramiz asked again.

'Yes,' Celia whispered, for it was the truth. She had missed him enormously. She had spent hours and hours wrestling with her conscience over the Consul General's proposal, concluding time and again only that she must do nothing she would later regret, nothing which would compromise her integrity, nothing she could not undo. Which meant avoiding exactly the sort of situation she was now confronting.

But it was all very well to think such thoughts and to hold such high-minded opinions when alone. In Ramiz's disconcerting presence she had no such control. Her mind—that disciplined, logical part of her which had ruled her life until now—was in real danger of surrendering control to her body. And her body was not slow to take advantage, so that without meaning to, without realising she was doing it, Celia closed the tiny gap between them and tilted her head up and put her arms around him. And that was it. She kissed him. She had to. There was nothing, nothing at all she could do about it, for if she did not kiss him she was afraid she would stop breathing.

And when his lips met hers she stopped breathing anyway, just for a moment, so literally breathtaking was the feel of his mouth and the scent of his skin and the complex magic of his just being there. She murmured his name, she pressed herself into the hard lines of his body, and he groaned. And then he kissed her back—a surprisingly gentle kiss, feathering its way along the line of her lower lip, licking into the corners, then the softness inside. His free hand was stroking the nape of her neck, the hollow of her collarbone, the column of her throat.

Then it was over. Ramiz stepped back. He unwound her hair from his hand. He rubbed his forehead, pushing back his headdress so that it fell to the floor. 'I must go and change,' he said reluctantly. 'I must see Akil.'

'Don't go. Not yet. Stay and talk to me. Please.' Celia held out her hand. His hair was rumpled. Without the frame of his *gutra* his face looked younger, almost vulnerable. Her own needs vanished, superseded by the desire to erase Ramiz's lines of fatigue, to ease the tension she could see in his shoulders, just to have him to herself for a little while.

He hesitated, then allowed her to lead him into one of the salons. She made him tea on the little spirit stove there, taking care with the ritual of measuring the leaves from the enamelled chest into the silver samovar, serving it just as he liked it, with no sugar but lemon and mint. And as Celia busied herself with the tea she talked—of her visit to Yasmina, of the books she had read, of her letter to Cassie. Ramiz listened at first with detachment, simply enjoying the graceful way she went about the small domestic task, the sound of her voice and her gentle wit, and then he was smiling over her description of the play Yasmina's children had put on for her, and making her laugh with his description of the English emissary's falling asleep on the cushions over dinner, relaxed enough to tell her about his trip into the desert.

As before, she listened with understanding—sympathetic without being fawning, contributing her own opinions without being asked, contradicting him without offending. Tea was taken, the lamps were lit, and still they sat on, talking and laughing in unperceived intimacy until Ramiz yawned and stretched and said he should go. They both realised that was the last thing they wanted.

'Five nights on a carpet in someone else's tent,' he said, rolling his shoulders. 'I'd forgotten how uncomfortable it can be.'

'Would you like me to give you a massage?'

Ramiz looked as startled as she herself was, for she hadn't meant to offer—only she hadn't wanted him to go, and she wanted to do something that would preserve this unaccustomed intimacy. 'Do you know how?' he asked.

Celia nodded. 'Fatima has shown me what to do, though I've not really had a chance to practise. I find it helps me sleep. Perhaps it would help you too?'

He doubted Celia's touch would make him sleepy. He knew it was one of the things which breached the boundaries he'd told himself to establish, but then so too was talking to her alone like this. And he *was* tired. And sore. And in no mood for anything other than sleep. Not really.

Ramiz got to his feet. 'Where?' he asked, and when she indicated they use the large circular divan on which she slept he allowed himself to be led into that salon, watched as she spread a fresh silk sheet over the velvet cover while he pulled off his robe, wrapping his lower half in a linen towel, lying down on his stomach and closing his eyes. A swish of material told him Celia had discarded her caftan. He could smell the orange and amber in the oil as she rubbed it onto her hands. When she leaned over him a long strand of her hair brushed his cheek. She tutted and swept it back. Then she leaned over him again. He could feel the heat emanating from her skin, the feathering of her breath on his. Then he surrendered to the supple kneading of her fingers.

She started at his shoulders, where the tension knotted his muscles together like rope. Carefully at first, her touch experimental, she leaned over, trying to keep the contact to her hands, though the temptation to brush her breasts against him, to prostrate herself on top of him, skin to skin, was strong. His eyes were closed tight. His lashes, sooty and soft, fanned onto his cheeks. His hair grew in a shape like a question mark on the back of his head, tapering down like an arrow to his nape. The veins on his neck stood out, so bunched tight were his shoulders. Celia pressed into them with her spread fingers as Fatima had shown her, rolling her thumbs up his spine, circling back down and round again in a soothing motion, pressing harder as she felt Ramiz relax, kneading him with her palms, concentrating on levelling out the twisting stress, smoothing and kneading, pressing and soothing in a smooth rhythm so that she forgot everything except the feel of her hands on his body.

Breathing a little harder with the effort, she leaned a little closer, and a little closer yet, to get just the right angle—until she was kneeling on the divan beside him, then kneeling between his legs as she worked her way down his back, then over him, so that her breasts brushed his heated skin, slick with the delicately scented oil, and her nipples budded through the thin layer of silk which contained them. Below her, Ramiz kept his eyes tight shut. She could feel the steady rise and fall of his chest. Sleeping? The scent of him, a subtle something, male and other, rose like a whisper of smoke from his skin.

She worked her way down to the base of his spine, pulling away the towel which covered him, waiting for a sign that she should stop which did not come. His buttocks were firm and slightly rounded, his flanks were firm too, with a feathery smattering of black hair, surprisingly soft. The softer flesh at the inside of his thighs was hot. Tender from the time spent in the saddle. Heat. It was not just coming from Ramiz.

A trickle of sweat shivered down between Celia's breasts. Wiping it away, she trailed oil over her own skin. She picked up the bottle to trickle more oil onto her hands. A drop escaped onto Ramiz's shoulders. She leaned over to rub it in. Her breasts pressed into his back, her stomach onto his buttocks. Skin slick with oil. A sensual sliding. She lay motionless, relishing the melding of skin on skin, of heat on heat. Below her, Ramiz lay still as a statue.

She had convinced herself he was asleep. Then, as she sat up, he turned underneath her, so quickly she would have fallen had he not grasped her by the arms, rolled her with him, so that somehow she was under him and he was on top of her, and he did not look at all as if he had been asleep.

His eyes blazed like molten bronze sparked with gold. A slash of colour highlighted his cheekbones. His chest rose and fell, rose and fell almost as rapidly as her own. She could feel the pounding of his heart. Then he kissed her, wildly and passionately, yanking away the strip of silk which covered her breasts. And then he devoured them.

His mouth was on her nipples, hot on their aching hardness. His hands moulded her breasts, shaping them and stroking them, and his mouth was sucking and nipping, making her writhe and moan, strange little gasping pleas she didn't recognise as she bucked under him. Her own hands were grasping and pulling at him. The hardness of his erection was pressing solid and insistent against her thigh. In minutes, seconds, it would be too late. She knew that absolutely—as she knew absolutely that she would not stop him. She wanted this with an urgency she had not dreamed possible. Something as fundamental as the stars urged her on, made her push against him, arch into him, pluck at him as if she would spread him over her, all the time gasping and moaning his name. His mouth on her nipples forged a burning path of sensation, stirred up a cauldron of heat in her belly, and their oiled skin slid and glided and clung.

Her gauzy pantaloons were pleated into a sash at her waist. Ramiz pulled it open. She struggled free of their constraints with neither shame nor modesty, wanting only to feel him against her, beside her, inside her. They lay facing each other, kissing. Mouths fervent with need, eyes burning with desire, fingers seeking out secret creases, stroking into them, until she felt his hand between her legs, cupping her, stroking her, and the hot surge of wet pulsing need made her clench and clench again as he touched her exactly where she needed him to touch her. No teasing this time, no drawing out, just there, and there, and *there*, reading her wants as she moaned and dug her fingers into his shoulders, and jangled like a puppet on strings which Ramiz pulled, until she felt that plundering, plunging sensation build. She jolted as her climax took over, barely noticing that he had rolled her onto her back, that he was between her legs, pushing them up, angling himself over her until he thrust hard and powerfully into her and she screamed out—not with pleasure but with pain.

Ramiz froze. The expression on his face was ludicrous in its intensity. Sheer disbelief, swiftly followed by horror. As the sharpness of the pain receded, and she realised he was going to pull away, Celia clutched at him. 'No.'

But she could not hold him. He cursed long and viciously in his own language, pushing her hands away and pulling himself from her in one move. He grabbed his robe from the floor and pulled it over his head. There was no mistaking the anger which froze his face into rigid lines. His eyes were cold too, glinting chips of amber. Celia sat up, clutching the sheet around her. Bright beads of blood showed crimson on its pristine white, like berries in snow. Hastily she twisted the sheet, but Ramiz had already seen them. He wrenched it from her grasp, forcing her to scrabble for her caftan to cover her nakedness.

'A sheet any bride would be proud of,' Ramiz said through gritted teeth, holding it up so that the traitorous blood spots could not be avoided. 'But you are not a bride. Why in the name of all the gods did you not tell me? Do you think I would have? Do you think I would have let you—allowed myself—? You don't know what you have done.'

'What I have done?' Celia stood up, glaring at him.

'What *I* have done, then. Something your husband evidently did not!' Ramiz ran his hand through his hair. 'Why didn't you tell me?'

'You didn't ask!' But even as she threw the words at him she knew how unfair they were. The reality of the situation came crashing down like a sudden cloudburst. *What had she done?* 'George didn't want—we didn't— he said it would be easier if we waited until we knew each other better,' she said quietly. 'But we never did.'

'Evidently,' Ramiz said bitterly.

'No.' Celia blinked, determined not to allow the tears which burned her eyes to fall. 'I doubt we ever would have, to be honest. I'm sorry. I'm sorry I didn't tell you. I didn't mean this to happen. I should have stopped you. I'm sorry.'

She brushed the back of her hand across her eyes. The defiant little gesture touched him as tears would not have. 'Celia, did I hurt you?'

She shook her head.

'Are you sure?'

She managed a weak smile. 'Just a little.'

'Next time it won't be so—' Ramiz stopped. There would never be a next time for them. There should not have been a first. He should be thanking the fates that he had managed to stop—that shock had allowed him to stop. Only he didn't feel like thanking the fates. Horrified by his own base desires, by the persistence of his erection, which nudged insistently against his belly, he realized that what he wanted to do was to finish what they had started. To sheath himself in the luscious delight of her, to thrust deeper and deeper, until he spent himself inside her, to claim her as his. As his own. As her first.

No! He could not. He would not. Not even if it meant another would take what rightfully should be his.

No! No! No! He would not think of Celia with another. Looking at her trying so hard not to cry, the flush of passion fading from her cheeks, her mouth bruised with his kisses, the delicate creamy white of her breast showing the imprint of his touch, Ramiz fought the urge to take her in his arms and soothe away the hurt he had caused. The stain on his honour, the tangible evidence of that stain on the sheet he gripped, held him back. 'What have I done?'

'It wasn't just you. It was my fault as much as yours,' Celia said resolutely.

'I have deflowered you. The dishonour!'

'Ramiz, as you have already pointed out, I was married. In the eyes of the world I was already deflowered. There is no dishonour because no one will know.'

'*I* will know!'

'Well, I'm sure you'll learn to live with it.'

'Is that all you can say?'

She bit her lip. What she wanted was to know how it felt to really make love. How it felt to have him move inside her. What she wanted was to complete and to be completed—because that, she realised, was what it was really about. Two people as one. That was what she wanted to say, but she couldn't, because for Ramiz it had clearly been nothing more than the easing of tension. The natural conclusion to her massage.

'I think you should go now,' she said instead, wresting the horrible evidence of her virginity from his hands. 'I think we should agree to forget all about this.'

'Forget?'

'Yes. It's for the best.'

'Is this your famous British stiff upper lip? It doesn't suit you.'

'It's what we British call being practical. You're tired. Exhausted, in fact. Go to bed.'

'But you...'

'I will be fine.'

She was right, but it felt wrong. He didn't want to leave her—which was exactly the reason why he should. Nothing about this was right. Staying would only heap more wrong on wrong.

He didn't like the way she was so determined to take

her share of the blame. And he definitely didn't like it that it was she and not he who insisted he go. It was all the wrong way round. Where was the clinging vine? Why must she be so stoically independent? He didn't like it, but there wasn't a thing he could do about it either.

Ramiz shrugged. 'Goodnight,' he said coldly. Then he left without another word.

Alone, Celia picked up his headdress from where he had dropped it carelessly on the floor. The square of white silk smelled of him. She clutched it to her chest. Then she curled up on the divan and gave way to racking sobs and blinding tears.

Peregrine Finchley-Burke's confidence in the efficiency of the Royal Navy was not displaced. Lord Wincester's despatch reached England less than three weeks after it had been written. The special courier arrived mud-spattered, his horse's flanks speckled with foam, at the country estate of Lord Henry Armstrong just as its owner was preparing for a long overdue meeting with his bailiff. The contents of the missive, perused in the seclusion of his study, were shocking enough to require sustenance in the form of brandy, despite the early hour. Throwing back the large snifter, Lord Henry read the letter for a third time. A frown marred his normally serene countenance, for the consequences of the matter were potentially far-reaching. A delicate situation. Very delicate indeed, he thought, scratching his bald pate. It was a good thing his sister Sophia was here. He could trust her to manage the girls. But what to do about it all was another matter.

'Damn the man,' Lord Henry muttered, staring at

Lord Wincester's signature. 'Bloody fool. Only reason he's out there is because of that fracas in Lisbon. He thought it was all hushed up, but *I* know the real story.' He poured himself a second snifter. 'Damn the man,' he said again, more loudly this time. 'And damn George Cleveden too! You'd have thought he'd have more wit than to get himself killed in such a manner.' Lord Henry leaned over to ruffle the fur of his favourite pointer bitch, sitting obediently at his feet 'Bloody stupid thing to do, if you ask me.' The dog whined. 'You're quite right. Time they were all told,' Lord Henry said, bestowing another affectionate pat upon the animal before he got to his feet and left the library in search of his family.

He entered the blue drawing room to find the collective eyes of his four daughters and sister Sophia upon him. Not for the first time he wondered at his own inability to father a son. Girls were all very well, but he couldn't help thinking five girls excessive. And expensive. 'Well, well, here you all are,' he said, with an air of false bonhomie which he mistakenly imagined would reassure them.

Cassandra, the beauty of the family, had been rather too aptly named, for she had a propensity for prophesying tragedy. She clutched dramatically at her father's coat sleeve, her lovely eyes, the colour of cornflowers, already drowning in tears. 'Papa! It is Celia, isn't it? She is—oh, Papa—tell me she is not—'

'Celia is absolutely fine,' Lord Henry said, detaching her fingers from his coat sleeve. 'It is George, I'm afraid. Dead.'

Cassandra collapsed back into a convenient chair, clutching her breast, her countenance touchingly pale. Caroline gave a little gasp of horror. Cordelia and Cressida simply stared with mouths wide open at their father. It was left to Lady Sophia to seek clarification. 'May one ask what happened to result in such an unfortunate outcome?' she asked, rummaging in her reticule for the vial of *sal volatile* she kept there for such occasions.

'He was murdered,' Lord Henry replied flatly.

This shocking news gave even the normally redoubtable Lady Sophia pause. Casting a baleful look at the two youngest of her nieces, who had squealed in a most unrefined manner, she thrust the *sal volatile* under Cassie's nose.

'May I?' asked Sophia, holding her hand out imperiously for the despatch which Lord Henry was only too happy to hand over. She read it with close attention, her eyebrows rising fractionally as she digested the content. 'You may leave this to me, Henry,' she said to her brother.

Only too happy to obey, Lord Henry left the room.

'I am sorry to inform you that George has indeed been murdered,' Lady Sophia informed her nieces. 'Brigands. It seems he and Celia were on their way to a place called A'Qadiz, which is somewhere in Arabia, on a special assignment which entailed a journey across the desert. That is where poor George met his fate. He died bravely, serving his country,' she said with an air of assurance and a complete disregard for the truth. 'That fact will, I do most sincerely trust, mitigate the rather vulgar manner in which he was slain.'

'And Celia?' Faced with a genuine crisis, Cassie had abandoned her vapours and, though prettily pale, was composed enough to join her sisters on the sofa, putting a comforting arm around the two youngest. 'What does the despatch say of Celia? I take it she is now under the care of the Consul General? Or perhaps she is already on her way home?' she said hopefully.

'Hmm.' Lady Sophia inspected the lace of her sleeve.

'Aunt?'

'Hmm,' Lady Sophia said again. 'Celia is still in A'Qadiz, I am afraid.'

'What? In the desert?'

'She is apparently resident in the royal palace there. As a guest of a Sheikh al-Muhana. Prince al-Muhana, I should say.'

This information was met with stunned silence. Lady Sophia twitched at her lace.

'Cassie, is Celia being held prisoner?' Cressida's chin wobbled.

'Cassie, will she be locked away and have to tell the Sheikh a story every night to stop her getting her head cut off?' Cordelia, aged twelve, asked. Too late she remembered that Aunt Sophia had forbidden them to read *that* book. Cordelia blushed. Cressida pinched her. Caroline drew her a look.

The ensuing reprimand distracted Cassie temporarily from the question nagging away at her. 'Why has Celia been left alone with Sheikh al-Muhana?' she asked, when order had finally been restored.

'A very pertinent question,' Lady Sophia answered dryly.

'A very pertinent question indeed,' Lord Henry said as he re-entered the room. 'Wincester is a buffoon and a liability, which is why I'm going out there personally to sort this mess out. Don't worry about your sister's safety in the meantime. No foreign power would dare harm the daughter of a senior British diplomat.'

'Papa, Celia has witnessed the murder of her husband. She has been kidnapped by a man who for all we know could have her under lock and key in his harem,' Cassie said, her voice rising as the full horror of her sister's plight began to sink in.

'Now, now,' Lord Henry said, eyeing his daughter warily, 'no point in letting our imagination run away with us. Celia is a sensible gal, and I'm sure the Prince is an honourable man. I'm sure there's no need to worry on that score.'

'No need to…' Cassie stared at her father in disbelief. 'I take it you *are* going to Egypt at once?'

'Well, of course I am.'

'Then I am coming with you,' Cassie said resolutely.

'Don't be ridiculous, girl.'

'I am coming with you, Father, and nothing you can say will dissuade me. Celia is my beloved sister. Heaven knows what she has gone through—is going through even now,' Cassie said with a shudder. 'She will need me to support her. I am coming with you and that's that.'

'Sophia, can't you talk some sense into the girl? The desert is no place for a young lady of breeding.'

'You might have thought of that before you despatched your other daughter, then,' Lady Sophia said witheringly. 'Cassandra is quite right. Celia will need her sister. And what's more she will need her aunt too. I am also coming with you.'

'Eh?'

'You heard, Henry,' Lady Sophia said, fixing her younger brother with one of her glacial glares. 'Now, since time is of the essence, I will go immediately to attend to my packing. You will summon Bella Frobisher to look after the girls. Since it is your intention that the woman is to be their new stepmother, she might as well make a start in getting to know them. Come, Cassandra. We will leave in an hour, Henry.'

Lord Henry Armstrong was renowned as a tough and unyielding negotiator, who had faced down the most cunning and powerful courtiers in all of Europe, but he was no match for his sister and he knew it. 'As you wish, Sophia,' he said resignedly, before leaving to go in search of the brandy bottle for the second time that morning.

CHAPTER TEN

RAMIZ wandered alone in the gardens of the royal palace. The relatively compact area was divided by a series of covered walkways and winding paths, linked with fountains and small pavilions to give it a sense of space. Watered by an ingenious system of sprinklers fed by underground pipes, it combined the traditional plants of the East, such as fig, oleander and jasmine, with a number of species brought back by Ramiz from his travels. Amongst these were several roses. One of his favourites, the lightly scented pink rose which climbed round the gilded trellis by the fountain where he sat now, had been given to him by the Empress Josephine herself, from her treasured garden at Malmaison. The petals appeared almost white when furled, the pink revealing itself like a blush only when the flowers opened fully.

They made him think of Celia. Three nights had passed since his last visit to the harem, and the only conclusion he had reached was that it was best to keep away from her. He had taken something precious, and there was nothing he could do to recompense her for the loss. What he had done was wrong, without a doubt, and Ramiz was unused to being in the wrong. He had never before been in a position where he could not put a wrong right, and he was wholly unused to the position in which he now found himself—torn between the desire to make amends and the equally strong desire to make proper love to Celia.

That was the most shocking thing of all. He had done wrong, commited a sin of honour, but he was struggling to regret it.

The fact that Celia herself refused to accept his crime didn't help. Why had she not stopped him? Why had she not confessed? Why was she determined to brush it off as something trivial? Didn't it matter to her? What did she want of him? Could it be that she was a pawn in some diplomatic game, ready to cry ravishment in order to gain advantage for her country? But she had already insisted she would *not* cry ravishment, and one of the few things he was certain of was that she did not lie.

So why? The last time he'd asked her, after the visit to Katra, she had blamed it on the harem. *Unreal*, she'd said. As in a fantasy? From the start she'd shown a fascination with the harem, or with her perception of the harem drawn from that set of fairytales *One Thousand and One Nights*. Like her compatriots on the Grand Tour, perhaps she was indulging in a fantasy safe from the prying eyes of her peers. It made sense. It made a lot of sense.

The only way to eliminate temptation is to yield to it. An old saying of his brother's. As the eldest son and his father's heir, Asad had been much indulged. Asad had preferred action to words. 'Women talk, men act,' he'd used to say. 'The sword is the instrument of the Prince. To his subjects falls the task of writing down his words.' Too quick to the flame, their father had always said of Asad, but he'd said it in such a way as to make his pride in his eldest son clear.

If truth be told Ramiz and Asad had rarely seen eye to eye. If truth be told, Ramiz thought wryly, nor had he and his father, but that didn't stop him missing them both. Nearly two years now since Asad was killed, and in that time Ramiz's life had been turned upside down. While he had always felt strongly about what he would do differently were he to become ruler of A'Qadiz, he had never seriously considered it happening. Putting his long-considered policies into action had gone some way to help him through the loss of his last remaining close relative, for his mother had died when Ramiz was a teenager, but it had also prevented him from thinking too much about the loss itself. He missed Asad. Why not admit it? He was lonely. He was a rich prince, with thousands of loyal subjects, and he had everything except someone to confide in.

He hadn't noticed until Celia came along. He'd been too immersed in state policy and state negotiations and state legislation. No time to think about anything other than A'Qadiz. No time to think that maybe he needed something for himself. Someone for himself. Perhaps Akil was right. What he needed was a wife.

But the idea of marrying one of the princesses from Akil's list was even less appealing than ever. Such a wife would be taken for the sake of A'Qadiz. Such a wife would not give him anything other than more responsibility, one more thing to worry about. Such a wife would not be like Celia—would not *be* Celia.

Ramiz growled with exasperation. A whole hour wasted thinking, and he was right back where he started. *The only way to eliminate temptation is to yield to it.* One thing Asad had always been good at was getting to the nub of a problem. Lady Celia, with her copper hair and her creamy skin and her forthright opinions, was in danger of becoming an obsession. If she did not think herself dishonoured, why should he worry about it? Why not indulge her in her Arabian fantasy and at the same time rid himself of his unwelcome obsession?

The problem was he didn't like being thought of as *unreal*. He didn't like the idea of her thinking of him only within the confines of his harem. If he was to be her first lover, he wanted her memory of him to be very real and lasting.

Ramiz looked up at the sky, where the sun was just coming into view on its slow arc over the northern wall of the garden. A slow smile crept over his face. He would bring her into the light of day, away from the shady confines of the harem. Seeing her more clearly would surely speed the cure along.

'You wanted to see me?'

Celia stood before Ramiz, his desk serving as a barrier between them. She wore a caftan of cerulean blue, with slashed sleeves pulled tight at the wrist, over a pair of pleated *sarwal* pantaloons the colour of the night sky. It was the traditional costume of a woman at home, but with her mass of copper hair uncovered and dressed in its usual fashion, piled in a knot on top of her head with wispy strands curling over her cheeks, the simple outfit seemed exotic. A lady dressed in the garb of an odalisque. Though she was draped with propriety from head to foot, the fluttery fabrics drew attention to the softness of her body underneath. He caught a glimpse of her forearm through the slashed sleeves of her tunic. Creamy skin. Ramiz dragged his eyes away. It was only her arm! But already he could feel himself hardening.

'Sit down,' he said, annoyed to find that his voice sounded harsh, while Celia looked composed as she took the chair opposite. 'You are well?' he asked.

'Certainly I am well cared for,' she said carefully.

'What does that mean?'

She raised an eyebrow at the tone of his voice. 'Is there something wrong, Ramiz?'

'That is what I have just asked you.'

Celia clasped her hands in her lap. 'I told you, I am well. In fact I'm so well looked after that I'm in danger of forgetting how to do anything for myself. Adila and Fatima anticipate my every need.'

'You mean to tell me you are bored?'

'I was trying to be tactful about it, but yes. I am not used to having nothing to do save embroider and read.'

'But you have been visiting Yasmina?'

'Yes, where I embroider and play with the children—which is lovely, but...' Celia bit her lip. The last few days, without so much as a glimpse of Ramiz, had given her ample opportunity to try and put her feelings for him into perspective, but it was almost impossible to do that within the confines of the harem, redolent as it was with sensuous overtones, not to mention the scalding memory of their previous fevered couplings. There, she was in thrall to him, obsessed by the feelings he could arouse in her. If only she could see him in more mundane surroundings—or what passed for mundane surroundings, given he was a prince. Then she would be rid of this continuous need to be with him, able to acknowledge that she was lonely, and she was bored, and that her body, having discovered something new and enjoyable, was quite naturally wanting to experience it again. That was all it was. Absolutely nothing else!

'I've been thinking,' Ramiz said, interrupting her musing. 'It would be a good idea for you to see more of A'Qadiz, to learn more of the problems we face—I face—in trying to bring our country into the modern world of the nineteenth century.'

Celia stared at him in astonishment. *Was he a mind-reader?* 'But what about—? You said because I am a woman that...'

Ramiz shrugged. 'If I choose to bend a few traditions, that is up to me. You said so yourself, did you not?'

He smiled. Perfect white teeth. Eyes cold glinting metal. Had he guessed what Lord Wincester had asked her to do? Her stomach clenched at the very idea. But if he knew he would surely not be offering her such an opportunity to observe. Was he testing her? She knew with sudden blinding clarity that it was a test she would not fail. She could not possibly betray this man who had saved her life, made her feel alive for the first time in her life and who clearly trusted her. 'I would love to see more of A'Qadiz,' Celia said excitedly. 'What did you have in mind?'

'A significant number of my people belong to Bedouin tribes. They live in the desert, moving from place to place with their livestock according to the season and their own inclinations. We have a tradition here of allowing them to petition the crown for alms. Three times a year they can come to me and ask for assistance.'

'You give them money?'

'Sometimes. Although more often it is food or animals. Money doesn't mean much to the Bedouins. It's not just that, however. I act as arbitrator in their disputes between families and between tribes. It is an opportunity for me, too, to see how things really are and to assess where I can best help them. You must not be thinking these are simply poor nomads. Some of them are very powerful men. It would not do to offend them.'

'So you go to them rather than ask them to come to you?'

'Exactly. We will be away about a week or so. You will come?'

'I would love to.'

'Good. You may go now. I will see you first thing tomorrow morning. We will start before dawn.'

The caravan which snaked out behind them put the one with which Celia had arrived in Balyrma firmly into the shade. She counted at least twenty guards on camels, and it looked like double that number of servants with mules. Akil took on the role as leader of the train. To Celia's surprise Ramiz insisted she ride ahead with him, mounted on a camel as snowy white as his own, its saddle draped with a bejewelled cloth of crimson damask, silver bells jangling on its reins, which were adorned with golden tassels. Covered by an *abeyah* of gold silk—a long robe with side slits to make riding astride easier—and with her hair and face protected from the sun and prying eyes by a headdress of the same colour, Celia felt like an Arabian princess.

She said so to Ramiz, who laughed and said no one looking at her could ever mistake her for what she was:

an English rose disguised as a desert flower. He was in a strange mood. She would almost call it relaxed. They would dispense with the formalities and deference while they were in the desert, he told her. She was to remain by his side at all times. She was to address him as Ramiz. She was free to ask whatever she wished to know. He valued her opinion.

At first she thought he was teasing her, but as they rode through the day she discovered he meant it—telling her unprompted all about the meetings to come, the ritual and the forms, even sketching out the main personalities for her. He was altogether charming, showing a side of himself she had not seen before. As the miles of the desert stretched out behind them he became almost carefree. The tension in his shoulders eased. The lines around his eyes relaxed. The formidable air departed, leaving a stunningly attractive man who was frankly beguiling.

And Celia *was* completely beguiled. Perhaps even mesmerised, for she noticed no one but Ramiz. The caravan might as well not have existed. As far as she was concerned they were alone in the desert, riding forever onwards across the sands under the blazing sun, to a destination which would remain elusive, for to arrive would be to break the spell, and she didn't want that to happen.

But when they arrived at the oasis where they would rest for the night the magical atmosphere continued. Instructing Akil to see to things, Ramiz led Celia away from the braying mules and bleating camels and muttering guards to a secluded part of the oasis, where a small pool lapped around a group of palms. The stars above them were like saucers of beaten silver.

'It's a full moon,' Celia said, sitting down by the edge of the pool and removing her sandals to trail her bare feet in the water.

'*Qamar,*' Ramiz told her, sitting beside her. 'A time for wishes to be granted.'

His thigh was pressing against hers. Her shoulder brushed the top of his arm. Celia circled her ankles in the cool of the water. 'What would you wish for, Ramiz?'

'A starry night. A tent to cover me. A beautiful woman to share it with.'

She tried to laugh, but it sounded more like a choke. 'Well, you've got the first two, at least.'

'No, I have it all.' Ramiz cupped the back of her head, gently turning her towards him. 'See—above us the starry sky. Over there the tent. Beside me a beautiful woman. And I intend you to share it with me, Celia. All of it.'

Before she could ask him what he meant, he kissed her. His kiss made his intentions clear, and as she kissed him back she signified her agreement with no thought of refusal. It was why she was here. In his desert. In his arms. It was why he had brought her, and it was why she had come. It was what she wanted more than anything. She saw that now with a brilliance and clarity to match the very moon suspended above their entwined bodies.

Celia put her arms around Ramiz. She nestled into the familiar stirring scent of him. She parted her lips at his bidding, and kissed him in such a way as he could be under no misapprehensions. She would share the night with him. All of it.

They kissed for long, languorous seconds, their arms entwined, their tongues tangling, their toes touching in the cool of the water. Then Ramiz broke away and got to his feet, pulling her with him. 'You understand?' he said. 'There is no going back from this moment.'

Celia nodded.

'It is what you want?'

'Yes.'

'Though ultimately it can mean nothing?'

She knew that! Why did he have to say it? But she knew that too. Ramiz was a man who liked the rules of any pact clear cut and neatly drawn. 'Yes,' she said again. 'I understand, I assure you.'

He nodded. For one ridiculous moment she thought he would shake her hand, so formal had he become in that moment, but then she realised he was almost as tense as she was. She followed him back to the camp, where a small village of tents had appeared and fires were burning. The smell of goat and rabbit roasting should have been appetising, but though she was hungry it was not for food.

Two larger tents sat at a distance from the others. Ramiz led her towards one, pulling back the damask cloth which covered the entrance to usher her inside. Celia gave a gasp of amazement. Like the tent in which they'd had lunch the day Ramiz took her to the lost city of Katra, the walls were covered in tapestries and the floor in rich carpets. But this tent was much bigger, the coverings in the soft lamplight richer and more colourful.

'Do you like it?' Ramiz asked, smiling at the look of wonderment on her face.

'It's amazing. Like a mobile palace.'

'I must go and speak to Akil. Make yourself at home. I won't be long.'

Alone, Celia wandered around the tent, running her fingers over the tapestries, curling her toes into the luxurious carpets, stroking silken cushions and rubbing her cheek against velvet throws. A second room was obviously intended as a sleeping area. Here her luggage sat and her dressing case had been placed on a low table, beside which stood a full-length mirror. A smaller room led off from this one, where she was astonished to find a copper bath, already filled with water and scented with petals. Without further ado she stripped her dusty clothes off and sank into the water.

Clean, scented, and dressed in a loose caftan of organdie the colour of the setting sun, Celia returned to the main room. In her absence someone had set out dinner—an array of covered dishes from which delicious smells wafted towards her. She was investigating their contents when Ramiz entered the tent.

Like her, he had bathed and changed. His cropped black hair sat sleek on his head. He wore a robe of his favourite dark blue velvet. Though the tent was large, it seemed suddenly very small. His very presence seemed to fill it. It felt incredibly intimate, much more so than the harem. Against the soft drapes and jewelled colours of the hangings Ramiz looked very male. Very intimidating. Celia was assaulted by a jangle of nerves, taking up residence in her stomach like a cloud of little birds.

'Dinner's arrived,' she said. 'Are you hungry?'

'No,' Ramiz replied baldly.

'Would you like something to drink, then?' She reached for a jug of sherbet.

'No.'

'How is Akil?' Celia asked, realising even as she spoke just how ridiculous was the question.

'Celia, come here.'

She put down the jug, but made no move towards him.

'If you're having second thoughts, now would be a good time to tell me.'

'I'm not.' She adjusted the sleeve of her caftan. 'I'm just a bit—well, as you know, I've never done this before.'

She tried to smile, but her mouth trembled. Her eyes were mossy green, fixed on him with a combination of appeal and defiance that he found irresistible. Ramiz strode over to her and swept her into his arms. 'There's no need to be nervous. I'll show you.'

He nuzzled the tender skin in the crease behind her earlobe. The scent there was pure Celia. He tasted her with the tip of his tongue. Such a vulnerable spot—the softness of her lobe, the delicate bone of her ear behind it, the endearing little crease they formed together which he licked into. Something clutched at him, piercing its way into his heart like the lethal tip of a dagger. He would remember this always.

'Ramiz?'

'Come.' He took her by the hand and led her through to the sleeping chamber. He dispensed efficiently with Celia's robe, tugging it over her head before she could protest. She stood before him naked, blushing, fighting the urge to cover herself with her hands.

Her eyes betrayed her confusion at his lack of tenderness. His instincts were to be tender. It was what she needed. What she wanted too. But it was not what this was about. It was about finishing what they had started. It was about taking what he needed from her in order to cure himself of her too-tempting presence.

'Lie down.'

She did so without a word. He glanced down at her and caught his breath. She looked like the moon goddess, all creamy flesh and blushing curves, with the dark shadow of curls between her legs, the rosy tips of her nipples, the lush pink of her mouth, the deep copper of her hair spread out behind and over her. 'Beautiful.' The word was drawn from him, harsh and grating. He was hard. More than ready.

Ramiz hauled his robe over his head and stood before her, hugely aroused. Celia stared up at him. Wanting hurtled through her, fierce and hot, made urgent by the undertone of fear she was trying desperately not to acknowledge. He looked so remote. Like a conqueror standing over the vanquished—which was exactly how she felt. Except that the blade which would claim her as his was no scimitar. Her eyes were riveted on the curving length of his erection. It seemed impossible that she could contain such a size.

'Ramiz,' she said, sitting up. She wanted him to kiss her. 'Ramiz…' She held out her hand to him.

He stared at her for a long moment, an expression like pain slanting across his face. Then he was beside her. On top of her. Kissing her. Pressing her down under him, his mouth hard, his hands rough, his manhood insistent between her thighs. She was overwhelmed by the intensity of his passion, but excited by it too, and as he kissed her and touched her she became infected by a carnal need of her own, feverishly stroking and nipping and licking, until she was aware of nothing but skin on skin, heat on heat, the scent of him, the sound of his breathing, harsh, rapid, shallow, the thrumming of her blood raging like a torrent through her veins, the clenching pulse of her muscles hurtling her forward,

upwards, mercilessly on to some destination of which
she was only vaguely aware.

Ramiz grazed her nipples with his teeth. She dug her
nails into his back. He moulded her breasts in his hands.
She stroked the taut sloping muscles of his buttocks.
His fingers found her entrance and slipped carefully
inside. She moaned. He slid over the swollen centre of
her, around and over, around and over, so that she could
scarcely bear the tightening, clenching, sharpness of her
response, resisting it, holding tight to it like a swimmer
to a rock. But his fingers stroked and circled remorse-
lessly, and she let go with a cry, arching under his touch,
barely aware of him readying her, tugging her to him,
until she felt the nudging of his shaft.

She closed her eyes and waited for the thrust and the
pain, determined not to cry out, but he entered her so
slowly, so carefully, she felt only a sort of unfolding as
the aftermath of her climax drew him in. She opened
her eyes. Ramiz was watching her, the strain of the
care he was taking etched on his face. He pushed further
into her and she moaned. He stopped. She reached for
him, pulled his face towards her and kissed him deeply,
tilting her hips encouragingly, moaning again, with
pleasure this time, as he sheathed himself in her slowly,
slowly, until she thought he could go no further, pausing, pushing again, waiting until she could not bear the
waiting. He withdrew from her slowly, and thrust back
into her again, slowly and deliberately, watching her,
and she knew that she was going to lose herself again.
This time she clung to him, felt the frisson of her
muscles on his shaft from base to tip, then tip to base
as he pushed back into her. She tilted instinctively,
wrapping her legs around his waist, and he pushed

higher, harder, making her moan and clutch at his back as the ripple of her climax started to build again, or started to finish, and still he continued to thrust, each plunge more deliberate, higher, until she could feel the tip of him touching some tender spot high inside her and she lost control instantly, crying out. Her surrender acted like a trigger. Ramiz lost control almost as she had, thrusting fast and hard with abandon, until she actually felt him swell before he pulled abruptly from her, spilling hot over her belly before collapsing on top of her, wrapping his arms so tightly round her, kissing her so hard that there was no space at all between them as their skin and mouths clung to each other, because to let go would be to die.

She lay exhausted, saturated with a bone-deep heaviness that pinned her to the bed, feeling weightless, as if she was gliding. As Ramiz's breathing steadied he unwrapped himself from her. As he rolled away from her, Celia felt as if her wings had been clipped, so suddenly did she plunge back down to earth.

'Did I hurt you?'

'No.' She wanted him to hold her again, wanted reassurance, words of endearment, but she knew she could have none of those things, so she lay still, holding herself instead.

'Are you hungry now?'

She was, surprisingly, but it seemed rude to say so.

'I'm starving,' Ramiz said with a grin. 'Come on.'

Before she could move, he scooped her up in his arms, striding with her held high against his chest to the other room. 'We can't eat like this,' Celia said, for they were both still naked.

Ramiz grinned again. 'Trust me—we can.' He kicked a heap of cushions together on the floor, and picked up the huge silver tray upon which the dishes were held, placing it on the carpet in front of the cushions before sitting down. 'Come here.' He patted a cushion invitingly. When Celia didn't move, hugging her arms around her breasts, he caught her hand and pulled her down beside him, so that she sprawled, half lying, half sitting, on a huge tasselled velvet cushion.

Ramiz lifted the cover from a dish and took out a *pastilla*, breaking it open so that some of the pastry flaked onto Celia's arm. He leaned over her to lick it off. Then he offered her a bite of pastry, licking the crumbs from her lips when she bit, before popping the rest into his own mouth.

A pomegranate salad was flavoured with lime juice and finely chopped onion. He fed her from a silver spoon. The lime gave their kisses a tangy taste which sparkled on their tongues.

Roasted aubergines and sweet peppers drizzled with olive oil were next. The oil dripped over her fingers and Ramiz sucked at them, drawing each one into his mouth and licking it clean before moving to the next.

The juice of a pineapple which had been roasted with sugar and ginger he deliberately allowed to trickle down the valley between her breasts. By this time they had given up all pretence of eating. It was a game of call and response. Where Ramiz led Celia followed, so that what had started as his teasing was in danger of turning into his own undoing.

He feasted on her breasts, tasting pineapple juice and salt and sugar, and underneath the delicious tang of what he had already come to think of as essence of

Celia. She lay beneath him, aroused, flushed, her hair tangled, her eyes alight with the passion he knew she could see reflected in his. He had never known this feeling before. He couldn't put a name to it. It was as if she was drawing something out of him, mixing it with something of her own, so that she mingled in his blood, so that he felt mingled in hers. As if he knew her. Was inside her. As if she was inside him somehow.

He fastened his mouth around her nipple and sucked, then tugged, then sucked again, delighting in the way she cleaved to him, the way he could make her arch or jolt or writhe, depending on how soft or hard he licked or sucked or nipped. He sucked again, and cupped his palm over the mound of her curls between her legs. Damp. Hot. He pressed the heel of his hand against her in a little circling motion, felt the responding clenching at the base of his shaft. He wanted her again. Now. Urgently.

He nudged her legs to part them, but Celia resisted. Before he could stop her she had pushed him over onto his back. Before he could resist her she'd dipped her hand into a dish of something and trailed it neatly in a line from the middle of his ribcage. Down. It was cold. Creamy. Yoghurt of some sort, he thought vaguely. Then he stopped thinking as Celia began to lick it, daintily flicking her tongue along the path across his abdomen, dipping into his navel, down to where the path ended, at the point where his hair began to thicken. Ramiz closed his eyes and held his breath. There was a pause, during which he thought he would cry out with frustration, and then her tongue flicked over the tip of his shaft. Stopped. Another flick—a little longer. Another. Down. Down. Down the length of him and then back up, in one fluid movement that made him jolt with pleasure. Blood surged. He felt the tightening in his groin that presaged his climax. Dear heavens, he thought he would die with the pleasure of it. If only she would—now—like—just exactly like that! And like that. And—oh—like that!

'Celia.' She stopped. He didn't want her to stop. Ramiz reached down to grip her by the shoulders. The look of surprise on her face would have been funny if he had been in the mood to be amused. He wasn't. He pulled her down over him. Her knees brushed his shoulders. Her breasts were crushed into his stomach. Her mouth was back where he wanted it. And his was exactly where he wanted it to be too. He put his palms on the delightful swell of her bottom, he put his mouth over the delightful mound of wet curls and tender folds between her legs, and moaned as he tasted her and breathed her and sought out the nub of her. He moaned again as she followed him, reflecting and echoing every lick and stroke, resisting, but only just, the urgent clamouring of his climax until he felt hers, and then he let himself go as she came, and he had never, ever felt anything quite so heady as that feeling of her sweetness in his mouth as he surged and pulsed into hers.

It felt right. Which was absolutely wrong. But for now Ramiz cared for nothing, nothing—at all.

CHAPTER ELEVEN

RAMIZ did not sleep in her tent but returned to his own. For a long time Celia gazed at her reflection by the light of the lamps. She barely recognised the woman staring back at her from the mirror. Her hair was a tangled mess. Her eyes were huge—a darker green than she had ever seen them. Her bottom lip seemed swollen. Her skin was flushed all over, with the faint marks of Ramiz's fingers on her breasts, a slight bruise on her bottom. Between her thighs she was tender. Under one of her nails was a trace of blood where she had dug her fingers too deep into his back. Something else she couldn't put a name to shone from her face too. A different kind of glow she hadn't experienced before. Sensual, that was what it was, she finally decided. Wanton, even. For the first time since she had arrived in the East she saw the point of the veil. She would certainly not like anyone else to see her like this. They'd know straight away.

Sliding between the silk sheets of the divan, she wondered if Ramiz looked the same. Somehow she doubted it. None of this was new to him. They had done nothing he had not done before, and no doubt he would do it again. The idea of him with another woman made her feel sick.

She must be careful. Though she had pleased him, though he had seemed most reluctant to leave, she must remember it meant nothing to him. And he was just a passing fascination for her. She would do well to remember that, too. It meant nothing. No matter how right it felt, or how amazingly he had made her feel. Ramiz was an oasis of sensuality in the desert of her life.

Celia chuckled at that, for it was the sort of thing Cassie would have said. She wondered if he was sleeping. She wondered if he was thinking about her. Celia drifted into a deep sleep, most certainly thinking about him.

When she awoke, the sun was rising and the caravan was already being prepared to depart. She ate a hurried breakfast alone in her tent, conscious that the men were waiting to take it down. Ramiz was waiting with her camel, anxious to make a start, leaving Akil to lead the caravan which would again follow in their wake.

She expected Ramiz to ignore her. She expected him to be brusque, to have returned to his princely remoteness now he had what he wanted from her, but he surprised her, helping her onto the camel with a smile so warm it might as well have been a kiss. They set out as yesterday, in companionable closeness. If this were not Ramiz she would feel she was being courted. But it *was* Ramiz, and he could never court her.

They made camp that night in the same manner as before, but this time they were not alone. 'Sheikh Farid and his tribe,' Ramiz told Celia, nodding over at the cluster of tents about five hundred yards distant. 'We must pay our respects tonight. Dress up. It is expected.'

'You want me to come with you?'

'If you don't he will be insulted. You think they haven't heard of the mysterious English lady travelling with me?'

She hadn't given it much thought, though she realised now that she should have. 'What will they think of me?'

'I have asked Akil to put out the word that you are here as an emissary of the British Government.'

'A woman! They'll hardly believe that.'

Ramiz shrugged. 'Just another Western quirk—treating a woman as a man. It is why we have separate tents. You would not want them to think you my concubine.'

'No, of course not. I—thank you, Ramiz.'

'It is my own honour as much as yours I must protect. Besides,' he added, acknowledging Akil's summons, 'Sheikh Farid's daughter is one of the princesses on my council's list of brides.'

She had been touched by his care for her reputation. Now she saw it was care for his own, and was angry—not at Ramiz, but at herself for reading something into nothing. Celia made her way to her tent, mortified and fighting a wholly unaccustomed feeling which she realised, as she stepped into her waiting bath, was jealousy. 'Of a woman I have never met,' she muttered in disgust, 'and whom he may not marry in any event.'

The bath calmed her, and the oil she rubbed into her arms and legs afterwards soothed her. She must find out the receipt for it from Fatima. Cassie would like to try it, and she knew they would not be able to buy such a thing at home.

Home! The word startled her. Soon she would be going back to England. Far away from the heat and the smells of this beautiful land, from the contrasts of barren deserts and green oases, from A'Qadiz and its exotic foods and vibrant colours. And far away from Ramiz. She wasn't ready to go, not yet, but, counting up the days, she knew it could not be long before her father arrived in Cairo. 'Home.' She said it out loud, experimentally, but it still didn't work.

She couldn't bear the thought of leaving Ramiz. She couldn't imagine her life without him. 'Because I might as well admit it,' she said to her reflection. 'I'm not just beguiled. I'm not just in thrall to him. I'm in love with him.'

Her reflection smiled. A soft, tender smile, which crept warily across her lips. 'I'm in love with Ramiz.' Her smile spread. Her skin tingled. 'I'm in love with Ramiz. Oh, God, I'm in love with Ramiz.' Celia tottered backwards onto the divan. 'I'm in love with Ramiz, and I'm just about to meet the woman he may well marry.' A hysterical little bubble of laughter escaped her, followed by a large solitary tear which trickled like acid down her cheek.

She was in love! Who'd have thought it? Certainly she'd never considered herself capable of such a thing. Not this kind of love, at any rate. She'd always thought of love as something comfortable, something that grew slowly over time, something stolid, dependable, rather than essential. But this, this thing she called love, was nothing at all like that. It glowed inside her like a living thing, pulsing and throbbing with life, the source of her being rather than a pleasant appendage. The reason for her being. Ramiz completed her. He was the heart which beat in her, the sun around which she revolved.

Celia laughed. Such fancies were the stuff on which Cassie thrived, and she had always mocked them, but now she found they were true. It was all true. She had been waiting to be woken. The way he made her feel, the way only *he* could make her feel, was nothing to do with the harem and everything to do with Ramiz. Her body was in thrall because she was in love. Her body responded to him at some elemental level because it had recognised, long before her mind did, what he meant to her. She loved him.

And Yasmina was right too. She would always love him. She was not the type to love twice. There would never be anyone else. She loved Ramiz. He was the beginning of her story and the end.

Except there could never be a happy ever after.

Fortunately Celia had never allowed herself to hope for one. There would be an end to this, and she would have to cope with it. Cope with it and never allow Ramiz to know. For if he thought she cared he would feel responsible, and that responsibility would touch his honour and—no, she could not allow that.

Celia dressed with care in a pair of lemon pleated pantaloons bound at the ankles with silver and pearl beading. The same design was embroidered onto the long loose sleeves of her caftan, which was velvet, in her favourite jade green, and on the matching velvet slippers too. Around her neck and wrists she roped her mother's pearls, and there were pearls in her hair too, which she wore up, but with a loose knot over one shoulder.

Passable, she thought, looking at herself again in the mirror. The caftan, which was slashed to the thigh, drew attention to her height, and the length of her legs. The pearls lent their lustre to her skin. Her hair was glossy from the care lavished on it by Adila and Fatima.

She looked exotic, she realised. Although the outfit covered more of her than a ballgown, the diaphanous material of the pantaloons, visible through the caftan's vents, made her legs clearly visible. The soft folds of the caftan itself hinted at her uncorseted shape beneath. Celia laughed, wondering what Aunt Sophia would think of her going to pay a visit without her stays!

Ramiz might not love her, but he desired her, and in this outfit even Celia could see that she had a certain allure. Which was consolation enough, she told herself firmly as she left the tent.

Ramiz was conferring with Akil. Dressed in his formal robes, white silk edged with gold, the state scimitar glinting at his waist, he looked every inch the regal prince. He was preoccupied, giving her a cursory glance only as he rapped out instructions to the guards, inspected the gifts which were to be given to Sheikh Farid, and listened impatiently as Akil read through his seemingly endless notes.

The procession they formed to walk the short distance to the Bedouin tents was impressive. Ramiz took the lead, preceded by his Head of Guards, a great hulk of a man whose robes, Celia thought, were large enough to form a tent of their own. She herself followed Ramiz, with Akil behind her, flanked by the remainder of the guards carrying blazing torches to light the way.

Sheikh Farid was a small man of about the same age as Celia's father. He was simply dressed, in a black robe and red-checked headdress, but his womenfolk more than made up for his lack of ostentation. Celia counted six wives, bedecked in so many gold anklets, bracelets, necklaces and earrings that they jangled when they moved. Bedouin women covered their skin with complex ink and henna tattoos—swirling designs encompassing leaves and flowers, mixed in with ancient symbols. Their nails were stained red with henna, and their eyelids stained black at the corners, much in the way the eyes of the pharaohs were painted. They did not wear the veil, and stared with blatant curiosity at Celia, though when she smiled in their direction they giggled and lowered their eyes.

She kept discreetly in the background, under Akil's watchful eye. Though he had said nothing, she was aware that Akil did not approve of her presence here. No doubt he fretted over the propriety of it, and she could not blame him—especially since his suspicions had all too recently been proved correct. He would think her a loose woman. No doubt he would be glad when she was gone, for he could not approve of her relationship with Yasmina. It saddened Celia, and she determined to do all she could to ensure she intruded on official business no more than necessary.

As it turned out, she enjoyed her role as onlooker immensely, for it gave her the opportunity to observe Ramiz the Prince. It was a role he performed with the assurance and dignity she had come to expect of him, but as the ritual of the alms-giving got underway what impressed her most was his complete lack of arrogance. Throughout the long process of receiving each person who wished to make a plea, Ramiz showed only patience and concern. He had that rare ability to talk without talking down, taking time to calm the most nervous of the supplicants or the most aggressive of the litigants, treating the ancients with touching deference, joking with the younger men as a contemporary.

Despite the long line of supplicants, there was no sense of hurry. Every case was given due consideration, every decision proclaimed formally to the audience before the next commenced. Not everyone received the outcome they'd hoped for, but all seemed to be treated fairly, and Celia realised that this, and not the sums of money given out in alms, was the point. Prince Ramiz was seen to be fair and just, as well as accessible.

She was impressed and touched—not just by Ramiz's humanity, but by his vision, for he was obviously intent on demonstrating to his people the principles by which he ruled. The principles to which too many other rulers, in Celia's experience, paid merely lip-service. He truly was a remarkable man. She loved him so much.

Humbled, and slightly overcome by the strength of emotion which enveloped her, Celia crept unnoticed from the ceremony. Away from the blaze of the torches which lit Sheikh Farid's tent, the full moon cast a ghostly light across the Bedouin encampment. She wandered a little distance from the tents, absorbed in her thoughts, enjoying the cool of the evening and the scents of the desert which came to life after dark. The vast stretches of sand which surrounded her began to have their usual effect, imbuing her with a strange combination—a sense of her own insignificance and at the same time a feeling of endless possibilities. Desert euphoria, she called it, for it was both exhilarating and chastening, like flying in Signor Lunardi's balloon, which Papa had been fortunate enough to witness on its inaugural flight from Moorfields.

A shuffling sound alerted her to the presence of another person. A glint of steel showed the shadowy figure to be one of Ramiz's guards, no doubt instructed to keep an eye on her. Strange to think that when first they'd met she would have been insulted by this apparent lack of trust. She knew better now, and recognised it for a combination of deeply embedded chivalry and an equally strong duty of care which was an essential part of him. She had come to like it.

Nodding to the guard as she passed, Celia made her way back to the Bedouin camp. The line of people was coming to an end. Fires had sprouted up outside many of the tents, and the smell of cooking filled the air. Women were gathering around the glowing embers, chatting and laughing. A group of semi-naked children were playing a ball game. As Celia stopped to watch, the ball landed at her feet, and before she knew it she was embroiled in the game, whose complex rules were explained with many gestures and much hilarity.

Her regular visits to Yasmina's extended family had given her a smattering of the language, and when the ball game petered out Celia recognised the word for story as the children gathered around her and tugged pleadingly at her caftan. Sitting cross-legged on the sand, surrounded by a circle of expectant faces, she prayed that her enthusiasm and the children's participation would make up for her lack of vocabulary, and launched into one of Samir's favourite stories, which happened to be one of her youngest sister Cressida's too. *Ali Baba and the Forty Thieves.*

'*As-salamu alaykum,*' Ramiz said to the last of the supplicants, a man seeking arbitration over the return of his divorced daughter's dowry. 'Peace be with you.'

'*Wa-alaykum as-salam*, Highness,' the man replied, bowing backwards out of the tent.

Ramiz rubbed his temples and looked around. 'Where is Lady Celia?' he asked Akil sharply.

'She left some time ago.'

Ramiz glared at him. 'I told you to keep watch over her.'

'I did, Highness. A guard is with her.'

Ramiz made to leave.

'Majesty?'

Ramiz eyed the restraining hand on his arm with a cold hauteur which made Akil step hurriedly back. 'Well?'

'I have arranged with Sheikh Farid to have his daughter formally presented to you tomorrow. I apologise if I speak out of turn, but you would do well to leave the Lady Celia to her own devices,' Akil said, blanching at his friend's glacial expression but remaining firm. 'No-one believes this story you have had me put about,' he hissed, ushering Ramiz to one side, away from listening ears and prying glances. 'Anyone with eyes can see what you are to her. She turns to you as a flower does to the sun. And you, Highness, if you are not careful you will fall under the spell she casts. Her father is an influential man. Do you think he will take kindly to having his daughter used as a concubine?'

'How dare you speak to me on such a subject? Just because you are my friend, Akil, do not think I will tolerate interference in my personal life.'

'Ramiz, you are a prince. Unfortunately you do not have a personal life. It is because I am your closest friend that I dare to speak. You think I don't know how tirelessly you have worked in the last two years? You think I don't know how much you have done for A'Qadiz? How much more there is still for you to do? It would be foolish to offer insult to the English over such a trivial matter as a woman, and equally foolish to insult Sheikh Farid, whom you know holds sway over almost all of our Bedouins. Trust me on this matter. Leave that woman alone, or if you must go to her bed at least have the discretion to do so away from the eyes of those who hold power.'

There was a long silence. Furious as he was to be spoken to in such a way, Ramiz was even more furious at himself. He rubbed his eyes. 'If I have been indiscreet it shall be remedied, but you are making a camel out of a flea. Lady Celia is under no illusions about our—our relationship. She is perfectly well aware of its temporary nature and will make no trouble.'

'Ramiz, I tell you she is in love with you.'

Ramiz shook his head. 'You are quite wrong. Like all foreigners she is obsessed with the sensual elements of our culture, and who can change her, coming as she does from a people who make a virtue of indifference, who equate virtue with frigidity and passion with vice? Lady Celia is indulging her passions safe from the prying eyes of her compatriots. She is simply taking advantage of the situation.'

'Is that what you're doing?'

Ramiz clenched his fists. 'You overstep the mark, Akil. What I am doing is enjoying the company of one who wants nothing from me except myself. A rare enough thing since I came to power, you will agree.'

'Ramiz, if it is just a woman you need, you could—'

'Enough! That is quite enough!' Ignoring the sudden hush around them, ignoring the guards who had rushed towards him at the sound of his raised voice, even ignoring Sheikh Farid, who was making his way towards the commotion, Ramiz gripped Akil by the

shoulders. 'She is not *just a woman*! If I *ever* hear you speak so discourteously of Lady Celia in my presence again, I will have you banished—do you understand?' he said through gritted teeth.

Akil nodded.

'And if I ever hear from Lady Celia that you have treated her in any way disrespectfully, or if I hear from her that you have allowed your wife to see your own prejudices, I will have you banished. Yasmina is Celia's only friend here. It would be a great shame if she were to lose her. Do I make myself understood, Akil?'

White as his master's headdress, Akil nodded again.

Ramiz released him. 'Then let us put this behind us. We go too far back to allow it to come between us.'

Akil straightened the *igal* which held his own head-dress in place. 'I hope that is true,' he murmured, but he did so very quietly.

Ramiz's anger had shocked him to the core. For once Akil was certain he knew better than his friend. The sooner Lady Celia was on her way back to Egypt the better, so Ramiz could get on with the serious business of taking a suitable wife.

In search of a little quiet before the feasting began, for it would last much of the night, Ramiz encountered Celia in the centre of a circle of ragged children with rapt expressions on their faces. Taking care to remain out of sight, he watched, fascinated, as she recounted a tale, amused by the clever way she encouraged the children to join in with words and gestures when her own surprisingly large stock of vocabulary failed her. He hadn't known she could say anything other than good morning and thank you, but she'd picked up a lot more than that in the time she'd been here. From the maids, he presumed. And Yasmina, of course.

Akil's words had angered him, but he knew his friend well enough to understand how strong his feelings must be for him to have spoken in such a way. He was wrong about Celia, though; it was a ridiculous notion to think her in love. Almost as ridiculous as the idea that he, Prince Ramiz al-Muhana of A'Qadiz, could feel such a thing. Princes did not fall in love except in fairytales. English roses did not fall in love with Arabic princes except in fairytales—which was almost certainly how Celia saw it, and exactly what he'd just said to Akil.

He looked at her now, absent-mindedly stroking the hair of the little girl who sat by her side while balancing another on her knee. He'd noticed it the day she'd arrived at the port, and again the day they went to the market in Balyrma—how children were drawn to her, how naturally she talked to them, stooping down to their height, never using that patronising tone with them which so many childless women used. Affinity—that was the word. It must come from looking after her sisters.

Akil worried too much. He was so focused on his great plan to tie up their hard-won peace with a good marriage that he couldn't see clearly. No matter how comfortable Celia might look here, A'Qadiz was not her home. No matter how incredible last night had been, it was just a temporary passion. Like all passions, it would take flight sooner rather than later. Sooner, if he continued to indulge it. She would be gone soon enough. He would do his duty to A'Qadiz, as he had always done his duty. After thirty-five years of doing so he deserved these few days.

The privilege of sitting in Celia's lap was now being disputed by a little boy. Without pausing in her narrative Celia managed to accommodate both children, but it left her no hands free. 'Open sesame!' she declared, but without being able to throw her arms wide the English version of the words fell flat. The children looked puzzled.

'Iftah ya simsim,' Ramiz said, unable to resist joining her, much to the children's awed delight. 'Open sesame,' he said carefully, lifting up a small boy to clear a space by her side.

'Open sesame,' the children repeated gleefully.

'Thank you,' Celia whispered. She smiled at him—a smile he hadn't seen before. Tender. It must be the children. She was thinking of her sisters. Akil was wrong.

Akil was definitely wrong, Ramiz thought again later, much later, as they made their weary procession back to the tents after a long drawn-out dinner. He nodded goodnight to his friend. Akil bowed stiffly and retreated to his own tent without a backwards glance, still piqued by the dressing-down Ramiz had administered.

Celia would be asleep by now. She had eaten separately, with the women, and been escorted back at least an hour ago. Ramiz had intended going straight to his own divan, but Akil's unspoken disapproval and the need to prove him wrong sent him to Celia's tent. If she was asleep he would not wake her.

But she was not asleep. When he pulled back the curtain the lamps were lit in the main room. She was reclining, still dressed in her velvet caftan, on a heap of cushions, reading a book which she put immediately to one side as soon as he appeared in the doorway, holding out her hand invitingly.

Ramiz hesitated. She didn't look any different to him. Beautiful. With more awareness, maybe, in the way she smiled at him—but that was because she was more aware of her body. Of how it could feel. Of what he could do to it. Of what she could do to him. His manhood stirred.

'Celia, you do not—you know this cannot last?'

She lowered her eyes. 'Of course not. Are you come to tell me our fairytale is over already, Ramiz?'

'Fairytale?' he repeated, taken aback by her repetition of the very word he himself had used.

'That is how I think of it. Don't you?'

He took her outstretched hand, allowing himself to be pulled down to join her on the cushions. 'A fairytale? Am I your prince?'

'Yes.'

'Then you must do my bidding,' Ramiz said, pulling the pearl pins from her hair and running his hands through it.

'Your wish is my command, master.'

'Excellent,' Ramiz said, pulling her caftan over her head. He ran his palms down her shoulders, across her breasts, skimming the indent of her waist to rest on the curve of her hips before tugging his own robe over his head. 'Though tonight I think it should be your wish which is my command. What would you like me to do with this?'

Sheikh Farid presented his daughter Juman the next morning. The visit was obviously expected. Watching from the shade of her tent, Celia saw Akil fussing over the positioning of the furnishings in the tent in which Ramiz slept. The whole front of the main room had been lifted up to reveal an interior bigger and much

richer than the one she enjoyed. Akil was supervising
the placing of a tea service, watching carefully as one
of the servants polished the gold samovar to his satisfaction, while Ramiz sat in a corner reading.

Sheikh Farid arrived on horseback—a magnificent
and extremely rare black thoroughbred which con-
trasted perfectly with the grey on which his daughter
was mounted. A third horse, another grey, pranced delicately on a leading rein behind them. Even from a
distance Celia could see that father and daughter rode
well—hardly surprising since she had learned last night
that the thoroughbreds, with their distinctively arched
necks and high, swishing tails, formed a significant
part of Sheikh Farid's livelihood.

The Sheikh's daughter was younger than she had
expected—nearer Caroline's age than Cassie's, perhaps
only sixteen or seventeen. Though Yasmina had told her
that girls married young here in A'Qadiz, Celia could
not help thinking that sixteen was far too young for
Ramiz. The girl would bore him to death. What on
earth were Akil and the council thinking about, suggesting such a baby for a man like Ramiz?

But, watching her spring lithely from the horse, she
began to see exactly why this girl had been recom-
mended, and when she was invited to join them for tea
in Ramiz's tent her understanding was completed.
Juman Farid was extraordinarily beautiful, with ebony
hair that shone with health, almond eyes which managed to be both mysterious and seductive, and vermilion lips which no matter how hard Celia stared at them
showed not a trace of artifice. She had a figure which
was a perfect hourglass too, and not only that she was
quite obviously as blue-blooded as the horse which had

carried her here. No doubt, Celia thought bitterly to herself, she had a pedigree just as long and impressive, for she was the firstborn of Sheikh Farid's first wife, and even Celia knew how important such precedence was.

Though she was dressed in the traditional *sarwal* trousers and tunic under the *abayah* which had cloaked her upon the horse, Juman's charms were nonetheless subtly on display, for the gauzy gold and crimson chiffon left little to the imagination.

So Celia thought—until she realised what she was thinking and castigated herself for it. She was jealous! It was hardly Juman's fault that she was so attractive and so eminently suitable a princess for Prince Ramiz. It was not as if she was behaving with anything other than perfect propriety either. Juman spoke only when spoken to, insisted that Celia pour the tea, and kept her eyes discreetly lowered. Only when Sheikh Farid suggested she show Ramiz the horse they had brought for him to try out did she leap up excitedly and clap her hands, her enthusiasm shining through in a way so entirely genuine that Celia was mortified.

It was Akil who suggested to Ramiz that he try out the horse's paces, and Akil who suggested to Sheikh Farid that he allow Juman to accompany Ramiz. Sheikh Farid agreed, but only on the proviso that he go along as chaperone. Celia was ashamed to find herself relieved by this, but it was still with a heavy heart that she waved them off.

She retired to her tent, occupying herself with the embroidery of a caftan which she intended to leave as a present for Ramiz when she left. As the sun rose to its apex she fell asleep, waking in the afternoon to discover that the trio had gone straight to the Bedouin camp, where a new tribe of supplicants had arrived.

'You may join them if you wish,' Akil told her, in a voice which suggested she should not. She took heed of it, eating a lonely supper and retiring early to her divan with her book.

But Ramiz arrived as he had the night before. And, as he had the night before, he made love to her with a fervency and a passion which took them both by surprise all over again.

So it continued the next day and the next, as each new tribe arrived, with Celia spending some time alone, some time at the camp with the children, but avoiding Ramiz in public. Ramiz's spare time was monopolised either by Akil or Juman, but his nights were reserved for Celia.

They made love. They talked. She read to him. He told her of the more interesting cases he had adjudicated that day. She shared with him her ideas for a school camp which could be set up like the alms camp, where Bedouin children could come for at least a smattering of education, even if they did not stay long.

'If you chose one of the bigger oases, where they are likely to stay longer, and made sure the teacher did not mind that one day her class might be five strong, another fifty, then I think it would work,' she said eagerly. 'They are such a huge part of A'Qadiz's population, yet they have virtually no schooling. Yasmina told me one of your sayings: not having the opportunity to test your talents does not mean you do not have them. It's not as if they don't want to learn; it's just that they don't get much opportunity. Their parents have no education either, and cannot teach them.'

With Ramiz's encouragement, she went on to outline

in more detail the practicalities of how her 'tent school', as she thought of it, would work.

'You've thought this all through very thoroughly. I'm impressed,' Ramiz said, looking at her with new respect.

'Will it work, do you think?'

'With the right teachers, I don't see why not. But where am to find people willing to take on such a challenge?'

'I would do it,' she said, without thinking.

'Live in a tent teaching Bedouin children? I don't think so. Your father would never permit it.'

'Probably not.'

'What will you do when you go back to England?'

'I don't know.' Celia looked away, biting her lip. 'I don't know. Perhaps I will teach at a charity school there. There is no shortage of children in England needing education, and I seem to have a gift for it.'

'You should have children of your own,' he said, then wished he had not, for the idea of Celia bearing anyone's child but his was unexpectedly painful.

'Ramiz, let us stop this conversation,' she said gently.

'You mean it is none of my business.'

'Ramiz, don't! I do not ask you whether you will marry Juman, but it does not mean I don't think about it. It does not mean I don't feel horribly guilty thinking about it, and what we do here in this tent every night. I don't feel guilty enough to stop, but that is because I know it will end anyway—and soon. I do not ask you because I don't want to know, and because, as you say, it is none of my business—as my life will be none of yours when I leave here.'

His expression darkened, his anger arriving without

warning and whipping him into a stormy rage. 'I won't
be marrying Juman. She is a child, and she bores me
rigid with her endless talk of horses, horses, horses and
nothing else. I cannot contemplate taking her or any
other woman into my bed when I have you waiting for
me. You obsess me! Do you not understand? I cannot
get enough of you—yet I must, for you must return to
your homeland.'

'Ramiz, it is the same for me.' She gripped his arms,
shaking him so that he looked at her. 'Can you not see
it is the same for me? I want you. All the time I want you.'

'Celia, I...'

'For heaven's sake, Your Highness, just shut up
and kiss me.'

And, for once in his life, Ramiz did exactly as he
was commanded.

CHAPTER TWELVE

LORD HENRY ARMSTRONG, who had hitherto considered himself in robust health, had been much worn down by the journey across the Mediterranean in the cramped and infested quarters of His Majesty's frigate *Hyperion*, suffering grievously from *mal de mer* exacerbated by some rather vicious fleabites. While the redoubtable Lady Sophia flourished under the conditions, her brother and niece were laid low, forced to remain below decks upon their bunks for much of the voyage. Lady Sophia it was who saw to it that the invalids were provided with what little nourishment their delicate stomachs could tolerate, and it was she who obtained a salve from Captain Mowbray himself, which rid Lord Henry of his unpleasant infestation.

And upon their arrival in Alexandria it was Lady Sophia again who rose to the occasion, conjuring up the transportation which hurtled the travellers onwards so quickly that Lord Henry had no time at all to recover from the pitching of the ground beneath them before being besieged by the bone-jolting experience of an unsprung carriage travelling an unmetalled road with his daughter rather vulgarly urging the driver to 'spring 'em' every time they stopped for a change.

They had arrived at Lord Wincester's residence in Cairo at some God-forsaken hour last night, and now here was Cassie, having made a remarkable recovery, demanding that they resume their journey not twenty-four hours later.

'Absolutely not!' Lord Henry exclaimed. 'I cannot journey another inch without a day's rest.'

'But, Papa, you cannot have considered—'

Lord Henry looked at his daughter with an eye which was considerably jaundiced. He had the tic. He had a splitting headache. In fact there wasn't a bit of him that didn't ache in one way or another. 'You worry too much. What is another day, after all this time?'

Cassie who, after seven hours' rest and a bath had made a remarkable recovery, was back in full Cassandra mode. She wrung her hands. 'Another day of suffering, Papa. Another day of Celia wondering when we will come to rescue her. Another day of gazing through the bars of her prison and *praying* for her release.'

'For God's sake, daughter, you should be on stage! You know, I can't understand how someone who looks as if a puff of wind will blow her away can survive such a journey as we have made with so little visible effect. I congratulate you on your constitution but—*but*, I say—I do not share it. I need another day before I go traipsing off across the desert. Apart from anything else, I must consult with old Wincester. The negotiations that George Cleveden was sent to conclude are extremely important—far too important to make a mull of because I didn't have time to receive a proper briefing. Damned inconvenient of George to get himself killed in the middle of it all, I must say.'

'But, Papa, surely my sister is the more important

issue at stake? Aunt Sophia!' Cassandra turned large blue eyes, wide with appeal, upon her aunt. 'I beg you, let us make haste today. Apparently it is only a very short trip to the Red Sea, where we can take a boat to this A'Qadiz. A gentle sail, Lord Wincester says it is.'

'What the devil does old Wincester know about it? He's never been,' Lord Henry exclaimed exasperatedly. 'Instead of treating me to histrionics, you'll make far better use of your time talking to that fellow—whatshisname—Finchley-Burke. He saw Celia only a week or so ago. Now, go away and allow me the dignity of recovering my health in private.'

Recognising the note of finality in his voice, Cassandra was forced to retreat, stopping only to press upon her father some most efficacious powders, before returning to the drawing room with her aunt.

There, Peregrine awaited her nervously, torn between a desire to pay homage at the temple of her beauty and an equally strong desire to avoid her terrifying aunt, whose baleful eye reminded him rather too much of his mother.

'You will accompany us, naturally. We need someone who knows the ropes,' Cassie informed Peregrine, putting her new-found seaman's slang into use. 'You've done the journey before, and you know all about camels and such. In fact compared to everyone else here, including even Lord Wincester, you are quite the expert,' she said, conferring upon the young man one of her most beguiling smiles.

Peregrine blushed. Now that Lord Henry Armstrong, with his reputation for honesty and integrity, was actually here in Cairo, the Consul General was regretting the liberties he had taken in suggesting that the

Lady Celia's incarceration in A'Qadiz could be of service to her country. In fact Lord Wincester had forbidden Peregrine from mentioning it, putting Peregrine in a very awkward position indeed. Not even Lady Cassandra's charming countenance and nymph-like figure could tempt him into spending any more time in her presence than necessary, lest he betray himself.

'Thing—thing is, Lady Cassandra,' he stammered, appalled at the very notion of having to keep her, her esteemed papa and formidable aunt company on a trek across the desert, 'thing is, I have to go to India.'

'Mr Finchley-Burke!' Cassandra exclaimed. 'Surely you would not let us down?'

'Eh! No, no, didn't quite—that is—you don't need me. You'll need a guide for the desert, but you'll be able pick one up at the port—don't want me along, keeping you back.' But Peregrine knew he was clutching at straws.

'India will wait, Mr Finchley-Burke. My sister cannot. You, I am sure, will not wish to think of her incarcerated in that place a moment longer than necessary.'

Peregrine's memory of Lady Celia was of a female perfectly content to stay where she was, but he did not quite know how to put that to her sister.

'How did you find my niece, Mr Finchley-Burke?'

Peregrine jumped, for he had quite forgotten Lady Sophia's presence. Now, faced with her gimlet gaze, he quailed. 'Well, it was quite simple, really, once I got to the palace.'

Lady Sophia rolled her eyes. 'No, you nincompoop, I'm referring to her health, her mental state.'

'Oh! Yes! Quite! She actually seemed remarkably well. Very composed young woman, Lady Celia. Seemed to be handling it with real aplomb,' Peregrine said bracingly.

'Ah, that does sound like Celia,' Lady Sophia said placidly.

'Of course it does, Aunt Sophia. Celia is not the type to have hysterics, you know that, but just because she does not show her feelings it does not mean she has none.' Cassandra clasped her hands to her bosom, unwittingly drawing Peregrine's attention to her curves. 'Remember, this man—this Sheikh al-Muhana—has her in his harem. I picture him rather old, with a black beard and a sort of grasping look.'

'As to that,' Sophia said with pursed lips, 'I have been making enquiries, and believe harems are not all decadent places. It may be that he has placed Celia in his harem simply to keep her safe. Do not let your imagination run away with you, Cassandra. I have every confidence in Celia's sense of propriety and her good sense. You must rid yourself of the notion of her as some sort of concubine.'

'But, Aunt, what if Celia's choice is to submit or surrender her life?' Cassandra asked tragically, once more allowing *One Thousand and One Nights* the upper hand.

'There is no point in wasting our time on idle speculation,' Lady Sophia said acerbically. Realising her niece was genuinely upset, and upon the brink of tears, she softened her expression marginally. 'Really, Cassie, you know your sister well enough. Celia is hardly the type to appeal to a sheikh, for she is not in the least exotic— and even if she did, which I strongly doubt, she is not the type to simply submit. Celia,' Lady Sophia said with authority, 'is not a tactile woman.' She got to her feet. 'We will leave you to your arrangements now,' she said to Peregrine. 'Come, Cassandra, what you need is some rest. Fortunately I have some laudanum in my reticule.'

* * *

'Sheikh Farid has requested an audience with you.'

The servants were packing up the camp in preparation for the journey back to Balyrma. 'With me?' Celia closed the lid of her dressing case, and turned towards Ramiz, who was standing in the doorway. 'What can Sheikh Farid wish to say to me?'

'I've been telling him about your idea for a Bedouin school. In amongst that gaggle of little admirers who follow you about wide-eyed, begging for stories, are three of Sheikh Farid's youngest children, and their mothers have been singing your praises.' Ramiz grinned. 'You've made quite an impression on them.'

'But what can I say? You said yourself the problem is finding teachers.'

'*"To him that will, ways are not wanting."* If Sheikh Farid wants a school for his people, teachers can be found. He has not until now believed it is what his people want. It looks as if you may have changed his mind.'

'You will be coming with me, won't you, Ramiz?'

'Yes, but you don't need me to tell you how to behave any more than I need to remind you of the honour Sheikh Farid is conferring upon you. You have a very charming way of making whoever you speak to feel as if they are the most important person in the world. Even me.'

'In your case it is because it is true.' The words were out before she could stop them.

Ramiz stilled.

'I mean,' Celia said lightly, 'in the eyes of your people, of course.'

'Of course,' Ramiz said thoughtfully.

'Does Sheikh Farid wish to see me now?'

'Yes, now. Akil can go ahead with the caravan. Tonight will be our last night in the desert. Tomorrow we will be back in Balyrma.'

'It will be strange, being back in the harem.'

'Celia, you don't regret what has happened? Between us, I mean?'

He looked troubled. *Was it he who had regrets?* She could not bear that. Though she rarely took the initiative, even in the most commonplace of touches, Celia took Ramiz's hand and pressed a kiss onto his palm. His skin was warm, his taste tantalisingly familiar. 'I will remember it always,' she said, rubbing his hand against her cheek. 'This last week has been magical. I will never regret it. Never.'

'Celia…'

She had a horrible suspicion he was going to apologise. Or, worse, offer her some sort of reparation. 'Please, Ramiz, don't.'

'Don't what?'

'Don't spoil it. As an interlude from reality it has been perfect.'

He pulled his hand away. 'That is still how you see it?'

She looked at him in bewilderment. 'Do not you?'

Ramiz shrugged. 'We will take the camels to Sheikh Farid's camp. That way we will waste less time.'

'Ramiz…'

But he was gone. She stared at the spot in the tent where he had stood. In the last week she'd thought she had come to understand him completely, but today she had no idea what he was thinking—what it was she had said to him to make him look so…what? Angry? A little, but not just that. She pulled an *abeyah* the colour of cinnamon, embroidered with russet and gold, over her caftan, and checked her appearance in the mirror. He had seemed almost disappointed. But why?

Tonight would be their last night in the desert. Their last night together in her tent. When they returned to the palace would it all be at an end? Was that what he meant? That he would not visit her in the harem? Had he had enough of her? Was he letting her down gently?

A horrible sick feeling made her slump down onto the divan. When he'd said it was their last night in the desert, he'd meant it was to be their last night. Ever. There could be no other meaning. Celia blinked rapidly to prevent the hot tears which welled up in her eyes from spilling. She'd known it would end, but she'd hoped it would last until she had to leave. Now she saw he was right. To drag it out, waking each morning wondering if it would be this day or the next when her papa would arrive, would be unendurable.

Her papa would take her home. But home was here, with Ramiz. Without him she might as well be condemned to a nomadic life, just like the Bedouins. Celia sniffed and blew her nose, and chastised herself for the fanciful turn her imagination had taken. She had tonight. She had the memories. Things could be worse, she told herself bracingly, though she wasn't exactly sure how.

The meeting with Sheikh Farid went well. Celia was nervous beforehand, worried she would let Ramiz down. 'It's not possible,' Ramiz had said reassuringly, surprised to find that he meant it. 'I trust you.'

He had meant that too, which was more of a surprise, for the truth was he didn't normally trust anyone com-

pletely to act on his behalf, to act without his explicit
instructions, to think for themselves—not even Akil.
Yet he trusted Celia. He trusted her judgement and he
trusted her ability. Sitting by her side, translating only
when consulted, he watched with admiration as she set
about charming Sheikh Farid as she seemed to charm
everyone she spoke to, from the market traders in the
souk, to Yasmina, his servants, every child who came
within a hundred yards of her, and now this wily old
Bedouin, who was already smiling and making jokes
after just fifteen minutes in her company—something
it had taken *him* many visits to achieve.

Sheikh Farid summoned his wives and younger
children. Ramiz recognised the little girl who made a
beeline for Celia's lap as the one he'd seen her with the
day before. They had been counting out numbers using
pieces of straw. Now Celia encouraged the child to
show her father what she had learned.

The meeting concluded with a promise on Sheikh
Farid's part to give thought to the problem of finding
teachers—a giant leap forward as far as Ramiz was
concerned.

'You are blessed in your visitor from the West,'
Sheikh Farid told Ramiz. 'She has the brains of a man
in the body of a beautiful woman. If only you could be
persuaded to stay,' he continued, turning towards Celia,
'I would be happy to take you as my next wife. Though
I fear that Prince Ramiz here would have something to
say to that.' Sheikh Farid smiled sadly. 'I should not
grudge him, for I already have six fine wives and this
poor man has none, but you must understand I speak
as a father. I had hoped my Juman would please the
Prince, but I can see she is not to his taste.' The Bedouin

touched his hands together and bowed. 'Safe journey, my friends. Peace be with you.'

Celia returned the gesture. '*Wa-alaykum as-salam*, Sheikh Farid. May our paths cross again one day.'

'I will pray for it.'

Celia's farewells to the many Bedouin children who crowded round her, tugging at her *abeyah* for attention, were less formal and more protracted. Ramiz watched almost unnoticed, content to remain in the background, a strange emotion tugging at his heart. It was pride, he thought. He was proud of her, and proud to be in her company. It felt good, this sharing. A taste of what it could be like to have a consort. A partnership.

'*She has the brains of a man in the body of a beautiful woman.*' Sheikh Farid's words were a high compliment indeed, and Celia deserved it. She was exceptional. She deserved to be recognised in such a way—as herself, on her own terms. It was only in seeing someone else do so that he realised he had long since stopped trying to slot her into any preconceived role himself. She was Celia. Unique. He would never meet anyone like her again.

She finally escaped the clambering embraces of the children and allowed Ramiz to help her up onto the high saddle of her camel. Smiling and waving, the children followed them for about a hundred yards, Sheikh Farid's little daughter being among the last to give up the chase. Celia, touched immeasurably by the affection she had been shown, was dabbing at her eyes with a scrap of lace. Beside her, Ramiz kept his camel to a slow trot to allow her to regain her composure. The reality of her leaving was beginning to dawn on him with cold clarity.

This 'interlude', as she called it, he had intended as his cure. *The only way to eliminate temptation is to yield to it.* Asad's words, which only a few days ago had seemed to be the answer to his prayers. Now they mocked him. He had yielded to temptation, he had abandoned his principles to do so, but far from being sated, he was now addicted. Addicted to Celia's body. Addicted to her company. Addicted to her mind.

He needed her. He craved her. He could not imagine how it would be without her. Loneliness loomed like the vast desert plain stretched out before them in the rising heat of late morning, scorched of life, bleached of colour, dusty and arid.

A messenger had come in the night. The English had arrived at the port. The escort Ramiz had organised to attend them was even now leading the caravan across the desert to Balyrma. By the time they returned to the city tomorrow Celia's father could be waiting to take her home. They had only tonight. Just one more night.

Ramiz could hardly bear to look at the bleakness which was his future. Almost he resented Celia for doing this to him. Until she'd arrived he hadn't even known he was lonely. Until she'd arrived he hadn't needed anyone or anything. Only A'Qadiz mattered. A'Qadiz was his life and his reason for being. Now A'Qadiz without Celia seemed as drained of colour as an English morning in November.

Tonight would be their last together. Tomorrow he would cut her from his life. Why did it feel as if he would be severing a part of himself? He didn't even know what she felt about it all, not really. He hated the way she looked so cool and collected, when he ached with something horribly akin to love. But he could not love her and he would not—any more than she could or would love him.

Tonight was all they had left to them. Tonight must be enough, for there was no more to be had.

When Ramiz joined her in the tent he seemed different. Celia couldn't say how, just that he was. He had been in a strange mood since the morning's visit to Sheikh Farid. Distant, but watchful. Every time she looked at him he was looking at her, his eyes slits of amber, the tiny lines at their edges more pronounced than usual, as if he were frowning, but he did not seem angry. He seemed tense. And now, prowling around her tent in a dark blue caftan, restless as a caged tiger.

Neither of them had eaten much over dinner. They had not spoken much either. Celia was aware—too aware—of the fact that this was the last time. She could feel her heart beating, marking time like a pendulum, swinging inexorably back and forth, back and forth, counting out the seconds and the minutes and the hours.

She was apprehensive, waiting for him to make the first move as he always did when they came together. Excitement lay like a sub-strata beneath the layer of tension. Tonight she wanted it all. She did not care about the risk. She did not care about the possible consequences. She did not care about anything other than knowing, experiencing the completion of their union inside her—something Ramiz had been extremely careful never to allow. She loved him for it, and knew she should be grateful for his self-control. She was, but it left her feeling as if something was missing, something lacking. It left her feeling empty. She wanted him to make complete love to her. Just once.

But she was nervous. And if she hadn't known him better she'd have said Ramiz was nervous too. Something was bothering him, though he denied it when she asked him.

'I've made you a present,' she said, pulling the caftan she had so carefully embroidered out from under a cushion and handing it to him.

Ramiz shook it out and examined it. Dark blue silk, she had copied its pattern from one of his others. The long sleeves were embroidered in shades of blue in the traditional pattern which Yasmina had shown her. The same pattern was repeated around the hem and at the neckline, delicate but unobtrusive, designed to give weight to the garment rather than adornment. The most intricate work was on the motif she had sewn on the left breast. A crescent moon and a falcon—Ramiz's own insignia—but the bird was in full flight, and in its beak it carried a rosebud.

Ramiz gazed at it in silence, tracing the image with his finger.

'Do you like it?'

He laid the caftan down carefully on a divan. 'It is a very evocative image.'

'It's how I think of you. Me. This.'

'Us,' Ramiz said softly, stroking her hair behind her ear so that he could lick into the little crease behind her lobe, inhale the scent of her that lingered there, feel the strength and the fragility of her that seemed to be encapsulated at that precise point, in that combination of soft flesh and delicate bone.

'Us,' she said breathlessly, allowing herself to feel the word, to think the word, to believe that it could be true just for tonight.

Ramiz pushed back the heavy fall of her hair to flutter kisses onto the nape of her neck, his fingers kneading her shoulders, stroking the wings of her shoulderblades. He pulled her against him, slipping his hands down to her waist, wrapping his arms around her, folding her into him.

She could feel his erection pressing against the base of her spine. She could feel the wall of his chest, his heart beating slow and sure against her back. Her head nestled into his shoulder. She closed her eyes and drank in the scent, the feel, the soft sound of his breath—drank it all in so that she would remember it for ever.

Ramiz turned her round in his arms and kissed her. So tenderly. So softly. Holding her as if she were something precious, his hands on the side of her face, his thumbs caressing her jaw, his eyes warm and golden, with such a look that she felt as if she were melting. She closed her own eyes and surrendered to the moment, which was like no other moment that had passed between them. A long, languorous moment, as if they had all the time in the world just to kiss and kiss and kiss. Gentle kisses, gentle caresses, as if they would soothe rather than arouse, as if they would coax and cajole, a slow burn—so slow that they barely noticed the flames rising.

Her clothes disappeared as if they had melted. His hands were on her breasts, touching her as if he had never touched her there before, his fingers marvelling at the roundness, the smoothness, the creaminess of her skin, the pink puckering of her nipple. His mouth landed like the whisper of a butterfly, sipping and sipping and sipping until she was nectar, trickling hot and sweet in a path downwards from her nipples to her belly to the darker, more sumptuous heat between her thighs.

He was naked. She was naked. Liquid with desire, molten with it, she lay touching and being touched, kissing and being kissed, stroking and being stroked. His shaft throbbed under her caress, but he seemed in no hurry, intent on tending to every curve and dip and swell, every crease and pucker, rolling her onto her stomach to kiss down her spine, the curve of her bottom, the back of her knee, the hollow of her ankle bone, then on to her back, to work his way up again, reaching the softness of her thighs, the damp heat between them, jolting her from floating bliss to jagged desire in an instant.

Celia moaned and clenched back on her climax, catching Ramiz unawares when she wriggled out from under him, rolled him onto his back, placing herself on top of him, leaning over him so that her breasts were crushed into his chest, her nipples taut and hard on his skin, his shaft taut and hard between her legs. She kissed him urgently. She saw the urgency reflected in his face, his eyes dark with it, his skin flushed with it, and then as she kissed him she felt herself lifted, his hands gripping her waist, and he thrust up and was inside her, deep inside her, as he let her fall on top of him at the same time.

She gasped her pleasure, lying still over him. He pushed her gently upright, steadying her by the waist, and the action allowed his shaft to forge deeper. His thrust forged it deeper again, touching something, a spot high inside her, that triggered an instant clenching and pulsing climax, sending her over in a headlong rush so that she was barely conscious of him thrusting inside her still, of the tension of his control etched on his cheekbones, on the rigid muscles of his shoulders, the corded sinews of his arms as he gripped her and thrust, and she lifted and fell in the same rhythm, lifting and falling, feeling him building and thickening as with every thrust he hit that same spot again and she trembled and shuddered.

She could determine the moment when he would push her from him by the way his eyes lost focus. She could see the resolution in him in the way his grip changed. She could feel his climax tightening in the base of his shaft. She could feel him swell, her own muscles gripping and holding, furling and unfurling against him. Ramiz groaned. She fell on top of him, pushing him down as he thrust up, pushing him hard down so that he couldn't move, and with a harsh cry he came, pouring hot and endlessly, high and deep inside her, and it was more, more than she had ever imagined it would be—for it was as if their essences mingled, and for now, in this instant, they truly were one.

They lay melded together for long moments, breathing fast, hearts thumping in wild unison, limbs entangled. Celia's hair trailed over Ramiz's shoulders, over his arms, which were wrapped tight around her waist in an iron grip, pressing her against him as if he would never let her go. She floated on a cloud of ecstasy, glided on a current of the sweetest, warmest air, heavy yet weightless, finally understanding the word *sated*.

Gradually their breathing slowed. Ramiz's hold on her relaxed. She waited, but the anticipated rejection did not come. He smoothed her hair back from her head. He kissed her gently on the mouth. He turned her onto her side and cradled her into him—two crescents fitting perfectly together. He ran his hand possessively down her flank and held her thus until she slept. And when she awoke in the dark of the night, when the lamps had burned out, he was still there. Still holding her.

'Celia.' Ramiz kissed her neck.

She tensed. Now he would leave. Now he would say something. But he didn't. Except her name. 'Celia…' in that husky voice, raw with passion, brushing over her skin like velvet, and he turned her to face him and then he kissed her, and it started over again—except this time Ramiz took control, Ramiz lay on top of her. It came harder and faster, their joint climax, as he thrust with her legs wrapped around him, and he poured himself into her with no need for her urging, his cry one of abandon she had never thought to hear and would never forget.

In the morning when she awoke he was dressed, sitting on the edge of the divan, with his formidable look back in place. She stretched out her hand. 'Don't hate me.'

Ramiz shook her away. 'If I hate it must be myself. A man must take responsibility, since a woman must bear the consequences. It should not have happened.' *It should not, but he could not regret it.* His own intransigence confused him.

'It was my fault.'

'No. The fault was mine. We must trust to the fates that you are not punished for it.'

Celia bit her lip. Punished! He was talking about the possibility of a child, their child, as punishment. She sat up. 'I should get dressed. You wanted to make an early start.'

His mind seethed with words. His heart seethed with emotions. He couldn't understand it—any of it. He couldn't think straight. He wanted to shake her until she told him what she really felt. He wanted to make love to her again, to experience that sweet perfection of their union, a perfection he hadn't known possible until last night.

Ramiz got to his feet, running his hand through his hair. 'A messenger arrived yesterday. Your father is here in A'Qadiz. He arrived at the port two days ago. He will be at Balyrma shortly—perhaps even before us.'

'You knew last night?'

Ramiz nodded curtly. 'This is the end.'

'You knew last night?' Celia repeated stupidly.

Her eyes were like moss damp with dew. Her hair curled like fire over the creaminess of her skin, over the soft mounds of her breasts. She looked like Botticelli's *Venus*. He had never seen anyone so beautiful or so irresistible. Having her, taking her so completely, possessing her, had made it worse, much worse. Knowing did not satisfy. It only made the wanting more painful, for he knew now what he would be missing.

'Why didn't you tell me, Ramiz?'

He had no answer—none he could give which would not force him to confront—what he did not want to confront—so Ramiz shrugged. 'You know now. There are two women with him also. One young, one old.'

'My aunt? The other is probably a maid.'

Another shrug. 'Get dressed. You will find out soon enough.' He turned to go.

'Ramiz?'

'Well?'

'You were saying goodbye, weren't you? I understand. It was perfect while it lasted—our fairytale. I want you to know that.'

He blanched. The words were almost his undoing. A fairytale. That was all it was. Ramiz left the room.

In the main part of the tent he saw the caftan she had embroidered for him. He picked it up. The motif dug like thorns into his heart. He could never wear it. Never. But he folded it carefully and took it with him all the same.

It came to him then, as he strode across the sand to his own tent. He loved her. That was what it was—this craving, this need to be with her. It was because she was part of him.

She was his. He felt it more fiercely than the burning heat of the sun. She was his. He loved her. And soon she would be gone.

CHAPTER THIRTEEN

CONTRARY to Ramiz's expectations, when they arrived at Balyrma there was no sigh of Celia's relatives. In fact dusk was falling and Celia was beginning to think they would not arrive at all that day when the doors of the harem were flung open and, to her astonishment, not just Aunt Sophia but Cassie stood before her, looking extremely dusty, exhausted and bewildered.

'Celia? Is that you?' Cassie was the first to speak, standing transfixed before the exotic-looking creature who bore a distant resemblance to the sister she had come so far to rescue. She hesitated, unaccountably nervous.

'Cassie!' Celia flew across the courtyard to embrace her sister. 'Cassie, I can't believe it's really you. Are you well? I can't tell for all the dust. Cassie, it really is me, I promise.' Celia kissed her sister's cheek. 'And Aunt Sophia. You've come all this way, and so quickly. You must be exhausted. Please come in. Fatima, Adila—here are my aunt and my sister. They will want food.' Celia broke off to issue instructions in Arabic, before ushering Cassie ahead of her to her favourite salon.

'You have learned the language?' Cassie said in amazement.

Celia laughed. 'A little only.'

Cassandra paused at the fountain, trailing her fingers in the water and looking around her at the lemon trees, the tiled pillars, the symmetry of the salons running round the square, one leading into another. So strange, yet Celia looked so at home here. Even the way she walked in her jewelled slippers was different. She seemed to float and ripple.

'You look like Scheherazade in these clothes,' she said, regarding her sister with a mixture of envy and awe. 'So very glamorous. I hardly recognise you.'

Celia made a little twirl. 'Do you like them? They are so much more suited to the heat here, and such lovely colours.'

'Celia, are you—can it be that you have *abandoned* your corsets?' demanded Lady Sophia, looking at her niece's all too obvious curves, revealed by the clinging fabrics. 'I do trust you do not leave your rooms in such a toilette?'

Celia laughed. 'No one wears corsets here, Aunt, it is far too hot.'

'And your hair—is it the custom to wear it down like that?'

'Not outside. Then it is covered by a veil.'

'And you have no stockings. What are these things under your robe? They look remarkably like pantaloons. Do you tell me it is also common to have one's *undergarments* on display?'

'Dearest Aunt, they are called *sarwal* pantaloons, and, yes, I am afraid it is quite acceptable. Oh, Cassie, Aunt Sophia—I can't tell you how wonderful it is to see you. Please do sit down. Adila will bring you some sherbet. You will like it; it is most refreshing.'

'Where do we sit?'

'On the cushions. Like so.'

Celia floated gracefully onto the carpeted floor. Cassie followed suit, but Lady Sophia took a seat with extreme reluctance. 'Only heathens sit on the floor.'

'Where is Papa, Aunt?'

'He has an audience with the Sheikh.'

'How are the girls? Are they well? Did you get my letters?'

'Yes, they are all very well and send their love. But, Celia—' Cassie looked anxiously at her sister '—are *you* well?'

'Do I not look it?'

'Yes. Very. In fact I don't think I've ever seen you look better. You look—older, but more beautiful,' Cassie said, sounding as confused as she felt. 'Not in the least like our Celia. I have to confess I am a little intimidated by you.' Her laugh tinkled like the cold water of the fountain. 'What do you think, Aunt?'

Lady Sophia pursed her lips. 'Hmm.' She took a cautious sip of the sherbet which Adila had handed to her on a silver tray. 'Do they speak English?' she asked, nodding at the maidservants.

Celia shook her head.

'And this place we are in—is this what is known as the harem?'

Again Celia nodded.

'Where are the other women?' Cassie asked, looking around her as if she expected a flock of scantily clad females to suddenly appear.

'Sheikh al-Muhana is not married. He has no wives,' Celia said with a smile.

Lady Sophia cleared her throat. 'Celia, I must ask

you. Has that man committed any—any improprieties with you? You must know that your sister has been most concerned for your—your... I told her not to worry, of course. I told her you would not—but you must put her mind at rest. Tell us plainly, child, have you—have you been forced to—? In short, Celia, this man has not laid a hand upon you, has he?'

Though she tried desperately to stop it, when she was faced with the frank blue eyes of her sister and the worried grey of her aunt, Celia felt a blush steal over her cheeks. 'Sheikh al-Muhana has treated me with the utmost respect,' she replied falteringly. 'He was conscious from the first that I—that my family—that Papa... He has done nothing to compromise the relationship between our two countries,' she finished with a tilt of her chin. 'In fact it was Ramiz—Sheikh al-Muhana—who saved my life when we were attacked by the brigands who killed George.'

Needless to say this statement produced a welter of questions from Cassie. Though Celia tried to gloss over George's role in events, Aunt Sophia's sharp nose scented scandal. 'George Cleveden was reputed to be an excellent shot,' she said. 'I cannot understand how he came not to defend himself.'

'He did not have the opportunity to fire his gun. It was all so sudden.'

'And it was early morning, you say? How came it that you were not in the tent with him?'

'I found the tent claustrophobic and chose to sleep outside.'

'Had you and George quarrelled?'

'No, Aunt Sophia, nothing of that nature. We had not long been married. We were still...well, getting used to each other.'

'Hmm.' Lady Sophia treated Celia to her Sphinx look. 'You should know that your sister and I came all this way in anticipation of having to support you through the trial of your husband's death and your subsequent incarceration here. Cassie in particular has been most upset by the idea of your suffering inopportune advances from this Sheikh al-Muhana.'

Celia pressed her sister's hand. 'Have you been worried about me, Cassie? Poor thing. There was no need as I have been very well looked after, I promise. I am so sorry to have caused you to fret.'

Cassandra examined the intricate silver *passementerie* braiding on the sleeve of Celia's caftan. 'What is it you're not telling us?' She lifted her eyes, meeting her sister's with a puzzled look. 'It's true I've been worried sick about you, and I can't tell you what a relief it is to see you in one piece, looking so well, but—but that's just it, Celia, I don't understand it. What has happened to you?'

Celia pulled her sister into a tight hug. 'Cassie, nothing bad, I promise.'

Cassandra sniffed. 'You've always told me everything.'

'Hmm,' said Lady Sophia once more. 'Celia, I believe Cassandra would be the better for a wash and change of clothes.'

'Of course she would.' Celia clapped her hands to summon the maids. 'Cassie, go with Fatima and Adila. You will be amazed by the bathing chamber, and they will give you some of my clothes to try if you wish. Then you will see that they are just clothes, and I really am your sister. Go on—you will feel much better.'

Cassandra left. 'Well,' Lady Sophia said when they were alone, 'since it is obviously not George Cleveden who is responsible for that glow you have about you, young woman, I presume it is this sheikh. You will tell me, please, now that your sister's blushes have been spared, what exactly is going on here.'

Lord Henry Armstrong's meeting with Ramiz was conducted on much more formal terms, in the splendid surroundings of the throne room. Ramiz, clad in his royal robes of state, sat on the dais, with Akil standing in attendance. To Peregrine's relief two low stools had been placed in front of the throne, and to these Ramiz graciously waved his visitors.

'I think we have met before, Your Highness,' Lord Henry said, sitting cautiously down, having made his bow, 'though I can't recall where.'

'Lisbon, about four years ago,' Ramiz replied. 'Until my brother was tragically killed in battle I spent much of my time abroad as my father's emissary, and my brother's too.'

'Thought I recognised you,' Lord Henry said with satisfaction. 'Don't often forget a face, though I'm not quite so good with names. Well, now, tragic business this, but no point in dwelling on it, so we might as well get straight to the point. George Cleveden came here with the objective of agreeing rights of passage through A'Qadiz's port. I've been authorised to conclude those negotiations.'

'I am sure we can reach terms agreeable to us both, Lord Armstrong,' Ramiz said smoothly. 'I know how very important the route is to your East India Company.'

A lesser diplomat would have expressed surprise, but Lord Henry's experience stood him in excellent stead. Like a good gambler, he knew when he had been trumped. 'Quite so,' he said. 'Three months is a considerable advantage over two years. What is it you seek from us in return?'

'We will discuss the details tomorrow, but let me just say it pleases me to be able to conclude a pact which I believe will be to the long-term advantage of both our countries. Tonight I am sure you wish to rest after your journey. The desert can be unkind to those unfamiliar with it. And you will obviously wish to see your daughter.'

'No rush on that. Celia and Cassie will have their heads together, happy to wait until our business is concluded.'

Peregrine frowned. His instructions from the Consul General were clear. The Lady Celia was to be questioned prior to the treaty for any pertinent information. Acutely uncomfortable as he was with the damnable position in which Lord Wincester had placed him, he was even more terrified of disobeying the explicit orders of such an influential man. He tugged on Lord Henry's sleeve. 'My Lord, would it not be wise for us to speak to Lady Celia now?' Peregrine said with a significant look. 'Find out how she is, what she has been up to, et cetera. She'll be anxious to tell you all about her adventure, if you get my drift.'

'Dammit, man, I said it can wait,' Lord Henry said, frowning.

'But, My Lord—' Peregrine persisted awkwardly.

'*I said not now,*' Lord Henry said furiously. He turned towards Ramiz. 'You will forgive my assistant. He is rather tired,' he said, drawing Peregrine a censorious look.

Ramiz clapped his hands together and the doors at the far end of the throne room were flung open.

'Indeed—as I am sure you are too, Lord Armstrong. My servants will escort you to your quarters, and to the men's *hammam* baths. I will join you later for dinner.' He nodded his dismissal. 'Akil, a word, if you please.' Waiting until Lord Henry and Peregrine were safely out of earshot, Ramiz got to his feet and cast his jewelled headdress onto the throne. 'Get that idiot assistant on his own. There is something going on and I want to know what it is.'

'And the treaty?'

'As we agreed. Lord Armstrong knows his position is not strong. Give a little to massage his ego, and he will not argue with the main points. Are Lady Celia's sister and aunt with her in the harem?'

Akil nodded. 'If things go well, Lady Celia can leave tomorrow.'

'Why do you dislike her so much?'

Akil hesitated. 'It's not that I don't like her. Under different circumstances I would like her very well. But she does not belong here, Ramiz.'

'You saw how Sheikh Farid took to her. And his wives.'

'And many other people—my own wife included. The Lady Celia is undoubtedly charming.'

'But?'

Akil shrugged. 'You know what I think. Do not let us quarrel over it. It is not just that she doesn't belong here, Ramiz, her family would no more accept it than your own people. In the eyes of the likes of Lord Armstrong we are heathens. It wouldn't surprise me to find that he suspects his daughter has been kept in your harem as a concubine,' he said with a smile.

'If he thought that he would hardly have been so polite just now,' Ramiz snapped.

'He is a statesman first, a father second. He will get the treaty signed to advance the British cause, and then he will worry about his daughter. Mark my words, Ramiz, he says nothing for the moment, but that does not mean he will remain silent. We must hope the Lady Celia has nothing to complain of.'

Ramiz cursed. '*You* must rather hope for your own sake that *I* have nothing to complain of. Find out what Finchley-Burke was so cagey about and report back to me before dinner. And bring Yasmina to the palace tomorrow, Celia will wish to say her farewells.'

'She *is* going, then?'

Ramiz ran his hand through his hair. 'Would it be so impossible to imagine her staying?'

Akil shook his head and made for the door. 'You don't really want me to answer that,' he said, and left.

For a long time afterwards Ramiz stared absently into space. The problem was not that it was impossible to imagine Celia staying; it was that it was impossible to imagine her leaving. He did not know how it had come about, but she had become indispensable to him. He, Ramiz al-Muhana, Prince of A'Qadiz, did not want to contemplate the rest of his life without her. Now he wondered if he had to. If Sheikh Farid accepted her, why not others? As his consort, with the fulfilment she would bring to his life, would she not more than make up for any potential backlash which failure to marry to one of his neighbours' daughters would inevitably bring?

After last night he was as certain as a man could be without hearing the words that she loved him. Last night she had made love to him, as he had made love to her. Last night had not been about the pleasures of the flesh—it had been something more fundamental, almost religious. The worship of a lover by a lover. The desire to create one being from two separate halves. The need to celebrate that union with the planting of a seed. How much he had derided that idea until now. He wanted Celia by his side. He wanted her to be his and only his. He wanted children—not as the means of cementing the succession, but as the fruit of their love.

It would be asking much of her. To stay here in A'Qadiz, to surrender her family, to exchange her loyalties from one country to another, to commit herself not just to him but to his kingdom, a place steeped in custom and traditions alien to her. It was not something she could do half-heartedly either, if she was to be accepted. There would be changes, and with Celia by his side some of those changes would come more quickly than he had planned, but some things would never change. As his princess she must not just pay lip-service to their traditions, she must embrace them. It was much to ask. Perhaps too much.

Ramiz forced himself to imagine life without her. His mind refused to co-operate. She was his—had always been destined to be his. Tomorrow, in the clear light of day and before her family, he would claim her.

Filled with determination, and a lightness of heart which it took him some time to realise was a foretaste of happiness, Ramiz retired to his chambers to change. He wondered how Celia's reunion with her sister was going. He wondered what she was saying of him, if she was confiding anything about him. No, she would not. His Celia—for already he was thinking of her thus— was fiercely loyal. She would tell nothing which might compromise his relationship with her father. Nothing which would put his treatment of her in anything other than a favourable light. She loved him. He was almost sure of it.

The urge to seek her out and declare himself was strong, but duty forbade it. As Ramiz finished bathing and donned a clean robe in preparation for dinner, Akil arrived, looking sombre.

Dismissing the servants, Ramiz turned to his friend. 'Well?'

'I spoke to Finchley-Burke as you suggested, Highness.'

'You call me Highness. It must be bad news,' Ramiz said with an ironic smile. 'Spit it out.'

'Ramiz, you must understand if I was not absolutely sure of this…'

Ramiz's smile faded. 'What is it?'

'The Lady Celia.'

'What of her?'

'She has been spying on you.'

'Don't be foolish.'

'Perhaps spying is the wrong word. She has been collecting information about our country.'

'A natural curiosity, Akil.'

'No, Ramiz. I'm sorry, but it's more than that. They left her here deliberately, with instructions to make use of your attraction for her.'

'You are being ridiculous.'

'I'm not, I assure you. Oh, nothing improper was asked of her. According to Finchley-Burke it was all neatly veiled—her duty to her country, the memory of her dead husband…you know the kind of thing.'

'You are saying that Celia was instructed to extract information from me that might prove useful to the British government by—? No, I can't believe it.'

'Ramiz, I'm sorry.' Akil put a hand on his friend's shoulder but it was shaken off. He took a step back, but met Ramiz's eyes unflinchingly. 'I *am* sorry, but you must ask yourself why else would a woman of her birth have allowed you such liberties? Come on, Ramiz, it's not as if she put up much resistance, is it?'

Ramiz moved so quickly that his fist made sharp contact with Akil's jaw before he had a chance to defend himself. Akil staggered back against the wall, frightened by the blaze of anger he was faced with.

Ramiz took a hasty step towards him, his fists clenched, but stopped short inches away. 'My hands are shamed by contact with you. You deserve to be whipped.'

'Whip me, then, but it won't change the truth.' Akil spoke with difficulty, for his jaw was swelling fast. There was blood on his tongue. 'She has used you. It is as well we found out before tomorrow, for you can be sure her father would have found an opportunity to allow her to brief him. She has used you, Ramiz, we are well rid of her.'

'Get out! *Get out of here!*'

'Ramiz…'

'Now!'

Akil bowed, still clutching his jaw, and fled. Alone, Ramiz slumped down on his divan, his head in his hands. There must be an explanation. But Akil would never lie to him. He knew that for a certainty. There was no reason either for Finchley-Burke to concoct such a story if it was not true. He would not demean himself by asking the junior diplomat to repeat it. Celia would answer to him personally.

* * *

Lady Sophia, having much food for thought, graciously agreed to permit Fatima to help her bathe, after much encouragement from Celia. 'Please, Aunt, I promise you will find it a most amenable experience.' Celia had also been fulsome in her descriptions of A'Qadiz, and her recent trip to the desert in Sheikh al-Muhana's caravan, but despite being pressed had said little of the Sheikh himself—even less of her relationship with him.

Cautiously lowering herself into the scented water of the tiled bath, Lady Sophia realised that it was Celia's very reticence which gave her most grounds for concern. The girl was smitten, it was obvious. She would consult Henry in the morning, for the sooner Celia was removed from this sheikh's beguiling presence the better.

Left alone together with Cassie, Celia gave in to her sister's plea to be allowed to try on her exotic outfits. She was sitting on her favourite cushion, watching Cassandra parade before her, laughing and telling her she looked rather like the Queen of Sheba, when the crash of a wooden door slamming with force onto tiled walls made the smile die on her face and had her leaping to her feet.

Celia reached the doorway in time to see Ramiz stride across the courtyard. His face was set and white with fury. 'What's wrong? Is it my father?'

'Traitor!' He stood before her wild-eyed, his chest heaving.

'Ramiz! What on earth is the matter?'

'I trusted you! Dear heavens, I trusted you. I who trust no one. And you betrayed me.'

Anger glittered from his eyes, mere slits of gold under heavy lids. His mouth was drawn into a thin line. Celia clutched a hand to her breast. 'Ramiz, I have not betrayed you. I would never—what has happened? Please tell me.'

'You lied to me,' he snarled.

'I did not lie to you,' Celia responded indignantly. 'I would never lie to you. You're frightening me, Ramiz.'

'I doubt it,' he flashed. 'I doubt anything frightens *you*, Lady Celia, consummate actress as you are. I should have known. Akil was right. I should have guessed from the start that such a delicate English rose would not subject herself to the brutal caresses of a heathen like myself without reason. Do they *know*, my lovely Celia?' he hissed, nodding contemptuously at Lady Sophia and Cassie, paused on the brink of intervention in the doorway of the main salon. 'Have you told them the price you paid for whatever pathetic little snippets of information you have garnered for them?'

As realisation dawned Celia began to feel faint. 'Mr Finchley-Burke,' she said, her voice no more than a whisper.

'Precisely. He is here with your father. You didn't expect that, did you?'

Horribly conscious of the presence of her aunt and her sister, Celia shook her head miserably and moved a little further down the courtyard. 'Ramiz, it's true. Mr Finchley-Burke asked me to—to keep my eyes and ears open. Those were his words. It is also true that I thought about it—but only for a few moments. I was just relieved to have an excuse to stay here, Ramiz. I never intended—I would never use—especially not now, after...'

'I don't believe you.'

'Ramiz, please.' Celia took a step towards him, her hands held out in supplication, but he shrank away from her as if she were poison. She swallowed hard. Tears would be humiliating. 'It's the truth. Even if I did consider it at first…'

'So you admit that much?'

Celia hung her head. 'I thought if I could salvage something from George's death… But it was a thought only—a fleeting one. I never really intended—I know I never would have. And that was before you and I…'

'There *is* no you and I. Not now.'

'*Ramiz!* Ramiz, you can't seriously believe that I would have made love with you for any other reason than—' She broke off, realising that what she had been about to say was exactly what she had sworn never to say. That she loved him. Looking at him in anguish, she could think of nothing *except* that she loved him.

Now he did touch her, pulling her into his arms, pushing her hair back from her face, forcing her to meet his hard gaze. 'So why did you, Celia? Why did you allow me such liberties? Why did you give *me* what you gave no other man?'

'You know why,' she whispered. 'I couldn't stop myself.'

'How can I believe that when you obviously had no such difficulty in denying your husband?'

'George has nothing to do with this.'

'But he has everything to do with it. Was it not for the sake of his memory that you did all this?'

'Ramiz, have I ever asked you anything remotely sensitive when it comes to A'Qadiz? Have I prodded you for information? Have I ever attempted to cajole secrets from you? You know I have not!'

But he was beyond reasoning. 'You have done worse than that. You have forced me to betray my honour. You gave yourself to me. You threw yourself at me in the hope that I would succumb and I did. I do not doubt for a moment that your intention is to cry ravishment now, thus allowing your father the moral upper hand, which he will have no hesitation in using to his advantage.'

Celia stared at him in absolute astonishment. 'I truly thought you knew me. I thought you understood me. I thought I understood you too. But I don't. I would die rather than do such a thing.'

'I didn't expect you to admit it. I just wanted you to know that I'd found out. It is I who would die rather than allow you to take further advantage of me. There will be no treaty. Never. Now get out of my sight.'

He threw her from him contemptuously. Celia staggered. 'Ramiz, please don't do this. Please.'

'I am done with you. All of you. You will leave Balyrma tomorrow. I will have an escort to see you out of my kingdom. I don't want to see or hear from you ever again.'

The harem door clanged shut behind him and he was gone. As Celia crumpled to the floor, covering her face with her hands, Lady Sophia and Cassandra rushed towards her, helping her to her feet and back to her salon, seating her on her divan and wrapping her in a velvet throw.

'It's all right, Celia,' Cassie said, holding her tight and casting a bewildered look at her aunt.

Almost oblivious of their presence, Celia huddled under the soft caress of the velvet. It would never be all right. Nothing she could say would make any difference. Ramiz despised her. It was over.

CHAPTER FOURTEEN

'LET me in! Open up at once, I say.'

Celia raised a weary head from her pillow and listened.

'Open up! Dammit, my daughters are in there. Will you open the door?'

'Papa?' Celia stumbled from her divan to the courtyard, to find Cassie and Aunt Sophia staring in consternation at the closed door of the harem. 'Is that Father I can hear?'

'We can't get the door open,' Cassie said. 'There's no handle on this side.'

'Open up,' Celia called to the guards in Arabic. 'It is my father.'

The door swung open, revealing an irate Lord Henry with a red-faced Peregrine beside him. The eunuch guards had drawn their scimitars and were barring the way. 'For goodness' sake, Celia, tell these men to let us through,' Lord Henry said testily.

'This is a harem, Papa. Sheikh al-Muhana is the only man who is permitted to come here. Why did you not just send for me?'

'Couldn't get anyone to understand a damned word I was saying.'

'But where is Ramiz?'

'If you mean the Prince, I have no idea. Didn't turn up for dinner with us last night—haven't seen him this morning. Took us the best part of the last hour to track you down here. I've never seen so many corridors and courtyards in my life. This place is like a maze.'

Celia spoke softly to the turbaned guards, gesturing to her father. Reluctantly, they sheathed their scimitars. 'I've told them to leave the doors open and promised we will remain in full view in the courtyard,' she said, gesturing her father in. Peregrine, who looked as if he would prefer to stay on the other side of the door, entered with some reluctance.

Lord Henry looked about with interest. 'Well, so this is the harem. Where are all the other women?'

'There aren't any. Prince Ramiz is not married. What has happened, Papa? You look upset.'

'Well, and so I bloody well should be,' Lord Henry said, casting a contemptuous look at Peregrine. 'Come here, Celia, let me look at you.'

Lord Henry inspected his daughter, who was dressed in a green caftan of lawn cotton, with her copper tresses flowing down her back, in some state of disorder from sleep. Perfectly well aware that the trauma of the scene with Ramiz and her consequent disturbed night showed in the dark shadows under her eyes, Celia put her arms round her father's neck, avoiding his scrutiny. 'It is lovely to see you, Papa. I'm sorry you've had to come all this way.'

'Aye, well, providential as it turns out. Or at least,' he said, glowering once more in Peregrine's direction, 'I thought it was until this damned fool told me what he and that idiot Wincester had cooked up.'

'Lord Armstrong, I assure you I was just the messenger,' said Peregrine. 'Wouldn't dream of— Would never—' He broke off to look beseechingly at Celia. 'I beg of you, Lady Celia, to inform your father of what passed between us.'

'Let us sit down,' Celia said wearily, clapping her hands to summon Adila and Fatima, and asking them to arrange divans in the courtyard for her guests, much to Peregrine, Lady Sophia and Lord Henry's relief. Celia and Cassie, who was dressed in one of Celia's outfits, though she retained her corsets, sat on cushions, leaning against the fountain.

Once coffee was served, and the maidservants had retired, Celia took a deep breath and recounted her original interview with Peregrine. 'I assure you, Papa, he was most circumspect in his request, and most painfully embarrassed by it too. I admit, I did consider the possibility of disclosing any information which I obtained here—not by subterfuge but simply because I *was* here—but after Peregrine left I decided I could not. Lord Wincester may consider my first loyalty is to my country, but while I am a guest of Sheikh al-Muhana, my country is A'Qadiz, and I would not insult him by betraying him. If I did, would I not be betraying my country rather than serving it?'

'Quite right, quite right,' Lord Henry said. 'Well said, daughter—exactly as I would have told old Wincester myself, if I had been consulted. Call me old-fashioned but diplomacy is an honourable vocation. I'll have no truck with stooping to nefarious methods. Britain can fight her corner without resorting to that.'

'Yes, Papa. I only wish I had said as much to Mr Finchley-Burke at the time,' Celia admitted, shame-faced.

'And why did you not, may I ask?'

She coloured, but met her father's gaze. 'I wanted to stay here. I was glad of the excuse not to leave. I didn't say as much to Mr Finchley-Burke, but I think he guessed.' She turned to Peregrine. 'Did you not?'

He shrugged in agreement.

'But why?' Lord Henry looked at his daughter afresh, seeming to notice for the first time her loose hair and traditional dress. His eyes narrowed. 'Why are you dressed like that?' He cast a worried glance at his sister. 'Sophia?'

Lady Sophia, looking unusually disconcerted, in turn cast a warning glance at Peregrine. 'Perhaps if you are finished with Mr Finchley-Burke, Henry…?'

Immensely relieved, Peregrine rose from his seat, but Lord Henry detained him. 'He made this mess— damned fool confessed all to that Akil chap last night— so he can stay where he is until we've agreed how to patch things up. Which I won't be able to do until I know all the facts.' Lord Henry got to his feet, dipping his hand into the fountain as if to test the temperature, and sat back down again. 'Out with it,' he said, looking at Sophia. 'What is going on?'

'Papa, there is nothing going on,' Celia said hurriedly. 'Only that I—that Ramiz and I—that Sheikh al-Muhana and I…'

'Celia thinks herself in love with the man,' Sophia said testily. 'That is why she stayed.'

'In love! With a sheikh! Are you out of your mind, Celia?' Lord Henry leapt to his feet once more, looming over his eldest daughter. 'I hope—I do most sincerely hope—that you have not lost all sense of propriety as to have been spending time alone with this man.' He

eyed his daughter's guilty countenance with astonishment.

'I am afraid, Henry, that after the scene Cassandra
and I witnessed last night there can be no doubt at all
that she has,' Lady Sophia said grimly.

'Eh? What scene?' Lord Henry demanded, now
looking thoroughly bewildered.

'Sheikh al-Muhana came here last night, presumably
as soon as he had discovered the Consul General's little
subterfuge,' Lady Sophia explained, with one of her
gimlet stares which made poor Peregrine quake. 'While
Celia chose to keep the detail of what passed between
them private, it was obvious from the—the manner in
which they spoke that Prince Ramiz and your daughter
are no strangers to one another's company.'

'Dear heavens.' Lord Henry staggered back into his
chair. 'What on earth are we to do? The treaty,' he said,
staring at Celia in horror. 'That treaty—you have no
idea how important it is. A long-term commitment like
the one we're aiming for is crucial. Fun-da-mental,' he
said, banging his fist on his knee, 'is that we trust one
another. Now I find that the Prince thinks my daughter
has been spying at our government's instigation, and
not only that she has been behaving like some sort of—
of…'

'Papa!'

'Father!'

'Henry!'

'I say, sir…'

Lord Henry glared at the four shocked faces surrounding him. 'Well, how the hell do you think it looks?'
he demanded furiously. 'Must I spell it out for you?'

'No, Henry,' Lady Sophia said hastily. 'I don't think that is necessary.'

Lord Henry mopped his brow with a large kerchief and sighed heavily. His Lordship was not a man prone to fits of ill temper. Indeed, his success as a diplomat was in large part due to his ability to remain level-headed in the most trying of circumstances, but an arduous trip by sea and sand, the incompetence displayed by everyone involved in this sorry matter, and now the scandalous and highly uncharacteristic behaviour of his eldest daughter had sent him over the edge. 'What were you thinking, Celia?' he said, his voice heavy with disappointment.

Celia, who by now was feeling about one inch tall, bit her lip. 'I wasn't thinking, Papa, that is the problem,' she said stiffly. She got to her feet with as much dignity as she could muster, shaking out her caftan and pushing her hair back from her face. 'Ramiz is an honourable man, and one who values the welfare of A'Qadiz over everything else. I am sure, with a few concessions on your part to compensate him for the misunderstanding, he will still be prepared to come to an agreement over the use of the Red Sea port. It will do your cause no harm to inform him that the matter has been a cause of estrangement between you and I, for upon that subject I think you will find you and he are in complete accord.'

'On the contrary, Lady Celia, I would be most upset to discover that I was the cause of your estrangement from your family. I know how much they mean to you.'

All eyes turned to where Ramiz stood, framed by the doorway. A night alone under the stars in the desert had done much to cool his temper, and with an element of calm had also come rationality. It was true Celia had never made any attempt to extract information of any sort from him, but more fundamentally he felt in his bones that she would not lie to him.

In his determination to be rid of her, Akil had exaggerated. With the discovery of his love still young, and Celia's feelings for him as yet undeclared, the situation had punctured Ramiz in his most vulnerable spot, but with the dawn had come renewed certainty. He loved her. He was sure of it, though he had never loved before—and never would again. He loved her. She was his other half, and as his other half could no more do anything untrue than he could.

Ramiz had returned to the palace filled with hope. Making immediately for the harem, he had come upon the open door, through which he had witnessed most of the courtyard scene. He had not stopped to wash or change. His cloak and headdress were dusty, his face showed a blue-black stubble, and there were shadows under his eyes. Ignoring all but Celia, he now strode into the room.

'I must speak with you,' he said urgently, taking her by the arm.

'You will unhand my niece at once, sir,' Lady Sophia said brusquely. 'You have done quite enough damage already.'

Confronted with a sharp-eyed woman bearing a remarkable resemblance to a camel dressed in grey silk, sweeping down upon him like a galleon in full sail, Ramiz stood his ground and kept his hold on Celia. 'Lady Sophia, I presume?' he said haughtily.

'And you, I take it, are Sheikh al-Muhana. I do not offer my hand, sir, nor do I make my bow, for you do not merit such courtesy. Unhand my niece, sir. She has suffered quite enough of your attentions.'

Ramiz's eyes narrowed. He took a step towards Lady Sophia, who flinched but did not give ground, then halted abruptly, snapping out a command in his own language. The two eunuchs came immediately into the courtyard, their swords drawn. Before they could protest, everyone except Ramiz and Celia had been ushered with varying degrees of force from the room. The harem door banged shut.

'Ramiz, what…?'

'I'm sorry.'

'What?'

'I'm sorry.'

'I've never heard you say that before,' Celia said, with a fragile half-smile.

Ramiz took her hand between his, holding it in a warm clasp. His face was stripped of its mask, leaving him exposed, raw, and there was something more there—something she recognised but had never dreamed to see, had never even allowed herself to hope for. It looked like love.

Celia caught her breath. 'Ramiz?'

'Celia, listen to me. I heard what you said to your father just now, but you have to believe I came here to ask you to forgive me for doubting you before I heard the words. What I heard just confirmed what I knew. What I should have realised last night—' He broke off and ran his hand through his hair, pushing his headdress to the floor. 'I wasn't thinking straight. I'd only just realized—only just begun to wonder if it was possible—then when Akil told me—I simply lost control. But there's one thing I'm sure of—will always be sure of. I love you. Without you my life would be a wilderness. I love you so much, Celia, say you love me and I will be the happiest man on earth. If you will just—'

'Ramiz, I love you. I love you. I love you.' Celia threw herself into his arms.

'Celia, say it again!'

'I love you, Ramiz.' She beamed at him. 'I love you.'

Finally he kissed her, his mouth devouring hers, the day's growth of stubble on his chin rasping against her tender skin, his hands pressing her so close she could scarcely breathe. She kissed him back with equal fervour, whispering his name over and over in between kisses, relishing the feel of him hard against her, the familiar scent of him, the wildly exhilarating excitement of him, and underpinning it all the simple rightness of it.

They kissed and murmured love, and kissed and repeated each other's name in wonder, and kissed again until, breathless and transformed, they sat together entwined in one another's arms on the floor of the courtyard, becoming dimly aware of an altercation on the other side of the door which seemed to have been going on for some time.

'My father,' Celia said. 'He probably thinks you're ravishing me.'

'If he would go away and leave us alone I would,' Ramiz replied with a grin. 'I did not like the way he spoke to you, or of me,' he said, his tone becoming serious. 'And your aunt too. They do not relish your choice of husband.'

'Husband?'

Ramiz laughed, a loud, deep and very masculine laugh of sheer joy. 'My love, light of my eyes, you cannot be imagining I mean anything else. You are the wings of my heart. I must tether you to me somehow.'

'But, Ramiz, what about tradition? I'm not a princess, and in the eyes of your people I'm not pure. Yasmina said…'

'Celia, what *I* know and what *I* think is all that matters. You *are* a princess—you are my princess. I will be a far better ruler with you by my side than alone. It is you who has taught me that, you who has made me realise that in order to be the man I ought to be I must have you with me.' Ramiz took her hand and bent down on his knee before her. 'Marry me, my lovely Celia, marry me. Because I love you, and because you love me, bestow upon me the honour of calling yourself my wife, and I will do you the honour of being your husband for ever, for even death will not part us. Marry me, and make me the happiest man on this earth and beyond.'

'Ramiz, that is the most beautiful thing I have ever heard.'

'Yes, darling Celia, but it was a question.'

'Yes.' Celia smiled and laughed and cried all at once. 'Yes.' She threw herself into his arms, toppling them both back onto the cushions. 'Yes, yes, yes,' she said, punctuating each affirmative with a kiss.

A loud thump outside the door startled them both. 'I think we'd better face your father before my guards are forced to use their scimitars on him,' Ramiz said.

It was not to be expected that either Celia's parent or her aunt would accept her marriage without protest. Ramiz listened with remarkable patience while first Lord Henry and then Lady Sophia asserted that such an alliance would end in disaster, would make Celia miserable, and would be the downfall of her sisters, who would be quite lost without her.

Celia countered by pointing out that her marriage to the ruler of a kingdom rich in natural resources with a port of immense strategic importance could hardly be deemed a misalliance. 'In fact,' she asserted, 'you should be honoured to have Prince Ramiz as a son-in-law, Papa, for association with him can only enhance your own career prospects—provided you can persuade him to forgive your rudeness.'

Lord Henry was much struck by his daughter's good sense. From that moment forward his affability towards Ramiz was marked. Indeed, in a lesser man such extreme cordiality might well have been branded obsequiousness.

Lady Sophia, whose objections were, to be fair, based upon her real affection for her niece, took rather more persuading. At Celia's behest Ramiz left the matter most reluctantly in her hands, concentrating his own efforts on discussions with Lord Henry on settlements, dowries and the all-important treaty.

'You talk as if I will be living here in isolation from the world,' Celia said to Lady Sophia as they walked in the palace gardens later that momentous day, 'but I hope you don't mean to deprive me of the company of either yourself or my sisters. I will be expecting all of you to stay here with us for extended visits—starting with Cassie, if she wishes,' she said, smiling at her sister. 'Though she may not wish to postpone her Season.'

Cassie clapped her hands together in excitement. 'What is a Season compared to this? Say I may stay, Aunt. I can come out next year, and anyway,' she said mischievously, knowing perfectly well what her aunt thought of Lord Henry's intended, 'I don't want to steal

Bella Frobisher's thunder by having my come-out ball in the same season as her wedding.'

As the day progressed, and Lady Sophia graciously permitted Ramiz to take her on a tour of the royal palace and its famed stables, her stance visibly mellowed. The following morning, a visit to Yasmina cemented the seal of approval. Yasmina's mother was visiting—a formidable woman of Lady Sophia's stamp. The two ladies spent a most amenable few hours together, with Yasmina translating, at the end of which Lady Sophia was able to declare herself happy with her niece's proposed marriage, and even prepared to remain in A'Qadiz in order to attend the nuptials.

'Ramiz came to call this morning,' Yasmina said to Celia over a glass of tea. 'Such an honour—our neighbours will be talking about it for ever.'

'He and Akil are reconciled, then?'

Yasmina nodded happily. 'He knows Akil only acted for the best. He loves Ramiz like a brother.' She pressed Celia's hand. 'I have never seen Ramiz so happy. You will forgive me if I spoke out of turn when we first met?'

'Yasmina, I trust you will always say what you think. Your friendship means a lot to me, I would hate it if you started treating me differently when I am Ramiz's wife.'

'Not just a wife, you will be a princess.'

'I will still be Celia, and it is as Celia that I ask you to be frank with me, Yasmina. What will the people really think about our marriage? Ramiz says that what makes him happy will make his people happy, but I know it's not that simple.'

Yasmina took a sip of tea. 'I will not lie to you. There will be some who will find it difficult to accept simply because it is a break with tradition. But Ramiz has come to symbolise change for A'Qadiz, and a Western bride will not be such a huge surprise as it would have been two years ago when Asad ruled.'

'You said that because I was married before—'

'"A prince's seed must be the only seed planted in your garden,"' Yasmina quoted. 'I remember. But it has been, hasn't it? The man you were married to was a husband in name only. You need not be embarrassed. I told you, I have the gift.'

Celia shook her head, blushing. 'No. Ramiz was the first—has been the only…'

'Then, with your permission, that is what I will say. People will listen to me as Akil's only wife,' Yasmina said proudly, 'and it is natural to talk of such things. You need not worry. I will drop the word in a few ears, and you will see. Now, we must go and talk to your aunt and my mother, and Akil's mother too. We have a wedding to plan.'

It took four long weeks to orchestrate. Four long weeks during which it seemed to Celia that she hardly saw Ramiz, what with the need for him to personally invite all the ruling families of all his neighbours, and the need for her to receive endless visits from the wives of Ramiz's most esteemed subjects, to say nothing of the terrifying amount of clothes which Yasmina declared necessary for a princess, and the equally terrifying regime of buffing and plucking and pampering and beautifying to which Celia was subjected.

At Ramiz's insistence, Celia and Cassie rode out every day, with only a discreet escort, signifying to the people of A'Qadiz the start of a new regime of freedom, and signifying to his beloved Celia and her sister the trust he had in their ability to treat such freedom with discretion.

Aunt Sophia left with Lord Henry for Cairo, promising to return in time for the week-long celebrations. Having heard her confess that her one remaining reservation was that the wedding would not be a 'real' one, Ramiz suggested that he would be happy for an English priest to participate if she wished. Suitably reassured, she informed him that she would not insult him by demanding any such thing.

Abstention from intimacy of any sort was part of the tradition surrounding the celebrations. This Ramiz and Celia managed with extreme difficulty, but were assisted by Ramiz's frequent absences, Cassie and Yasmina's perpetual attendance upon Celia, and the fact that the palace harem was suddenly overrun with female visitors.

By the time the week of her nuptials finally arrived Celia was beginning to think it never would, so slowly had the days passed despite the frenzied activity.

The formal betrothal, which took place in a packed throne room, was the first ceremony. Celia, dressed in richly embroidered silks and heavily veiled, was presented to Ramiz by her father. The ring, a fantastic emerald set in a star-shaped cluster of diamonds, was placed on her right hand.

Next came a round of pre-wedding visits and feasts, with the women and men strictly segregated. Lord Henry accompanied Ramiz on the most important of these, returning after each one more exuberant as the extent of his future son-in-law's wealth and influence was revealed.

The night before the wedding was spent by Celia in

the harem, where her hands and feet were painted with intricate designs of henna like the ones she had seen on Sheikh Farid's wives. Ramiz's formal wedding gift was delivered—a casket of jewels which it took two men to carry, including an emerald necklace, bracelets and anklets to complement her ring, each beautifully cut stone set in a star of diamonds.

Finally it was the wedding day. Dressed in gold, veiled and jewelled, and almost sick with anticipation, Celia stood before her sister and her aunt.

Cassie, in a traditional Arabic dress of cornflower-blue silk the colour of her eyes, hugged Celia tight. 'I'm so happy for you.'

'And I too.' Lady Sophia, splendid in purple, her grey curls covered by a matching turban in which feathers waved majestically, gave her a peck on the cheek. 'Good luck, child.'

Ramiz was waiting for Celia at the doorway of the harem, which she crossed for the last time, for they would share rooms in a newly decorated part of the palace—another tradition he had broken, having insisted that they would not spend another night apart. He was dressed in white trimmed with gold, the pristine simplicity of the tunic and cloak showing to perfection his lean muscled body, the headdress with its gold *igal* highlighting the clean lines of his face, the glow in his copper eyes which focused entirely on his bride.

They progressed under a scarlet canopy through the city, a band of musicians preceding them, family and close friends taking up the rear. Crowds sang and prayed, strewing their path with orange flowers and rose petals. Children clapped their hands and screamed with delight, jostling with each other for the silver coins which were thrown for them to gather. And through it all Celia was conscious only of the man by her side, of the nearness of him, of the scent of him, of the perfection of him.

Ramiz. Her Ramiz. Soon to be her husband.

The wedding ceremony itself took place in an open tent in the desert on the edge of the city, strategically placed on a hillside to accommodate the massive crowd. The bride and groom sat side by side on two low stools on a velvet-covered dais, while first Lord Henry spoke, in the hesitant Arabic in which Akil had coached him, before formally handing over his daughter. The *zaffa*, Sheikh Farid himself, declared the couple man and wife. Ramiz removed Celia's ring from her right hand and placed it on her left. Then he helped her to her feet and removed her veil. She was dimly aware of applause. Dimly aware of Cassie crying and of Aunt Sophia sniffing loudly. What she was most aware of was Ramiz. Her husband.

'I love you,' he whispered, for her ears alone, his voice sending a shiver of awareness through her. 'My wife.'

'I love you,' she said, looking up at him with that love writ large across her face. 'My husband.'

The applause became a roar as Ramiz kissed her. The music started, and she and Ramiz performed their first dance together—she nervously, he with aplomb. They sat together as the feast got underway, receiving congratulations, but as dusk fell and the first of the stars appeared Celia thought only of the night to come. They left, covered in rose petals, on horseback—a perfect black stallion for Ramiz, a grey mare for Celia, the wedding gift of Sheikh Farid. Their journey through the desert was magical and brief, silent with promise as the horses picked their way through the sand until the dark shadow of palm trees marked their arrival at an oasis.

A single tent. A fire already burning outside it. An ellipse of water lapping gently at the shelving sand. The stars like silver saucers. The new moon suspended in the velvet sky.

'*Hilal,*' Celia whispered to her husband, as they stood hand in hand looking up at it. 'New beginnings.'

Ramiz smiled tenderly. 'New beginnings. Come with me. I have a surprise for you—a gift.'

'Darling husband, you have done nothing but shower me with gifts since our marriage.'

'And I will continue to shower you with gifts for the rest of your life, since you are the greatest gift of all. Come with me.'

Ramiz led her over to the tent. As they grew nearer Celia could make out a strange contraption. It had a round base from which a wooden pole rose to support an irregular shape. It looked a bit like a very odd sundial. As they got closer Celia realised that the bulky shape was made of cloth. It was some sort of covering. She looked at Ramiz in puzzlement. He put a finger to his lips before carefully removing the cloth. There, on a perch, sat a hooded bird of prey, white and silver with black wing-tips. 'A falcon!'

'*Your* falcon, my beloved.'

'Oh, Ramiz, he's beautiful.'

Ramiz removed the hood from the bird and, taking Celia's hand, pulled a leather gauntlet over it. 'Keep very still.' She hardly dared breathe as he placed the bird carefully on her arm. 'The wings of my heart,' he said to her, 'my gift to you.' He jerked her arm and the bird flew high, its magnificent wingspan outlined against the crescent moon. 'Now, hold out your arm again, and whistle like this,' Ramiz told her, and Celia watched breathlessly as the bird glided back, landing delicately on her gauntlet. 'Like the falcon I fly, and like the falcon I will always return to you,' Ramiz said, putting the hood back on the bird.

He led her into the tent. 'I hope these are happy tears,' he whispered, gently kissing Celia's eyelids.

'I didn't know I could be so happy,' Celia replied, twining her arms around his neck. 'I didn't think it was possible. Love me, Ramiz. Make love to me.'

'I intend to, my darling. Tonight. Tomorrow. And tomorrow. And tomorrow, and…'

But he had to stop talking to kiss her. And to kiss her. And to kiss her. Until their kisses burned and the abstinence of the last few weeks fuelled the flame of their passion, and their love made that passion burn brighter than ever—brighter even than the stars in the desert sky which glittered above their tent. They made love frantically, tenderly, joyously, with an abandon new to them both, whispering and murmuring their love, shouting it out to the silent desert in a climax which shook them to the core, and which Celia knew, with unshakeable certainty, truly was the new beginning heralded by the crescent moon.

A new life together beckoning her.

And a new life growing inside her.

* * * * *

Historical Note

While I've tried very hard for historical accuracy, I've taken a few liberties with timings and some events referred to in the story, which I hope you'll forgive me for.

In 1818 Mehmet Ali had already wrested control of Egypt from the Ottoman sultan and the major powers, primarily the British and the French, were maintaining a local presence in the hope of rich pickings when the Ottoman Empire collapsed. The British Consul General was Henry Salt, a renowned Egyptologist who did, like my fictional Consul General, regard the relics of ancient Egypt as there for the taking, but there the similarity between my bumbling diplomat and the real one ends.

Obviously A'Qadiz is an invented kingdom. In my imagination it sits in what is now Saudi Arabia with a coastline a couple of days' sail away from Sharm-el-Sheikh, which would be an ideal port for the 'fast' route to India via the Red Sea. This route did play a significant role in reducing the overall journey from two years to three months, but it was about fifteen years after the story is set that this came into use and not until the 1880s that the Suez Canal made it commercially viable.

In real life, it could take anything up to three months to get from England to Arabia, depending upon the weather, the type of ship and the number of stop-offs, though at a push it could perhaps have been done in about three weeks. Since I needed Celia's family to come to her rescue, this proved to be a bit of an issue. I speeded up the process by giving them access to the Royal Navy, but there is no doubt that I've stretched credibility a bit by expecting a letter to get from Cairo to London and Celia's family to get to Arabia when they receive it all in the space of about six to seven weeks.

Richard Burton's (bowdlerised) translation of *One Thousand and One Nights* is the most well known, but it was not published until 1885. The French edition w .s published in 1717, however, and this is the one Celia has read.

THE

Balfour

LEGACY

Eight sisters, Eight scandals

VOLUME 1 – JUNE 2010
Mia's Scandal
by Michelle Reid

VOLUME 2 – JULY 2010
Kat's Pride
by Sharon Kendrick

VOLUME 3 – AUGUST 2010
Emily's Innocence
by India Grey

VOLUME 4 – SEPTEMBER 2010
Sophie's Seduction
by Kim Lawrence

8 VOLUMES IN ALL TO COLLECT!

 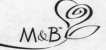

THE *Balfour* LEGACY

ℰIGHT SISTERS, ℰIGHT SCANDALS

VOLUME 5 – OCTOBER 2010
Zoe's Lesson
by Kate Hewitt

VOLUME 6 – NOVEMBER 2010
Annie's Secret
by Carole Mortimer

VOLUME 7 – DECEMBER 2010
Bella's Disgrace
by Sarah Morgan

VOLUME 8 – JANUARY 2011
Olivia's Awakening
by Margaret Way

8 VOLUMES IN ALL TO COLLECT!

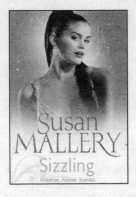

Secrets. Lies. Time to come clean...

Dani Buchanan is horrified when her father turns out to be a presidential candidate. And then the tabloids find out...

Katherine Canfield is unable to bear children. Dani's a reminder of what Senator Canfield could have had – and Katherine's jealous.

Adopted Canfield son Alex is tempted by Dani. With the scandal of the century brewing, can he pursue a relationship that could tear his family apart?

Available 3rd September 2010

www.millsandboon.co.uk

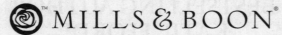